THE ETERNITY KEY

BREE DESPAIN

THE ETERNITY KEY

INTO THE DARK BOOK 2

EGMONT
Publishing
NEW YORK

EGMONT

We bring stories to life

First published by Egmont Publishing, 2015
443 Park Avenue South, Suite 806
New York, NY 10016

1 3 5 7 9 8 6 4 2

www.egmontusa.com
www.breedespain.com

Library of Congress Cataloging-in-Publication Data
Despain, Bree, 1979-author.
The Eternity Key / Bree Despain.
pages cm. — (Into the dark ; #2)
Summary: Haden, Prince of the Underrealm, is determined to defy his
fate to protect Daphne, even as they and their small group of friends
continue the search for the lost Kronolithe, the key of Hades—but his
undeclared love for a mortal girl is a terrible risk, and they must both
decide what they are willing to sacrifice to protect one another.
ISBN 978-1-60684-467-0 (hardcover)
1. Gods, Greek—Juvenile fiction. 2. Mythology, Greek—Juvenile
fiction. 3. Princes—Juvenile fiction. 4. Fate and fatalism—Juvenile
fiction. 5. Self-sacrifice—Juvenile fiction. 6. Love stories. [1. Gods—
Fiction. 2. Mythology, Greek—Fiction. 3. Princes—Fiction. 4. Fate and
fatalism—Fiction. 5. Love—Fiction.] I. Title.

PZ7.D4518Et 2015
813.6—dc23
[Fic]
2014034626

ISBN 978-1-60684-467-0
eBook ISBN 978-1-60684-468-7

Printed in the United States of America
Typography by Torborg Davern

To Michelle Sallay—
Because everyone should have a friend like you.
Love, Bree

THE ETERNITY KEY

chapter one

HADEN

Lord Haden, *prince of the Underrealm*, has ceased to exist.

I have ceased to exist.

Since I was a nursling, I'd been taught that life is nothing but a thin golden string. It's spun and entwined in a grand tapestry of the gods' design, then pulled and severed at a predetermined length. Nothing can be done to change this, nothing can be said, and no bargain can be made. Once your thread has been measured—that's it. No choice. It's the will of the Fates.

I'd believed this myth every second of my existence, and yet, as I'd learned all too recently, if you clawed at the design hard enough, the tapestry would unravel just enough that you could grab on to another string. Follow another path.

Since that realization, I have burned the connection between myself and my realm, ruined what little standing I had reclaimed as a Champion chosen by the Oracle of Elysium, and destroyed all hope of becoming my father's heir. I brought this upon myself with a single decision.

And I would do it all over again.

Because this is a fate of *my* own choosing.

I am rewriting my destiny.

Something I didn't even know was an option until I met *her*.

Daphne Raines—the girl who was supposed to grant me the chance to win back my honor. I had been Chosen for a quest to the mortal realm to convince her to come back with me to the underworld. It quickly became clear that there was something special about her. She wasn't a mere Boon to fill the harem of the Court.

Daphne is the fated Cypher—the only one who can find and retrieve the lost Kronolithe of my long-dead god: the Key of Hades.

I knew it was up to me to ensure that the Kronolithe was found, and use it to stop the Court of the Underrealm from breaking through the walls of the Pits and freeing the Keres. There would be terrible consequences if they were to take this action: all hell would break loose on the mortal world, spilling out from the schism created between the realms, and war with the Skylords would inevitably follow, not to mention the death toll and havoc the Keres would leave in their wake.

With the fate of the five realms hanging in the balance, I'd chosen to leave the safe haven we'd found in Ellis Fields in order to return to Olympus Hills to search for the Key.

Much to my surprise—and admittedly distress—Daphne and the others had chosen to go with me. "Even if you find it," she'd said, "you can't *get* the Kronolithe without me, so suck it." I'd known she was right, even though I had wanted her to be wrong. Because of our choices, our new destinies were now irrevocably entwined. If the realms can be saved, salvation will happen only if we do it united.

And so we'd escaped into the dark, together. . . .

Rain pounds on the hood of my car now as I sit outside Daphne's home in Olympus Hills. I realize I am gripping my steering wheel tight, as if I were once again silently maneuvering the Tesla Model X down an unlit canyon road in a torrential rainstorm without headlights. It had been a slow, tense, and quiet escape during the darkness of midnight. No one said a word for almost an hour, as if even a whisper might alert the Skylords of our presence or break my concentration on the wet, black road in front of us.

In our favor, Underlords see far better in the dark than Skylords do, and the Tesla, with its silent electric motor, had provided us the stealth we needed to make our exit. The Skylords, who can control rain as well as lightning and thunder, had intended the storm to prevent us from escaping, but instead it had provided the cover we needed to pass through the unlit canyon unseen. However, the mere memory of that storm is enough to raise the hairs on the back of my neck. I had never been so terrified in all my life—not even when facing the imminent destruction of my soul at my father's hands. Because, this time, the lives of Daphne, Joe, Tobin, Lexie, Garrick, and Dax—the only people left in all the realms who still believed in me—were in *my* hands as we crept along the cliffside road.

It may have been two weeks since that harrowing experience, but sitting in the rain now not only served as an unwelcome reminder of that long drive, but it also felt like a warning as to what is still to come.

I will one of my hands to release its death grip on the steering wheel and use it to take a swig from the coffee cup that's been my only company tonight. I gag, almost choking on the cold swill. I don't know how Simon could have loved this stuff. I take another sip, not because I want to taste it again, but because I need to stay awake. I've barely slept a scant few hours in the days since our return from Ellis. I may require less sleep than a human, but even I have my limits.

As if Dax can read my thoughts—which I am not entirely sure he *can't* sometimes—my phone lights up with a text from him.

Dax: You're there again, aren't you? Come home.

I stare at the screen, not sure I am going to reply, when another message comes through.

Dax: You've barely slept in weeks. You can't keep up this pace of looking for the Key all day and guarding Daphne's house all night.

I pry my other hand from the steering wheel to answer.

Me: I'm not at Daphne's. I am merely getting a bite to eat.

Typing it feels easier than saying it to his face. I've never been good at lying to Dax. I drop my phone in an empty compartment in the dash, hoping that will be the last of the conversation, and pinch my nose between my eyes. Sleep pulls at me, but I won't let my eyelids shut.

I grip my coffee cup with both hands, sending a small pulse of electric heat from my palms into it, hoping to warm it up enough to make it palatable again. An abrupt knock sounds against the passenger-side window. I jump in my seat, and a surge of electricity escapes my hands, nearly incinerating the cardboard cup before I drop it in my lap. I hold my hand out, blue light crackling between my fingers, toward the car door as it swings open.

A tiny gray cat jumps through the dark opening, landing on the passenger seat. She yowls at me.

"Hello to you, too, Brim," I say, knowing I've been caught.

I extinguish the lightning in my hand and pick up the cup from my coffee-stained lap, wishing I hadn't warmed the contents quite so much. Brim jumps over the center console onto my shoulder as Dax follows her into the car. He settles himself into the

4

passenger seat and pulls the door shut. His hair is damp, and rain has soaked the shoulders of his jacket.

"Liar," he says, not looking at me as he digs into a paper sack that he's brought with him.

"You used Brim to track me?" I ask, not realizing that is still a sore spot until I say it. Brim and I share a special bond, and because of it, she can find me anywhere. Simon exploited that fact to follow Daphne and me to the Oracle in Las Vegas, and that unfortunate choice had resulted in both Simon's and the Oracle's deaths. Brim might look like a harmless puff of fur, but Simon had made the mistake of ignoring one of the most steadfast rules of the Underrealm: never get a hellcat angry.

I scratch Brim under her chin to let her know there are no hard feelings about her being used to find me once again. Brim purrs next to my ear.

"I used my common sense to find you," Dax says. "Brim came along for the ride. We brought you something." He fishes in the paper sack.

"If that's another taco, Hades help me . . ." Since Simon is gone, Dax has taken over most of our meals, which means I've had more Mexican takeout in the last two weeks than I'd ever care to have in a lifetime.

"It's chamomile tea," he says, handing me a capped cup, and pulls out a second for himself. It smells sweeter than the coffee I've been nursing all evening, like flowers and honey. I'm about to take a tentative sip when he says, "It'll help you sleep."

I put the tea in a cup holder. "I don't need help sleeping."

"Those dark circles under your eyes tell a different story."

"What I mean is that I'm not going to sleep. Not when it's raining."

5

"You need sleep. *Go home.*"

Brim meows as if agreeing with Dax. *Furry little traitor.*

"Maybe you didn't hear me: *it's raining. I can't leave.*"

"Yeah, Haden, I can see that," he says, gesturing out the windshield. "And it's just rain. There's no lightning. No thunder. Rain doesn't always mean Skylords are about to swoop down on us. Relax. We're safe."

"You can't know that."

"It's been two weeks."

I don't like being reminded how much time has passed since we returned to Olympus Hills. I don't know why I really expected anything different, but part of me had thought we would have found the Key by now. Despite all our searching, we haven't made any progress. It's like I can feel every second that ticks by without the Key.

It's not just the rain that keeps me up at night. It's the nightmares. The visions of Keres ripping through the realms, devouring everything—and everyone . . .

I know if I tell Dax about my dreams, he will say that they were just that, *dreams*, but part of me worries they're a premonition of what is to come if we don't find the Key. Just like the rain feels like an omen now.

As if something else were coming . . .

"If the Skylords were coming for us, they would have come by now," Dax says, and I know my thoughts are painted on my face. All my life, I've practiced hiding myself behind an expressionless mask—a necessary skill for someone from a place where emotion and affection are considered weaknesses—but I seem to have lost my knack for it of late. Ever since I let Daphne see the real me . . .

"Deal with it, fearless leader; we got away," Dax says, and lifts his tea as if proposing a toast in my honor.

A sick feeling washes over me, and I know it's not from my steady diet of fast-food tacos and coffee. I hit the lever for the windshield wipers, wiping away a thick coat of rainwater. In the distance, I watch one of the lights go out in Daphne's house. It isn't her window that goes dark, but I wonder if she was the one who turned out the light. *Can she see me out here now?*

Her bedroom is in the back of Joe's mansion. I'd contemplated climbing the fence and camping out under her window, but I'd barely gotten past the point in which Daphne was referring to me as a creep and a stalker, so I didn't want to push my luck. Instead, I sit in my car like a sentinel. Making sure there's no sign of trouble.

Making sure she's safe.

"You should tell her." Dax's voice is so quiet when he says it, I almost wonder if he said anything at all. "No, wait, scratch that," he says, bolder now. "You *need* to tell her."

I raise an eyebrow with a noncommittal "Huh?"

"That you're in love with her, you idiot."

Panic rises up my throat, burning like vomit. Admitting to myself that I am in love with Daphne had been hard enough—and it had taken the imminent threat of my death to get me to do it.

"I can't," I say.

Affection is weakness, I hear my father's voice echoing in my head. My jaw aches as I remember his ringed hand slamming into my face when I was a small child. I'd been punished, disowned, stripped of my honor because I'd shown affection for my mother when she died. My love for her had caused me to take a stand against my father, and I'd lost just about everything because of it.

Dax shifts in his seat. "Despite what your father and Master

Crue and all the other Heirs may have taught you, loving someone isn't a sin. It isn't a crime, either."

Love gave you strength. That's what Daphne had told me when I related the story of my mother's death to her. Deep down, I'd known she was right. And I know that my love for Daphne was what gave me the strength to stand up to Ren once more—to try to weave my own destiny. But the idea of *telling her* terrifies me more than the threat of the Skylords and the wrath of the Court combined—because I turned my back on the Underrealm, my father, my chance to be his heir, gave up being a prince, and possibly endangered all the realms, because of my love for Daphne.

That love is all I have left.

It's the only thing that gives me hope.

And if I confess to her and learn that she does not reciprocate my feelings—then I will have truly lost *everything*.

My fingers shake as I reach for what remains of my coffee cup instead of the chamomile tea. "I can't," I say again. Even if I *wanted* to tell Daphne, I wouldn't be able to find the words.

Against my will, my thoughts flit to Rowan—my twin brother, the one my father and the Court would have chosen as the Champion to collect Daphne if the Oracle of Elysium had not intervened. *Rowan* was the one who had a gift for words. He was the smart one. The cunning one.

A small smile plays on my lips because I like to think that even Rowan, with all his manipulative skills, wouldn't have been able to trick Daphne into falling in love with him enough to return with him to the Underrealm. She'd have seen right through his lies. As far as I know, my brother is incapable of loving anyone other than himself. All he cares about are power and pride.

Then again, only four months ago, before I was sent to the

mortal world, before I met Daphne, before I refused to hand her over to my father, all anyone would have said I cared about was getting my honor back.

But I proved I wouldn't sacrifice her to do it. Rowan would have handed Daphne over without blinking, if he were in my place. He would have done anything necessary to succeed where I had failed.

Dax clears his throat, pulling my thoughts away from Rowan.

"So are you hoping that, by sitting outside her house every night, she'll figure it out on her own?"

"I don't sit out here every night. Only when it's raining."

"It's January in California. It's rained every night."

"It didn't rain yesterday."

"And yet you still found a reason to stay here half the night."

"There was rain in the forecast. I needed to know she was safe."

"Harpies, Haden. Sometimes rain is just rain. Come home. Unless you know something I don't know?"

I hesitate for a moment. There was something—something I saw when we stopped for breakfast at that diner outside Vegas. The same one where Daphne, Garrick, and I had stopped for lunch on our way to find Sarah, the Oracle, and ended up meeting up with Tobin and Lexie. Thinking we were in the clear after we escaped the rain, we'd stopped for sustenance and to retrieve Lexie's car. I hadn't thought anything of the trucker who had been in the diner when we stopped there the first time—just a man in a hat with a scruffy beard who seemed to like pink, creamy looking drinks—but when I saw him there again, at four in the morning no less, I'd started to worry.

I watched him down two of those pink drinks while the others ate piles of what Daphne had referred to as "buttermilk pancakes," then he threw a few bills on the counter and left without giving us a second glance. I'd let myself relax then, even grunted in response when Daphne dared me to try bacon dipped in maple syrup, thinking I'd been a complete lunatic for being anxious about the man—but then I could have sworn that, through the diner's dirty windows, I saw the man's truck rumble to life before he even got inside it. As if he'd started it with the brush of his hand over the hood. Like the way I could start my Tesla with my lightning powers.

Much to the others' protests, I'd insisted we leave as soon as the trucker pulled out of the parking lot. I didn't mention what I saw because I didn't see the man or his truck on the road. He wasn't following us, and he wasn't up ahead. I'd convinced myself that having my soul fried less than twenty-four hours before, followed by the tense drive out of the canyon, was making my mind play tricks on me. (For all I knew, there had been someone else in the truck to begin with.) And I didn't feel like contradicting my passengers, who were treating me like I was some kind of Hercules for successfully executing our daring escape from Ellis.

My pride had gotten the better of me then, but the more days that passed and the more rain that fell, I had started to wonder if we had really escaped at all.

"No . . . It's just a feeling," I say, my pride getting to me once again. "You know. As if I'm still being followed."

"They didn't follow us."

"You're the one who is always telling me to trust my instincts."

"Right . . . But, you know, if someone were watching us, you sitting outside her house every night is pretty much the same as erecting a huge, Vegas-style THE CYPHER LIVES HERE neon sign, right?"

I hadn't thought of that.

"And if you kill yourself via sleep deprivation, then you'll truly be no use to anyone." Dax places his hand on my shoulder, next to a now-sleeping Brim. "How about you let me take up the watch tonight so you can go home and sleep? There is that school thing tomorrow and all."

I try to take a sip of my coffee but all I find are the scalded dregs in my charred cup. Brim's purring snores next to my ear seem particularly hypnotic. My eyelids feel heavy as I look up at Daphne's house. All the lights are out now. I'm not going to be much use at school if I fall asleep in class. With Simon gone and Daphne knowing the truth, I normally wouldn't see the point in continuing with the school charade—except I don't like the idea of leaving Daphne unprotected all day long. Besides, I welcome the excuse to actually be close to her, instead of sitting outside her house at night.

I look out over the lake across the street from Daphne's quiet home and notice that the rain is finally starting to let up. I contemplate going home to sleep so I'll be prepared for tomorrow. My fingers are on the ignition button, ready to start the car, when a bolt of lightning rips the sky above the lake. Rolling thunder explodes with it, causing me to flinch at the nearness. But in the half second before my eyes clamp shut, I think I see someone standing on the lakeshore. Staring at me. When my eyes open another half second later, no one is there.

I jump out of my car and run toward the lake. The wet sand on the shore grips at my shoes, slowing my pace. Dax follows, calling, "What are you doing, Haden?" as if he hadn't seen anything. Brim yowls in protest over having been awoken so abruptly, sinking her claws into my shoulder.

I cast about in the rain, but I don't see anyone. I start to think I'd imagined seeing someone—perhaps I'd drifted momentarily asleep—but I make out what looks like a pair of boot prints in the sand before the lapping water of the lake washes them away.

"There," I say, pointing to the now-gone prints. "Didn't you see him?"

"*Him?*" Dax shakes his head. "I saw lightning, but nothing else."

I stand on the beach, frantically searching the shoreline with my eyes, that creeping feeling that I am being watched plaguing me. The rain, lighter than before but still a steady downpour, soaks through my thin shirt. Brim jumps from my shoulder and bounds back to the car, seeking shelter from the rain.

"Come on," Dax says. "It was just lightning. You don't want to be standing in the water if it strikes again."

I cross my arms for warmth and turn back toward Daphne's house, watching for any signs of trouble. Any thoughts of leaving, and any sleepiness, have vanished. I don't care if I have to stand in the rain all night; I'll do whatever it takes to keep Daphne safe.

chapter two

DAPHNE

I ask the raindrops on the windowsill to dance, and they listen. Four little drops pucker and roll along the painted wood to form a circle of dots just below my fingertips. They twist and twirl, like they're performing a miniature ballet to the tune I hum. I raise my fingertip, along with my pitch, and one of the drops lifts off the sill and quivers and swirls in midair, following my command. I concentrate harder as I sing a high note, and the other three drops follow the first, leaping up into the air at my will.

I've always been able to hear the tones and melodies that every living thing puts off—like the world is a symphony that only I can hear—but learning that I can use those tones to influence the elements is a new and exhilarating feeling. A warm, pulsating sensation encircles me, and I feel calm, in control, for the first time since I was awoken by a crash of thunder in the middle of the night.

It's even more reassuring than knowing that Haden was standing guard outside during the night. I'd seen him sitting below my bedroom window, settled into one of the deck chairs beside the pool, when I'd gotten up to get a glass of water about an hour after the lightning crash had woken me. Only a few weeks ago, I would have called him on it—but the almost constant evening rain since we escaped the Skylords has me on edge.

Which is why being able to manipulate these raindrops makes me feel more in control. Like if I practice this newfound power enough, I'll be able to protect *myself.*

It's not that I don't appreciate Haden's efforts—the boy sleeps in the rain for me, after all. It's not that I doubt his abilities. And it's certainly not that his mere nearness doesn't make me acutely aware of his . . . prowess.

Maybe it's because of what happened with Joe. Maybe it's because I still don't understand the why of it all—*why* Haden would chose me over his father. Or maybe it's because I still have a hard time accepting the concept of fate. Even though Sarah had said that Haden's and my destinies were irrevocably intertwined, I don't want to rely on the idea that *someone* will always be there for me.

Even if part of me wants him to be.

The water droplets' dance slows with my lack of concentration. Returning my focus to them, I lift my voice in a few high, staccato notes, and raindrops jump along to the sound, almost as if I've given them life. A smile spreads across my face.

Yeah, I could get used to this.

"Oi, Daphne?" Joe says in his British accent from behind me.

I startle. The water droplets splat onto the sill, lifeless once more. I spin around, afraid I've been caught, and try to come up with an explanation for what he may have just witnessed. Whatever this new power is, whatever it means, I'm not ready to share it yet. Especially with someone I don't know how to trust anymore.

But Joe doesn't seem to have seen anything out of the ordinary. Instead, he's standing half in and half out of my bedroom doorway, looking down at the large package in his arms.

"I called up the stairs but you didn't hear me," he says, as if he's apologizing for invading my wing of the mansion. We've pretty much been keeping to our own parts of the house since we returned from Ellis. "My courier just dropped this off. It's the package from your mother. I thought you'd want it right away."

"Oh yeah, of course," I say, pulling the window shut, like I'm afraid the raindrops are going to start spontaneously dancing again behind me. "Bring it in."

Joe takes a few apprehensive steps into my bedroom and sets the hefty box on my bed. He backs away, wringing his hands as I approach, and stands again in that noncommittal fashion in my doorway. He acts like he isn't watching as I open the box.

Inside are two presents wrapped in red paper—the Christmas gifts from my mother that I never got to open—and a third present in sparkling silver paper, done up with more ribbons than should be legal (a gift from Jonathan, I know without even looking at the card). Tears prick at the backs of my eyes, and I set those aside, waiting to have my own private belated Christmas when Joe isn't watching.

The rest of the box is filled with stacks of papers and a few books and a small, carved wood figurine of a rose. They're all things that my Ellis Fields best friend, CeCe—who, it turns out, is really my Olympus Hills best friend, Tobin's long-lost sister, Abbie—left behind in her apartment before disappearing from Ellis. It makes me shudder as I think that the five years of her life she'd spent in Ellis Fields could all be fit inside this box.

I'd left Ellis with Haden and the others in such a hurry, I hadn't thought to look through CeCe's things, so when I got home and started kicking myself for the oversight, I convinced

Jonathan to send whatever he could find of hers. I was grateful that he agreed, especially since my mom hadn't been responding to any of my texts or messages since she'd returned from Salt Lake City with Jonathan to learn from her shopgirl, Indie, that I had returned to Ellis with some friends for only a few hours and then taken off again before even seeing her, and that I wasn't going to be there for Christmas break, after all.

That had been one of the two promises I had made to her when I chose to move to Olympus Hills with Joe: that I would be home for Christmas—the other promise being that "I cross my heart and hope to die, I won't go running off with some guy." And now after fleeing Ellis with Haden to go looking for the Key, I felt I'd broken both of those promises to her.

At the time, it had seemed vitally important that we leave Ellis immediately. The fate of the whole world seemed to rest on our quest to find the Key. But two weeks later, with nothing but raw fingers from flipping page after page in the town archives; newly healing blisters on my palms from digging up the grove— the place we had all thought to be the most likely candidate for where Orpheus had stashed the Key of Hades—and aching feet from walking every inch of Olympus Hills, searching out alternative possible hiding places; I was beginning to think I had broken those promises for nothing.

At least Joe had taken the bullet for me over the Christmas thing. When my mom found out I was skipping out on the holidays with her, the phone call that followed can only be described as epic. Luckily, Joe had taken the phone from me and informed her he'd become lonely without his only child around the house and ordered me back to California on the next flight out of Utah, or else he was going to revoke my tuition to Olympus Hills High.

I could hear her screaming through the receiver from the next room. The fact that he had just stood there, taking the verbal beating, had almost made me soften toward him.

Almost.

There's no time to really get into CeCe's things before leaving for school, but I give the box a cursory search, wishing for something—anything—that I might be able to offer Tobin when I see him at school. Something to give him hope that his sister can be found. Searching for the Key is proving more impossible than I could have imagined, which makes finding CeCe all the more important. Like it's something I can actually do.

Joe clears his throat. It almost sounds like he's choking. "I made breakfast," he says. "I even managed not to burn a couple of pieces of bacon. They're yours . . . if you want to join me?"

I look up from the box and meet his eyes just long enough to read the real question behind his words: *Have you forgiven me yet?*

I drop my gaze to the box again and see a green leather-bound book sticking out from under a stack of receipts. I pull it out, open it, and find pages filled with CeCe's flowery handwriting. I scan a couple of pages and realize it's a diary. This could actually be helpful.

Joe shifts heavily in the doorway, waiting for my answer about breakfast.

"I'm not hungry," I finally say, but the growl from my stomach at the smell of bacon wafting up the grand staircase gives away my lie.

Still, even if I could stomach a home-cooked meal—more like a home-destroyed meal when it comes to Joe—I'm not ready to share a table or a real conversation with my father.

As much as I would like to forgive him, I can't. And I'm afraid if we even talk about what happened, I'll feel just like I did when I first heard his confession. When the music in my head stopped and all I could feel was sorrow.

"Are you sure? I made blueberry pancakes. Well, I ran out of blueberries because I forgot to put eggs in the first batch and kinda scorched the second batch, so I had to use some strawberries to beef up the third. But they smell pretty good. Marta even tried one, and she's not dead yet, so . . ." He smiles, looking so hopeful, I almost don't want to burst his bubble.

"But *I* would die if I ate them," I say, tucking the diary into my tote bag. "Or at least get all puffy and need to go to the emergency room. I'm allergic to strawberries."

Joe goes from hopeful to crestfallen to panicked in a matter of a second. "What? I'm so sorry, Daph. I didn't know."

"How would you?" I zip up my bag and hitch it over my shoulder. "You sold my soul to the Underrealm in order to become a rock star. It's not like you're going to be up for any Father of the Year Awards anytime soon."

"Right," he says, going back to crestfallen. He wipes his hands on his apron and moves like he's going to leave me in peace. Reconsidering, he turns back. "Yesterday was New Year's, Daphne. Can't we leave the past in the past and start over fresh?"

I pick up my phone and send a text to Tobin, who's been in mother-imposed lockdown since we returned from Ellis.

I've got something you need to see. We're all meeting in the music room @ 7 a.m. Hope you can make it.

I slip the phone in my back pocket and glance at Joe. "I need to meet the others before class."

"It's been two weeks . . . ," Joe starts, but I lift my hand in a stop gesture.

"Two weeks isn't long enough in the past to leave it there," I say, and then bite my tongue. I am not going to talk about this. I can't talk about this. "I don't want to be late meeting the others. I need to go."

With school starting again today, we all know it is only going to get harder to find the time to look for the Key, so Haden called a "war meeting" of sorts before class so we can report back on the different angles we'd all been investigating over the break.

There was a part of me that had believed we would find the Key before winter vacation was over—that all this Underrealm-Cypher-Compass-Kronolithe craziness would be solved before classes started up again—but I realize now that had been a completely naïve notion. None of us even knows what the Key looks like—is it as big as a staff or as small as a car key? *And without the Compass . . .*

A hollowness fills me when I think of the Compass. Sarah had said that the Compass had been meant for me—that she had been waiting centuries to hand me my destiny—but it had been ripped away from me only minutes later.

I hadn't wanted it when Sarah had first offered it to me, but ever since the mysterious "Motorcycle Man" stole it during the fight with Simon at the hospital, I felt like a piece of me had gone with it.

And without the Compass, I fear we will never find the Key.

Joe gestures at the box of papers and scraps. "I can help you with your research."

"I don't need help."

Another lie.

"Play rehearsals start up again this week, Daphne," Joe says tentatively. "If you're going to continue in the part of Eurydice, you can't avoid me forever."

I sigh.

"That is, if you intend to keep the part?"

Once again, I catch the real question in his eyes. *Will you ever be able to forgive me?*

"We'll see," I say, heading for the door.

He steps aside and lets me go.

chapter three

TOBIN

Relief fills me when I find the house strangely empty this morning. Usually, on a school day, when I come down for breakfast, there's already a house full of maids, our latest cook trying to follow Dad's clipped instructions on how to make a proper vegan omelet (I have no idea what is in that shiz—and my dad isn't even a vegan) while my mother, Madam Mayor, sits at the table with an espresso and gluten-free toast, going over her schedule with her assistant, or squeezing in a FaceTime call with my brother, Sage, before he leaves his penthouse apartment for class at MIT. I used to love our morning routine. It was the baseline of normalcy to me. But I wouldn't be able to sit through it today, knowing it's all a lie.

Mom hasn't come out of her room yet even though she's usually up at the crack of dawn. I thought I heard her on the phone, or at least engaged in an exasperated one-sided conversation, when I passed her door. I definitely heard her say the name *Simon* before I ducked away. If she's trying to locate him, she's going to have a hell of a time. The house staff must not be back from their holiday vacation, and I have no idea where Dad is but he doesn't seem to be home, so my timing couldn't be better.

Skipping breakfast, I head straight for Mom's office. The door is locked—she's been doing that since she caught Daphne and me in there the night of the music department's party—so I grab the spare key that's hidden in a hollowed-out copy of Machiavelli's *The Prince* on the shelf in Dad's study. My parents don't know I know about that. Nor that I know our family's dirtiest secrets.

Once inside her office, I bypass the glass cases housing her antiquities collection and go for the built-in mahogany cabinets where she keeps her mayoral-related files. I figure if I can start where I left off, then maybe I can pick up the trail again. I'm not sure what I'm looking for—something that might help Daphne and Haden find this Key of Hades, or anything—anything at all—that might help Dax and me track down Abbie.

I don't have the foggiest idea of where they've gotten in either search, because I've been grounded (aka under house arrest) for the last two weeks for taking off for a couple of days without telling my parents. My incarceration was my own damn fault.

I'd gotten more than I'd bargained for on that trip—like the realization that my own mother was in cahoots with the real bad guys and the knowledge that my sister had been living under a false identity for the last few years in Daphne's hometown. Not to mention my joining up with a quest to find the Key of Hades before the end of the world comes. As far as my parents are concerned, I'd been yucking it up with friends in Las Vegas, so I can't really blame them, but the punishment has majorly cramped my ability to help out with both the search for Abbie's new whereabouts and this all-powerful Key.

But since the world hasn't ended yet nor my long-lost sister shown up on my doorstep, I figured both searches were probably still under way, so I've been conducting what little research I can do within in the confines of my internment. As in, sneaking into my mother's office whenever she isn't hovering over my shoulder.

With school starting up again and my finally getting some freedom back, I am determined to have something useful to offer the group when I see them again. Only, so far, all I've been able to find out is that the Olympus Hills master-planned community dates back only about sixty years. But the land itself has been owned by the rich and sometimes notorious for as far back as I was able to go. At one point, the land was even owned by a branch of the Spanish royal family in the 1700s.

I skim through the files in one of my mother's private cabinets. Another surge of anger flows through me when I see the file folder that holds the names of girls—my own sister's included—who've gone missing from town during the last fifty years. I skip over it and keep flipping through files until I see an older portfolio folder labeled O.H. SURVEYANCE. I pull out the folder, thinking it might be useful. Inside, I find a stack of what looks like old geological maps of the Olympus Hills area. A couple toward the back are yellowed and brittle, and look like they were hand drawn, with handwritten labels like what you'd expect on a pirate's treasure map.

I hear a door slam upstairs, followed by my mother calling my name. My phone, which I had only been granted back post-grounding from my mother's clutches late last night, chimes loudly with an incoming text. I curse myself for not setting it to silent before infiltrating enemy lines. I pull it from my pocket and see it's a message from Daphne, asking me to meet her at school, before I switch it off.

As quickly as I can, I slip the entire folder inside my old guitar case and close the cabinet drawer. I hear my mother calling me again, and this time it sounds like she's headed down the stairs. I jog quietly through the door with my backpack and guitar case, lock it, return the key, and head for the kitchen. As I round the corner, I almost run right into Mom. She jumps like I'm some sort of monster leaping out at her.

"There you are," she says, clutching her silk kimono to her chest. She's not wearing her usual makeup, and her face seems puffy and splotched, like she hasn't been sleeping well. "Why didn't you answer when I called?"

"Bathroom," I snap.

She blinks at my curt tone, and I realize I'm letting my anger show too much.

I try to dial it back. "It's my fault. I called back, but I must not have been loud enough for you to hear me," I say, with the politeness that she expects, but it physically pains me to do so when all I want is to yell and rage at her. But I'd promised Daphne and Haden I wouldn't let on that I know she's been aiding in the kidnappings of the daughters of Olympus Hills, not to mention that she was involved in what happened to my own sister.

"And what are you doing with that?" she asks, pointing at my guitar case. For half a second, I worry that maybe the Underlords have gifted her with X-ray vision, like the strange powers Simon had, and she can see the file folder inside the case. But then she goes on in her best tiger-mom tone: "I thought we agreed last year that you would give up guitar in favor of violin."

I hate the violin and she knows it. I want to be the next Frank Sinatra or Bruno Mars, not the next Hiroaki Yura. I swear sometimes my mom gives me this look like she questions if I'm really half Asian.

"I can do both," I say. "Mr. Morgan wants me to play a little in the opera. Daphne said she'd teach me a few new things after school."

She narrows her eyes, and I realize I've said exactly the wrong thing. "And when have you been speaking to Daphne? You were grounded for a reason, and I've told you how I feel about you spending extra time with that girl."

I'd never admitted it but when I didn't come home for two days, my mom had assumed it had something to do with Daphne. She'd been in a total panic when I finally returned. Maybe she'd thought I'd been spirited off by a group of Underlords. Though she hadn't seemed to mind that idea when she promised to trade my sister for the capital she needed to get her wind energy company up and running. I bite my tongue, forcing myself not to mention any of this to her. She takes my silence for insolence.

"I don't have time for your teen angst, Tobin. Clearly, you need to be further reminded of your responsibilities to this family and the proper behavior that your father and I expect. You will be home straight after school today, no excuses."

"But . . ."

"Don't even start with me today, young man. I do not have the patience. This house, your school, that fancy music program I indulge you with, even though you should be applying to MIT, like Sage; you have no idea the lengths I go to so you and your brother can have a good life."

My anger twists into a knot inside my chest. So she's saying that what she did to Abbie is *my fault?* So I can have this life? Her phone starts ringing in her hand. "Actually, I think I know exactly what you're capable of doing," I whisper under my breath.

"What was that?" she asks.

I shake my head. "Yes, ma'am. I'll be home right after school."

She eyes me for a second, and I worry she may have heard what I'd originally said over the shrill ring of her phone. She checks her caller ID, and a frantic look crosses her eyes.

"You should answer that," I say, and leave.

As I head into the foyer, I hear her say into her phone, "No, Marta, still nothing from Simon. I have no idea—" before she shuts herself into her office.

So my mother knows Marta as well as Simon? I shouldn't be surprised. Joe had postulated that the reason Abbie had fled from her life of hiding as CeCe Caelum in Ellis Fields is because she must have recognized Marta, Joe's assistant and Simon's lackey, when they came to move Daphne to Olympus Hills.

I make a mental note to look into what Marta might know about Abbie's second disappearance and then pull out my phone. On my way to the car, with my guitar case packed with stolen maps, I respond to Daphne's text: I might have something, too. Can't wait to see what you found. Be there in ten.

chapter four

HADEN

"You don't look so good," Daphne says to me as I enter the music room a half hour before school is supposed to begin. She's holding a green book open in front of her, and what looks like a breakfast of a protein bar and a can of root beer. "Rough night? Rain keep you up?" There's a challenging edge to her voice, and I wonder if she knows that I camped outside her window for most of the night.

My throat is sore, my ears feel strangely heavy, and I can barely keep my eyes open, but I only shrug in response. I don't feel like getting into it with her. I might slip and say too much.

She looks like she's about to question me further, but her attention is pulled away when Tobin and Lexie come through the door behind her.

"Tobin!" she says, jumping out of her seat, that green book still clutched in her hand. "Finally. Two weeks is too long."

A flash of jealousy runs up my spine as I watch her embrace Tobin in an enthusiastic hug. His face brightens for a moment as he greets her in return, then falls into an expression that I recognize as a mask used to hold back a flood of emotion. I know the look because it's one I've practiced all my life.

"Remind me to leave a note the next time we run off to Vegas, then," Tobin says. "My mom is the queen of grounding."

"At least she doesn't have the power to have you executed, like my father," I say. It was meant to be an aside to myself, but they all stare at me.

"No, but she does go around handing innocent teen girls over to him for profit," Tobin says, "so you don't exactly have the corner on the market of evil parents."

I glare at him. If he really wants to split hairs over whose parent is more—

"Okay, *awkward*," Lexie says, settling into her desk with some type of bright purple smoothie in one hand and a cup of steaming coffee in the other. "Who peed in your guys' Cheerios this morning?"

"I don't think Haden's been sleeping very well," Daphne says. She doesn't meet my eyes; instead, she traces her fingers over the cover of her book.

I blink and temper myself, realizing that my long night has me as cantankerous as a Gorgon. I should be as happy as Daphne to see Tobin, considering he risked his neck with the rest of us in coming back to Olympus, and was in an extra-precarious situation, living with his mother. Who knows what she would do if she found out we're onto her secret life?

"Gang's all here?" Dax says, ushering a very non-enthusiastic-looking Garrick, my Lesser half brother and recently former servant, into the room in front of him and breaking the tense mood. "We've only got a few minutes before classes start. Anyone find anything new?"

I shake my head. Not because I don't have anything to report to the group since our last strategy meeting, but because I don't want to tell the others about the person—or nonperson—whom I saw on the beach last night. Since Dax insisted he hadn't seen anything, and nothing had happened afterward, I was trying to convince myself that it was merely a mirage.

"I have my Sopranos researching different places in California that have either the words *devil*, *god*, *key*, or *hidden* in their names," Lexie says. "They're in the dark as to why, of course."

Leave it to Lexie to use her little mafia of minions to do her dirty work.

"There's a place called Devil's Pitchfork in the Mojave Desert that's topping the list at the moment. Maybe we need to take a little field trip this weekend."

"Sounds interesting," Dax says.

"I still think it's *here*," Daphne says, lowering her book. "It has to be."

It was Daphne's insistence that the Key must be hidden in Olympus Hills that sent us back here. Her logic had been solid: if Orpheus had escaped from the Underrealm with the Key through Persephone's Gate, which was located on the grove island of the lake in the center of Olympus Hills, while being pursued by a pack of Keres, he wouldn't have gotten very far with his contraband. Therefore he must have hidden it somewhere close or within the town's boundaries. Even after our searches turned up nothing, she still clung to the idea when the rest of us were ready to move on. The cursed Key could be all the way in Greenland, for all we knew.

"I still think it's in the grove," Daphne says. "I'm guessing Orpheus ditched it the second he made it through the gate. If we dig around a little more . . ."

"No way," Garrick says. "We've turned that place inside out."

"I'm with the kid," Lexie says. Garrick tosses her a death glare for being referred to as an infant goat, but she doesn't seem to notice. "My manicurist threatened to fire me as her client if I keep disrespecting her handiwork. I was not made for digging in dirt."

"I think Daphne's right," Tobin says.

Lexie and Garrick groan. "That's because you haven't been here," Lexie says. "You've been lounging about in the cushy king-sized bed of yours while the rest of us have been searching. I have blisters."

"My blisters have blisters," Garrick says.

"I haven't just been lounging in bed." Tobin's cheeks darken. "I've been investigating my mother's files. I took some maps from my mother's office, and I think I found something. One of the maps looks like the original plans for Olympus Hills, drawn up decades ago." He sets his guitar case on the desks in front of me and opens the latches. Just when I think he's planning on serenading us, he pulls a large folder from inside the case. He sets out map after map on the surrounding desks.

"I think this one is the oldest," he says, pointing at a map that is brittle and yellow. "And this is the most recent." He indicates one on clean white paper. "I think it matches the brochures my mom passes out to prospective residents."

"Oh, I think I have one of those," Daphne says, riffling in her tote bag. She pulls out a crumpled pamphlet and spreads it out with the other papers, then stands inspecting them while hugging her green book to her chest.

Dax and I huddle around the maps with her and Tobin as Lexie drinks her smoothie, watching us with uninterest. Garrick lies on top of a couple of desks, as if he's going to take a nap.

"Do you see it?" Tobin asks.

I study the maps in front of me. On the oldest map, the area is a wooded wilderness and there isn't a lake. I remember Simon telling me that the Olympus Hills lake was man-made, but I wonder when it was excavated. I scan the maps and land on one that's yellowed at the edges, but not yet brittle. I notice a handwritten note in the corner: *OH prospective ver.* 1. I compare it with the WELCOME TO OLYMPUS HILLS, A LUXURY MASTER-PLANNED COMMUNITY! brochure.

"Does anyone else notice something missing from this map?" Tobin asks, pointing at what I assume to be the original design for the Olympus Hills community.

I give it another inspection, and something catches my attention.

"The grove," Tobin answers his own question before I can respond. "The smaller island of the lake where the grove is, it's not in this plan. Everything else is the same as the brochure, the island for the school, Olympus Row, the walking paths around the lake. Everything except the grove . . ."

"Like someone changed the plan," Daphne says. "Perhaps someone who knew there was something special about the grove?"

"No way. You guys, get this," Lexie says, paying attention now. "After Pear was attacked and Tobin and Daphne found her on the grove's island, I overheard my dad talking to Bridgette's father—he's on the school board. Anyway, Bridgette's dad said that several parents had been lobbying for the board to make some sort of rule, banning students from cutting through the grove to get to school. He said there had even been a proposal to tear the island down, but that it would be *impossible*. And he said it like that, like it was all weighted, and my dad nodded like he knew what he was talking about. At the time, I thought they were talking about the expense. But what if it really is impossible to tear down the grove—and that's why the lake ended up different from what's on the original plans? Like when they tried to excavate the grove, it was, like, protected or something."

"Or that the grove *is* protecting *something*," Daphne says excitedly. "That makes total sense! I knew the Key had to be there."

Garrick groans from his makeshift bed. "Uh, yeah, the grove is protecting something: Persephone's Gate," he says, like we're all a bunch of addled idiots. "I imagine if there were Underlord emissaries involved in the design of the town, they wouldn't fancy the gate opening up underwater. It doesn't mean the Key is there, too. As we've already proven. If it were buried there, we would have already unearthed it."

I agree with Garrick's point but Daphne looks so crestfallen over his doubt that I contemplate placing my hand on her back in order to reassure her. But would she just find that too forward? Would it be more appropriate to place my hand on her shoulder? But the small of her back seems more appealing. More intimate. I shake the thought off and stretch my fingers toward her arm to give it a platonic but assuring pat, but she steps away before I get the chance. I tuck my hand behind my back as if nothing happened, and she flops down at her desk and flips open her green book with irritated abruptness.

"He's right," Lexie says, her interest returning to her smoothie. "My money is still on the Mojave Desert lead. Though I'm not picking up a shovel again. Not here. And certainly not in the desert."

"Whatever," Tobin mumbles, and picks up a couple of the maps as if he's about to pack them away.

"These are still useful," I say to him. "Can I hang on to them? I might be able to find some more inconsistencies. Perhaps there's another—"

"I think I've got something," Daphne says, cutting me off. She waves that book of hers in the air, excitedly.

"What is that?" I ask. She hasn't set the book down once all morning—almost like it has some strange hold over her.

"It's CeCe's—I mean, Abbie's—diary from before she ran away."

"Really?" Tobin and Dax say almost in unison.

"Look at this," Daphne says, handing the book to Tobin. "She talks about the grove in here."

Tobin takes the book from her. He stares at the lined pages for a moment, as though seeing his sister's handwriting is like looking at a ghost. He clears his throat and reads the passage Daphne indicates out loud: "'I feel as if the grove was created for keeping secrets. It's like I can feel them buried here. And it holds so many of mine. I tell everyone I go there to rehearse my lines for drama class, but that is only half the truth. I've been practicing using my powers. With Dax's help, I managed to create a few sparks in the palm of my hand last night. I wish I could tell Tobin—he'd probably think I'm like a character in one of his comic books. A superhero. He's the only one in my family who would get it—who gets me. He's not like Mom or Dad or Sage, who are so practical and analytical all the time. They have absolutely no imagination. But I can't tell Tobin, either. I just don't think he's old enough to understand what it all really means. He won't understand why I have to leave. . . .'" Tobin's voice catches, and it takes him a moment to go on. His eyes scan the page, and it seems as though he's skipped forward when he starts reading again. "'For now my secrets will have to stay buried in the grove with all the others.'" Tobin closes the book as if it pains him to read any more.

"You see, the grove," Daphne says quietly, giving Abbie's words reverence. "I'm telling you, that's where this town's secrets lie. The Key *is* there."

"That sounds like a pretty big reach to me," Garrick says, covering his head with his crossed arms. "So some half-Skylord chick used to go there to keep her dirty little secrets; doesn't mean the key is hidden there, too."

"That half Skylord is my *sister*. Don't talk about her that way," Tobin says, and I can practically feel anger rolling off him. I cannot help but worry that with all the new, not-exactly-pleasant information he's had to absorb in the last few weeks, Tobin is like a hellcat ready to "Hulk out" (as Daphne put it) if he gets pushed one too many times.

"I don't think it's a coincidence." Without any hesitance, Daphne places her hand on Tobin's shoulder as if she could sense him about to snap. Actually, knowing Daphne, I bet she could probably hear the notes of Tobin's anger filling the room. I still don't understand her ability to hear the tones and emotions that living things put off, but I do know that she's used it three times to save our lives, so I'm not going to question its oddness. But I also don't need to linger on the sight of her touching his shoulder.

I look away, clutching my own hand behind my back. Dax catches my eye and gives me a look like I should make some sort of decision. "Lead," he mouths, reminding me that I am supposed to be in charge of this bickering group. They'd all left the safety of Ellis in order to follow me.

"Daphne *is* the Cypher," I say in a tone befitting a captain. "She's the one who is supposed to be able to find the Key, so if she thinks it's in the grove, then we must have missed something."

Daphne smiles at me, and Tobin and Dax both give me nods.

Even Garrick deigns to uncover his face. Lexie takes a sip of coffee, but at least she seems to be listening.

I stand up straighter, ready to lead the charge. "I say we go to the grove now and we don't stop looking until we find something." I smack the desk beside me for emphasis.

"Um, now?" Daphne says, sinking back into her chair. "Class is about to start. You know Mr. Morgan is kind of insane about attendance."

"Who cares about Mr. Morgan?" I ask.

"Um, me," Lexie says.

"Me, too," Tobin says.

"Especially me," Daphne says.

"You were the one who was insisting that we needed to search the grove again," I say, my frustration edging into anger.

"Yeah, but not this second. I told you I'd help you find the Key, but I'm not jeopardizing my standing in this program because of it," Daphne says. "I've told you before, I'm helping you because I want to go back to my normal life. Well, as normal as it was before I found out I'm the Cypher."

I want to argue with her, but I know it's pointless. I turn to Dax instead. He was the one who had wanted me to step up and take control. He was the one who declared, back in Ellis, that he would follow my lead anywhere.

He shrugs. "There's a new teacher starting today. I'm supposed to give him the grand tour and all that this morning. We can go after school."

I purse my lips and resist the urge to throw my hands up in the air. That would be expressing too much emotion.

"Wherever it's hidden," Dax says, "it's been there for a few millennia, and it will still be there in a few hours."

"Fine, after school, then. But nothing is stopping us."

"I'm out," Garrick says. "I've got plans to watch the cheerleaders practice after school." He jumps up from where he's been lying, with a newfound energy, and heads for the door.

"Garrick, wait. I'm not done—"

He reels around. "You're done as far as I'm concerned. You're not a Champion anymore, which means I don't have to listen to you anymore. I'll do whatever the Tartarus I want with my time. And breaking my back with your fool's errand doesn't fit into my schedule today."

I make a move to stop him—rebuke him for his disrespect—but instead I let him open the door to leave. He's right. I don't have any *real* authority over him anymore.

"Have any of you idiots stopped to consider that we can't find the Key without the Compass? Isn't that what the Oracle said?" Garrick says this like it's supposed to be a slap in the face and then goes, leaving the door wide open behind him.

"He's a real gem," Lexie says. "Remind me why we brought him back from Ellis with us?"

"I'm beginning to wonder that myself," I mumble.

"He has a point, though," Daphne says. "I've considered that possibility every waking moment since the Compass was stolen."

"Sarah didn't give you any clues as to how to get it back?" Dax asks.

"What she said is that I *will* get it back and that I *will* use it to seek the Key. But she didn't tell me how." Daphne sighs and stares out the window. Other students are starting to pull into the parking lot. We don't have much time left to ourselves. "Ever since the Compass was stolen from me, I've had this hollow ache gnawing at my heart. Like I lost a piece of myself when the Motorcycle Man stole the Compass. And how am I even supposed to find it when I have no idea how to find him?"

A similar feeling fills my chest as I think of her pain. I realize now that we've all been dancing around that issue—trying to ignore the hydra in the chamber—until Garrick threw it in our faces. That without the Compass we will fail.

"I wish I'd gotten a look at that motorcycle's license plate," Daphne says, "but I never saw it from behind because it was always chasing us. All I know about it is that it was a black, shiny bullet bike."

Lexie laughs. "That was not a bullet bike. Do you even know what you're talking about?"

"Isn't that what you call bikes with a weird racer front that really douchey guys drive?" Daphne asks.

"Um, I'm not sure what you're describing, but that motorcycle was a Ducati Superbike 1199 Panigale. That's, like, a thirty-five-thousand-dollar bike."

I blink at her.

"What? I'm a poor little rich girl with daddy issues. I have a thing for hot, douchey bad boys with motorcycles. Can you blame me?"

"Um . . ." Daphne makes a look like she's actually considering answering that question but then reconsiders.

"And it wasn't just 'shiny'—that thing was in mint condition. Brand-new, if you ask me."

I stand up straighter. "As in recently purchased? Probably from a dealer nearby?"

Lexie nods. "I don't know how nearby, but there are probably only half a dozen dealerships between here and LA that sell that kind of bike."

"Do you think if we found the right dealership, they might tell us who bought it?" Daphne asks.

"We could try," Lexie says. "I'll have one of my Sopranos research it during lunch and draw up a list of Ducati dealerships in the county. I'll visit a few after school to see what I can find out while you all go and dig around in the mud."

"You really think you'll get them to hand over someone else's personal information?" Tobin asks, sounding incredulous.

Lexie puts her hands on her hips and gives him a little wink. "I do have a way of getting what I want."

Tobin's cheeks darken again, and I wonder if there's a story behind Lexie's insinuation.

"Sounds like it's at least worth a try," I say. "We'll go to the grove after school; you'll work on tracking down that bike."

A few students enter the classroom through the door that Garrick left open. Class is starting soon.

"Gotta go," Dax says, checking his watch. The group disperses, with Dax heading to the counselor's office, and Tobin, Daphne, and Lexie going to the back of the room to check their cubbies for the new sheet music Mr. Morgan had promised before Christmas break. I collect the maps and stick them in my bag for safekeeping.

A sharp scream goes up in the back of the room, and I expect the worst, but find Lexie with a gaggle of her Sopranos. From the squealing and exclamations that follow, I gather there had been a note in Lexie's cubby indicating that she had landed a choice role in the musical written by Daphne's father. Fittingly, it is about the tragedy of Orpheus and Eurydice, of Orpheus's journey into the

Underrealm to retrieve his wife. Risking everything for the one he loves . . .

Daphne and Tobin had already been chosen to play the roles of Orpheus and Eurydice last fall, but I knew Lexie had been campaigning for Persephone's. Sounds to me like she's gotten it.

"Settle down, settle down," Mr. Morgan says, coming into the room. "I see that a few of you found your belated Christmas presents. If you didn't get a note in your cubbie, don't despair; there are still a few parts left to assign. I'm still looking for a Hades, a handmaiden, and the Three Sisters Fate. I'll be hosting one last round of auditions next week, so if you've been holding out on me, be sure to bring your A game. After that, rehearsals will begin in earnest. We're only eleven weeks out from curtain." He sits at the piano on the small stage at the front of the room and hits a key. "Daphne, will you lead the class in our vocal warm-up?"

Daphne takes the stage, and the others follow her lead. I'm not in the mood for singing, but I still watch as she sings a scale of notes from high to low. She looks so natural up there, calm—not on edge like she was only a few minutes ago when we were discussing the Key. Part of me gets why she didn't want to skip music class, but her insistence on clinging to normalcy concerns me. We shouldn't be singing warm-up notes when our time to find the Key is wasting away, but she is so stuck on her plan for her future that I am afraid she doesn't realize that particular future may never come. What if her life never goes back to normal—how will she handle that?

And if by some miracle we *do* find the Key, stop the Keres, and escape the Court, will she really just go back to her regular-life plan? Forget about everything that has happened to her?

And what about us? Where do I fit in her grand plan? Will

she even want anything to do with me when this is all over? Or will she walk away from me, too?

You should tell her. I haven't been able to get Dax's words out of my head since last night. Maybe if Daphne knew what she was walking away from, she'd reconsider.

Mr. Morgan catches my eye and gives me a cross look for not participating in the warm-up. I join my voice with the others, but I can tell mine sounds unsteady. The idea of telling Daphne about my feelings has me shaking again.

Between that and having lost control of that so-called strategy meeting, I'm not exactly feeling like the fearless leader that I need to be.

When class ends, I wait for Daphne, ready to escort her to our next class. Tobin stops her. He has the green diary in his hands. I realize now that he'd been holding it all through class.

"Can I keep this?" he asks Daphne.

"Of course," she says, placing her hand on his arm. "You have more right to it than anyone."

I know Dax would probably like to have a look at the diary, too, but I don't say anything. Tobin squeezes Daphne's hand and then takes his leave with the book.

Daphne lets me walk beside her on our way to humanities. My thoughts drift to when she held my hand before we left Ellis. The way her skin felt pressed against mine . . .

Daphne comes to a sudden halt in the classroom doorway. I hear a quick intake of breath through her lips. "What is it?" I ask.

She shakes her head. "Nothing," she says, and quickly takes her seat. She almost seems embarrassed. I take my seat in the back of the class, wishing, not for the first time, that my desk were closer to Daphne's. But being in the back at least means I might be able to sneak in a few minutes of sleep. Ms. Leeds has proven herself to be somewhat nearsighted when it comes to my faults.

"Greetings, class," a voice rings out just as I lay my head on my humanities book for a pillow. The voice is booming and male. A strange yet familiar energy buzzes in the air, sending an ominous shiver up my back. I snap upright, clenching the sides of my desk, as if bracing myself for a blow to the face. A very tall, very tan man with a close-trimmed beard stands at the podium where Ms. Leeds usually begins the class lecture. Tingling electric heat shoots through my arms.

I've seen him before.

"My name is Ethan Bowman. But you can call me Ethan. I don't care for formalities. Your regular teacher has come into an unexpected . . . windfall. I will be teaching this class for the remainder of the year." He looks through everyone else in the class and locks his eyes on me. A slight smile plays on his lips, like he's letting me in on a joke. "I hope we can all get along just fine."

His beard is shorter, his hair has been cut, and he's dressed in crisp slacks and a button-up shirt rather than the grungy hat and coveralls that had been his disguise the last time I saw him.

He's the trucker from the diner outside Vegas.

chapter five

DAPHNE

I can't take my eyes off the girl sitting in the front row of my humanities class. She's new—I know I've never seen her before, but when I first walked into the classroom, I thought for almost a full three seconds that CeCe—oh yeah, Abbie—was sitting right in front of me. I almost dropped my tote bag and sprang at her for a hug before I realized how mistaken I was. The hair is totally different. Abbie's hair was flame red and curly as could be, while this girl's hair is a dark brunette, almost black, and her skin is a deep olive complexion. Not to mention that her tone is all wrong. CeCe had a jazzy, friendly tone like Tobin's (when he isn't angry), while this girl puts off a jumbled mesh of notes that sounds chaotic.

But everything else about her, from her face to the way she sits in her chair with both legs crisscrossed on top of the seat to the way she tugs on her hair while she reads, is so much like Abbie that for another two seconds I thought she was in some sort of elaborate disguise. But watching the girl now from my seat in the second row, I realize that she is far too young and too tall to be Abbie.

I am so distracted by the girl that I don't notice the new

teacher until he starts talking. I stare at him and notice that he has almost the same look as the new girl. A connection that makes sense when after he finishes introducing himself, he says, "And one of the perks of being a teacher here is that I get to spend more time with my niece and nephew, who just started attending today. Both of whom happen to be in our class." He indicates the girl. "This is Terresa Gordan." And then he points to a teenage boy near the windows, whom I also hadn't noticed before. "And this is her cousin, Calix."

The boy scans the classroom with his dark eyes. The hair stands up on my arms, as if there's an abundance of static electricity in the air. I look at Haden, but it's like he's intentionally not looking at me. A thought starts to form in my head, but before I can finish it, a silent message pops up on the iPad that sits on my desk with my textbook cued up. I keep my phone turned off at school but forgot that my texts get sent to my iPad when it's left on. I figure the message is from Joe, wanting to see if he can bring me lunch like he used to before winter break—before I knew the truth—and almost dismiss the text without reading it. Then I notice it's from Dax.

Skylords, the text says. There are Skylords in your classroom.

I almost jump out of my seat when I read it, but a second text pops up almost immediately. This time, it's from Haden: Do not react.

I start to look at him, but a barrage of further messages stops me:

Haden: Don't look at me.

Don't acknowledge me.

Pretend you barely know me.

I nod slightly, even though I know Haden isn't looking at me.

My first thought is that we should try to run, but then I realize that with Terresa by the door and Calix by the windows, they've got all the exits covered. We're basically trapped.

My second thought is to play sick and ask for a hall pass, or maybe to text Dax to call us down to the office. . . . But, no, both of those would look suspicious. And what if they tried to stop us? That would be three against one. Well, two, if you count me, but it's not like I know how to use my burgeoning powers for anything more complex than making raindrops dance. Maybe I could will chalk dust to fly in their eyes?

Yeah, that would be really useful against demigods who can wield lightning and thunder. In a room full of mortals no less. I have a feeling Skylords don't have much of a problem with the concept of collateral damage.

I'm about to stealth-text Haden to discuss strategy when I hear a measured, symphonic tone hovering above my head. I look up to see the Skylord named Ethan standing in front of my desk. "I hope you're studying the lesson on that contraption and not idling away your time on other concerns," he says, smiling down at me in a seemingly knowing way.

"Uh, yes," I say, quickly exiting out of my texting app. A textbook page pops back up on my screen, and I set my iPad on top of my desk to show him that I was scanning today's lesson.

"Daphne Raines, is it?" he asks.

I nod.

"Can I borrow this?" he says, and his bronze fingers snatch up my iPad before I even have the chance to answer. My heart drops into my stomach like a rock as he looks at the screen. I can see his finger swiping on the surface, as if he's looking for something. Was he onto my and Haden's texting? The muscles in my

44

legs tense, getting ready to bolt. But it's not like I'd get past the CeCe-sort-of-look-alike in front of the door. I wish more than anything that I could see Haden's reaction.

"What can you tell me about this?" Ethan says, holding my iPad aloft for the class, or maybe just for the other two Skylords in the room.

I look up at it, expecting to see the texts from Haden on display for everyone's view, but instead I see a picture of a sculpture from our Greek mythology unit. It's of a tall, thin, curly-haired young man with wings embracing a nubile woman, who is reaching up to cup her hands around his face. The two look as though they are about to kiss.

"Daphne?" Ethan asks, prodding me for an answer. Out of the corner of my eye, I see the female Skylord eyeing me. I'm sure the one named Calix is watching me also, but I don't dare look toward the back of the room.

My thoughts are too clouded by the adrenaline leaving my body to come up with anything. I shake my head dumbly. Maybe behaving like an idiot will help my cover.

"Anyone else?" Ethan asks.

"He's an angel," Bridgette says, her sentence arching up at the end so I'm not sure if it's a statement or a question.

"Well, he's certainly divine, but, no, not an angel. That is a common mistake, I'm afraid. Anyone else?"

Lexie's hand goes up with a confident flick of her wrist, showing her disdain for those of us who couldn't get the answer. We may be pseudofriends now, but I'm sure she's happy for the opportunity to show me up. "*Psyche Revived by Cupid's Kiss*, by Antonio Canova, circa 1777. It resides in the Musée du Louvre," she says, accenting her French at the end.

"Very good . . ." He checks the seating chart on the podium. "Lexie?"

She nods, and I can tell by the melody spiraling up from her that she is wholly unaware of his Skylord status and might be developing a teacher crush. For the moment, I figure it's better if she doesn't know anything.

"But isn't Cupid supposed to be some fat little baby in a diaper who goes around shooting people with heart-shaped arrows on Valentine's Day?" Bridgette says. "I mean, the dude in that sculpture is kinda hot."

An amused smile edges Ethan's lips. "Another common misconception. I am afraid Cupid—or Eros, as he probably prefers to be called—is the mythological god who has had his image most distorted by modern commercialism. He was, in fact, a man, and was part of one of the greatest love stories in all of history. Many of the most famous fairy tales and love stories—Rapunzel, Romeo and Juliet, Beauty and the Beast, Rumpelstiltskin, and even Sleeping Beauty—all find their roots in Cupid and his beloved Psyche's tragic tale."

Ethan tells the story of how Cupid fell in love with a woman named Psyche, and how their love was forbidden by Cupid's mother, Aphrodite. We hear of the many obstacles and tragedies that befell their love and kept them apart. The other girls in the class are watching Ethan dreamily as he speaks of true love, and I am almost distracted from his clutch on my iPad by the absurdity of it all, but my ears perk up when Ethan mentions Psyche's journey to the underworld. Apparently, in order to prove her love for Cupid to Aphrodite, she was tasked with retrieving a portion of Persephone's beauty in a box.

"Persephone freely gave Psyche the box and warned her not

to open it. Unfortunately, when Psyche returned with the box, her curiosity got the better of her, and she opened it to see what was inside, perhaps hoping to claim some of Persephone's beauty for herself to further strengthen Cupid's love. But as soon as she opened it, she fell into a deep sleep, like unto death. None could wake her, save true love's kiss from Cupid himself. Upon rescuing her from the enchanted sleep, Cupid, with Psyche, fled to Zeus, hoping to find refuge and seek intervention from any further punishment dished out by Aphrodite.

"Now this is where scholars differ on how the story ends. Some say that Zeus granted the two amnesty and convinced Aphrodite to drop her wrath against them. Others say that Zeus was angry with Cupid for allowing this forbidden love to continue, and cast them both out, cursing them never to be together again. So I guess it is up to you to believe whichever story you choose. Do you believe that tragedy comes to those who disobey the will of the gods, or do you believe that true love conquers all?"

It is almost as if every girl in the room sighs at once.

"Interesting side note," Ethan says, waving my iPad with the picture of the two characters on the screen. "The names Cupid and Psyche represent the ideas of the heart and the soul. These two mythological beings symbolize the two halves of what makes us who we are—our heart and our soul."

A languid tone swoons through the room from the other female students, but all I can concentrate on is the fact that Ethan has gone back to swiping his finger across the screen of my iPad. If he were to click on my texting app . . .

I wave my hand in the air, catching his attention. "Mr. Bowman, may I have my iPad back?" I ask. "Um, I'd like to bookmark that passage."

"Ethan, please. And thank you for the use of your handy device, Daphne." He sets the iPad on my desk. The screen has gone dark, so I'm not quite sure what he's seen.

"No problem," I say. "Ethan."

Ethan smiles, his large hand resting on my desk. "'Daphne, Daphne, why dost thou run? What grievest thou to be undone?'" His words make me feel like my rib cage is too tight, and my hand begins to shake, but his voice is lilting and lyrical, and I realize that he's reciting poetry. A collective tone wafts throughout the room, another sigh from all the female students. Ethan leans down close to my ear. "Daphne, are you as hard to catch as your namesake?" he asks, his measured tone dipping colder, darker, as he speaks.

I resist the urge to shiver and give him a befuddled look instead.

"You do know *that* myth, don't you?" he asks. "The girl who would rather be turned into a laurel tree than to be caught up by an enamored Apollo?"

I nod. "I know the story."

"Good," he says, and returns to his podium. He relays the story of Daphne and Apollo to the rest of the class, but I'm too shaken to listen. I'm about to tuck my iPad into my bag when a new text from Haden comes up on my screen: When the bell rings, I want you to take Lexie and walk out of here as casually as you can. Go find Dax. Do not come back to this classroom under any circumstances.

I nod, letting him know I got his message. I don't dare attempt to text him back, even though I'm dying to know what he's planning to do.

The bell rings, and I stuff my things in my bag, wondering how I'm going to get past Ethan, when half the girls rush toward the front of the room to talk to him. It reminds me of that scene in Indiana Jones when all the archeology students want a piece of Harrison

Ford. I catch Lexie by the elbow before she can join the throng.

"I wanted to ask Mr. McHottypants over there . . . ," she starts to protest, but I give her the most pointed look I can muster and say, "Hey, girlfriend, I really need your help with . . . something," and propel her toward the door.

"Are you feeling okay?" she asks.

I hold my breath as we pass by Terresa. She stands up but lets us pass.

"Yeah, I just forgot my trig notes. Can I borrow yours?" I say to Lexie as we exit through the door.

"Sure. I didn't know you had trig."

I glance slightly behind me and see Calix coming down the hall behind us.

"I do. Last period. Are they in your locker?"

"Yeah."

I lead her through a crowd of students heading the opposite direction and then make a sharp turn down the next hall.

"My locker is the other . . ."

"Shhh. Don't say anything," I whisper. "We're headed toward the counselor's office. We need to find Dax."

"Why?"

I glare at her for saying something after I told her not to. "Because your Mr. McHottypants is a freaking Skylord," I whisper. "And his Skylord nephew is behind us."

Lexie's eyes go wide. We turn down another hall and duck into the counselor's office before Calix comes around the corner.

"What about Haden?" Lexie asks.

"He'll be okay," I say. I hope that I'm not wrong.

chapter six

HADEN

I watch Daphne leave, taking Lexie with her, and the Skylord named Calix leaves shortly after. It takes everything I have not to go directly after them, too. But I can't. Not if I don't want to blow Daphne's cover. But what if it's already blown? What if Calix is tailing them? What if there are more Skylords in the school and he's flushing them out into a trap? That is a common hunting practice in the Underrealm—make your prey think it's getting away, when you're really herding it into the waiting sights of a comrade. I can't help it. I grab my stuff, and I'm about to follow after them despite my better judgment when Ethan calls my name from the crowd of girls who surround him.

"Haden, may I have a word with you?"

As if he were just going to let me walk out of here?

"I am sorry, ladies. We will have to continue our discussion tomorrow," Ethan says, ushering the gaggle of very disappointed girls to the door. After they've reluctantly left, only he, Terresa, and I remain in the room.

So it is to be two against one? In an empty classroom? Those odds I like better than trying to take on all three in a room full of bystanders. What I don't like is not knowing what Calix is up to.

Nor do I like the idea of fighting in the school, but I will if I have to. I concentrate some of my energy into my hand, preparing a bolt to be flung when I need it.

Terresa advances toward me. I can feel her energy pulsating in the air.

"Terresa," Ethan says, "you should be getting on to your next class. I need to have a word, alone, with this student."

Terresa turns her menacing glower from me to Ethan.

"Pardon?" she asks.

"*Leave.*"

"He's Underlord scum. He knows what we're looking for—"

"I am your commander, and I *command* you to get out. Leave teaching this Underlord scum a lesson to me. Guard the door if you think it necessary."

Ethan ushers Terresa out and shuts the door behind her, but I can see her silhouette in the mottled glass window as she stands guard. I hear Ethan click the lock into place. It's not the kind that would prevent me from getting out, but it would temporarily stop anyone else from entering.

So it's to be one against one? Even better.

Ethan turns toward me.

I raise my hand, a swirl of blue lightning crackling in my hand as a warning.

"I know who you are," I say. "I saw you watching me in the diner two weeks ago. And I imagine you know who I am or else you wouldn't have asked for this little *meeting*. I will tell you right now, I no longer have allegiance to the Underrealm. I am not a threat to you. However, if a fight is what you want, a fight is what you'll get."

"I am not looking for a fight, if I can help it. But if you know who we are, then you know what we want."

For half a heartbeat, I consider playing dumb.

"The Cypher," I say instead. "You want the Cypher so you can find the Key of Hades and destroy the Underrealm once and for all."

"That is what the *Skylords* want."

"Know this," I say, the lightning in my hand pulsing brighter. "I risked death at the hands of my own father in order to prevent him from getting her, so if you think I'm going to tell you who she is . . ."

Before I can finish, Ethan's hand juts out and grabs me by the throat. He yanks my head close to his as if he is about to slam his forehead against mine, but instead he growls a low whisper next to my ear, "I already know who she is."

I take in a sharp breath and start to raise my hand to blast him.

"You don't want to do that," Ethan says. "Or else Terresa will break down the door and it will all be over." He grips my neck tighter, but not enough to crush my windpipe. "She's itching to kill somebody today."

His eyes flick toward the window in the door. I can tell by her outline that she's facing the door, trying to watch us through the thick, distorted glass. "I know who the Cypher is. But the others do not. The message from our Oracles was distorted and a name was never given. All they know is that the Cypher is a person close to you. I won't tell the others who she is, and I will let you walk out of here and go find your pretty blond friend if you make me a deal," he says, and I realize he's holding back because he's putting on a show for his comrade.

I claw at his hands, but not enough to actually cause him harm. "What do you want," I whisper, "that you think I will give you?"

"I will come to you in the near future, and you will grant me a favor."

"Which is?"

He shakes his head, indicating that he will not say.

"I am not a fool. I'm not going to grant you a favor carte blanche. My father has already offered me glory and the seat at his right hand as his heir in exchange for the Cypher, and I turned him down, risking my own death in the process. I will not give her to you, nor the Key. If that is the 'favor' you are asking for, you best change your mind right now."

"Impressive," Ethan says. I almost hear a tinge of respect in his voice. "However, let's put it this way: either you agree to grant me the favor of hearing me out when I come to you in the future, or I will have my compatriots kill you all now and I will snatch the Cypher up and let them do whatever it takes to get her to lead us to the Key."

I want to ask him why he doesn't go through with that second option right now and be over with it, but I don't want to put the idea in his head.

"That option is a lot messier," he says, as if he can see the question written on my face.

"Why don't you just tell me whatever it is that you want me to hear now?"

"The timing isn't right."

"When will it be?"

"That depends on you and your little gang of friends," Ethan says. "Now do I have your consent?"

I don't get what he means by the timing being dependent on me, and agreeing to his terms may be foolish, but what he is truly offering me is time. And that's exactly what I need. Time to find the Key, time to figure out how to save the five realms, time to protect my friends.

"Fine," I say. "One favor, that is all."

"Wise decision," he says, and pushes me away from him. "And don't say a word of this to anyone, not *Dax*, not your precious Cypher, not even your cat. Say one word, and the deal is off. Got that?"

"Got it," I say, shrugging the strap of my bag back onto my shoulder. "So what happens in the meantime? Until you come calling for this favor?"

"Act normal. Lie low. Steer clear of Terresa and Calix. Or whatever other cliché mortals use for staying out of trouble. Terresa and Calix are under my command, but the Key is quite the prize, and Terresa, especially, is ambitious. Try not to lead her right to it."

So many things confuse me that I am not sure how to respond. He'd said Dax's name with such familiarity, it makes me wonder if they'd known each other in Dax's past life as a Champion. If he already knows Daphne is the Cypher, then why not snatch her up immediately instead of pulling off this teacher charade? And why doesn't he want someone in his command to get her hands on the Key? Isn't that why he's here in the first place? What could he possibly want to tell me that can't be said now?

"Now, if you don't mind, this is my free period and I have some lessons to plan."

He unlocks the door and tries to show me out, but Terresa blocks the doorway. "Don't you have a class you need to attend, Teri?" he says. She flinches as if that nickname makes her want to punch him. "*Now.*"

She turns away, and I think I catch a growl under her breath. I follow her out.

"I recommend reading pages two hundred thirty-four through two hundred eighty-five for tomorrow's lesson," Ethan says. "I expect a lot from my *students*."

The way his demeanor flips so easily from hardened commander to dashing teacher reminds me of Simon and his dual personality. The comparison makes my skin crawl. I notice Terresa watching me in the hallway, so I head for my locker instead of going to meet the others in Dax's office. She stays a few paces away, pretending she's looking through her new class schedule. At least two minutes pass as I leisurely exchange the books in my locker, waiting for her to get bored and move on, until the vice principal notices us lingering in the hall and barks at us to get to class.

She leaves, a cross look on her face. I look back at the classroom I've just come from and see Ethan's outline behind the glass, as if he's listening at the door.

I walk away, not knowing what to make of this seemingly rogue Skylord, nor of what the future will hold when he comes to collect his favor.

chapter seven

DAPHNE

Instead of welcoming us into his office, Dax instructs us to head to our next classes as usual. I'm sitting in US history, my knee bouncing up and down uncontrollably, when a text from Haden finally pops up on my iPad. It's a group text, addressed to me, Dax, Tobin, Garrick, and Lexie.

Haden: Go to all the rest of your classes like normal. Lexie, stick with your dealership research, the rest of you, meet me in the grove after school. Everyone should go there separately. Make sure you're not being followed.

Me: What happened? Are you okay?

Haden: Everything is fine. I'll tell you when I see you at the grove.

I don't realize how few breaths I've taken in the last half hour until I read that Haden is okay. My lungs ache as I sigh with relief.

Dax: I'll be there.

Lexie: Will do. Glad you're not dead.

Tobin: What are you guys going on about? I'm in the middle of a chem quiz. Oh and btw, freaky new chick in my class keeps checking me out.

Garrick: Stop with the texting. I'm trying to nap.

Haden: Grove. After school. And, Tobin, DON'T bring the scary new girl with you.

Tobin: Bro, you can't try to keep all the new girls to yourself.

For some reason, I blush. And then duck my head, even though none of them can see me.

Me: Tobin, he's serious. Make sure she doesn't follow you.

Tobin: All right. GTG.

Haden: One last thing. If you see me in the halls, pretend you don't know me. We should all be seen together as little as possible for the time being. For Daphne's protection.

Time passes at a snail's pace until the last bell of the day rings. I get waylaid by Mr. Morgan, who wants me to bring some line notes to Joe for the opera's libretto, and I don't see anyone else around by the time I leave the school. I hop on my lemon yellow cruiser bike, make sure no one is watching, and pedal off toward the grove as fast as I can. The grove had been the first place I'd explored when I moved to Olympus Hills, its ethereal lullaby drawing me to it. But ever since Tobin and I had found Pear Perkins unconscious on its shore, and Lexie and I had been attacked by a Keres nearby, I haven't exactly enjoyed being here during our little treasure hunts. I have to admit that I'm glad when I hear the others' voices in the grove as I approach. I don't know that I would have had the courage to go in alone.

I get off the bike, look around again, and then wheel it between the tall poplar trees that surround the grove in a perfect circle, and find the others waiting for me. Haden stands in the center of a group that consists of Dax, Tobin, and Garrick. The latter of whom I am surprised to see, considering his blowup at Haden earlier.

Haden looks up when he hears me approaching. I notice a particularly relieved tone swirl about him. Like he was worried about me. I smile, feeling that tightness in my chest finally loosening at the sight of him safe and sound. The urge to hug him grips me, but I look away instead.

I wouldn't want to lead Haden on.

I'd never been into the idea of dating. My music and my goals had always come first, and having a mother who had been royally screwed over by the only guy she'd ever loved, I never saw all that lovey-dovey stuff as anything other than a distraction.

Until I met Haden.

Or I guess I should say until I got to know him—I'd hated him at first. But once he'd started to open up to me, I'd started to try to picture how he might fit in with my future plans. But now, with everything that is happening, I don't know what that future holds. With all the dread and searching, and not even knowing how all of us—especially me, who according to a somewhat sketchy prophecy was supposed to use my heart and soul to unlock the Key—are going to come out of this unscathed. I don't even have the emotional capacity to entertain the idea of a relationship at the moment. And depending on how all this shakes out, I'm not sure if there really is a place for Haden in my future. We're too different—we're literally from two completely different realms, after all.

It would never work.

Or at least that's what I tell myself, despite not being able to breathe properly when I don't know if he's okay. . . .

I take a few measured breaths as Haden passes out shovels. There are holes in the ground that make it look like the place has been attacked by Godzilla-like gophers, large rocks turned over, and little saplings pulled up by their roots. They lie, shriveled and songless, strewn across the ground. I can hear the aching pulse of the grove's pain. I know some of this damage was done before we started looking for the Key—Haden had reported that he'd found the grove trashed when he came back to investigate the night Lexie and I were attacked—but guilt still pulls at me for our contribution.

When Haden told me about what he'd found here that night, I'd thought maybe it was the Keres that had caused the damage, but now that we've landed on our theory about the grove, I'm starting to think maybe someone else had been digging around here on purpose. Looking for the Key.

It's a plausible and extremely freaky prospect since we already knew the Motorcycle Man had been following us before we left for Vegas. And now he has the Compass. Or perhaps the Skylords arrived in Olympus Hills earlier than today.

What if either party finds the Key before us?

"So what's going on?" Tobin asks. "Why are we being so clandestine? Nobody in town ever comes to the grove anyway."

"There's been an incursion," Haden says. "That new girl in your class, Terresa; another student named Calix; and our new humanities teacher, Ethan Bowman, they're all Skylords. . . . I . . ." He seems to have something more to say but hesitates, like he doesn't want to.

"Whoa, that Ethan guy is a Skylord?" Tobin asks. He has humanities last period of the day. "He did seem a little too suave for a substitute teacher."

"So . . . there's something else you should know about Ethan," Dax says, looking at Tobin. "He's Abbie's fiancé."

"Wait, what?" Tobin says, dropping his shovel. "She's engaged to a Skylord?"

"I thought she was in love with you?" I ask Dax. CeCe—I mean, Abbie—hadn't struck me as the "get engaged before you graduate high school" type. Then again, I'd had no idea she was a half Skylord in a self-appointed witness relocation program, either.

"She is in love with me. Or at least she was when we parted ways." An unsure tone flows under Dax's words. "I guess her *betrothed* is a better title than *fiancé*. Important Skylords pair their children off before they are even born. Political alliances, that sort of thing. Abbie's biological father is named Taran, the son of a pretty high-ranking Skylord official. He went through a bit of a rebellious stage during his youth, fathering Abbie with your mother before returning to the Sky Court to take over his father's position. Abbie was all but forgotten until Taran got word that the Underrealm had made a deal with your mom to make Abbie a Boon—and suddenly Taran remembered that his first-born daughter had already been promised to someone else. And not just any someone, but the eldest grandson of the Sky King himself."

"You mean Ethan isn't just any Skylord, he's a Sky Prince?" Haden asks.

"Wait, Ethan is Zeus's grandson?" I ask.

"Zeus is the Sky God," Dax says, "but if you've read the myths, he prefers spending his time on *other* activities than actually managing the day-to-day dealings of his realm. He leaves that to his adopted son, Life, the very first Skylord—or the Sky King, as he prefers to be called."

"You mean Life is still alive? How old would that make his grandson?" I say.

"The Skylords are immortal under Zeus's protection. Just

60

as the Underlords would be if Hades's Kronolithe had not been stolen," Dax says. "Ethan could be the age of twenty-three that is listed in his school file, or a millennium and a half, for all we know."

"So my sister was not only promised to the Underrealm as breeding stock but was also betrothed to some possibly super-old prince from the Skyrealm?" Tobin asks.

"You see why she needed to go into hiding?" Dax says.

"And you didn't think this betrothal business was pertinent information to share before now?" Tobin asks, clenching his fists. "For all we know, either group has her."

"Or she could have just found a better spot to hide after she recognized Marta," I say, trying to calm Tobin down. The angry notes that have been tumbling off him today are so thunderous, I don't get how nobody else can hear them.

"So what do the Skylords want?" Garrick asks.

"The Key, I assume," Dax says.

"So what do we do?" I ask.

"We find it first," Haden says, handing me the last shovel.

"Okay. But please be mindful of the trees," I say, listening to the worried little tones they put off.

We search until the sun starts to go down and my arms ache so much, I can barely lift them to wipe the sweat from my face. My throat is so dry, it feels like sandpaper. I reach for the water bottle I'd bought from one of the school vending machines after class but find that I've already drained it. I groan.

"Here," Haden says, holding out his own bottle. "Take mine."

"It's yours. I couldn't take it from you."

He shrugs, and I notice that even though he's dug three times as many holes as I have, he's barely broken a sweat while I feel like a dripping, dirty mess. "You need it more than I do."

The tone coming off him is so earnest; I know he isn't being rude. His concern makes me hesitate. "I don't need—"

"Don't be addled," he says, pressing the water bottle into my hand.

I'm careful not to let my fingers brush against his as I take it, but as the cool water soothes my parched throat, I can't help lingering on the thought that my mouth is pressed where his warm lips had been only moments before.

Heat rushes into my cheeks as I finish off the water and set the bottle aside.

I wipe my neck where water has spilled over my lips and run down to my collarbone in my exuberance in quenching my thirst. Haden glances away as if he weren't watching.

"This is stupid," Garrick says, collapsing against one of the larger trees. "How are we even supposed to know if we find the Key? Nobody even knows what we're looking for. Is it large or small? Are we looking for a box that it's hidden in? I am supposing it's locked up somehow, considering Daphne's supposed to use her heart and soul to open it up? What does that even mean?"

"I have no idea on any of those," I say, because even though his attitude stinks, his words echo the thoughts that have been running through my head for the last two weeks. I sit on the ground and use my foot to push dirt back into one of the holes I've dug. I hate the idea of leaving the grove ripped up, but I know I don't have the energy to clean up all of this mess today. "I can only hope Lexie has had more luck. Speaking of which . . ." I reach for my tote bag and dig my phone out. There are two texts from Joe, who's wondering when I'll be home, and a voice mail from Lexie.

I hit the speaker button and play the message out loud. "So it turns out there are eight dealerships that sell Ducatis between here and Redondo Beach. I emailed you a copy of the list. I only had time to make it out to the closest one. . . . And this is going to be harder than I thought. I even flashed around my dad's black AmEx and said I was trying to buy him a special birthday present, and I couldn't get anyone to give me the time of day. It doesn't help that most of the sales staff are female. Anyway, got to get to my Pilates class. Talk at you tomorrow."

I delete the message and rub my hands over my face, forgetting they're wet and dirty until it's too late.

"I'm guessing teenagers aren't worth their time," Haden says.

"That's what I thought," Tobin says, kicking a pile of dirt.

"I can give it a try," Dax says. "Clean me up enough, and I could look like an up-and-coming starlet."

I crook a smile. "Starlets are girls . . . but that gives me an idea. . . ." It just involves bringing in the one person I was hoping to leave out of my life at the moment.

I dial Joe.

"Daphne?" he asks. "What's wrong? Where have you been? Are you okay? Do you need help?"

"Nothing is wrong," I say, realizing with a pang of guilt that Joe thinks that's the only reason I would call him on my own accord. "I do need your help with something, though. How much do you know about motorcycles?"

"Not a bleeding thing. But my drummer has one."

"How do you feel about looking into one for me?"

"Um . . . I guess. What kind did you have in mind?"

"A black Ducati Superbike 1199 Panigale."

Joe sounds like he's choking on his own spit. "Right, I know enough about motorcycles to know that your mum is going to kill me if I get you one of those."

"It's not for me. It belongs to your new bass player—or at least the one you want to hire."

"What are you talking about?"

"We have a theory that the Motorcycle Man may have recently bought his bike from one of the nearby Ducati dealerships. I'm thinking that if *the* Joe Vince goes swaggering into the dealership looking to find the name and address of someone who purchased a black Ducati Superbike in the last three months—say, because you recently saw that person play at an open mike night and you want to hire him for your band, but all you got was the make of his motorcycle, and you just happened to be offering a finder's fee—they might be more willing to give his personal information to you rather than a bunch of teenagers."

"Sounds like a decent theory," Joe says, his voice much brighter now. "I'll give it my best shot."

I tell him that I'll send him the list of dealerships, and then hang up the phone, hoping he means it, because this shot may be the only one we've got left.

chapter eight

HADEN

It takes four days to visit all eight of the dealerships before Joe is able to procure the information that we need. He calls me as I am leaving Ethan Bowman's latest lecture on Greek art. I watch Daphne walk away, pretending she does not know me for the sake of Terresa and Calix, before I duck into a restroom to answer the phone.

"Between all the dealerships, five black Superbikes have been sold since September. Two went to a movie set, one a supermodel bought for her boyfriend, another was bought by someone replacing a bike with an insurance claim, and the fifth, get this, was sold to an overly chipper man who somehow talked the manager into a discount so mad that he later got sacked for it. Remind you of anyone we knew?"

"Simon?" I say. "However, we know for sure he wasn't the Motorcycle Man, so that means they must have been working together."

"Simon had the bike delivered to a luxury condo complex at the edge of Olympus Hills. I'm guessing our Motorcycle Man was the recipient."

"Did you get a full address?"

"I had to agree to give the saleswoman—who wants to be an

actress—an audition for my new music video, but, yes, I got an address. It's 1472, apartment 7, Icarus Court," he says, like he's dictating it off a piece of paper.

"Good work," I say, heading out of the restroom to the parking lot.

"Oh, by the way, do you happen to know what Daphne's favorite color is?" Joe asks.

"Um . . ." I stop at the school exit, realizing that I don't know the answer to that unexpected question. Here I'd been wishing I could confide in her my feelings, but she hasn't even confided in me something as simple as her favorite color. "She wears a lot of green," I say. "Teal green." I almost say *jade green*, but that is the same color as my eyes and that seems oddly presumptuous of me.

"Right. Have fun catching the bad guy." Joe sighs. "But do me a favor, mate? Don't bring Daphne with you."

"Don't worry. I won't."

I stand in front of the door of 1472, apartment 7, Icarus Court, with Dax standing behind me as backup. Three against one would normally be better odds, but Garrick is completely untrained and more likely to be a liability in a fight.

I don't want to knock and alert the Motorcycle Man of our presence. By the will of the Fates, the lock on the door is electronic, requiring a pass code to gain entry—but I don't need one. I cup my hand over the electronic box above the doorknob and send a pulse of crackling blue lightning into it. I can hear the circuits sizzling. The lock clicks open.

I turn the knob and shove the door, going for speed and surprise, with Dax close on my heels, as we burst through at the ready. Lightning swirls inside my chest; a confrontation could be only seconds away.

What we find is an abandoned apartment.

A black leather couch is the only thing that sits in the front room. An empty closet stands open. An inspection of the kitchen and the bedroom yields only empty cabinets and a bed with a plush mattress, which has been stripped of its sheets. There are no pictures on the walls, no television, and nothing in the fridge but a container of Greek yogurt. If it hadn't been for that last thing, I would have thought this apartment had never been occupied.

"This yogurt is still good," Dax says, testing the white goop with his finger. "This apartment hasn't been empty for long."

"*Kopros*," I hiss under my breath, and kick the closest thing. The trash receptacle sails across the room and slams into the oven. It falls over, and its contents topple out onto the tile floor.

"Good thinking," Dax says, crouching to inspect the mess. It looks mostly like food waste, but he fishes a piece of paper out from under a banana peel. "Look at this."

I take the slimy paper. It looks to be nothing but a grocery list—only it isn't written in English. "This is Underlord writing."

A sinking feeling grips me. The suspicion that the Motorcycle Man was another Underlord had plagued me ever since Daphne had mentioned seeing someone with fiery eyes at her audition that first day I'd met her. She'd thought I'd stalked her all the way to the auditorium, but if it wasn't me and it wasn't Dax or Garrick, that meant there had to be another Underlord at play in Olympus Hills. The fact that this unknown lord was also the Motorcycle Man, whom I'd seen following me on more than one occasion, made perfect sense. But it also made him all the more dangerous.

"Heads up," Dax says, looking out the window. "Olympus Hills security just pulled up. Someone must have seen us busting in."

"Or they knew we were coming."

"Either way, we need to get out of here. *Now.*"

chapter nine

TOBIN

I sit in the far corner of Olympus Brew, the coffeehouse next to the gelato shop on Olympus Row, observing my prey from over the brim of my gingerbread spiced latte. Marta sits at her usual table—or at least where she's usually sat for the last three days that I've been following her after school—near the door. Her iPad and several documents are set out in front of her. She has shiny black hair slicked into a tight bun, and she wears a dress suit that fits her like a glove. She wears high, high crocodile heels that match her purse. Under normal circumstances, I might think she was attractive in a sexy librarian sort of way, but considering she might be responsible for my sister's disappearance, the sight of her sipping her daily 4:15 p.m. espresso makes me ill.

I haven't actually drunk any of my own coffee, but having something to hold keeps my hands steady. For the last three days, I've been building up the nerve to confront her. Or building up the nerve to go against Daphne's wishes to not let anyone know that we're onto Olympus Hills's deep dark secrets. If I were to say something to Marta, she most definitely would tell my mother, and then where would I be?

My mom would probably lock me in my room and throw away

the key if she knew that I'm onto her extracurricular activities—or possibly cart me off to that mathematics-and-engineering boarding school in Virginia that she threatened me with when I got into that fight with Haden back on his first day of school. Back when I thought he was the one responsible for what had happened to my sister and I'd gone in swinging.

But it's not like I could do that with my mother—nor Joe's personal assistant, who looks like she barely weighs 115 pounds. But as frail as she might appear, the sight of Marta may have been what sent Abbie running from the haven of Ellis Fields to a location (or fate) unknown.

Or maybe Marta had kidnapped Abbie herself.

In that case, boarding school seems like a small price to pay for the truth.

I place my coffee cup on my table, straighten my tan fedora, and decide to make my move. But I get only two steps in her direction when Marta receives a phone call. I stop, listening in on her clipped responses, while trying to look like I'm merely getting a napkin from the condiment bar.

"Really?" she says into the phone. "Finally. I've been looking everywhere. Where?" She grabs her iPad and stuffs it into her crocodile purse. "I'll leave right away."

She hangs up and gathers her papers in an almost frantic haste. She's out the door and getting into an Audi before I make it out onto the street. My car is parked only a couple of slots over. I should follow her. But as I stick my hand into my jacket pocket, I realize I've left my keys on the table next to my latte.

I'm cursing myself as she speeds out of the parking lot. I'd never make it back with my keys before she's out of sight.

It's for the best, I try to tell myself as I head back into the coffeehouse. What was I going to do anyway? Follow Marta to some clandestine location, grab her, and demand she tell me where she's hidden my sister? She might look defenseless, but very well could be hiding some sort of supernatural power like Simon's. Or one even more deadly. I shudder at a vision of Marta sprouting a couple of extra fire-breathing heads while I've got her cornered in an alley.

And if that weren't the case, I can't assume she'd even tell *me* anything. She seems loyal to Simon and the Underrealm, and my five-foot-five—with a hat on—stature isn't exactly intimidating.

No, I'm not going to be able to *force* the truth out of Marta. I pull out my wallet and dig for some cash. *But everyone has a price.* Which means I'm going to have to do some more surveillance to figure out what Marta's is.

I place a couple of bills on the table.

"See you again tomorrow, Donna Lee," I say to the barista as I leave.

chapter ten

DAPHNE

"'Ello, Daphne, come here," Joe calls from the kitchen as I come in the house after school. I hadn't seen Haden again since after humanities and I'm just about to text him, but Joe's voice is filled with so much urgency, I tuck my phone in my pocket and head for the kitchen. I expect to find some sort of disaster, but instead I discover stacks of papers and notebooks lined up on the kitchen table. Each pile has its own brightly colored Post-it tab protruding from the pages.

Joe has a fluorescent yellow highlighter tucked behind his ear, and he's sucking on the tip of a blue pen. He scribbles a note on a loose notebook page. "Hand me a green sticky tab, will ya?" he says. I pull a tab off the dispenser and hand it to him. He slaps the tab on the page and then sets it on top of its color-coded pile. The only time I've seen Joe this intent on anything is when he's composing a new song, but none of this looks even remotely musically related.

"What's all this?" I ask.

"Detective work," he says, a buzz of manic notes flitting off him. "I've been going through that box of stuff Jonathan sent. I've read just about everything, and I've been sorting them by date and importance."

"You mean the box of CeCe's stuff?" I ask, a wave of anger seizing me. "The box that Jonathan sent me? The box that was in my room? The box that I told you I didn't need your help going through?"

"Yes. But you've been so busy looking for the Key, I know you haven't had a chance to touch any of this stuff."

"Doesn't mean I wanted *you* to. And what about Marta? If she sees this stuff—"

"I called and told her that Simon showed up out of the blue and wanted her to meet him at the studio in LA. She won't be back for hours," he says, like he thinks he's so clever.

"And what happens when Simon isn't there? She'll know you lied to her, and then she'll know that we know what happened to Simon."

"Oh, right. Didn't think of that."

His manic tone picks up more excitedly, and he doesn't even notice that I'm annoyed. "I'm just trying to be helpful. Like with the dealership. You should have seen me smooth-talking that saleswoman. She was dead set against sharing another customer's information at first, but by the time I was done with her, I had not only the Motorcycle Man's address but her number as well."

"A rock star getting a woman to give him her number doesn't exactly sound difficult."

"Yes, but she was eight months pregnant," he says, wiggling his eyebrows up and down. "That's a hundred extra points, according to Bobby."

"Um. Gross."

"Not that I'm planning on pursuing anything, mind you . . ."

"I should hope not."

"There is the audition thing after she has the baby, though. . . ."

Anyway, I did such a good job with tracking down the bike, I wanted to show you that I can be helpful in other ways. I saw this box and thought I would help." He picks up the stack marked with pink tabs. "I think I might be onto something."

I am about to ask Joe why the hell he was in my room to begin with and why he thinks I'd be okay with him not only invading my privacy as well as CeCe's, but his excited melody increases tenfold. I am genuinely terrified when he tosses the stack of papers back on the table and says, "Oh, but I almost forgot to show you your surprise! You are going to love this!"

"What are you talking about?"

He grabs my hand and pulls me toward the elevator that leads to his basement garage. "Oh, Daphne, you are going to love her so much!" he says, pushing the button that will take us down.

"Her?" *Oh crap, oh crap, oh crap, what has he done?*

"Ta-dah," Joe says, sweeping his hands out as the elevator door opens into the garage. I half expect to see a very pregnant saleswoman standing there or, like, a puppy or something *living*, but, instead, in front of the row of his six different sports cars sits a teal green Vespa with a bow as big as my head tied to the handlebars.

"What is that?" I ask.

"Your Christmas present. You and I didn't celebrate together, so I thought . . ."

"You'd buy me a motor scooter? You know I don't even have a regular driver's license yet, right? Let alone a motorcycle one? I can't drive this thing."

"The saleswoman told me that most scooter drivers never even get their license. I bet you could drive this all around Olympus Hills without getting pulled over once."

"I don't feel like taking my chances," I say. "What possessed you to buy me a Vespa?" I have to admit that the scooter is a thing of beauty and just happens to be in my favorite color, but I also know that Vespas costs thousands of dollars. My mom and I have a fifty-dollar budget for Christmas. I mean, I hadn't even gotten Joe a Christmas present. I'd planned on bringing him back something from Ellis Fields, like a T-shirt, but number one, I'd never got the chance because my Christmas plans had been completely derailed by an Oracle's declaring that I'm a Cypher and my finding out that there's an impending apocalypse that only I can stop— and number two, what exactly do you get for the man who sold your soul so he could become a rock star?

"It's not as grand as a Ducati—your mother would murder me—and scooters are much safer, and since purchasing something made it easier to get the people at the dealership to talk, I thought maybe you'd appreciate something nice from your dad. You know, with all we've been through lately, I thought you might like it. . . ."

And there it is. The reason I'm not jumping up and down with joy over my pricey new gift. Because it isn't a present. It's a bribe. I'd learned the hard way, promises and presents from Joe—my tuition for school, living in this mansion with him, the starring role in his rock opera—always came with strings attached. My *Christmas present* is no different. He's trying to buy my forgiveness.

"I got us matching helmets," he says. "Let's take her for a spin around the lake."

"No," I say, backing away.

"Come on, Daph. I'll teach you how to drive it in the school parking lot."

"I don't want to take it for a spin. I don't want to learn how to drive it. I don't want it. Take it back."

"But, Daph. I thought you'd—"

"What, that I'd love it so much that I would forget what you did to me? I'd forget that being famous was more important to you than having a kid? That you lured me to Olympus Hills with the promises of a world-class musical education—the chance to make all my dreams come true—when you knew what was really waiting for me?"

"I had no choice," Joe says with a pleading urgency.

"Yes, you did. You just made it seventeen years ago."

"Daphne, please. I'm so sorry—"

"No, Joe. I'm done. I don't want your apologies. I don't want the Vespa. I don't want the lead in your play—I'm quitting! And I don't want to live with you anymore." I pull a packet out of my tote bag and shove it at him.

"What is this?"

"I was waiting to tell you until I got the verdict, but you might as well know: I'm going to apply to live in the dorms with the scholarship kids." It's a cruel card to play, and I know it. The packet had been sitting in my bag for days, and I hadn't even decided if I was going to use it until this very moment.

Joe blanches. "Your tuition was contingent on you living here!"

"I picked up a packet for a scholarship, too, if you decide to stop making my payments. I bet Mr. Morgan will write me a recommendation."

"You're really going to leave me?" Joe's whole face crumbles. "I am so sorry, Daphne. You have to let me say it. You have no idea how sorry I am. That's why I started drinking . . . just something, anything, to try to drown out the guilt. I wanted to tell you, I *should have* told you, but even if Simon hadn't been preventing me, I still don't know if I would have . . . because I knew you'd hate me even more. . . . You wouldn't want me. . . ." The notes of pain wafting off him are palpable. They snake around him, wrapping him in a coil of hurt, and my anger makes me happy that I've wounded him.

And that's when I realize it: that I could eviscerate him right now with my words. Unleash the full brunt of my anger onto him. Hurt him more than he ever hurt me. Cause more damage than he ever caused himself. Make him feel so unwanted that he would need to drink himself into oblivion. Or worse . . .

So I go. I leave. Before I *allow* myself to hurt him more.

I turn back toward the elevator and hit the up button. It opens, and I step inside.

"Where are you going now?" Joe calls desperately as the door closes between us. "Just tell me where you're going."

"I don't know," I say.

Anywhere but here.

chapter eleven

TOBIN

As far as Mom is concerned, I've been coming home straight after school every day this week—but that's only because I make it a point to be home by 6:25 p.m., because I know she pulls in at 6:30 on the dot every evening. That usually gives me enough time to kick off my shoes and set up my homework in the great room before she walks in the door. However, I make it home today just before 5 p.m. only to find two Olympus Hills security vehicles, with lights flashing, in my driveway. They're parked right behind my mother's Lexus.

The front door of the house stands wide open.

Oh no.

The only other time I've seen security cars in my driveway like that was when Abbie had gone missing—just shy of six years ago—and my first thought is that something equally terrible has happened. Like maybe Dad had another heart attack. Or Mom came home early to check on me and had a bad fall.

My anger and frustration are replaced by fear as I jog to the open front door. "Mom?" I call as I launch into the front hall— only to literally run right into one of the security guards. He's hefting a large box in his arms that I almost knock out of his grasp. "Sorry," I say when he steadies himself, and I grab a stack of papers that slides off the top of the box.

I recognize the top document in my hand—it's from my mother's files in her office. The ones I've been snooping through for the last couple of weeks.

"I'll take that," the security guard says as he indicates for me to put the documents back on top of the box.

As I do so, two more guards enter the hallway from my mother's study. One carries another box of files while the second guard, Travers Johnson, head of OH security, is cradling a glass case that holds one of my mother's prized antiquities from her collection.

What is going on here?

"Be careful with that vase, Johnson," my mother's voice rings out as she comes around the corner. "It's over two thousand years old, and your yearly salary wouldn't begin to cover it if you drop it."

"Yes, ma'am," Johnson says, but I catch the roll of his eyes as if babysitting a crusty old vase isn't worth his time.

"Oh, Toby!" Mom says when she sees me in the hallway. The relief in her voice almost startles me. "I was so worried when you didn't come home," she says, clutching me to the lapels of her ruby red power suit. "First, my office, and then you not being here. I was beginning to fear the worst."

"I got waylaid with a project after school," I say, not quite lying, as I extricate myself from her grasp. "Did something happen?"

"We've had a break-in," she says, waving her manicured hand toward the boxes the security guards carry out of the house. "Either that or one of our house staff has sticky fingers. But I think someone must have come in my office while you were at school. A few of my government files are missing."

"Oh," I say. I take a step back, keeping my eyes from meeting hers. I don't know whom she suspects, but I know exactly who stole those files.

"What are they doing?" I ask, referring to the guards.

"The thief only took a few files this time, but I can't risk them getting the idea to come back here and take something from my collection. I'm having everything moved to my office at town hall where the security is much tighter, in order to remove the temptation for our burglar to return. My antiquities are too precious to be left vulnerable to undesirables." She squeezes my arm. "And so are you, Toby."

Her voice drips with concern. I swallow hard, trying to gulp back the anger that rises inside of me. My mother wasn't the one who had called security when my sister had gone missing all those years ago. It was me. When three days had passed with no word from Abbie, I'd been the one to call the police—only to have my call rerouted to OH security. My mom had been angry that I was making such a big deal out of it. She claimed Abbie had simply run away from home and there was nothing we could do. I imagine she didn't know yet that she really had run away rather than go to the Underrealm, as was my mother's deal with King Ren. No, that realization had come later and had resulted in my mother acting as if Abbie had never existed. Even having her scrubbed out of our family photos.

Where had been her concern then? Where had been her desire to protect her precious things? My hands begin to shake like they had when I'd been watching Marta. From my feeble memories of my sister and from reading her journal entries, it was plain to me now that my mother had never loved Abbie. My sister had merely been a commodity for my mother to barter with. A means to an end.

And if the roles were reversed, she'd see me that way, too. Hell, she'd taken steps to secure her collection today before thinking of sending someone to come look for me.

To make matters worse, I have no idea how much my dad is involved in all of this. He has always been the quiet, overly-in-volved-in-his-scientific-research type, while my mother takes care of business. He walks out the door looking like a normal human being only because my mother dresses him each morning as if he were a dapper little Japanese doll. Or puppet. My father didn't need to know anything about what happened to Abbie; he'd just think and react to Abbie's disappearance however my mother told him to.

"Tobin, are you okay?" Mom asks. She reaches out like she's about to test my forehead for a fever. I must look pale.

I step away from her touch and head for the front door.

"I need some fresh air," I say, and put some distance between us as quickly as possible.

chapter twelve

HADEN

Dax and I managed to duck past the security guards at the Motorcycle Man's former apartment complex and take a roundabout way back to our residence. I sit at the kitchen table, typing out a message to the others, informing them that the lead was a dead end—that we'd lost the trail on the Motorcycle Man, maybe this time for good—and then delete it before pressing send. I know I need to tell them, and I know his getting away wasn't my fault, since he was gone before we even got there.

However, it still feels like a failure on my part. If I'd thought of tracking down the Motorcycle Man myself, if I knew more about things like motorcycles in the first place so I didn't have to rely on Lexie's intel, or if I'd gone to the dealership on my own instead of waiting for Joe, maybe I would have gotten there soon enough. Maybe I'd have the Compass in my hands right now.

I decide to grab the hydra by the tail. I type out the text and finally hit send. Now they all know that I've failed.

"We'll figure something else out," Dax says, looking at his phone, which just beeped with my text. I looped him in on it even though he'd already witnessed what happened firsthand.

"As in what?"

"I don't know. But if Sarah, the Oracle said that we'll find the Compass, then we'll find it."

"You expect it to magically appear out of thin air?" Garrick says sarcastically from where he's been perched in front of the Xbox. The amount of disrespectful comments I've been getting from him lately makes me wish I still had the authority to put him in his place. I contemplate smacking the controller out of his hand, but I'm trying to show more restraint when it comes to Garrick.

The doorbell rings, and Dax gets up to answer it without being asked. I wonder if he realizes that, if I am no longer a Champion, then he is no longer my servant.

"Haden," he calls. "It's for you."

I go to the door and find Daphne standing on the porch. She's hugging her tote bag to her chest, and tears streak her face. "Can I stay here tonight?" she asks, wiping her eyes.

I can feel my mouth pop open and heat rush up my back. I don't know how to respond. She shouldn't be here. We shouldn't be seen together, lest Teresa or Calix figure out who she is, but I'm not about to send her away in this state.

"Of course," Dax says, ushering her into the house before I can even find my voice. He glances around the yard, making sure no one is watching, before closing the door, and escorts her to the family room. She takes a seat in the same armchair she'd been standing behind when she swore she didn't want anything to do with me.

"I'll make up one of the extra rooms upstairs," Dax says. "And then Garrick and I will go pick up some tacos for dinner."

Dax disappears for a few minutes and then returns, swinging his Roadster keys in his hand. "Let's go," he says to Garrick.

"No way," Garrick says, mashing the buttons on his controller.

"I just made it to level thirty-seven. I'm not moving from this spot."

"I'll let you drive," Dax says.

I gape at him in surprise. He won't even let *me* drive Venus.

"Seriously?" Garrick says, tossing aside his controller.

"Only if you get your butt out the door right now."

Garrick grabs his jacket and bolts out to the garage.

"You're really going to let him drive?" I ask.

"The sacrifices I make for you," he says. "Just make sure it was worth it."

"Meaning what?"

"*Tell her,*" Dax says, giving me a very loaded look.

I glance at Daphne in the next room. She's still hugging her tote bag to her chest. "Now hardly seems like the right time."

"Now is the perfect time."

"She's clearly upset about something."

"Exactly."

I give him an incredulous stare.

"She's upset. She wants to be comforted. And where did she choose to go?"

"Here," I say. "But that doesn't mean anything—"

"It means *everything*, you idiot. She could have gone home or to Tobin's or Lexie's, but she didn't. She came here. And I can guarantee it wasn't to see Garrick or me. She came for you." He raises his eyebrows, and his meaning starts to dawn on me. "I'll make sure Garrick drives real slow. I'll make sure we don't come back for at least an hour. Don't waste it. *Tell her.*"

"Maybe you should stay here," I say, feeling suddenly panicked. Daphne and I haven't really been alone together since the brief, few moments she held my hand before we left Ellis. Now that it's been nearly three weeks of our lives being all consumed with finding the Key, I am not sure I know how to pick up where we left off. I don't know where I stand with her. And it feels like I don't know how to talk to her about anything other than strategy anymore.

"No way, man. Now's your chance." He slaps me on the back. "Make me proud."

I watch him leave, horror-struck, to say the least. They're gone for a good two minutes before I have the presence of mind not to just leave her sitting on the armchair by herself. I walk into the family room. She glances up at me.

"Would you like something to drink?" I ask.

"Yeah," she says softly.

It takes a bit of searching to find a clean cup, what with the takeout containers everywhere, and dishes overflowing from the sink and strewn all over the house. I finally find a clean water bottle in one of the upper cabinets and bring it to her.

"Thanks," she says, and takes a sip. "You guys aren't big on cleaning up after yourselves, are you?" She wrinkles her nose. "What's that smell?"

"Oh yeah." I grab the to-go containers and trash off the coffee table in front of her. "It's been a bit of an adjustment without Simon around. Three guys all on their own for the first time. It's been all taco heaven all the time, and we've been out looking for the Key and such so much, it's like we're only here long enough to make a mess and then leave again without cleaning." I carry the trash to the kitchen and shove as much of it as I can in the compactor. "Garrick isn't too keen on taking orders right now, either."

"Have you seriously only been eating fast-food tacos for the last three weeks?" she asks, sniffling, but it sounds like that idea amuses her.

"There may have been a chimichanga or a burrito mixed in there somewhere, but they all taste the same to me. Dax is a little obsessive about Mexican food, and since none of us knows how to cook—"

"None of you knows how to cook?" she asks.

I shake my head and then scoop some of the refuse off the kitchen counter into the trash bin. Daphne sits on the armchair for a moment, silently brushing tears from the corners of her eyes. Just when I think she's about to close herself off from me completely, she sets aside her tote bag and stands up.

"We need to do something about that," she says, coming into the garbage heap of a kitchen. She clicks her tongue as she throws open a cupboard under the oven and pulls out a large pan that I didn't even know was in there.

"What are you doing?"

"I'm going to give you your first cooking lesson." She smirks and goes to the fridge. "You guys are going to die of malnutrition otherwise."

"Um . . ." I'm not sure how I feel about this proposal—lords do not prepare their own food—but the idea of it seems to amuse her, so I go along with it. "What are we making?"

"Let's see what we've got to work with." She opens the fridge and starts rooting around in its contents while I stand behind her. She opens a drawer and closes it. "Well, that looks like nothing but turnips. And that's just plain disgusting," she says, pointing at a molding green smoothie that Simon left behind. "Ooh, eggs. These look like they're still good," she says, checking a series of numbers on the side of the oddly shaped container. She hands the eggs to me and then reaches for a bottle of milk in the door. She pops off the lid and makes a gagging face at the sour smell that wafts out of it. "Ugh. When was the last time you went grocery shopping? Oh yeah, never."

She thrusts the milk bottle back in the fridge and then opens the freezer. She pulls out a frosty package of Multigrain Superbread and hands that to me also. "We're looking good so far . . . and I'm guessing since Simon was a health nut, there's probably some almond milk. . . ." She walks into the pantry and comes out half a minute later with an armload of objects. "Jackpot! We've got almond milk, *real* maple syrup, and cinnamon. We are going to eat like kings tonight."

She sets her bounty on the corner of the counter that I had cleared off a minute ago. I put the eggs and the bread with it. "What in Tartarus are you going to make with all this?"

"French toast. And *you're* making it, not me." She places her hands together, gives me a short bow, and says in a strange voice, "I am here merely to instruct and observe, young grasshopper."

I roll up my sleeves and follow Daphne's instructions. I am used to learning through mimicry—Underlords have a natural talent for watching, absorbing, and mimicking actions much more quickly than humans—but she insists that I do everything myself rather than observing her. She has me crack eggs into a pot since we can't find a clean bowl, and then I add a cup of the creamy-colored almond milk and mix it together. I want to ask how exactly it is that someone milks an almond, but I figure it is a stupid question so I merely wait for her next instruction. She makes me dip the bread in the concoction and place each slice in the heated pan. They sizzle when they hit the butter that's been melting in the pan. I go along with it, watching the way she twists and puckers her lips and tries not to laugh at my awkwardness in the kitchen, until she tells me to sprinkle cinnamon over the cooking bread.

"Are you sure?" I balk. "That sounds disgusting."

"Trust me, it's divine. Just shake it all over the top."

I give the spice container a small shake and watch tiny flecks of brown speckle the top of the eggy toast.

"No," she says. "Don't be afraid of it. There's no such thing as too much cinnamon. Give it a good shake. Like this." She clasps her hand over mine to take control of the cinnamon, but her touch is so unexpected that a shock of electricity sparks out of my fingertips. She pulls her hand back at the same time that I let go of the cinnamon. It falls into the pan, dumping a heap on one of the bread slices.

"Okay, so maybe *that's* too much cinnamon," she says, shaking her hand.

"Sorry," I say sheepishly. I don't like the idea that I may have failed my first cooking attempt, but I am even more chagrined over shocking her—and she most definitely noticed. If the way she makes me feel isn't written on my face or screaming out through my tones, which only she can hear, then the fact that I shoot lightning out of my hands at her simple touch is probably as obvious as it gets.

Hades, I'm hopeless.

"It's okay," she says, with a laugh. "We'll just give that piece to Garrick and watch his face when he bites into it."

She smiles so deviously that I can't help but laugh, too.

"There it is," she says. "You really should laugh more often."

She seems to be staring at my lips, so I give her a small, tight smile. She seems happy, but I know she's just using me to distract herself from whatever had her upset when she came over.

At the moment, I am okay with that.

"Oh, it's time to flip 'em over," she says, turning away. When she turns back, she's holding out a flat-headed cooking tool.

I temper myself as I reach for it, making certain I don't shock her again. I let my fingers linger longer than necessary against hers as I take the tool from her. She doesn't pull away.

But I do when I feel a sharp pain at my ankle. Brim yowls at me when I almost step on her.

"Whoa, it's okay," Daphne says, scooping up little Brim in her hand.

"She must have smelled the food," I say, flipping the bread over. "I think she's pretty sick of taco meat."

"Poor baby," Daphne says, scratching Brim's ears. Brim leans into it. "I'll scramble some eggs for you as soon as Haden's done."

When the French toast and eggs are finished, Daphne wraps the extras in foil to keep warm for Dax and Garrick, and then she and I take our food to the coffee table. Brim eats her eggs straight out of the pan while Daphne and I opt to share the one clean plate I can find. She sits crossed-legged beside the table and digs into the syrup-covered French toast with her fork. I tuck my legs behind me and lower myself down next to her.

She laughs, covering her full mouth with her hand.

"Pardon?" I ask.

"You're so formal sometimes," she says, with her mouth full. "Even the way you sit down. You're so stiff. Like a soldier who's afraid his drill sergeant is watching and giving him demerits."

I don't know what a drill sergeant is, but I do know what she means. "To be fair, I was raised a soldier, and there usually is someone watching and judging me at every moment."

"Good point," she says, and takes a second huge bite. She chews and swallows and then cocks her head to the side, looking at me. "It must be nice, then," she says. "I mean this place is a wreck and you're going to need some serious lessons in how to be human and all, but I'm sure it's nice not to have Simon over your shoulder anymore. That guy was a real psycho."

She takes a third bite, savoring it like it's the best thing she's eaten in a long time. I'm betting it hasn't occurred to her that she's eating a dead man's food.

However, her statement makes me stop and think. I've spent so much time being paranoid about the Skylords and obsessing over finding the Key that I haven't really had a chance to think of it that way. "Yes," I say. "It's the first time in my life that I haven't had my father or his guards or his emissaries watching me. I've never really been . . ."

"Free?" she guesses.

I nod.

"Does it feel good?"

"When I was boy, after my mother died, I used to sit up in the owl roost in one of the palace's towers and watch the owls fly in and out. I wanted to be able to fly like them. To escape whenever I wanted, to be light as a feather. That's what I always imagine freedom would feel like. But this, it feels different. It feels . . . heavy."

"How so?"

I look down at the scar in the palm of my hand. It's the imprint of the talisman I'd had to electrocute in my grasp in order to break free from Father's hold in the Underrealm. "Don't misunderstand me; I'm grateful for it, but freedom begets responsibility. Everyone is looking to me to figure out the answers, to know what to do. They want me to lead, and I don't want to fail them. I don't want to fail . . . you."

I look up and meet her eyes over the plate of French toast. Her bemused attitude is gone, and I notice tears pooling in her eyes again. Whatever distraction she had found before has been broken.

"What is it?" I ask. "What's wrong?"

Why did you come here?

My instinct is to grab her up in my embrace. To wrap my arms around her and tell her everything is going to be okay, but I don't have the right to presume that she would be receptive to this. Instead, I place my hand near hers on the coffee table. "Are you hurt? Did something happen?"

I imagine all sorts of terrible things involving Skylords or the Motorcycle Man, and I curse myself for letting her teach me how to cook instead of asking her right away. I feel like a complete *koprophage*.

"Nothing," she says, and picks up her fork. She sets it back down. "*Everything*. From Joe trying to buy my forgiveness to having my whole grip on reality turned upside down. To missing home. Missing the holidays with my mom and Jonathan because it was so important that we come back here, and now we're not any closer to finding the damn Key than we were then."

She wipes away her tears with the back of her hand. "You know what I miss the most, even though I never thought I liked it in the first place? Jonathan always throws this big New Year's Eve party every year. Practically the whole town comes, and he spends all night trying to find just the right person for everyone to kiss at midnight." She shakes her head. "Jonathan thinks he's a real matchmaker, going around trying to pair everyone off. He usually picks out some jock from my school for me or one of the bag boys from Sunup Market, and goads me all night long until I agree to give the poor boy at least a peck on the lips at the stroke of midnight. Man, I thought I hated that, but when I spent this last New Year's Eve alone on the couch with some stupid Ashton Kutcher movie, I started crying in my microwave popcorn because I didn't have anyone to kiss."

"Oh," I say, because I suddenly can't find any other words. I'd spent all of New Year's Eve sitting outside her house in my car. If I had known she didn't want to be alone, I would have . . . I don't know what I would have done.

We sit in silence for a moment, me feeling uncomfortable in my own skin.

"Are you going to eat any of this?" she asks, cutting off another bite. "I eat when I'm emotional, so you had better dig in before it's gone."

I nod and take a tentative bite. It's sweet and rich, but I know I want more. The flavor of the cinnamon and the maple are the perfect combination. After a couple of more forkfuls, I feel my courage building.

"Why do you kiss someone at midnight?" I ask, feeling my cheeks flush with heat at the thought of her kissing other guys. I should have realized I wasn't the first.

"Oh yeah, you probably don't do that in the Underrealm, huh? You know, with the lack of females and all." A strange half smile quirks her lips, and I can't imagine what she's picturing.

"We don't celebrate the new year," I say. "Not the way you do anyway. We count time by the equinoxes. The Leaving and the Returning of the Champions . . ." I trail off, already regretting reminding myself of the impending deadline hanging over us. If we don't find the Key before the spring equinox, then surely Ren will send his soldiers after it when the gate opens—after us. And that is only if the Court doesn't get its way and rips through the walls of the Pits before then.

That isn't what I want to dwell on at the moment, so I return my attention to her. Her tears have dried up, but her cheeks are flushed red.

"Kissing someone at midnight is supposed to bring you good luck for the year to come. I guess I realized that I could have used some good fortune, these days."

She tugs on the end of her golden hair, and I watch the curve of her lips as she wavers between a frown and sheepish grin. Electricity pricks my fingertips. If I had been with her that night, would she have let me kiss her if I'd tried?

Would she let me kiss her now?

"Or maybe I just don't like feeling so alone," she says.

"You still have your father. . . ."

And me, if you want, but I can't bring myself to say it.

"I told Joe that I'm quitting the play and moving out."

"Oh. Where will you go?" I pull my hand away slightly. My thoughts immediately go to her returning home to Ellis Fields. Leaving here. Leaving our quest. Leaving me.

"The dorms, if they'll accept my application. I'll go back to Joe's until they do, but I couldn't handle being there tonight. I'm sorry for just showing up."

"Don't be. You can stay here as long as you want."

"Just tonight," she says. "You'd get sick of me."

"I'd never get sick of you—" My throat catches, and my whole face feels hot. I had not intended on saying that out loud. It probably sounded saccharine to her, but it's the truth.

A quirk of a smile plays on her lips again. "I shed more than Brimstone, and I probably snore."

"You don't," I say. "At least you didn't that night in Vegas." Heat swirls in my chest as I think of the night I spent lying next to her bed in the Crossroads Hotel, her hand dangling over the side, clasped in mine.

That was one of the best nights of my life is what I want to say, but this time the words don't come tripping out of my traitorous mouth.

Daphne's lips curve again, and that strange smile falls into a more concentrated expression. Seemingly, something heavy weighs on her mind. I curse myself for not expressing the thought out loud. I am reminded of Dax's words. That I should tell her how I feel while I have the chance. The idea sends fear shuddering through me.

Daphne shivers as if her body is responding to mine. She rubs her hands up and down her bare arms as though she is cold. Once again, I wish I could embrace her, this time to share the warmth that ripples under my skin.

She licks some maple syrup from her lips. I imagine they taste just as sweet.

You need to tell her, Dax's voice echoes in my mind.

I lean in closer to her and she moves closer to me. My courage surges. Gathering all of my control so my lightning remains in my chest instead of flowing up my arms, I raise my hand to cup it against her face. She leans into my touch. Her warm cheek presses against my scarred palm, soothing the pain that always aches behind it. I breathe deep, steadying myself. I caress r her bottom lip with my thumb. Her mouth puckers against my touch.

She lets out a breath as if she'd been holding it. My skin tingles as her air brushes over my fingertip. I smooth my hand back over her cheek. She leans even closer.

Hades, I want to kiss her.

But I need to tell her first. She needs to know.

Her lips part.

"I need to tell you something," I say as quickly as possible, but my words get jumbled with the question that comes tripping out of her mouth at the same time. "Can I show you something?" is what I think she asks.

We laugh slightly at the awkward timing.

"What did you say?" she asks, her lips still only inches from mine.

I drop my hand and pull back slightly, realizing my nerve is waning. "You first," I say, hoping to build my courage back up again in the meantime.

Daphne puts her hand on my arm. While I've lost my resolve, she seems to be filled with a confidence that wasn't there a few moments ago. "I need to show you something."

She stands up quickly and goes to the kitchen. I follow her, tentatively, not knowing what to expect. She plucks a few leaves from Simon's wilting herb garden on the windowsill above the sink.

"Watch this," she says, and begins to hum.

"Watch what?" I say, stepping closer.

"Be quiet. This takes concentration."

She continues her humming, getting louder, all her focus concentrated on those little leaves. I start to wonder if all the stress is making her a bit addled, but then, for half a second, I think I see one of the leaves in her hand begin to quake.

The doorbell rings, the chime echoing through the house. Daphne jumps like she's forgotten where she was and drops the leaves.

The bell rings again. Brim yowls at me to respond.

"Must be Dax," I say, rushing to the door, about to curse him out for coming back sooner than expected, but when I open it, I find one of the last people I expect to see.

"Tobin?" Daphne says from behind me. I didn't know that she'd followed me into the foyer.

"I went to your house first, but Joe said you were gone." He kicks the front step a couple of times. "Do you think I could stay here tonight?" he asks, looking up at us sheepishly.

I have never wanted to slam a door in someone's face more than I do at this very moment.

"Of course you can," Daphne says. She looks at me for my approval.

All the heat that had been building up inside of me washes away in two seconds flat. This was not how any of this was supposed to play out. "Of course," I say. "Let me make you up a room."

Daphne pulls Tobin inside the house. "We made French toast; Dax is coming back with tacos; and I've got something to show you. We'll make an evening of it."

"Thanks," Tobin says quietly. "I just can't be in the same house as my mom tonight."

"I know how you feel," Daphne says, leading him into the family room while I head upstairs.

Apparently, we're taking in strays with parental issues tonight. I just hope there aren't any more unexpected visitors planning on stopping by. The house is suddenly feeling crowded as it is.

chapter thirteen

DAPHNE

Tobin digs into a piece of French toast like he hasn't eaten all day. He's just polishing it off when Dax and Garrick come back with their contribution to the meal. Garrick complains about how slow Dax made him drive until he smells the luscious goodness Haden and I have prepared.

"You cooked, Daphne?" Dax asks. "It smells better than anything Simon ever made."

"Actually, Haden did," I say proudly. "I might turn him into a decent facsimile of a human being with enough lessons."

"*You* cooked?" Garrick asks, giving Haden a look like he'd done something that made his standing lesser in his eyes. Then I realize that where they come from, probably only Lessers cook. But it doesn't stop Garrick from wanting to eat the end results.

Garrick and Dax eat their French toast straight out of their foil wrappers. I laugh when Garrick bites into his extremely overly cinnamoned piece. His reaction is priceless—he spits it out and wipes at his tongue, letting go of a string of what I assume are Underrealm swear words. I glance at Haden with a devious smile, but he doesn't seem to appreciate the joke anymore. He just sits quietly on the couch, watching us.

"Don't worry; I saved you a better piece," I tell Garrick, feeling like a jerk all of a sudden, and present him another foil packet. "There's even some eggs that Brim didn't eat."

He gives me the stink eye but eats the new piece anyway. Tobin and Dax are the only ones who touch the tacos. When we're done eating, Tobin knocks his foot against mine. "You wanted to show me something?" he asks.

Haden sits up when he hears this, but what I want to show Tobin isn't the same as what I was going to share with him.

I open my bulging tote bag. My phone sits on top of the papers that I'd shoved inside on my way out of Joe's house. It lights up with a text from Joe asking me to please come home—that he'll leave the house if I'll just come back. I move my phone aside and pull out a stack of color-coded papers. I spread them out on the family room floor because the coffee table is covered with our dishes. "I was kind of in a hurry, so this isn't everything, but all of this belonged to Abbie. Joe had been sorting through them and said he was onto something, so I thought if we went through them, we might be able to figure out what that was."

"Why don't you just call him and ask?" Garrick says, licking syrup from his fingers.

I shake my head. "Not happening."

Haden joins us, sitting on the floor all stiff and proper, as we pick through the papers. Many of them are old receipts, but there are also notes, and pages that seem to be torn out of a composition book. Joe's color-coded system doesn't seem to make much sense, but that's Joe for you.

It's getting late and I'm fighting to keep my eyes open when Dax waves one of the pink-tabbed papers in the air. "I've got something," he says. "Everything tabbed with pink has a mention of some place called Old Sutton Mill or an Old Sutton Road."

"What's that?" Garrick asks before I can. I'd thought he'd fallen asleep because he'd been just lying there with a brochure for Zion National Park tented over his face.

Tobin grabs the paper from Dax. "I wonder . . . When we were younger, before we moved to Olympus Hills, Abbie and Sage used to play at this old abandoned mill with their friends. They let me go with them a couple of times. We used to pretend it was haunted and play hide-and-go-seek. There were the best hiding places there."

"Hiding places?" Dax asks.

"I bet Old Sutton Mill is the same place," he says, typing the address into his phone. "Yeah, I'm pretty sure it is."

"How far is it?" Dax asks.

"Right now about a twenty-five-minute drive. During rush hour, it would take a lot longer."

"Feel like taking a drive?" Dax asks Tobin.

He nods and jumps up.

"Anyone else want to come?"

I want to be there for Tobin, but I'm so tired, I feel like I'd just slow them down. My phone buzzes from another pleading text from Joe, and I feel ill on top of my exhaustion.

"It's okay," Tobin says, watching my face. "I doubt we'll find anything anyway. Just ruling out leads." I can tell by the tone that comes off him that he's disappointed, but he smiles regardless. "We'll call if we need backup," he says to Haden. I realize if I'm staying here, then so will Haden.

chapter fourteen

TOBIN

Dax and I are walking out to Dax's Roadster parked in the driveway, when a green BMW pulls up to the curb. "Having a party without me?" Lexie calls out the window. "Where was my invite?" For a moment, I almost think I register a bit of disappointment in her voice. Or maybe it's just irritation, though I can't imagine why she'd be bothered that we had all been hanging out together. On a normal basis, we don't usually hang in the same social circles. *At least not anymore.*

"It was a spontaneous gathering," Dax says, like he's worried about her feelings.

I am not as inclined at the moment. "What, like you don't have better things to do on a Friday night?" I ask.

"Whatever, I just got off a date with Derek Van Houser from the lacrosse team." She tosses her blond hair over her shoulder. "Saw you guys and thought I might grace you with my presence if you were up to anything interesting. Where are you boys off to now? Wine cooler run? You know I prefer Cristal," she says, with exaggerated indifference.

"We're not having fun. We're headed out to investigate a lead on Abbie," I say, my voice indicating that I'm trying to politely dismiss her. I'm not in the mood to be her postdate entertainment.

"Ooh," she says, suddenly interested. "Get in. I'll drive."

"We've already got a ride," I say, pointing at Dax's *two-seater* Roadster.

She scoffs. "That thing is tiny. I suggest you let me drive . . . unless you *want* me to sit in your lap."

I am suddenly too flustered to respond. What makes her think she's coming? Or that I'd want her to sit on my lap?

"She does have more room," Dax says with a chuckle, and heads for the backseat of the BMW. I blink at him, wondering why he's going along with letting her come.

"Lap or Beemer, Tobin?" Lexie croons out the window. "Lap or Beemer?"

I can feel my face burning. For all the help she's offered us in the last few weeks as part of our team, it didn't erase the fact that Lexie had mastered the Soprano art of irritation by sophomore year.

Sometimes, I wonder how we had ever been friends before that.

"Beemer," I say, getting in the passenger seat next to her, since Dax is sprawled out in the backseat.

"Where to?" she asks excitedly.

"Old Sutton Mill," Dax says before I can answer.

"It's supposedly haunted," I say, making a last-ditch effort to deter her. "It could be dangerous."

"Neat!" Lexie says, hitting the gas and flying away from the curb.

I give her the side eye as we drive. I expected Lexie, queen bee of the Sopranos, to balk at the idea of poking around an old, abandoned mill in the middle of the night, but instead it seems she can't wait to get there. Either her date with Derek Van Housitwhatsits had been a real snooze fest, or perhaps the old Lexie, the one I'd spent the summer before freshman year with, making our own faux documentaries about swamp people in the Olympus Hills lake, was still in there somewhere under all the designer clothing and hair products.

It strikes me a few minutes later, as we pull onto Old Sutton Road, approaching the mill, that, even though in the last few months, I had come to consider Daphne to be my closest confidante when it came to Abbie, it isn't she who is with me now, following this lead—but Lexie Simmons, the last person I expected to want to help me.

chapter fifteen

DAPHNE

After Tobin and Dax leave, I wander off to find a spare room upstairs. I choose the one with a small balcony that looks out over the lake. I stand, leaning my elbows against the railing, looking out at the rippling water, and feel a surprising pang of disappointment that Haden isn't standing next to me. I smile a little to myself, remembering when he'd shocked my hand while we were cooking—and that horror-struck look on his face that he'd tried to pass off as sheepish. Then, with encircling warmth, I think about the touch of his hand against my face. The closeness of his lips to mine. The thrumming notes pulsing off his body, as if an electric current had been building in his chest.

I don't know exactly why I'd chosen to come here tonight.

Or maybe I do.

Haden had been a welcome distraction when I had lost my hope that night in Vegas, and had treated me with such concern since. Perhaps part of me had been looking for that kind of diversion again—or maybe something *more.* . . .

I had pretended to be fine with Tobin's intrusion because from the broken notes that were coming off him, I knew he needed my friendship, but his timing couldn't have been worse. It had taken a stroke of courage for me to finally work up my nerve enough to share my secret with Haden—to show him my new power, but then I lost my chance when Tobin arrived.

I'd been more than disappointed when the doorbell had interrupted my concentration, but at the same time, I have to admit that I am also relieved. In the moment, I had wanted to share with Haden. I had wanted to open up to him.

Hell, if he'd tried to kiss me, I might have let him, despite my better judgment.

But maybe it was better that I didn't get the chance for any of that.

CeCe—I mean, Abbie—had always teased me about having a wall around my heart. I'd put it there after being disappointed by my father time and time again as a kid, but over the last few months of living with Joe and getting to know Haden, I had let some of my defenses down. Opened up. But now that I know what Joe did to me, now that my trust has been so thoroughly betrayed by the one person who is supposed to want to protect me above anything else—my father—how am I supposed to truly trust anyone else again?

And now that I know that my heart and soul might need to be sacrificed to get the Key, I don't want to just rebuild the wall around my heart; I want to line it with battlements and cannons.

Would my secret be safe with Haden? Would he tell the others? Would he still be my ally, or would he only see me as a more valuable prize?

I try to shake that last idea off. Haden had traded everything he'd ever wanted to keep me out of his father's hands. The feel of his scarred hand he'd held against my cheek had been a reminder of his refusal. Even if I didn't know why he'd given it all up for me, that was the reason I'd almost opened up to him earlier this evening. It was the reason I felt safe staying here now. . . .

And yet, I still don't know if I can let him in.

It's a clear night, and I can see all the way out to the smaller island of the lake. It sits silent and dark in the water, no longer singing the lullaby it sang to me the first night I arrived in Olympus Hills, the song that drew me to it the next day—the day I met Haden, and the same day Tobin and I found Pear almost drowned in the lake at the edge of the island. The song had seemed fractured then, broken notes and distressful strains, as if the island had been calling out to me that something was wrong. Pear—who is still in a coma at the Olympus Hills Medical Center—might have died if not for that. But after that night, the grove fell silent, like it had gone into hibernation. I hadn't heard its song since that first day, but it was still etched inside my heart.

I hum the melody I remember to the grove and then listen for a moment to see if it responds. I hum again, louder, as if I can wake the grove up from its slumber. I want it to know that I'm still here, that I'm still listening if it wants to sing to me again. "Tell me your secrets," I whisper to the grove.

After a few minutes, my exhaustion gets the better of me, and I nestle my head on my arms on the railing and think about CeCe's words from her journal about all the things the grove is hiding. I'd been so sure that we would find the answers we needed there.

chapter sixteen

HADEN

A strange pall of anxiety falls over me after Dax and Tobin leave. Garrick disappears to wherever the Tartarus he wants, and Daphne goes upstairs to find a bedroom. I wake Brim from where she slumbers, curled in a tiny ball, on top of a stack of blue-tabbed papers. She sits up, stretching, and quirks one eye open at me, as if asking, *What's going on?*

"Follow me," I say, and the two of us go out the front door. I walk the perimeter of the grounds with Brim close at my feet, both of us listening, watching for anything out of the ordinary. Anything that might explain the anxiousness that hangs over my shoulders.

Nothing strikes me as strange as we round the house back into the front yard, and I resign myself to accepting that the dark cloud that follows me isn't a warning from an impending threat but from a storm of emotions brewing inside of me.

I had almost done it. I had almost told Daphne how I feel. It had taken all of my courage to get to that point—like it was an act of bravery—but then my effort had failed.

And now it left me feeling more raw and vulnerable than ever. Weak.

That's where the anxiety came from. If I am weak, then how am I supposed to protect her? How am I supposed to save us all?

Brim gives a little meow, and I follow her upward gaze to find Daphne standing on the balcony of Simon's old bedroom above us. She leans her arms over the railing, staring out over the lake, and is oblivious to my presence.

Brim nudges my leg with her head, trying to prod me into action, as if she knows how badly I long to climb the balcony stairs to stand beside Daphne. To get a second chance to tell her.

Instead, I watch Daphne until she turns away and goes inside.

"Come on," I tell Brim. "Let's go in."

There will be no more brave actions from me tonight.

chapter seventeen

TOBIN

Lexie pulls into the debris-strewn lot in front of the mill, gravel crackling under her tires. She parks in front of a NO TRESPASSING, VIOLATORS WILL BE PROSECUTED TO THE FULL EXTENT OF THE LAW sign on the chained entrance to the fence that surrounds the crumbling stone-and-adobe building.

"What now?" Lexie whispers, as if she's afraid we'll get caught if someone hears her.

"There's a hole in the south fence," I say. "Or at least there was when I was a kid."

"Let's hope it's still there," Dax says, getting out of the car. He can see better in the dark than the two of us, so Lexie and I follow his lead as we search for the opening. It doesn't take long. "Someone's been here recently," Dax says, indicating the bent and broken tall grasses that surround the hole in the fence.

My heart starts to race. There could be any number of other people who would sneak into this spot—little kids from my old neighborhood, so-called ghost hunters looking for a thrill, or even just teens looking for a place to party—but I can't help but hope that this lead will actually pan out.

I climb through the fence, not caring as the broken chain link rips my sleeve. Lexie follows behind me. I don't wait for Dax, who, being much larger than the rest of us, has to take more care to squeeze through the opening. I jog toward the mill and then break into a run when I see that the old wooden door of the south-side entrance is standing partially ajar. That was the entrance we'd always used as kids because the latch on the lock never caught properly.

Abbie is here. She has to be here.

I throw the door open and hurtle inside. "Abbie?" I shout, my voice echoing in the dilapidated stone building.

There's a flutter of movement in the loft above. But it's only pigeons, startled into flight by my shout. I use a flashlight app on my phone and shine it in their direction.

"Abbie!" I shout again, spinning in a circle, swinging my light as I inspect the corners of the large room that had once served as the main production room when this was a paper mill decades ago.

"Shhh!" Lexie says, coming in behind me. "Do you want to get caught?"

I ignore her. "Abbie!" I shout again. "It's me, Tobin. You can come out. You're safe."

"Tobin," Dax says with a warning voice. He's about to say more when a heavy creaking noise echoes behind me.

I turn toward the noise and catch a swaying movement in the dark. I shine my light in its direction and find the old tire swing—strung from the rafters by some kids at least twenty years ago—in the middle of the room, swinging back and forth seemingly on its own accord.

"What was that you said about this place being haunted?" Lexie asks, sounding like she's no longer finding any of this amusing.

"This place used to be a paper mill," I say, approaching the swing. "It supposedly caught fire on April first back in the 1890s. Because of all the paper and the fact that many of the workers thought the alarms were an April Fool's joke, a lot of people didn't make it out. Another owner started rebuilding it a few years later but abandoned the project because weird accidents kept happening."

"And you used to play here?" Lexie asks.

"Mostly Sage and Abbie. She liked the drama of it all."

"Sounds like Abbie," Dax says, reaching his hand out to stop the swing. The swaying motion stops, but it spins slowly a couple of times before coming to rest. "Must be a draft," he muses, looking up at the rafters.

"We never believed this place was really haunted. We just liked to tell stories. Made hide-and-go-seek all the more thrilling."

Hide-and-go-seek. I picture myself as an eight-year-old boy, standing under the loft and shouting, "Come out, come out, wherever you are!" after a long game of searching—because Abbie had always been too good at hiding. She'd burst out from wherever her latest spot had been and run for the tire swing—our home base—while I tried to tag her. Sometimes, she even let me win.

I insist on searching the various rooms of the mill but turn up nothing more than old beer bottles and a stained mattress that must have been used by a vagrant at some point in the loft.

It's about a half an hour until midnight when Lexie insists that we leave. "It's getting cold," she says, rubbing her arms. "And my voice coach is coming in the morning. And since I'm your ride, that means you have to come with me, Tobin." She gives me a pointed look.

I knew I shouldn't have let her come.

"I'll stay," I say. "I can walk."

"Don't be addled," Dax says.

"Maybe we should check the storage rooms again—"

Dax places his hand on my shoulder. "I'm sorry, Tobin. There's nothing here," he says with resignation.

I hang my head, knowing he's right, and let them propel me toward the exit. Before pulling the door shut, I look back at the tire swing, which has begun swinging in the dark on its own once more.

I may have never believed this place was haunted, but I can't help feeling like a ghost of Abbie's memory is watching me leave.

chapter eighteen

DAPHNE

I wake up at least an hour later. A chill breeze swirls through the room. The doors to the balcony are ajar, even though I don't remember leaving them that way before I went to bed. But it isn't the breeze that awakens me; it's the song it carries through the open doors. The lilting, soothing lullaby of the grove, calling to me from the lake, answering my song from earlier. I follow it out to the balcony. A strange light seems to surround the island, dancing to the song that emanates from the trees. It reminds me of the pictures I've seen of the aurora borealis—the northern lights. The grove's beckoning notes surround me, pushing me toward the spiral staircase leading down from the balcony to the stone patio below. I can feel the song telling me to come, its draw getting stronger with every step I take. It pulls at me. Anxiously, I hesitate, wondering if I should go back for Haden. No, there isn't time. What if the song stops if I turn back?

I follow the notes to the lakeside paths and then over the footbridge to the grove's island. I hadn't stopped for shoes, so I am grateful that I'd fallen asleep in my socks. The song grows stronger and more urgent with every moment that passes, prodding me to move faster. The light that surrounds the island engulfs me as

I enter the grove. The light shifts and swirls, creating different shapes that dance in front of me. Not just shapes, but the outlines of people. One of them takes a form that I know instantly is a portrait of CeCe, with her crazy, springy hair. She holds her hand out, almost as if she's offering it to me, but then something that resembles a small burst of lightning crackles up from her fingertips. She rocks up on her heels in excitement, and another formation of light—looking very much like Dax—embraces her, swirling her around with joy. The light shifts again into another couple, this one I don't recognize, heading hand in hand toward the two arched trees at the edge of the grove before disappearing. A thought strikes me like the lightning that CeCe had been practicing with—these images are echoes of people who had been in the grove before.

The grove is showing me its secrets.

Just as I'd asked.

The light shifts again, as if confirming my conclusion. It shows me another scene that had played out here not too long ago. I see the echoes of Haden and me the first time we met. I watch as Haden lifts his hand, seemingly to touch the face of the ethereal version of me, and then pulls back when he realizes who she is. I step toward the vision, but the light swirls away toward the tree arch once again. The light grows brighter, swirling pink and yellow and orange until it snaps suddenly into the echo of a man bursting through the archway. He holds a bundle against his chest with one arm and a long, two-pronged staff in the other. It looks like a bident.

The Key!

I watch intently as the man places the bundle in a crop of bushes, looking over his shoulder, as if he knows he is being pursued. I step closer to get a better look and realize the bundle is a tiny, sleeping baby, and I know for sure now that I am watching the echoes of Orpheus and his infant son—*my ancestors*—having just escaped the Underrealm with the Key. I catch my breath as Orpheus holds the staff out in his hands, trying to figure out what to do with it. I can only hope that the image doesn't shift into a new one before I can witness where he hides it. *How* he hid it, without anyone being able to find it.

I watch, completely still, afraid to disrupt anything, as Orpheus stakes the bident into the ground next to a young sapling, driving the staff into the tiny tree's roots. Then he takes something that had been strapped to his back—a lyre—and strums it as he holds it out toward the tree. Swirls of light flit out of his moving mouth, and I realize that he is singing. The ground vibrates under me, and I watch, astonished, as the branches of the sapling reach up and wrap themselves around the staff of the bident. The tree grows and grows, until the entire bident is encased inside the trunk of it. Light shoots out from the crevices and knots, and the ground feels as though it is quaking under my feet, and then it fades away.

Orpheus steps away from the tree and moves as though he is about to go for his son but then whirls around in the other direction, taken by surprise. I watch as he seems to be attacked by a barrage of invisible monsters. The Keres. His body contorts and writhes as if they are trying to rip him apart, and even though I know it is all just an echo and not real, I find myself crouching over the sleeping child, protecting it from the monsters, and I cover my own eyes from the terrible scene.

The light fades away from behind my eyelids, and the urgent notes of the grove's song lessen into a soft melody again. I open my eyes to find the baby gone, and all the other echoes, too.

The aurora is gone also, but the resonating vibration of the trees remains. No, not from the trees, but from one tree. I recognize it not only from the vision the echoes had shown me, but also from my first encounter in the grove when I thought the tree had looked like a giant tuning fork. But it isn't a tuning fork that gives it shape.

It is the bident encased inside that caused it to grow that way.

The grove had answered my plea. It had shown me its biggest secret.

I've found where the Key of Hades is hidden.

I reach toward the resonating tree, not believing that any of this is real, when I hear the snap of a twig behind me. I whirl around, realizing that I am not alone.

chapter nineteen

HADEN

I lie awake only two bedrooms away from Daphne's. My phone is next to me, waiting for a call from Dax or Tobin if they find anything at the mill, so I can't allow myself to sleep. However, it is not as if I can when I know that *she* is so close.

I look up at the clock on my wall, easily making out the numbers in the dark. It's 11:58 p.m. I find myself fantasizing about knocking on her door at exactly midnight and offering to help with a do-over of her New Year's Eve.

Ugh. I pull my pillow over my head. *I'm an idiot. What kind of addled idea is that?*

I hear what sounds like the creak of a door down the hall, and sit up quickly. My heart beats erratically as I allow myself to think, just for a moment, that maybe Daphne has decided to come to me instead. However, I don't hear any footsteps in the hallway, and lie back down and smack my fists against my forehead.

Idiot. Idiot. Idiot.

Of course she isn't going to come to me.

That would mean she actually likes—

A crashing noise makes me bolt right up again. I expect Brim, who always sleeps at my feet, to bristle beside me, ornery at being awoken once again this evening, but she isn't there. *Kopros. How did she get out without me noticing?* She probably went looking for Daphne herself. She is almost as smitten with her as I am, but Daphne doesn't need to be awoken by a hellcat sitting on her face.

Another crash, followed by a growl.

Or worse, a grumpy hellcat trying to break down her door.

I bolt out of bed, realizing that I am only in my pajama bottoms, but don't stop for a shirt. I stumble into the hall to find Brimstone bristled and growling outside Daphne's closed door. "Calm yourself, Brimstone," I hiss at her.

She spits at the door, ready to ram it again with her head. I make to grab her, but then I hear what's got her so upset—a rustling and banging behind the door, like things are being shoved around.

I grab the doorknob, hoping it's unlocked, and throw open the door. I half expect to see a startled Daphne sitting up and glaring at me, but instead I find her bed empty, the nightstand tipped over with a broken lamp lying beside it, and the balcony doors wide open.

Oh Hades. What happened here?

I step into the room, careful not to step on the broken glass from the lamp. All the drawers have been pulled from the dresser, and the closet door is partially open. I catch something shifting in the shadows behind it. It looks like someone dressed in all black, and entirely the wrong build to be Daphne.

"Who are you? Where is she? What do you want?"

"You busted into my place this afternoon," an all-too-familiar voice says. "I thought I'd return the favor."

He pushes the door open so I can see him fully now. I first

take in the glint of the moonlight cascading in from the balcony on the visor of the motorcycle helmet he holds under his arm, and then look up to meet his mocking smile. I feel as though my stomach has tied itself into the shape of a noose.

"Hello, *little* brother," Rowan says. "Aren't you happy to see me?"

chapter twenty

DAPHNE

A calloused hand closes over my wrist, but all I can see of its owner is a small, bright, smoldering circle seemingly floating in the air in front of his face.

I shriek and reel back, ready to unleash one of my now-famous right hooks, when the hand lets go and raises in the air. "Whoa, whoa, whoa," someone says, stepping out of the shadows of the aspen trees. "It's just me." He pulls the cigarette from his lips and blows a puff of smoke away from my face.

"Garrick?" I say, not quite completely relieved. "What are you doing here? Did you follow me?"

He nods, taking a puff on his cigarette. The smell makes me want to gag. "I was out on the porch, having a smoke, and saw you leaving. It looked like you were in some sort of trance, or like you were sleepwalking, so I followed. Looked like you were having full-on hallucinations, so I thought I'd try to wake you up. Didn't mean to scare you."

"Oh." I realize that he wouldn't have seen or heard any of the things in the grove that I had and how I must have looked pretty bonkers, crouching over an imaginary baby who was invisible to anyone else. Garrick isn't exactly my favorite person, but it still surprises me that he cared enough to look out for me.

I rub my arms for warmth and find streaks of mud on my wrist where he'd grabbed me. I notice his hands look dirty, as if he'd been digging around or something.

"Fell over a root back there," he says, seeming to anticipate my question. "Apparently, I can't smoke and walk at the same time."

"You shouldn't be smoking at all. Rule number one of the mortal world: those things will kill you."

"Whatever, *Master* Daphne. I'm not exactly into following rules these days."

"I gathered that. You smell lovely, by the way."

"Why, thank you very kindly," he says, bowing deeply, his hand holding the cigarette sweeping up in the air.

I'm tempted to say something like *bite me*, but there's a strange look in Garrick's eyes that makes me think he might actually do it. Garrick sometimes reminds me of an angry little junkyard dog.

He takes a long drag on the cigarette and then flicks it on the ground. "So if you weren't sleepwalking, what in Tartarus are you doing out here?"

I stamp out the cigarette butt. The last thing we need is for the grove to catch fire. Part of me doesn't want to share the grove's revelation with Garrick, but he's going to know as soon as I call Haden anyway. Everyone needs to know.

"I found it," I say, placing my hand on the bident-shaped laurel tree. It vibrates under my touch, almost as if greeting me. "The Key of Hades is hidden inside this tree."

"Inside?" he says incredulously, but I can hear a slight, wavering tone of excitement coming off him. This pricks my curiosity, since Garrick is normally silent—no inner song to speak of. "How do you know?" He circles the tree, inspecting it. I don't know if he can feel the tree's vibration or not.

"The grove told me," I say. "It brought me here."

I can hear a curious quirk in his tone, but I don't care to elaborate any further about my new powers.

"Look at the shape," I say. "This tree has grown up around the bident. It's inside the core of the tree."

I don't listen for his reaction. I don't care if he believes me or not; I know what I saw. "Now, how to get it out of there is a whole other mystery."

I guess I could try asking? I lean my ear against the trunk of the tree, soaking in the resonating notes that ripple off it and then hum the same tone back at it. "Open," I whisper into its bark. "Give me the Key."

The tree quivers, but nothing else happens. I know I shouldn't have thought it would be so easy.

"We should call Haden," I say, realizing my phone is still in my jeans pocket. At least I'd fallen asleep in my clothes and am not standing out here in a silky white nightgown as if I'm in some gothic movie.

"Let me try," Garrick says from behind me. "I've got an idea. Step back."

I turn and see that he has a ball of crackling blue lightning in his raised hand.

"No!" I say, but he doesn't listen. I barely have time to jump out of the way as he lobs it at the tree. The lightning hits the trunk and then explodes, sending both of us flying with a forceful shock wave. I land hard on my wrist about ten feet away from Garrick. He sits up, panting, inspecting himself for burns. I look back at the tree. It stands unharmed as far as I can tell, but I can't hear its tone anymore. It's grown silent as if in shock. Or perhaps retribution.

"You idiot!" I yell at him. "You almost killed us both. And now the tree is pissed off."

"The *tree* is pissed off?" he asks. "And I'm guessing you think your shoes have emotions, too?"

I give him a death glare, hoping he can see as well in the dark as Haden does.

"Maybe a second blow will work better." Garrick raises his hand, preparing a second bolt.

"No," I say, pulling out my phone. My wrist twinges with a sharp pain at the effort. "I'm calling Haden."

I dial the number, excitement almost making it hard to press the right numbers. But the line rings and rings until it goes to voice mail. I know that's not unexpected. It's the middle of the night, after all, but when the recording picks up instead of Haden, dread fills my chest.

chapter twenty-one

HADEN

"What's the matter, little brother?" Rowan says. "Hydra's got your tongue?"

He calls me *little* even though I am bigger than he is. He means to imply that I am the younger twin—something neither of us knows for sure—the *Lesser* brother.

"What are you doing here?"

That mocking smile of his grows thick with satisfaction. "You didn't really think you were the only Champion, did you? I told you I'd be the one they'd send to clean up your mess."

Lightning ricochets through my chest, down my arm, and into my hand. I want to lunge at him and shove my electrified fist down his throat, but it's the empty bed separating us that stops me.

"Where is she?" I demand, energy surging in my voice. "What have you done with her?"

If he's so much as touched Daphne, I'll—

"Tell me where it is, and I'll tell you what I did to her." Rowan speaks with confidence, but I know him well enough to know when he's bluffing. Either he isn't planning on telling me anything, or he doesn't even know what I'm referring to.

"It?" I ask. "What do you want?"

Whatever *it* is, it must be valuable if Rowan wants it. Then I realize he must be after the Key, but he doesn't know much if he thinks we've found it already.

"The communication talisman."

The talisman? That's . . . unexpected.

"Give it to me or you'll never see her again," he says.

That's it. I start to lunge at him, my hands ablaze with lightning, but a sound catches my ear. My phone ringing from inside my bedroom. The ringtone is the one I assigned to Daphne's number. "Falling Slowly." Wherever she is, she's calling me for help. I turn toward the sound, my cold relief extinguishing the bolts in my hands.

A sudden shove from behind sends me sailing into the doorjamb. I collide with it temple-first and sink to the ground.

"Haden? Haden?" Dax's voice rings in my ears.

Someone shakes me back to my senses. My head is still hot from the impact; only a few minutes must have passed since I fell.

"Gah . . . Rowan," I moan.

"Is he saying *growan*?" Tobin says. They're both leaning over me like I'm some specimen to be examined. "Where's Daphne?"

"Rowan," I say as clearly as I can. My tongue feels thick and slow.

"Are you saying *Rowan*?" Dax says. "That's his brother," he tells Tobin. "He must be really out of it. Do you know where you are, Haden?"

I nod. "Rowan. He was here. He came out of the closet." I look toward the open closet door where Rowan had been standing only moments before. He's gone now. Probably out the balcony doors as soon as I hit the floor.

Tobin makes a snerking noise. "You mean your brother came all the way from the underworld to tell you he plays for the other team? Did you faint or something?"

"What?" I slur. "What other team?"

"Haden has difficulties with euphemisms," Dax says. "But I think what he means is that Rowan came out of the literal closet." He stands up and goes to the closet. "Look at this." He holds up the helmet that Rowan left behind—it's the kind with the full-face visor that our mysterious Motorcycle Man always wore.

"Does that mean what I think it means?" Tobin asks.

I nod, my head throbbing from the movement.

"But where's Daphne?" he asks, springing up. "Did he take her?"

"He claimed he did, but I think he was bluffing." I try to push myself up, using the wall for support. "I heard my phone ringing just before he hit me. I think it was her." I point toward my room.

"I'll get it," Tobin says. He returns a few seconds later. "Missed call and a text."

I take the phone from him and look at the screen.

Daphne: Come to the grove ASAP!

"Can you even walk?" Dax asks, grabbing my elbow to steady me. "Maybe Tobin and I should go, and you stay here."

"I'm going," I say.

If Daphne needs me, nothing, not even my inability to stay upright, is going to stop me.

chapter twenty-two

DAPHNE

A text from Haden finally comes in, saying that he's on his way. Less than five minutes later, he, Dax, and Tobin show up in the grove. Dax and Tobin look as though they have only just returned from the mill—and I assume from the flat notes of disappointment coming off Tobin that the lead had been a bust—but Haden is dressed in pajama pants and a sweatshirt that is only half zipped up over his naked chest, as if it had been an afterthought. It would be impossible not to notice the taut olive skin of his bare chest and upper abs, but what is more arresting are the flowing, pulsing notes that coming rushing off him when he sees me.

I can't tell if it's the sound of relief or something else.

For half a moment, I think he's going to catch me up in a hug, but then he stops himself. Had getting a text from me in the middle of the night, when I was supposed to be down the hall, freaked him out that much?

"What's going on?" Haden asks, instead of embracing me. I note that his speech is slow and staggering, like he isn't fully awake despite the waterfall of notes surrounding him.

"You won't believe it," I say, buzzing with excitement.

"We found the Key," Garrick announces, totally stealing my thunder.

The others look completely dumbfounded.

"Truly?" Haden asks. I like that surprised look on his face.

"Well, where it's hidden anyway." I point out the tree and give them the same explanation I'd given Garrick. "It's getting to it that's the trick."

Tobin shrugs. "Anybody got a chain saw?"

"Not a good idea. Mr. Genius over here," I say, thumbing in the direction of Garrick, "already tried a lightning blast, and that almost resulted in us losing our teeth, but it didn't even leave a scratch on the tree. It's like it's being guarded by some sort of force field or protection spell."

"Sweet," Tobin says.

"Not sweet," I say. "Check this out." I crouch down near the base of the tree. My right wrist is still tender from falling on it when Garrick's lightning experiment went awry, so I can't help wincing as I pull back the long grasses in front of the tree. I use my phone as a flashlight for those of us in the group who don't have night vision, and point out my discovery. "See that knot near the base of the tree? Notice anything weird about it?"

I'd found the knot while trying to stop Garrick from using one of the shovels we'd left behind in the grove to try to dig up the tree's roots. Not that he'd gotten anywhere with that plan—the roots were as impervious as the trunk—but I didn't like the idea of him hurting something that had protected my ancestors' secrets for so long. I'd thought the knot at the base of the tree had been just that, but then I'd noticed the strange markings inside of it. I'd almost dismissed them as just scratches.

"Are those symbols?" Haden asks.

"Yep. The same symbols that are on the Compass. It's the same shape, too. Like it would fit right into the knot if you lined up the impressions of the symbols just right. I think I know what the Oracle meant when she said I'd use the Compass to seek the Key. I didn't need it to find its hiding place, but I do need it to get the Key out." I sigh. "So, good news: we found the Key. Bad news: we still need the Compass. Any more thoughts on where we might find the Motorcycle Man? Do we need to stake out some biker bars or something?"

Haden bristles beside me. "About that," he says. "Other good news: we know who the Motorcycle Man is." He takes a deep breath. "Other bad news: he's my psychotic twin brother and he has the Compass."

"Um, what?"

Haden tells me about finding Rowan in my bedroom and the motorcycle helmet he left behind when he escaped.

"But how did he get here?" Dax asks.

"I think he's been here all along. He called himself a Champion. I think the Court sent him through the gate soon after us."

"But if he's been here this whole time, why reveal himself now? He could have put the helmet on and escaped without you being the wiser," I say.

"He wanted something," Haden says, holding his hand to the side of his head as if it's throbbing. I realize that he must have left out part of the story and feel a pang of sympathy over the idea of him being hurt. "He was pretending to be holding you captive in exchange for a communication talisman."

I nod, feeling an additional ache of . . . *something* . . . when I realize why he had been so relieved to see me. But had he been worried about losing the Cypher, or was it the idea of losing *me* that had caused him anguish?

"He wants a communication talisman?" I ask instead of the question that is forefront in my mind. "You mean that medallion that you found next to Simon's body that transported your soul from the hospital to the Underrealm?"

When Haden's whole body had gone limp after grasping the talisman, Dax had explained to me that the device was used to make realm-to-realm calls by the Underlords—only it transported a person's soul, not just their voice. Haden had to fry the talisman, along with himself, in order to break the connection to free himself from his father's throne room.

"Did you tell Rowan that Simon's talisman has been destroyed?" I ask, pointing to his scarred hand.

Haden shakes his head. "I am starting to question whether or not the talisman was Simon's to begin with. It could have been either Simon or Rowan who dropped it at the hospital, and thinking back on it, I am not sure whom my father was expecting when I answered the call."

"But it had to be Simon's, right?" I look at Dax. "You said he made a call to the Skylords before he came into the hospital room. He would have needed a talisman for that, so it had to be the one we found on the floor."

Dax shakes his head. "He made the call on an ordinary iPhone. That didn't strike me as odd until now."

"I have a feeling some Skylords enjoy posing as humans, so it's not that strange," Haden says. "Look at Mr. Bowman, for example. I doubt this is his first sojourn in the mortal world. . . ." It seems as though he's about to say more but then trails off.

"But Simon had been in communication with your father while you were here, so that means he at least owned a talisman," Dax says. "But if he didn't have it with him at the hospital,

I wonder if he ditched it because he was planning on running off with the goods—namely Daphne and the Compass—and the talisman could be tracked somehow?"

"Or he didn't want to accidentally answer a call like I did." Haden shudders at the memory. "The room I caught Rowan in was Simon's old bedroom. . . ."

I cringe at the idea of having slept in a dead man's bed but let Haden go on.

"If Rowan lost his own talisman at the hospital, that means he either needs to find his or get a new one, so it makes sense that he would break into the house. He either thinks we still have his, or he was looking for Simon's. And if he was willing to reveal himself in order to try to bargain for a talisman, that means he's desperate."

"But why?" Tobin asks.

"Because if he's lost his talisman, he's flying blind," I say, putting it together. "He might have the Compass, but he has no idea what to do next without being able to communicate with King Ren."

Haden nods. "Which means he has something we want, and we have something he wants—or at least he believes we do. Which means he's going to show himself again."

"And in the meantime," I say, "we need to figure out how to get the Compass from him when he does."

"Exactly," Haden says.

"But more importantly, even if we get the Compass, how are we supposed to use it to get the Key?" I ask. "I doubt it's as easy as plugging it into the tree, or else you wouldn't need me. I'm not exactly looking forward to giving up my heart and soul for the thing."

"We'll worry about that later," Haden says. "For now let's focus on the Compass."

Easy for him to say, I think. The idea that I might need to give up my heart and soul to get the Key to the Underrealm doesn't exactly make it easy to focus on anything else at the moment. And it doesn't fill me with ease when I know that both the Skylords and Haden's crazy-loyal-to-the-Underrealm brother are after it, too. Both parties would probably shove me right through the lock if they need to.

"I think we have company," Dax whispers, and covers the light on my iPhone with his hand. He nods toward the path that leads into the grove from the footbridge. Two orbs of flashlight beams dance along the path. It's either Olympus Hills Security or someone worse. . . .

Haden tries to take me by the wrist, but I wince and pull away.

He gives me a concerned look, but I just shake my head. Now is not the time to explain how I hurt it. Instead, I follow him and the others into the thick trees at the north end of the grove. We crouch down behind a few boulders and watch as Calix and Teresa enter the grove, swinging flashlights and surveying the damage we've caused with all of our digging.

"I told you no one was here," Calix says. "We should go back. I don't like being out at night."

"Stop being a suckling," Teresa hisses at him. "It's obvious someone has been here." She swings her light across the trees, the beam barely over our heads. "Ethan is an idiot if he thinks those Underlords aren't looking for the Key on their own. We know they have the Cypher. If he'd let us tail them, then they'd probably lead us to its location."

Its? I think. *Does Teresa think the Cypher is an object like the Compass? Or does she mean it as in she doesn't know if the Cypher is male or female?*

"Do not speak of Ethan that way," Calix says to her. "He is your commanding officer—"

"Only because his grandfather granted him back his position after he came crawling home from his walkabout in the mortal realm. He's been gone for six years, while I've been the loyal lord. I should be the commanding officer, not him."

"I wouldn't call what he did crawling back. More like sweeping into a room and announcing his return."

"And just like that, he's back in charge," she says, bitter notes mixing with her already chaotic tone.

"I guess being a prince has its perks." Calix turns around with his flashlight aimed at the tuning fork–shaped tree. I hold my breath as he steps toward it. He stumbles into one of the holes we'd left in the ground and falls forward on his knees, muttering what I suppose are Skylord curses. He picks himself up and brushes off the dirt. "If you think I'm going to keep stumbling around in the dark against Ethan's orders, you're mistaken. I'm heading back."

"Suit yourself, suckling," she says as he picks his way back to the path. She shines her light again in our direction.

"We'll see how Ethan feels about your insolence."

Her shoulders drop, and she almost loses her grip on her flashlight. "Calix, wait." She follows after him up the path. "Don't tell Ethan."

"Come on," Haden whispers, once they're out of sight. "Let's get out of here before she decides to come back."

chapter twenty-three

HADEN

After we leave the grove, Dax drives us back to the house in the Model X, taking a longer route with several unnecessary turns and side streets just in case Terresa and Calix's leaving the grove was a feint. The conversation between the two Skylords makes me quiet with contemplation. Either what they said meant that Ethan had told me the truth—that he was attempting to keep his two lackeys off our scent—or the conversation was staged to make me think that is the case.

Either way, Terresa is getting far too close for comfort. And knowing now that Rowan is the one who has been tailing me for the last few months makes me shiver with paranoia. How are we to continue researching the Key with more than one adversary watching our every move?

It was a mistake for us all to have been in the same house tonight. What little cover we'd been keeping may have already been blown.

Daphne's head lolls as she sits next to me, reminding me how late it is. I can see her fighting to keep her eyes open. I wish I could tell her that she is welcome to rest her head on my shoulder if she wants to sleep. Instead, I shake her awake.

"Hmmm?" she breathes.

"Daphne," I say. "I need you to do me a favor. However, you are not going to like it."

Her drooping eyes open wider. "As in?"

"I need you to go home tonight. Back to Joe's, I mean."

She starts to shake her head.

"I also need you to ask him to give you back your part in the play."

"I don't want—"

"I know you don't, but it's important. We can't be seen together like this. That was a pretty close call back there in the grove with the Skylords, and letting you stay at my house nearly put you in the same room as Rowan. I also know that we aren't going to be able to solve the Key and Compass quandary if we cannot get together. . . ." Plus, I can't stand the idea of staying away from her. "Which means we need a *reason* to all be together where no one will question what we're doing. We need to bring Joe in on this. He hasn't made all of his final casting decisions yet, right? Do you think he might be willing to give me a part?"

"You want to be in the opera?" Tobin asks.

"We're all going to be in it," I say.

"What?" Garrick balks. "I am not going to be singing or dancing or any such thing."

"Then tech crew," I say to him, and then meet Dax's eyes in the rearview mirror. "I'm sure Mr. Morgan will take on a new faculty advisor and a tech hand if Joe puts in a request. Rehearsals start in earnest next week, which means we'll have two hours after school each day with a plausible reason to be together."

"Good thinking," Dax says.

"But it will only work if we're *all* involved." I place my hand tentatively over Daphne's. "You're going to have to talk to your father."

"Fine," she says, pulling away from me. *For the second time tonight.*

"Circle the lake a couple of times," I instruct Dax, "and then take us to Joe's."

chapter twenty-four

DAPHNE

It's nearly one thirty in the morning when we pull into the driveway at Joe's, but all the lights on the main floor shine through the windows. Dax and the others pull away, leaving Haden and me on the front porch. Haden stays without my asking, as if he thinks Joe and I need an intermediary.

"You might want to zip that up," I say, pointing at Haden's hoodie, which has come open almost all the way to his navel. It's not an unpleasant sight, but I don't think showing up in the middle of the night with a half-naked companion is going to get my conversation with my father off on the right foot.

"Oh yes," Haden says, his voice sounding garbled, as he zips his jacket up to his collarbone.

I pull out my house key and let the two of us in through the front door.

"Joe?" I call tentatively, my voice echoing in the white marble foyer. "I'm home."

"I don't care what you have to say. I'm done with you!" Joe's shout echoes from somewhere up the grand staircase.

I am taken aback for a moment and almost bolt right back out the door, but Haden's hand against my shoulder stops me.

"You don't have any control over me anymore!" Joe's voice climbs in anger, but from the sound of it, he's moving through the second-floor hallway toward the stairs. "Simon is gone, which means you have no place in my life." Joe appears on the landing and makes his way down the stairs, his phone pressed to his ear. "I'm sorry, Marta. I don't care what you do with yourself now. You're fired."

"Joe?" I call again.

"Daphne?" Joe drops his phone. It lands hard against the marble, but he doesn't seem to notice as he bounds down the stairs, two at a time, to meet me. "You came back." He stops short of hugging me and stands awkwardly in front of us. "I can leave the house. Sleep somewhere else tonight if you don't want me here."

I shake my head. "Can we talk?"

I sit Joe down in the main-floor family room. Haden lingers in the entryway, seeming to be fascinated by Joe's collection of all-white artwork. It takes me a few moments to get the courage to speak, but then I relate to Joe everything that has been going on for the last three weeks, from our search for the Key to the Skylords at school, and Rowan's revealing himself as the Motorcycle Man after Haden and Dax broke into his vacated apartment.

"So the lead I provided ended up being useful?" Joe asks.

I nod. In a way, it had. "And now we need something else from you." I launch into my explanation of Haden's idea to use play rehearsals as a cover for our group to meet without interference from the Skylords or Rowan.

He nods along with the idea, showing he sees the logic in it.

"Which means you'll need to find places for Dax and Garrick on the crew," I explain. "And Haden wants a part in the play."

I expect Joe to agree right away, based on the hopeful tone he puts off, but instead he leans forward, clasping his hands over his knees. "I'm going to need three things from you first," he says, like he has all the bargaining power in the room. "First of all, I want in on these meetings. I told you back in Ellis that since I got you into this mess, I want to do everything in my power to help you get out of it. I've already proved I can be helpful, so I need you to trust me enough to let me into your circle."

I push my hair behind my ears, not sure how to respond.

Haden takes a step into the room. "He should be a part of this, Daphne. We could use all the help we can get."

I sigh. Then nod. "And your second demand?"

"You'll keep living here. No dorms. No slumber parties with a bunch of teenaged boys."

That one I had expected already. "Okay."

"My third request is actually for Haden," Joe says, looking at him. "I'm going to need to hear you sing."

"What?" Haden asks. I can hear a tiny tremor of fear rolling off him.

"If you're going to be in my masterpiece, then I am going to need to hear you sing. I only have one male role left to fill, and it's a big one. Hades. I'm not handing that role over to just anyone. I'm going to need to hear you sing."

"Right now?" Haden asks.

"You've heard him sing before. At the Light-up Olympus Festival . . . ," I start to say, but then I remember that Joe hadn't exactly been sober the night Haden and I performed a duet in front of the whole town. More like wasted out of his mind.

Joe ducks his head in what I assume is shame.

"Couldn't you merely put me in the chorus?" Haden asks. I don't know exactly why he wants a part in the play rather than requesting a spot on the tech crew like Garrick, but I imagine it's because he wants to be on the stage with me as much as possible. He's been taking his self-appointed role as my bodyguard quite seriously.

Joe looks up at us again. "I've already submitted my chorus selections to Mr. Morgan. There's one last audition for the role of Hades on Wednesday. You'll have to impress me as well as Morgan if you want to be in the cast. Take it or leave it."

"I'll see you then," Haden says, accepting the challenge. "Good night, Daphne."

Haden heads for the foyer and lets himself out. I am about to head up to my wing of the house when Joe stops me. "One more thing, Daphne . . ."

"Haven't you made enough demands for tonight?"

"This isn't a request," he says, reaching into the breast pocket of his shirt. He pulls out what looks like a large gold coin. "I want to give you something."

"I don't want any more bribes. . . ."

Joe presses the coin into my hand. "This isn't a bribe. It's a commitment."

I look at the coin. There's a number 1 engraved in the middle with a triangle around it. On the top of the coin is the inscription TO THINE OWN SELF BE TRUE.

"What is this?" I ask.

"It's a sobriety coin. That one signifies one month of complete sobriety, but it's been six weeks since I've had a drink. Not since that night . . . the night of the festival, when I was so drunk you had to protect me instead of me protecting you."

Joe had almost been killed by a Keres that night. If it hadn't been for my vocal powers—in the form of a shrieking scream—that had made the shadow monster become solid enough for Haden to blast it to smithereens with his lightning, Joe would have had his life force sucked out of him by the parasitic Keres. I didn't think he'd remembered any of it.

"I see now why you got so mad about the scooter. You don't need gifts and bribes from me; you need me to be a better man. A better father. I'm giving you that so you can see that I'm trying to change. For you. I've been going to meetings. I don't even feel like touching alcohol again—because I need to be sober for you. I fired Marta. . . ."

"I heard."

"And with Simon gone, that means nothing else has control over me anymore. Nothing is stopping me from being who you need me to be. I understand if you don't want me. I understand if you want to kick me out of your life. But I want to be your father, Daphne—if you'll let me."

Tears flood my eyes. I press the coin tight in my hand. My anger is still there, sitting in my chest. I know it's going to take time to go away. I know the wall around my heart won't come down all at once. I know it will take me time to trust him again. But seeing him standing there in front of me, hearing the notes of sincerity that accompany his words, I know there is only one thing I can do at the moment.

I step toward Joe and wrap my arms around him. I hold him tight in a hug, crying against his chest, his hot tears landing on top of my hair while he shakes in my arms, and I cling to that coin in my grasp.

chapter twenty-five

HADEN

Over the next few days, I long for Daphne's help with preparing for the audition, but since getting together with her outside of the play would defeat the purpose of our clandestine plan, I stick it out on my own. I alternate my time between practicing the first song Daphne ever taught me with a loaner guitar of Joe's, and worrying over when or if Rowan will choose to reveal himself again.

The fact that he hasn't yet by Monday makes me fret even more. What if I had been wrong about supposing that we could use his desire for a talisman to help us get our hands on the Compass? Knowing where the Key is hidden and not being able to access it make my patience grow thin. But at least as long as Rowan stays away, the Skylords won't be able to steal the Compass out from under him, either.

Wednesday comes, along with my audition. I take the stage with my guitar, the last of the auditions for the day. Daphne sits in the audience with a few other students who have come to watch the proceedings. She seems to be careful not to give me too much notice, as if we are merely acquaintances instead of comrades—either that or she still has not forgiven me for making her go back to Joe's.

I approach the mic and address both Joe and Mr. Morgan, who sit in the middle of the auditorium. "I'm Haden Lord, and I am auditioning for the role of Hades, god of the Underrealm . . . er, I mean, underworld."

As I start to strum the guitar, I notice a presence in the room that I didn't expect. Ethan Bowman stands in the back of the auditorium, his arms crossed in front of his chest as he watches me with an intent stare. If he's going for intimidation, I won't let it deter me. I launch into the song, pretending Daphne is sitting next to me like when she taught it to me, and try to sing as if it were only for her.

It seems like no time until the song is over. There's a spatter of applause from the few students in the room, and Joe and Mr. Morgan put their heads together, conferring. Then Joe looks up at me and calls, "Congratulations, Mr. Lord, the part is yours."

I nod a thank-you and let my sight drift to Daphne for the first time since I finished singing. She gives me a small smile before her gaze darts to the side of the auditorium in warning. Terresa stands in the shadows of one of the east-side doorways. I duck my head and walk with my guitar to a back exit instead, not giving Daphne a second glance.

Ethan nods as I pass him. "Interesting talent you have for an Underlord," he says quietly. "I hope keeping your end of a bargain is another one."

"It is," I say under my breath, and push my way out the exit door.

chapter twenty-six

DAPHNE

The first group rehearsal starts on Saturday. Tobin and I are paired off for most of the morning, working on a duet from the opening act of the play, while Lexie and Haden are supposed to run lines for one of the underworld scenes. Garrick is assigned to be a stagehand, while Dax volunteers as the assistant for the props and costume master—a job he seems to be taking quite seriously, considering he's only using it as an excuse to be here. Only, we're so busy all morning, I start to worry that using rehearsals as a front for secret meetings isn't going to work, until we finally break for lunch. Mr. Morgan and the other students leave campus to find food, but Joe orders pizza so the rest of us can stay behind.

I sit on the stage, waiting for the delivery and nursing a bottle of apple juice. Mr. Morgan ran us through our paces so many times this morning that my voice is starting to feel strained. I realize I'm already letting this Key and Compass business adversely affect me because I've been skipping out on my self-mandated daily vocal exercises in favor of angsting over whether the Skylords or Rowan is going to suddenly decide to kidnap me.

Which is why I groan when someone finally brings up the subject at hand.

"Any sign of Rowan?" Joe asks as he sits down between Lexie and me. Haden, Dax, and Garrick sit across from us in a circle. The only one who hasn't joined us in our pseudohuddle is Tobin. He sits with his legs dangling over the edge of the stage while he studies pages from Abbie's diary. He must have read that thing five times over by now. I'm starting to worry that he's becoming obsessed.

But, really, could I blame him?

"Nothing," Dax says. "It's like Rowan is a ghost in the wind."

"It doesn't make sense," Haden says. "Why would he show himself only to disappear again? What is his endgame?"

"He probably knows we can't get to the Key without the Compass," Dax says. "Perhaps he's biding his time."

"But for what?" Haden asks. "He seemed desperate enough for a talisman; I thought for sure we would have heard from him again by now."

"Do we *want* to hear from him again?" Lexie asks. "From what you've described, this guy doesn't sound like someone you want to have a family reunion with."

"We need him if we're going to get the Compass."

"How's the search for Simon's talisman coming anyway?" I ask. "We're going to need it if we have any hopes of making a trade."

Dax shakes his head. "Haden and I have turned the house over looking for it. Simon could have ditched it somewhere in Vegas, for all we know."

"I'm tired of waiting for Rowan to make the next move," I say. "There has to be another way that we can try to track him down."

"But how?" Lexie asks. "The motorcycle lead was a bust. What else do we have?"

The group falls silent for a moment until Joe checks his phone.

"The pizza guy is out front." He reaches into the back pocket of his skinny jeans. "Bugger, I must have left my wallet at home." I can tell by the tone that comes off him that he's worried he's made himself look bad in front of me—like I'll think he's being irresponsible. "I might have cash in my car."

"Don't worry about it," Haden says, pulling a black credit card out of his back pocket.

Joe shies away from it. "I couldn't let you pay for the pizza I ordered."

"It's not a big deal. It's Simon's account anyway."

"In that case . . ." As Joe plucks the card from Haden's fingers, an idea hits me.

"Simon's account?" I ask. "How come the card is still working, then? He's been gone for weeks and if he's not here to make the payments, then where is the money coming from?"

Haden shrugs. I wonder if I need to add paying bills along with grocery shopping to Haden's How to Human lessons.

"He's probably got all of his bills set up as automatic payments from his bank account," Joe says. "Marta set the same system up for me—speaking of which, I should probably change my passwords, considering I just canned that evil minioness. Simon's money will run out eventually, but knowing him, it'll be a while before you have to worry about that." He looks at his phone again. "Pizza guy is getting impatient. I'll be right back."

He jogs down the stage steps and out the auditorium doors. As he goes, I turn to the others. "So if Simon is the one who bought Rowan's motorcycle, don't you think that probably means he was bankrolling Rowan?" I ask. "He's probably got one of those cards, too."

"I bet you're right," Dax says.

"Which means you can track his movements through his purchases," Lexie says excitedly.

"You can do that?" Haden asks.

"Yep," Lexie says. My dad does that to me whenever he gets in a parental mood—doesn't happen very often, but it's a real pain in the ass when it does. It's like spending an afternoon on Rodeo Drive is a crime or something."

"Can we access Simon's accounts?" Haden asks Dax.

"I found his laptop while we were looking for the talisman. If we could hack his passwords, we'd probably be in business."

"I might be able to help with that," Tobin says, turning toward the group, even though I had assumed he wasn't paying attention. "I know a few tricks."

I remember now that he'd mentioned something once about wanting to hack the school's computer system to look for information about the Lord family.

"I'll bring the laptop to rehearsal on Monday," Haden says, the notes of his excitement filling the room as an actual *possibility* starts to take shape.

chapter twenty-seven

TOBIN

There's a reason my mother is perturbed that I'd rather apply to Juilliard than MIT. It's because if I put my mind to it, I *could* be a genius like my brother, Sage.

I just happen to enjoy singing and dancing more than solving math equations and writing code. That and not wanting to give my mother the satisfaction of being able to plan my life out for me. But that doesn't mean I don't know my way around a computer. Sage taught me a few tricks when he still lived at home, and I'd honed my skills over the last few years of searching for information about Abbie and the other girls who'd gone missing from Olympus Hills. I even hacked into the school's computer system a couple of times before they updated their firewall.

I've had Simon's laptop for almost a week, but with Mom in tiger hyperdrive since I managed to score my first-ever B on a chem quiz ("Oshiro-Winters do not settle for grades lower than A!"), I haven't had a chance to take a look at it until tonight. My parents are out late at some hoity-toity dinner or something, giving the house staff the night off, so I set up shop at the dining room table with my computer, Simon's laptop, a bottle of Mountain Dew Code Red, a bowl of Swedish Fish, and Abbie's diary for reading during my downtime. We don't know much about who Simon was, other than being a health freak, a possible satyr, and an emissary for the Underrealm, so it's going to take more than punching in his birth date or the model year of his first car in order to figure out his various passwords.

Unfortunately, I find, when I plug his computer in and turn it on, that it's password protected from the get-go. However, fortunately, the laptop runs on Windows and it takes only a minute for me to force a reset of the administrative password to give me full access to his laptop. Getting his credit account password is going to be trickier, though. Too bad Haden and Dax's search of his house hadn't turned up any bank statements or paperwork that could help me out. Either Simon had managed everything online, or Marta had handled all of that for him.

But also lucky for me, I have a few connections. Or one, really.

I open my email on my own laptop and pull up the latest message from Sage.

Here's that software you requested. Should I be worried about what you're going to do with it, little bro?

I send a reply: It's for purely educational purposes. And then download the software onto a stick.

My brother makes a small fortune freelancing out his services to companies who want someone to try to crack their security. If I can't figure it out on my own, I'll have to use Sage's "brute force" program to try to decrypt the password. But that could take anywhere from an hour to several weeks (or even years), depending on how strong Simon's password is.

When it's ready, I plug the stick into Simon's laptop and let the software start doing its thing. As I wait, I start poking around in Simon's files, hoping there might be some sort of lead there. My heart starts racing when I see a file marked *Abbie* in a documents folder. I'd been wondering for the past few weeks if Simon knew what had happened to my sister. And since Marta hadn't returned to Olympus Hills since Joe fired her—causing my only viable lead to go cold—I am overwhelmed by the possibility that the information I've been looking for might be stored right in front of me. I double-click on the file so fast that it doesn't register, so I have to try again. The file seems to take an eternity to open—probably because of all the memory Sage's software is using—and I find myself holding my breath until it does.

Only to let it out in a discouraged huff. The file is nothing but a resume for a woman named Abbie St. James, who appeared to be applying for a role as a backup vocalist for Joe Vince's band. The more files I open, the more I realize that they are mostly all band related (Simon was Joe's manager, after all), and I start to realize this computer must have been used purely for his day job. It's not like he would be getting emails all the way from the Underrealm. That's why Rowan needed his communications talisman.

It's been several hours and Simon's computer is running almost too hot to touch because of the brute force software and I am about to call it a night, when I notice a file named *PWs*. It reminds me of how Great-grandpa Oshiro writes down all of his passwords on a sticky note just in case he forgets them.

Old people do the weirdest things. . . .

Then it strikes me that, for all we know, Simon had been a very old man in a very young-looking man's body. Which is probably why he was so obsessed with his health.

I open the file and find a list of words written in a language that looks Greek to me. . . . Because it probably is Greek.

The first one in the list looks like two words combined by an underscore. I type them into Google Translate, and it comes back with the words *kale chips*.

Either this is a shopping list, or . . .

I open up the bookmark for Simon's credit card company. I type in his name and then *kale_chips* in the password field.

The computer is still running slow, but after a moment of thinking, a page opens, unfolding Simon's account information right in front of me.

"Seriously, his password was *kale chips?*" I say aloud, swinging my arms out in disbelief. My hand hits my half-empty bottle of Code Red. It spills right on top of Abbie's open diary.

I swear loudly and snatch the diary up. Which starts dripping on Simon's laptop. I swear some more and run for the paper towels in the kitchen with the diary in hand, leaving a trail of red drops on the white carpet in the dining room as I go.

"Tobin? What's wrong?" I hear my mother's voice echoing through the house from the mudroom. She must have opened the door from the garage just in time to hear my tirade. I cover the diary in paper towels—both to sop up the mess and to conceal the green leather book in case my mother might recognize it as Abbie's—and then scoop up both computers, juggling them frantically, and dash up the stairs before my mother has time to remove her jacket and shoes (a must before entering the house) and discover what I've been up to.

"Nothing, Mom," I shout down the stairs. "Just had an accident . . . with some soda. I'll clean it up in a minute."

"You'll clean it up right now!" she shouts from the dining room.

"Be right there!"

I wipe off the diary pages the best I can, and then toss it and the computers on top of my bed. I can hear my mother headed up the stairs, ready to give me a lecture about cleaning up after myself, so I grab my bath towel off the back of my desk chair and bound out of the room, closing the door behind me.

"I'm on it," I call as I jog past her on my way to the dining room. I throw the towel down on top of the table, soaking up the red soda.

"You should watch your language, young man. Even when you think you're alone. 'The true test of a man's character is how he behaves when no one is watching,'" she says, repeating one of her favorite mom proverbs.

I don't respond. The only thing I can think of is the list of names under which Simon had credit accounts that I had gotten the briefest of glances at before running the computer upstairs. *Rosemary Winters*, my mother, had been at the top of it.

Any inkling of a doubt that I could have entertained that my mother wasn't in the pocket of the Underrealm has been completely destroyed.

The next day, I sit alone backstage before rehearsal is supposed to start, with Abbie's journal and Simon's laptop in front of me. I know I should be running lines for the scene Joe suddenly decided to add to the play this morning, but instead, I can't pull myself away from Abbie's journal. I'd spent a good part of an hour last night carefully wiping Code Red soda from between the pages, feeling like an archeologist cleaning a precious artifact, and discovered an entry that I hadn't seen before.

Even though I'd read the diary through more times than I care to admit, I'd missed this page because it had been stuck to the one in front of it by what appears to be a couple of drops of clear nail polish.

What's so interesting about this entry is the drawing that (presumably) Abbie had made in a corner of the page. It's of a segmented circle with different symbols sketched in each block. One looks like a lyre; another resembles a trident. I know where I've seen something like this before. . . .

"Tobin?" I hear Daphne say, but from the sound of her voice, I can tell it's not the first time she's called my name. I hadn't even noticed her entering backstage.

"Hey," I say, tracing my finger over the drawing.

"How long have you been here?" she asks, pointing at the remnants of my lunch that sit beside me.

"Not long," I lie. Truth is, I skipped my last three classes today.

Daphne gives me this look like I'm not fooling her. I forget that she can read people's tones. Mine probably sounds as jittery as the three Mountain Dews I've downed so far this afternoon. I didn't sleep much last night.

Daphne sits next to me. She bites her lip as if thinking hard, and I worry she's trying to come up with the best words in which to stage some sort of intervention with me over the diary. *Like I need another lecture. . . .*

"I've missed you," Daphne says.

"Huh?"

She shrugs. "I just realized this is the first time we've been alone together since Las Vegas. I've missed my friend."

She gives a small smile, and it strikes me all over again what a beautiful person she is. It's not like I'm in love with her or anything. I knew there was no chance for anything to happen between us the second she gave me that speech about how she doesn't have time for boys because of her music and all that. And, really, I'm cool with being her friend, but I can still appreciate that she's a beautiful person—both inside and out.

"I've missed you, too," I say.

"How is everything?" she asks.

I know she means emotionally, but instead, I pick up the diary. "I think I found something," I say, my voice coming out much squeakier than I expected. I should probably cut down on the caffeine. "What do you make of this drawing?" I say, with a concentrated effort to make my voice lower.

"That looks like the symbols that are on the Compass," Daphne says excitedly. "And the tree."

"That's what I thought, but I'm pretty sure I've seen them somewhere else, too. I didn't realize it until now." I point at the paragraph at the bottom of the page. "Read this passage."

Daphne reads out loud: "'Mom got a new artifact for her collection today. It came in a wooden crate like something out of an Indiana Jones movie. She wasn't home when the courier service delivered it, so I thought I'd have a look inside. It was some sort of old scroll. Kinda lame for the $50,000 receipt that accompanied it. Extra, extra lame, considering Mom just told me she's cancelling my acting lessons because they're too expensive. Anyway, Mom freaked when she came home and saw the open crate. It's not like I touched anything inside of it. She acts like I'd be dumb enough to try to unroll some scroll that's been lying around in a cave somewhere for a few thousand years. She locked it away as soon as she got home. I don't know why she'd pay so much for something if she's not even going to put it on display like everything else. From what I could see, the only thing cool about it is this circle with all these weird symbols on the outside of the scroll. I keep finding myself drawing them when I'm not even thinking about it. Strange, huh?'"

"Definitely," I say.

Daphne stops and looks up at me. For a moment there, I had forgotten that she was reading and that Abbie wasn't speaking to me from the past.

"Look at the date of this passage," I say, tapping the page. "She wrote this shortly after we moved to Olympus. This would have been before she knew anything about Skylords and the Underrealm and all that."

"Have you seen this scroll she's talking about?" Daphne asks. "The fact that it has the same symbols as the Compass can't be a coincidence. Maybe it holds a clue as to how we're supposed to use it."

"That's what I was thinking," I say. "And, yeah, I've seen it. My mom keeps her more precious artifacts locked in her wall safe, rather than on display. I've seen a scroll in there once or twice."

"What, like you've broken into your mother's safe as well as her files?" Daphne punches me in the arm. "Hacking computers, cracking safes, why didn't you tell me that you're a regular James Bond?"

"Q," I say. "Q does the cool tech stuff; Bond just runs around looking good in a tux and drinking martinis. And I'm not really the Q in my family. I told you my brother is a mechanical genius. He made a combination cracker when he was fifteen."

"Wow, no wonder your mom treats you like you're the dumb one," she says, with a playful smile.

"Tell me about it." I roll my eyes. "But the point is, my mom has a scroll that might tell us something about the Compass. Maybe even how to use it."

"But *why* would she have it?" she asks.

"If I know my mother, she was probably looking for collateral.

She's been collecting artifacts for the last few years. I'm guessing she's been looking for something she might be able to use for more bargaining power if the Underrealm ever decides she outlived her usefulness. I wonder if she even *knows* what the scroll is for."

"You still remember the combination to the safe?" Daphne says, starting to stand. "Let's go get this scroll."

"I didn't think you were too keen on breaking and entering," I say teasingly. She'd scolded me big-time the last time we snooped around my mom's office.

"I'm not, but I'm hoping this scroll will tell us how to use the Compass without me having to cut out my heart or something not so pleasant like that." She's making a joke, but I sense the emotion she's trying to hide with it. The closer we get, this Compass, Key, and Cypher stuff is starting to freak her out.

"Unfortunately, it's going to be more complicated than that." I close the diary. "After I stole that file of maps from my mom's office back in January, my mom thought we'd had a break-in, and she moved her entire collection to her office in town hall. The security there isn't exactly as easy to bypass as stealing my mom's office key out of a hollow book and punching Sage's PSAT scores into her safe. Just getting into the building after hours would be impossible."

Daphne sinks back down to the floor next me. "Too bad you really aren't Bond," she says, and falls silent, as if lost in thought.

"What's with all the despair, you two? Did somebody *die*?" Lexie asks sarcastically as she comes backstage, carrying a box that seems to be loaded with poster paint and . . . glitter.

I look up at her.

She lowers the box. "Oh no, did somebody really die? I heard they were going to try to take Pear off her respirator today. Did you hear something—"

"Nothing like that," I say, because I see the terror in her eyes. She and Pear might have been rivals, but they had still been best friends since freshman year. Lexie was kind of complicated like that. "Just a problematic lead."

"No luck with cracking the password, then?" Dax asks as he and Haden enter the room after Lexie.

"Quite the contrary," I say, picking up the laptop. I'm glad to focus on something that doesn't seem so difficult for a moment. I pull up Simon's information and turn the computer around so they can see my handiwork.

"Impressive," Haden says.

"Only problem is, I don't see a Rowan Lord on this list of account holders," I say. "There is an R. King, though."

"That sounds about right," Haden says. "Rowan would choose King over Lord."

I click on the statements for that card. "The timing seems right. There are only statements dating back to September for this account. But, ugh . . ." I shake my head in frustration.

"What is it?" Haden asks.

"If this is your brother, he's a smart SOB. Look at this—he's been taking out large cash advances every few weeks and that's it. We can't track him by his spending because he's doing it all in cash—and every time he takes out an advance, he does it at a different location. His latest withdrawal was yesterday at a bank in Riverside. He's too damn smart."

"Sounds like Rowan," Haden says, not quite under his breath.

"But we can still use this to smoke him out," Daphne says, pointing to a link that says, *Report this card lost or stolen.* "How about we cut off his cash flow? See how long he stays in the wood-work when he finds out his card has been cancelled."

"You're brilliant," I say, clicking the link to go through the process to cancel the card. "Now, if only you could figure out how to get us into town hall on a Saturday night, I might propose to you."

"I got nothing on that one." She shrugs.

"If you want to get into town hall on a Saturday night," Lexie says, "then just buy a ticket to Cupid's Ball."

"Cupid's what?" Daphne asks.

"It's the school Valentine's dance," Lexie says. "Don't you guys pay attention to the posters around school? Me and the Sopranos have been working on them all week," she says, pointing at the box of paint and glitter. "Normally, I have one of the printers on my dad's payroll make up professional signs, but stupid Mr. Bowman volunteered to be our faculty advisor for the dance, and he's insisting we go all old-school, handmade posters and decor because it'll be more 'romantic,' but seriously, if you guys aren't even noticing the signs, this is a waste of time."

"I think we've all just had a lot on our minds . . . ," Daphne says. "But what does the dance have to do with town hall?"

"Well, if you'd read any of my posters or flyers"—she pulls a flyer out of her box and thrusts it at Daphne—"you would know that the dance is being held in the rotunda of the town hall building."

"When?" I grab the flyer from Daphne.

"In two weeks. You know, on Valentine's Day?" Lexie says with a "duh" sound to her voice, like we're all a bunch of idiots.

I exchange a look with Daphne. She smiles at me mischievously.

"Do you have a tux, Mr. Bond?" she asks me.

"Yeah . . ."

"You still have access to Sage's safe cracker?"

"He probably left one of his prototypes in his closet...."

"Do you have a date to the ball yet?"

I smile.

"What are you two going on about?" Haden asks, clearly more confused than usual. "Why is this dance so important?"

"Because," Daphne says, her smile going from mischievous to downright devious, "we're going to pull a heist."

chapter twenty-eight

HADEN

"Everyone needs to be there by seven thirty," Daphne says as she pores over a crudely drawn map of town hall that Tobin provided from memory. Our lunch break during this Saturday rehearsal is almost over, and the dance is tonight. We've spent the last two weeks coming up with a strategy to get in and out of the mayor's office during this so-called Cupid's Ball, but I still have misgivings about the plan.

"I still think I should be the one who goes for the scroll," I say.

"Doesn't work," Tobin says. "Ethan is the faculty advisor for the dance, which means it's inevitable that the Skylords will be there. They'll be watching you for sure, and the last thing we want to do is lead them right to the scroll."

I know he's right, but I don't like the idea of giving up so much control over the situation.

"Besides, if I get caught," Tobin says, "I'll be able to come up with a more plausible explanation for why I'm hanging out in my mother's office."

"Our diversion is planned for 8:07," Daphne goes on, reviewing our plan. "Do the Sopranos know what they're supposed to do?"

Lexie nods. "They'll rush the stage as soon as Joe and his band start their first song."

The diversion part of this plan is the one that has me the most dubious. We'd gone through several options for what would make the best distraction so Tobin and Lexie can sneak past security in order to get to the mayor's office. Garrick had gone as far to suggest an explosion in the town hall kitchen, but Lexie had wholeheartedly protested anything that might actually ruin the dance she'd spent the last month planning. "There will be no explosions at *my* dance! Besides, it'll make it even harder to get to her office if they have to evacuate the building because they think there's a bomb threat."

It was Joe who had finally come up with the idea that the others liked best. "What if Joe Vince and the Stargazers were to make a surprise guest appearance to the dance to perform a brand-new single from their yet-to-be-released album? Do you think that would create a bit of a ruckus? Especially if some overzealous fans were to rush the stage—that might keep security occupied for a few minutes."

Lexie didn't protest this idea at all. "Ooh, the surprise could be, like, my gift to the school or something!"

"Is anyone really going to buy it when a bunch of girls rush the stage?" I had asked. "Do people do such things over rock stars?"

"Uh, yes," Daphne had said. "Joe and I can barely make it in and out of restaurants outside of Olympus Hills without him being accosted."

"A lot of the students are getting used to seeing me around the school, but if the band is performing, I think that would cause a stir—especially if Lexie's Sopranos were tipped off to what we want them to do."

"I think we need a secondary option," I had suggested. "Something to split the security guards' attention in two directions."

Which is how Garrick had been reluctantly looped in on the plan.

"Garrick, your part needs to go off at 8:09," Daphne says as we look over the schedule now. "Garrick! Are you listening?"

He looks up from playing a game on his phone. "8:09, boys' bathroom, north hall."

"South hall," Daphne corrects.

"That's what I said," Garrick says, fervently tapping the screen of his phone.

A few students start returning from lunch break, so we huddle closer to review the rest of the plan before Mr. Morgan arrives.

"Everyone got it?" Daphne asks as we break apart.

"Got it," those of us who are paying attention respond.

"And make sure you look sharp, Tobin," Lexie says, wagging a finger at him. "I don't normally date short guys, so you'd better look pretty damn good if people are going to believe that we're there together. None of this basketball shoes paired with khakis that some guys try to pull off at dances."

"Um, I have a fedora to coordinate with every outfit that I own. You think I'd wear sneakers with a suit? Please. I own my own tux. And, by the way, you're, like, barely five feet tall. Compared to you, I'm practically in the NBA."

"NBA? Yeah, like you could score with me any day," Lexie says.

Daphne bursts into laughter. I blink at all three of them.

"I meant to say score *over* me," Lexie says, her face growing pink. "It was supposed to be a basketball reference."

"Freudian slip?" Tobin says, in a voice that I can't tell if it's mocking or teasing.

"You wish."

Lexie and Tobin glare at each other, and I start to wonder if pairing them up for a pretend date is a good idea. But I'm not about to suggest that he take Daphne instead. I wouldn't like the idea of her sneaking off with him to unknown parts of town hall without my protection.

"Whatever," Tobin says. "I'm going to look so fine in my tux, you girls will have a hard time remembering why we're even at the dance in the first place."

I hope that isn't the case. With Skylords possibly watching and Mayor Winters's security on the prowl, we can't afford any complications in our plan.

chapter twenty-nine

DAPHNE

I hitch a ride to Cupid's Ball with Tobin and Lexie, feeling like a third wheel even though they're on a fake date.

"Well, you look passable," Lexie says when Tobin picks us up. But she looks him up and down in his tux more than once—clearly liking what she sees. Tobin might be "too short" for Lexie, but there is something magical about a guy who can wear a tux well.

Tobin removes his black fedora and, with a grand bow, replies, "And you, sweetest Lexie, are as ravishing as ever." His voice drips with sarcasm, but the notes flitting off him suggest he's telling the truth.

I make a mental note to needle Tobin later about his history with Lexie—and possibly their future?

"You *all* look gorgeous!" Joe says, pulling out his iPhone to take some pictures. "Especially you, Daph."

Things are still weird and a little strained between us, but I return his compliment with a smile. Lexie had insisted on taking me shopping a week before the dance. "If you and I are going to continue being friends, we need to bring your fashion up a few notches. No more of," she said, waving her hand in my general direction, "this. I'm having my dress custom-made, but I've had a couple of my Sopranos draw up a list of glam boutiques in LA who cater to the big and tall."

She'd been kidding about the *big* part (I think), but compared to Lexie, I am pretty much a giant—I guess that's what happens when you're descended from the last of the Amazons. But I didn't put much stock in a dig from a girl who probably had her dresses custom-made so she didn't have to buy them from the juniors department. However, I have to admit that she did a pretty stellar job in helping me pick out a dress. It's red chiffon with a satin underlay. The bodice is a formfitting sweetheart neckline with capped sleeves, while the skirt is short in the front and long and flowy in the back. And because we'd bought it at a store for tall clientele, I don't have to worry about constantly tugging at the front of my skirt, because it isn't too short.

Lexie's dress has a similar skirt, but is pink and strapless, with intricate beading. I'm pretty sure it cost five times more than mine.

Joe insists on taking more than a few pictures. After about ten different poses, I remind him that he needs to go meet his band before they make their surprise guest appearance, and he lets us go.

"Shall we?" Tobin asks, holding out both of his arms to escort us to the car.

We arrive at the town hall shortly thereafter, but Tobin parks across the street rather than using the valet, in case we need to "bug out," as he phrased it.

As much as Tobin would probably like to walk into the dance with two girls on his arms, I insist on waiting a few minutes before following them in. I am supposed to be going to the dance stag, as is Haden, since we're not supposed to all be seen together.

When I finally walk into the entry hall, I find that it looks like a pink-and-red-heart-filled bomb has gone off. They're everywhere, from dangling like lanterns from the ceiling to masking the walls.

I show my ticket to Dax, who, as a faculty volunteer and a lookout for our little operation, is manning the ticket table.

"Everything looks well to have a good evening," he says. I think this sounds odd until he gives a slight nod behind him.

I follow his gesture with my gaze to find Haden standing in the rotunda of the building, just in front of the dance floor. I take in a quick breath that I hope Dax doesn't notice. I'd thought Tobin wore a tux well, but that was nothing compared to the way Haden looks in his. All dark and dashing and kind of regal.

It strikes me for a moment that he *is* a prince.

Or at least he could have been if he hadn't given it all up to save me.

I start to take a step in Haden's direction, but Dax clears his throat, catching my attention. "Don't forget to check your jacket," he says, even though I don't have one. I glance over to the coat-check station—a closet with an open window where students can pass their jackets to the clerk—to find Ethan and the other Skylords conversing—no, arguing—with each other. I can't tell what they're saying, but Terresa gives me a quick, sharp glance before returning to the argument.

Remembering that the Skylords are watching, I take a roundabout path to the rotunda, rather than making a beeline for Haden. I pass Tobin and Lexie, who've stopped to talk to Bridgette and her date, and give Tobin the smallest of nods as I go.

The rotunda is a large, circular room in the center of the building, with four sets of stairs that give access to a balcony overlooking the dance floor. A large crystal chandelier, as big as an elephant, hangs from the center of the ceiling, with glittering pink and red hearts dangling from its arms; and the floor and columns supporting the balcony are made of white marble. Tables, draped with black-and-white tablecloths, and adorned with arrangements of red roses, surround the outskirts of the dance floor, and an ice sculpture of a plump, little cupid with his bow and arrow guards the refreshment table that fills the space between two of the staircases on the south end of the rotunda. The space between the two north staircases is filled by a stage that has been erected for the DJ—and later for Joe and his band when they make their surprise appearance.

I give the rotunda a good once-over, expecting to see the mayor, but I don't. Instead, I spot the security guards, who stand at the top of each staircase. According to Tobin, their job is to keep students from wandering beyond the balcony to the corridors where the mayor and other town officials keep their offices. Below, the only security is that of the school faculty chaperones, who will be more than busy when Joe's band arrives. There is already a lot of excitement and speculation buzzing around the dance about a rumored surprise—and it's obviously a band, from the equipment set up on the stage.

I pick up a glass of pink fizzy punch from the refreshment table, where Garrick had grudgingly agreed to volunteer this evening. I don't see him at his post and quickly begin to worry about the plan. It may not work if he doesn't play his part.

I start to panic until I spot him, at the end of the table, slouching in a chair with his legs crossed and a plate of little sausages and cheese in his hand. He catches me glaring at him and gives me a sarcastic thumbs-up, then drops his attention back to his plate of food.

I take my glass and stand at one of the tall tables lining the dance floor and watch people who have come to the ball with dates dance to a slow song. It's 7:57 when Haden comes to stand at the table next to mine. His back is to me, but I still hear him say, "You look beautiful," over the music.

I am glad he cannot see me blush.

I watch the couples dancing, my anxiety growing the closer we get to eight, and I let out a too-loud laugh when something catches my eye. I clamp my hands over my mouth.

"What?" Haden says, turning toward me.

"Over there," I say, gesturing with my hand hidden by the table. "Check it out. Terresa and Calix are dancing together."

He turns slightly away from me again but looks at Terresa and Calix dancing only a few yards away. Their movements are mechanical and stiff, and I get the distinct impression that Terresa does not enjoy touching Calix.

"I mean, it's totally a ruse because they're obviously watching your every move," I say as Calix turns Terresa away so she isn't glaring at Haden for once. "But aren't those two supposed to be pretending to be cousins? Someone should tell them dancing together isn't the best idea, considering their cover."

Haden's shoulders shake a little as if he were silently laughing. I wish I could see his face. I start to move so I can face him, when the music comes to a stop and the DJ says into the mic that he has a special announcement on behalf of Lexie Simmons, the organizer of the dance. I can see Joe and his band waiting in the corridor behind the north stairs. I look to the other side of the rotunda and watch as Tobin and Lexie try to make their way through the crowd to the south stairs. I check my watch. It's only eight. We're seven minutes ahead of schedule.

I reach over and squeeze Haden's hand behind his table.

"Ready or not, here we go," I whisper.

chapter thirty

HADEN

The hysteria that fills the room when the DJ announces the special guests who will provide the entertainment for the rest of the evening is more than I could have predicted. Egged on by the over-the-top reactions from Lexie's Sopranos, a throng of students rush toward the stage. Chaperones and a handful of security guards descend on the crowd, holding them back just so Joe and his band can even get to the stage. The scene is almost as exhilarating as the fact that Daphne is holding my hand behind the table.

Joe takes the microphone from the DJ.

"'Ello," he calls to the crowd, which goes even wilder. "I'm Joe Vince, and we are the Stargazers. Some of you might have heard of us."

Excited screams echo through the rotunda, the crowd pressing even closer to the band. Someone, possibly Bridgette, tries to climb up onto the stage, requiring two security guards to pull her away.

Joe laughs charmingly into the microphone. "We're going to perform some of our old favorites tonight, but also a couple of new songs, to give you a little preview of the album we've been preparing, based on the rock opera that I've written for the school. The first of which features a very special guest vocalist." He swings his arm out in my and Daphne's direction. I pull my hand out of Daphne's grasp and step away from her. "Daphne, will you please join us onstage?"

A panicked look strikes Daphne's face. This is not part of the plan.

"Come on, Daphne," Joe coaxes.

She starts to shake her head. "We haven't practiced this song in weeks," she says, even though I am the only one who can hear her.

"All right, crowd, let's get her up here!" Joe leads the students in a rollicking chant of: "Daphne, Daphne, Daphne!"

"Go," I mouth to her.

Daphne starts to move toward the stage but gets mired in the crowd.

"Can we get a little assistance here?" Joe says, pointing to a couple of unoccupied teachers at the bottom of the south stairs. They respond by creating a buffer so Daphne can make it through the crowd.

I look at the time on my phone. It's 8:07 now. Joe has been buying us time and additional distraction. Tobin and Lexie are in place now, midway up the stairs, surrounded by a knot of students who are trying to get a better view of the band.

I look for Garrick, hoping I *do not* see him, but spot him headed down the south corridor with an empty food tray. A little late on his timing. He disappears through a doorway. I watch the time on my phone. If he does his part right, then something should happen in exactly a minute and a half.

Daphne makes it to the stage to join Joe. The drummer hands her a microphone.

The time turns over to 8:09. I look toward the south corridor. Nothing.

Harpies, I'm going to kill Garrick.

Five more seconds, and just as the band is striking up and the crowd is cheering in a frenzy, I feel a rumble under my feet and a popping sound, and Garrick comes dashing out of the boys' bathroom.

Never mind.

Even from this far away, I can see that his feet are wet. He approaches one of the security guards who has descended the south stairs. He swings his arms widely, gesturing toward the bathroom, and I presume that he is frantically explaining that a water pipe has burst under one of the sinks. Hopefully leaving out the part in which he had caused it to happen by boiling the water in the pipe with his lightning power.

The guard pulls out his radio and does exactly what I had hoped. In a matter of seconds, the guards at the top of the south stairs descend in a hurry. They follow Garrick in a rush to the bathroom.

The band starts playing, and with all the attention in the room focused on them, I am the only one who notices as Tobin and Lexie slip away from the crowd on the stairs and up into the corridor leading to the mayor's office.

I am inclined to follow them, my anxiety egging me on to make sure they don't mess up their end of the plan, but as Daphne's voice fills the rotunda, singing a duet with Joe, a calming sensation ripples through my body. My rationality returns to me. Calix and Terresa are watching my every move. If I were to follow Tobin and Lexie, it would only lead the Skylords right to them.

Instead, I hope to Hades that they can get the job done.

chapter thirty-one

TOBIN

When the band starts playing, Lexie and I rush up the remainder of the stairs. Lexie almost trips in her superhigh heels until I grab her hand to steady her. I don't know why she chose such ridiculous shoes for our mission, but I'm betting it's so she can get an inch of height over me. At the top of the stairs, Lexie slips off her terrible footwear and we disappear—sprinting—into the hallway that leads to my mother's office before anyone notices we've slipped past the no-admittance signs.

"We're clear," I say, looking behind us to check that we haven't been followed. "Let me just catch my breath for a second."

"Holy crap, that was a rush!" Lexie bounces up and down, clearly very excited. I glance away, not wanting to be caught in a stare. Maybe it's just the excitement of the evening taking over, but I can't help thinking about the first (and only other) time Lexie and I had snuck away from a party together. She'd dared me into jumping into a swimming pool fully clothed, and we'd swam under the moonlight, cracking jokes about the "cool kids" whose party we'd crashed.

But that was when we were only thirteen. Back before Lexie had joined up with Pear and the Sopranos freshman year—back when she'd still wear Princess Leia T-shirts to school and I thought she was the coolest girl in Olympus Hills.

I hear footsteps running toward us from farther down the hall.

"Someone's coming." I look back and forth, hoping to find a room to duck into quickly, but Lexie grabs both of my arms and shoves me against the wall. She kisses me, hard, and wraps her hands under my ears, nearly knocking my fedora from my head with her sudden movements.

Stunned, I almost push her away, but then rethinking, I kiss her back. The memory of my first kiss flits through my mind—a peck against Lexie's lips under the water of that pool. (Another dare from Lexie that I couldn't back down from.)

Had the memory of that night gotten to her as well?

A guard jogs past us, heading toward the commotion downstairs. "Nice, Tobin," he says under his breath, and I realize he must be one of my mother's staff whom I'm friendly with. Perhaps that's why he passes us without stopping. When he turns the corner, Lexie pulls away. My lips tingle as blood rushes back into them.

"Wow," she says.

I think she's echoing my thoughts until she goes on. "I can't believe that actually worked," she says. "I always thought it was so lame when they do that in movies, but it was the only thing I could think of when I heard that guard coming."

"Well, I'm glad you did," I say.

"I'm sure you are," she says, slipping on her shoes so she's taller than me again. She opens her clutch purse and pulls out a lipstick.

"I meant, I'm glad you thought of something in time . . . ," I start to protest.

"I'm so sure that's all it was," she says, freshening up her lipstick without a mirror. She gives off the air like deciding to kiss me was no big deal on her end.

This attitude, which she'd picked up from Pear, was the exact reason we had stopped being friends after that summer.

Lexie presses her lips together and then slips her lipstick back in her purse. "So where's your mom's office?"

"Just around that last corner over there."

We approach the door. I pull out Sage's Code Cracker Prototype 3.0—as it's labeled with masking tape and magic marker in Sage's once-juvenile handwriting—from my jacket pocket.

"Here's hoping this works," I say, attaching it to the door's electronic keypad.

Lexie grabs my arm and looks back and forth down the hall. I can feel her excitement trembling through her hands. I run the program on Sage's machine and watch as the numbers spin. Slowly, each number space locks on a specific digit, and I think about how nuts this situation is. I'm standing here in a tuxedo, a beautiful girl on my arm—one who just made out with me in the hall, no less—and I am cracking into a locked office with a techno gadget. Too bad we didn't rappel in from the ceiling.

Playing Bond is definitely more fun than being Q.

Now if only we can make our getaway in an Aston Martin that can shoot rockets . . .

The keypad on Sage's machine flashes green, and I hear a click.

"That was fast," Lexie says, squeezing my arm. But there isn't a guard coming this time to necessitate her touching me.

"We're not done yet. That was just the door to the office. We still have to get into the vault." I open the door, let the two of us in, and then close and lock it behind us as an extra precaution. I walk to the back of my mom's office and push at the side of the bookcase behind her desk. It glides out of the way, revealing a vault door large enough to walk through.

"Seriously? She hides the safe behind a bookcase?" Lexie says. "It's like we're in a real spy movie."

"I was just thinking the exact same thing," I say.

Lexie smiles at me, and I smile back. Maybe there really is still a bit of the old, geeky, *fun* Lexie in her somewhere.

I attach the code cracker to the vault's keypad and start the program again. This is clearly going to take much longer than the door. A few minutes pass in silence, but the device has only identified the first three numbers out of six. I start to worry about that guard who passed us in the hall—he might reconsider and come back to look for us.

Lexie starts to pace the room, her excitement shifting to anxiety. "How much longer?"

"I don't know. Maybe a couple of more minutes? Maybe more like ten?"

"I'm not sure we have that much time."

"I know." The excitement and adrenaline of the whole experience are wearing off. I hadn't anticipated it to take this long.

Two more numbers lock into place, one after the other. Only one left. With a gasp, Lexie stops pacing and looks at the door.

"Did you hear that?" she whispers.

"What?"

"Sounded like footsteps. I think someone's coming."

"It's almost done. Come here." The last number locks in place, and the vault clicks open. I push the door in and shove Lexie inside, just as I see a silhouette at the fogged glass in the office door. Someone is definitely coming. I step inside the vault and try and slide the bookshelf back over the door's opening, while leaving it open just a crack.

"What are you doing?" Lexie whispers frantically. "They'll see."

"I don't want to get trapped in here. If I close it all the way, I may not be able to get it open again," I say, realizing that I probably should have mentioned that I'm a tad claustrophobic when we started planning this heist. And Lexie wouldn't exactly be my first choice for witnessing my panic attack if we get trapped in a vault together.

"If you get us caught, I'll have the Sopranos skin you alive."

There's the Lexie I'm used to. "Shhh."

Even in the dark, I can see Lexie's scowl. I turn back and watch through the crack as the office door opens. I swear under my breath. It's my mother.

I figured if somebody catches us in her office, I'd try to pass it off as if I were running an errand for my mother (how else would I have been able to unlock the door?), but this is a more difficult complication to talk my way out of. Especially now that we're in the vault.

Mom walks in, carrying her briefcase and talking to someone on a walkie-talkie. "Yes, I know. Get maintenance down there and *fix it!*"

The other end of the line says something garbled that I can't understand.

"Then shut the water off to the south hall. I don't see why this is so hard, Johnson. Just get it done." She drops her briefcase forcefully on her desk.

Another garbled response.

"I've had it with your incompetence, Johnson. Do you really

think this is something I should have to deal with? I'm going to be there in three minutes. If this isn't resolved by then, you can bet we'll be freeing up your future."

That is my mother's favorite euphemism for firing someone. She storms out of the door, slamming it behind her.

"Holy Prada, that was close." Lexie lets out a huge sigh, like she'd been holding her breath the whole time.

"Let's get the scroll and get out of here before anyone else comes back."

"You mean this?" Lexie holds out a small wrapped scroll of papyrus, sitting in an open velvet box.

I raise my eyebrows. "How did you find that so quickly?"

"What? You didn't think I was just going to stand here and do nothing while we waited," she says, clearly impressed by herself.

I have to admit that I am equally impressed.

I take the scroll from her hands and check the markings on the outer seal. "This is it."

"I gotta admit, I expected it to be bigger," she says. "Aren't scrolls supposed to be big and long?"

"Size doesn't matter," I mumble. "It's probably a fragment of something larger." But I'm grateful for the small size when I slide the box containing the scroll in my inside jacket pocket.

"Good work, by the way," I say.

With one hand on her hip, Lexie cocks her head and blows me a kiss. She saunters past me and slides the bookcase out of the way. I pull the door closed behind me and make sure the bookcase is back in its original position, and follow Lexie out into the hall.

"That was fun," she says. "I could get used to this kind of thing."

"Thinking of taking the Sopranos to the next level?" I say, raising my eyebrows.

"Let's just say the wheels are turning."

Lexie and I start down the hall. She slips her hand into mine and leans her head against my shoulder. For a moment, I think she's being genuine with this show of affection, but then I see the guard from before coming around the corner. His name is Carson or Conway, and he's worked security for many of my mom's parties at the house.

"You two," he says, when he sees us. "Find a different spot to make out."

"Yes, sir." I give him a mock solute, and Lexie stands up straight and does the same. We both burst out laughing.

"Just get out of here, okay? This corridor is supposed to be off-limits for dance attendees."

I nod, and we walk away, back toward the balcony that overlooks the dance. Maybe it's just because she needs my support in her heels, or maybe it's because she remembers that there used to be something between us all those years ago, but to my surprise, Lexie keeps her hand wrapped around mine as we descend the stairs.

chapter thirty-two

DAPHNE

I manage to make it through the song with Joe's band, and no one in the audience seems to notice the one line I flubbed in the middle. Instead, they break into uproarious applause. I take a bow and excuse myself from the stage before Joe leads the band into a "slow song for all you couples out there" from his Saturn's Ring album. I've got my eyes on the south stairway, waiting for Tobin and Lexie to make their return, when I step onto the dance floor and a hand wraps around my elbow. A deep voice asks, "May I have this dance?"

The voice sounds like Haden's, but there's something off with his tone, and I turn toward the speaker, to find myself in the arms of a stranger.

I try to pull away, but he grips me tighter.

"Who are you?" I demand.

"You don't see the resemblance?" he asks, with smile. "My brother and I are twins, after all."

"Rowan?" I say, with a gasp, seeing it now. He's not an identical twin to Haden, but they are definitely brothers, Rowan being the blonder, brown-eyed, slighter-built one. I can feel the strength of his arms as he sweeps me onto the dance floor against my will.

"What do you want?" I ask. I don't want to go along with the box step he tries to lead me in, but it's preferable to being dragged, so I step in time with his movements.

He pulls me closer. "You know what I want."

I stomp on his foot, hard, with my heel.

He loosens his grip. "To negotiate a trade."

The hairs on my arms stand on end, and I look over Rowan's shoulder to see Haden approaching, through the crowd of dancers. Electric heat crackles around him, and the tone ricocheting off him sounds downright lethal.

I shake my head at him, telling him to stay back. I'd like to think that Haden would know better than to start a fight in a crowd like this, but I have a feeling Rowan knows exactly how to provoke him into doing just the wrong thing.

And if Rowan is ready to negotiate, I'm not going to risk losing this opportunity.

Haden stops midstride at my behest. But he doesn't leave, either. He stands in the middle of the dance floor, his fists clenched and red, while other dancers try to navigate around him.

"What are your terms?" I ask Rowan.

"The Compass for the talisman." He sends me out in a twirl and then brings me back into his arms. "Plus fifty thousand dollars, cash."

So he'd figured out that his funds have gone dry?

"You do have my talisman?"

"Perhaps," I say, trying to sound like I'm being coy and not like I'm lying as I swing under his arm. Rowan's talisman is still as fried as a charcoal briquette, and we are no closer to finding Simon's talisman than before, but Rowan doesn't need to know those things.

Rowan brings me back into his arms. "But there is one more thing that I want in addition to the money and the talisman." He presses his hand into the small of my back and leans me into a dip. "A kiss," he says, his lips almost touching my throat.

"Bite me," I say, losing any pretense of being polite.

"Is that an invitation?" he whispers, and pulls me back upright.

The song ends, and Rowan lets go of me. "Thank you for the dance," he says, with a bow that makes me wonder if he learned his party skills by studying Jane Austen movies. He is doing a fine job of impersonating Mr. Wickham. "Discuss my proposition with my brother. I will wait in the entry hall until nine for your . . . decision."

He turns on his heel and heads for the entry hall. Haden starts after him.

"Wait, Haden," I say, grabbing his shoulder. "I've made a deal for the Compass."

But I know he isn't going to like the terms.

"Who's the major hottie you were dancing with?" Lexie asks as she and Tobin approach the coat-check closet. I'd texted them to meet us here as soon as I saw them coming down the stairs. Dax had volunteered to take over manning the station from Ethan when Garrick reported that someone was trying to spike the punch.

"Rowan," I say, like his name tastes bad on my tongue.

"Seriously?" Lexie says as they squeeze into the closet with Haden and me. "And I thought Haden would be the more dashing of the two—"

"Did you get the scroll?" Haden asks, cutting her off. He seems to be barely holding himself together since I told him about Rowan's demands. I have a feeling that had been Rowan's exact intention when he'd demanded a kiss from me. Either that, or having to come up with fifty thousand dollars of Simon's money on the fly is what has Haden on edge.

Tobin pats his jacket. "Locked and loaded."

I nod with approval and then tell them about what happened with Rowan. "The only problem: I insinuated that we had a talisman. Now I'm thinking that was probably a mistake. How are we supposed to trade something we don't have?"

"I'm certain he will try to double-cross us as well," Haden says. "This can still work. We can use his same tactics against him. Dax went out the kitchen exit and is already outside in the parking lot, waiting to follow Rowan when he leaves. If we know where he's living, we can go for the Compass when he least expects it."

"What about the kiss?" Tobin says, looking at me. "That's a pretty creeptastic demand."

"You're not doing it," Haden says, his face reddening. "He only said that to rouse my ire. I can make it clear that he won't be doing it. . . ."

"And what, risk a fight in the middle of town hall?" I say. "He's not leaving here until he gets what he wants."

"You make it sound like you want to kiss him," Haden says, glaring at me.

"Who I kiss is none of your business," I say. "But, no, I certainly don't *want* to." I take in a deep breath and glance out the closet window where Rowan stands, leaning against a white marble column near the exit. He stares at the phone in his hand, as if counting down the minutes until nine. I am impressed with how he is able to convey that aura of arrogance just in the way he stands.

I guess I'm going to have to take one for the team. . . .

"I'll do it," Lexie says. We all look at her in surprise. "What?

He said he wanted a kiss. He didn't specify that it had to be from Daphne. We could send Tobin over to kiss him, and he wouldn't have the grounds to argue."

Tobin sputters. I don't know if it's over the thought of him kissing Rowan or Lexie volunteering to do it so nonchalantly that flusters him so much.

"It's not a problem," Lexie says, with a shrug. "He's tall, he's blond, he's hot, and he drives a Ducati. It won't take much of a stretch of my imagination to act attracted to him."

"Excuse me?" Tobin says. "Are you forgetting he's the enemy? Don't sound so happy to march over there and start making out with him. It's not like you can kiss a guy like it's no big deal and walk away. . . . "

"My life, my lips. You have a problem with that?"

From Tobin's expression and the chaotic tone coming off him, it seems he does, in fact, have a problem with that.

I raise my eyebrows, questioning him, but he turns away.

"So, let's get this over with," Lexie says, pushing her way out of the closet. Haden, Tobin, and I watch from the window as she approaches Rowan. When he sees her, he lowers his phone. He says something to her that I can't make out, but whatever it is, it doesn't deter her. She rocks up on her heels and reaches her hand behind his neck and pulls his head down toward hers—and kisses him with an intensity far beyond what I would have thought necessary. Tobin groans and turns away from the window.

Lexie slips her hand down Rowan's arm and wraps her fingers around his phone. He pulls away and tries to take it from her, but she holds up a finger and says something that makes him stop. She types something into it and then stretches way up on her heels again and whispers in his ear, while she slips his phone into his jacket's breast pocket. Rowan smiles as if he were Prince Charming.

Haden makes a noise like he's trying not to gag.

Lexie kisses Rowan one last time and then walks back toward us with an exaggerated sway in her hips.

"See you soon, *little* brother," Rowan shouts down the hall, then walks out the front doors with a satisfied swagger.

"That seemed a little over the top, don't you think?" I say as Lexie reaches us.

"Perhaps," she says, like she kisses random guys without regard all the time.

Tobin groans again, and I let him be the first to leave the coat closet. I follow a few seconds later, and then Haden waits a full minute before exiting just as Dax comes dashing through the front doors.

"I lost him," Dax says with a pant.

"Already?" Haden asks.

"I don't know how he did it so quickly, but he went around the corner of the building and was gone two seconds later."

"*Kopros*," Haden says, shaking his head. "We need to know where he's going."

"Well, I guess it's a good thing I sent his number to my Friends with Benefits app, then," Lexie says, pretending to blow dust off her fingernails.

"You did what?" Tobin and Dax ask almost simultaneously.

"I entered my phone number into his phone and told him to call me when he wants to make the exchange for the Compass. But while I had his phone, I sent his contact info to my Friends with Benefits app. It's this app one of my sophomore Sopranos' brother invented, where you can enter your . . . um . . . *special friends'* . . .

contact info into their database. And then any time that friend texts or calls you, it'll ping you with their location. It's for hookups, you know?"

"Hookups?" Haden asks, clearly confused.

"Booty calls," she says.

He looks even more bewildered. She rolls her eyes. "The gist is that when he calls me to set up the exchange for the Compass, the app will tell me where he is. Since he had absolutely no other contacts on his phone, I'm betting there's a good chance that location will be his house."

"That's brilliant, Lexie!" I exclaim a little too loudly, bringing the attention of a few too many bystanders to our small group.

"Tobin!" I hear a voice call over the crowd in the entryway.

We all look up to see the mayor in the archway that leads to the rotunda. Her hands are on her hips, and she seems particularly perturbed as she approaches. Tobin's hand goes to his jacket, like he's checking to make sure the scroll is still safe.

"You didn't think you were going to get away with that, did you?" she asks.

chapter thirty-three

HADEN

Tobin's face goes ashen. He steps away from the group like he doesn't want to incriminate the rest of us by association.

"Get away with what?" he asks his mother.

"You didn't think you could leave before I had a chance to get a picture of you and your date, did you? I've been looking for you two all evening."

"No," Tobin says, ducking his head in relief.

"Come this way, where the light is better," she says, leading Tobin and Lexie back to the rotunda. She doesn't give me, Daphne, or Dax a second glance.

"I guess we're sticking around a little longer," Daphne says, like she's anxious to get home. From the rotunda, I hear Joe announce the last song of the night: "Shadow of a Star." The crowd cheers in response. It's the band's most famous song, and the one Daphne had helped him write when she was a girl. "So grab that special someone before it's too late," Joe says in a deep, almost longing voice. "Don't let your Valentine slip away."

As the song starts, Daphne drifts toward the archway as if the music is calling to her.

Dax leans in close to me. "Tonight is a good night," he says.

"I suppose. Other than Rowan, things have gone according to plan."

"I mean, tonight is a good night for expressing one's feelings, that is." He nods toward Daphne. "Perfect occasion, if you ask me."

I sigh, shaking my head.

"Come on, man. Don't be a coward."

I scowl at him. "Why do you care so much anyway, if I tell her? You think you're Cupid or something?"

"I care, firstly because I want you to be happy, and secondly because I think Daphne is part of your destiny, and if that's true, then it's my job to help you along that path . . ." Dax trails off into silence. His eyes watch the dancers in the rotunda, and a strange sense of longing creeps into his face. That's when I remember that Sarah the Oracle had tasked Dax with the quest of helping me find my true path—and that if he succeeded, he would be reunited with Abbie.

A wave of guilt crashes over me, because I know that his happiness is dependent on me.

Dax nudges me with his elbow. "Ask her to dance."

"What about the Skylords?"

"I saw Terresa and Calix leaving when I was in the parking lot, and I can find Ethan if you want me to keep him busy. . . . So do it," he says, and disappears into the crowd.

I stand and watch Daphne as she sways to the music in the archway, her hands on her hips. I can't believe how much more stunning she seems to get every time I see her. I imagine asking her to dance and then clasping my own hands over those hips. I wouldn't force her to follow my lead as Rowan had; I would hold her in my arms and sway with her to the rhythm of the song.

I want to erase any thoughts of Rowan from her mind. I want

to hold her and let her lean into me, her head resting on my shoulder. Maybe I could whisper it to her then. Whisper the words I want to say into her ear—get them off my chest—and maybe she wouldn't be sure what she'd hear me say over the music. . . .

But none of that will ever happen if I don't make my move before the song is over. However, my feet seem to be stuck in one place.

I feel absolutely paralyzed until I see one of the tenors from our music class approaching Daphne.

Hades help me, I'm not letting someone else steal my perfect moment.

Gathering my courage, I take a step in her direction.

Only to be stopped by a hand on my shoulder.

"Can I borrow a moment of your time?" Ethan says. I look around, expecting Dax to be nearby, but he isn't.

I start to form the words to refuse, but he looks me squarely in the eye and says, "You promised me the favor of hearing me out, or have you already forgotten?"

"I haven't."

"I've come to collect. I would like to request a meeting with you and your compatriots."

"Right now?" I glance in Daphne's direction and see her take one of the tenor's hands and walk with him onto the dance floor.

My moment is gone.

"Not here. You meet with your friends in the workshop room behind the stage before rehearsals, yes?"

"How do you know that?"

"You will allow me to join you on Monday," he goes on, without answering my question. "Make sure all of your comrades are present, but do not tell them I am coming."

"What do you want?" I can't help but imagine that letting Ethan join us is the same as letting a snake into our inner sanctum. We would all be sitting targets in that small room.

"Only an audience. For you to hear me out, as I said before. I think you will find what I have to say . . . interesting." He claps me on the shoulder and says in a much louder, more jovial voice, "I expect to see that essay rewrite on my desk Monday morning."

I am surprised by the shift in his demeanor until I notice Tobin and Lexie approaching us.

"It'll be there, Mr. Bowman," I say.

"Oh, looks like I need to start helping with cleanup," he says, indicating that the last song is ending. "Good evening." He nods and takes his leave.

"What did he want?" Tobin asks me.

"Just to talk about a homework assignment."

"Come on," Tobin says. "Let's get Daphne and get out of here. This scroll is burning a hole in my pocket."

"I'm here," Daphne says as she approaches. I can't help but notice she sounds a little out of breath. "I, for one, would like to find out what's on the mayor's precious scroll."

chapter thirty-four

DAPHNE

Haden, Lexie, and I huddle around Joe's dining room table after the dance, waiting for Tobin to unroll the scroll. Maybe because it is his mother's property, or maybe because he'd worked the hardest to get it, or maybe it's just plain that no one else wants to take responsibility for possibly damaging such an old artifact, but we had all agreed to give Tobin the honor of being the one to handle the scroll.

He wears a pair of latex gloves and unfurls it with great care, one millimeter at a time. I find myself holding my breath and willing our only lead not to disintegrate in Tobin's hands. Once it's unfurled, it's about the size of a regular piece of printer paper. Tobin places it gingerly between two pieces of glass that I've stolen out of a couple of Joe's picture frames. He holds it in the glass sandwich in front of him.

"What is it? What does it say?" I ask, trying to see over his shoulder.

"I have no idea," he says, setting it on the table. "It all looks like ancient Greek pictographs or something just as archaic. It's useless unless anyone here knows an archeologist or something, because I doubt we can plug *this* into a translator app and get an answer."

"This sucks," Lexie says.

The bubble of excitement that has been building in my chest starts to deflate.

Haden clears his throat. "Or happens to know someone from an ancient Greek society. Archaic languages are kind of one of my specialties."

"Oh yeah, duh," Tobin says, sliding the glass-encased scroll over to him.

Haden studies it for a minute. "Do you have paper and a writing utensil?" he asks me.

I grab my notebook and a pen from my purse and hand them to him. "Just call it a pen."

"Noted," he says, and starts jotting a few lines in my notebook. He crosses something out and then keeps going. After about ten lines, he stops and reads it over.

"Out loud," I prompt. "Out loud."

Haden holds up the page and reads out loud. "'Cupid and Psyche are made as one. Your true self they will become. Cupid is courage, in the face of fear. Psyche is strength, to deliver all. Let them go. Let them flow, unfurling like the wind. Cupid and Psyche. Cupid and Psyche. Grant them both, and your will be done.'"

"What the crap does that mean?" Lexie says.

I shake my head.

"It appears to be nothing more than a poem about Cupid and Psyche," Haden says, and I can hear the disappointed notes rolling off him. "Just something some ancient poet jotted down, from what I can tell."

"But what about the drawing with the symbols?" Tobin asks. "That has to mean something."

"Or it could have just been a doodle," I say halfheartedly.

"That's it?" Lexie says. "A poem and a doodle? You mean I had to kiss Tobin so we could liberate some ancient person's purse trash?"

I look at Tobin. "You kissed Lexie?"

Tobin crosses his arms. "Only so we didn't get hauled off by security. Besides, she's the one who instigated it."

"Whatever," she says.

"Well, I'm pretty sure you enjoyed it, thank you very much," he says, tipping his fedora to her and winking like Frank Sinatra.

"You. Wish." For someone who had kissed a practical stranger with barely a second thought, I can't help but think this protestation seems a little strange.

I turn my attention back to the scroll. "You're sure that's what it says?" I ask Haden.

"It's a slightly different dialect than I've seen before, but I think the translation is as close as it's going to get."

I sit with my head buried in my hands, my bubble of excitement completely burst. I know it was totally silly and far too optimistic for me to have hoped, but in my fantasies of how this night was supposed to play out, I thought I'd be sitting here with an instruction book on how to use the Compass without sacrificing myself—and instead all I got was this crappy poem.

I'm glad when the others leave shortly after the revelation that our entire evening had been a waste of time—save for striking a deal with Rowan, that is. The energy I'd had at the dance is completely zapped, and the despair over having fewer answers now makes me feel as useless as an out-of-tune piano.

I can hear Joe and a couple of his bandmates pulling into the driveway, so I take the scroll and my notebook up to my room before they see me. I don't have the energy right now to try to carry on a conversation with Bobby Rox or Chris Trip. It really was pretty epic of them to agree to play at a high school dance, and I might burst into tears of frustration if they ask me if I had a good night.

I set the scroll on my desk and change into my pajamas, ready to go to bed and sleep off my disappointment when I find a red envelope on my bed. At first, I think it's from Joe or even, for a half a second, that Haden might have found his way up here before leaving with the others, but then I see the Ellis Fields return address and know it's from Jonathan. The man loves holidays— from themed costumes at Halloween, elf hats and caroling at Christmas, to his New Year's Eve matchmaking—but there is no holiday he revels in more than Valentine's Day. Being a florist and all, it is like his own personal Super Bowl.

I tear open the envelope, ready to see what monstrosity of a card he picked out this year, and find a picture of a chubby teddy bear dressed like Cupid with a big heart-shaped arrow pointed at me. *Grin and bear it, it's Valentine's Day!* the front of the card says. It is just like Jonathan to know that grinning and bearing it is how I face almost every Valentine's Day. I open the card and a puff of red, glittering confetti falls on my bed. Inside the card is a handwritten note from Jonathan.

> *All kidding aside, I hope one of these Valentine's Days you'll find everything your heart and soul desire.*
>
> *Miss you, sweetie!*
>
> *Jonathan*
>
> *P.S. I was going to send chocolates, but they somehow disappeared.*

I smile and shake my head, knowing exactly where my

chocolates ended up. I place the card, standing up on my desk, next to the scroll—and then something from Jonathan's message pops into my head. *Everything your heart and soul desire. Heart and soul. Heart and Soul.*

Hadn't Ethan said something about Cupid's and Psyche's names meaning the same thing as *heart* and *soul?* The two mythological characters represent the two halves of what made a person who they are—their heart and their soul? I open my notebook to Haden's translation of the poem. Taking a total shot in the dark, I cross out everywhere Haden has written *Cupid* and replace it with *Heart* and then *Psyche* with *Soul*. I read the entire poem with my edits:

Heart and Soul are made as one. Your true self they will become. Heart is courage, in the face of fear. Soul is strength, to deliver all. Let them go. Let them flow, unfurling like the wind. Heart and soul. Heart and soul. Grant them both, and your will be done.

I read the words over and over again, and as I do, they seem to sound more and more like, not just a poem, but a song. Though I imagine it's a much more beautiful-sounding one in its intended language. I speak the first few lines out loud in a singsong voice, not sure of the melody, and feel a surge of power with each word.

Another idea strikes me, and this time I sing the song using the melody of the grove. I can feel power rippling through the air, riding on the sound waves of my voice, as if reaching out to the world around me. I look at my geode collection that Jonathan had sent with my shipment of stuff from Ellis when I first moved here. The geodes sit on my desk, lining up from smallest to largest. I concentrate my voice on the smallest of them as I sing the song. It had taken all of my concentration to manipulate a few raindrops only a couple of weeks ago, so I don't expect much from the crystallized rock—maybe to lift a few inches off the desk—but when I beckon to it to come to me, *all* of the geodes lift off the desk. Even the largest rock, the size of a softball, swirls up in the air. They dance around me as I sing, as if they weigh nothing at all.

I remember Sarah the Oracle's words to me before she died. She had said that I was the Keeper of Orpheus's Heart and Soul, the Vessel of His Voice. But what if she had meant those things interchangeably? Orpheus's voice was what made him who he was—metaphorically, his voice was his heart and soul.

Hope rises up in my chest, and I want to sing out so loud that I would be heard all the way across town. The Oracle had said that I was the only one who could unlock the Key because my heart and soul are what is needed to obtain it. But what if she hadn't meant that literally? It wasn't my literal heart and soul that were needed to unlock the Key. It was my voice—and this song, I was willing to bet everything on it—was the pass code.

In my vision of the echoes in the grove, I had witnessed Orpheus use his voice to lock away the Key, so it makes perfect sense that I, his descendant, am meant to unlock it, using the Compass as a conduit for my voice.

Now all we need to do is get the Compass away from Rowan.

chapter thirty-five

HADEN

Brim is waiting up for me when I get home from Daphne's after the dance. She paces the counter in the kitchen, meowing in the direction of the fridge. Before I left, I'd fed her some canned concoction Dax picked up after we finally broke down and made a supply run to the grocery store—one of the more perplexing experiences of my life, because food in the Underrealm does not come as rows and rows of brightly colored boxes and cans—but I know what she wants. Eggs. Daphne had spoiled her with that treat, and now it's all she wants.

"You're getting fat," I tell Brim. "No eggs."

She glares at me, not amused. She really is getting awfully round, but there's no negotiating with a hellcat.

"Fine, you want scrambled?" I don't know why I bother to ask. Scrambled eggs and French toast are still the only things I know how to cook. I know I could probably become a master chef if I downloaded some cooking shows from the Internet . . . but I like the idea of letting Daphne teach me instead. I only wish I didn't have to be so careful about being seen with her outside of school. I'd like to learn something more advanced.

Brim gives a little purring meow and leaps off the counter onto my shoulder. She rubs her cheek against mine to show her appreciation. How do you say no to that?

Dax comes in through the garage. He looks haggard, with his tie loosened and his jacket slung over his shoulder.

"You know you're not *really* a school counselor. You didn't have to stay behind to stack all the chairs," I say.

"I do if I want to get a paycheck. Simon's money won't last forever. Especially if we have to withdraw fifty grand for Rowan."

Oh yes, there's that.

"How did it go?" he asks, dropping his jacket on the counter.

I'm not sure if he's referring to my attempt to ask Daphne to dance or with unraveling the scroll. I choose to respond to the latter because I don't feel like talking about the former.

"The scroll was nothing of import."

Dax sinks heavily into one of the chairs at the kitchen table. "Just when you think you're starting to get somewhere . . ."

I can hear the exhaustion in his voice and decide to make him some eggs, too. "There's still the deal with Rowan," I say, pulling a skillet from the dishwasher.

"Do you think he'll hand it over?"

"I don't know. Especially if we don't have the talisman to trade."

I open the fridge and gag. The rankest smell wafts out of it. Brim hunkers down on my shoulder and covers her nose with her paws. We'd stocked the fridge with more supplies but hadn't bothered to clean the old food out. I open one of the drawers and find a bag of turnips so far gone that they've started to liquefy.

"Ah Hades," I say, lifting it up. Gray moldy liquid drips on my shoes, and I can't help but think that an Underlord should not have to do such tasks as cleaning out a refrigerator. If only Garrick were still my servant . . .

As I head to the garbage with the reeking bag, I notice something glinting like metal in the turnip slop. Instead of into the garbage, I dump the bag in the sink. Something round and metal makes a clunking noise as it hits the bottom of the tub. I fish my fingers into the muck and find the end of what feels like a chain. I lift it up and see that it's attached to a large, oval-shaped medallion.

"What've you got there?" Dax asks.

"Simon's talisman, I think." I shake my head in disbelief. "He'd hidden it in a bag of turnips."

Dax crows with laughter—and relief. "Well, it is the last place his teenage houseguests would ever look."

We both have a good laugh at that, and for a moment our situation doesn't feel quite so dire.

"Find a good place to hide that," Dax says. He picks up his jacket and discarded tie. "If you don't mind, I think I might skip out on our group meeting on Monday. I'm thinking of taking a sick day and driving out to Santa Monica. I found an address for a pen pal of Abbie's out there. Thought I'd go check it out."

"Actually, can it wait until Tuesday?" I say, rinsing off the talisman in the sink. "I need you here on Monday."

He gives me an inquisitive look, but I don't elaborate. Ethan had warned me not to tip anyone off about his joining our meeting.

"It's a song," Daphne says as she explains her discovery about the scroll to us. Dax, Garrick, Joe, Tobin, Lexie, and I are sitting with her in the workshop room behind the stage. The crew stores and designs set pieces here, and it has become our regular meeting spot before rehearsals. I'm interested in Daphne's discovery, but I'm not sure how a song is supposed to help us any more than a poem would have, and my attention keeps wandering elsewhere: to the door of the room, actually, since I know that Ethan may arrive at any moment.

The others practically jump out of their seats when a thunderous knock raps against the door.

"Who is that?" Daphne asks.

"Company," I say.

I take my time getting to the door. I open it and find Ethan waiting. I look past him, almost expecting to find Calix and Teressa with him, ready to ambush us. Instead, he ducks his head like he's waiting for my invitation to enter.

"Come in," I say, and quickly close the door after he does.

"Everyone knows Mr. Bowman, right?" I ask. "Except you, Joe. This is Mr. Bowman, our humanities teacher."

"Your humanities teacher?" Joe asks. "You mean the one who's really a Sky—" He stops himself as if he's afraid he's said too much.

"You mean the one who is prince of the Skylords?" Ethan says. "Yes, that would be me. Although I prefer to be called Ethan."

"What is he doing here?" Tobin asks, suspicion edging into his voice. I wonder if he is thinking about the fact that Ethan is his sister's betrothed. Dax seems equally unenthused to see Ethan.

"I have requested an audience with you all, and Haden was kind enough to agree."

"You mean you knew he was coming?" Tobin asks, like an accusation. "And you didn't tell us?"

"That was by my request also," Ethan says, taking the chair that I vacated when I went to the door.

Tobin stands up as if he is going to leave if Ethan plans on staying.

"Please sit, Tobin," he says, sounding very much like a teacher.

"I have a proposal to discuss with your group, and I need all of you to be present."

"Proposal?" Tobin asks. "I assume you knew this was going to happen as well?"

"I promised to hear him out," I say. "But nothing more than that." I gesture to Ethan. "The floor is yours."

"I know you are close to finding the Eternity Key," Ethan says, crossing his legs and clasping his hands on top of his knee.

I gather Eternity Key is the name the Skylords use for the Key of Hades, but no one in the group gives any acknowledgment of knowing what he's referring to. I find myself thinking my little ragtag group might hold up well under interrogation.

But Ethan isn't deterred from his assumption. "I am hoping you will give it to me."

"Uh, yeah, right," Daphne says. "We know you Skylords want to use the Key to restart the war with the Underlords. That is exactly what we are trying to avoid."

"Actually, the Skylords want to use the Key to annihilate the Underlords where they sleep before *they* have a chance to restart the war," Ethan says with nonchalance.

"And you think we would help you with this?" I ask. "I may have turned my back on my father, but I will not be complicit in the destruction of my realm."

"I said, that is what the *Skylords* want. I, however, have allegiances to both the Skyrealm and the Metarealm. You see, while my mother is a Sky Princess, my father was one of the minor gods of the Metarealm—a dalliance that cost my mother greatly in her youth. I have never met my father, but over the years, I have found my allegiances shifting toward the goal of his realm: peace. As you may know, Apollo is the prime god of the Metarealm—a realm that exists within the other four realms, encompassing all things metaphysical, such as love, music, faith, hope, peace, and so forth. As such, Apollo took it upon himself to orchestrate the stalemate that put an end to the bloodshed of the Thousand-Year War between the Skyrealm and Underrealm. . . ."

"By enlisting Orpheus to steal the Key, causing the death of our god and our people to be trapped in the Underrealm for all eternity," Garrick says.

"True. There was some collateral damage. This was unfortunate. However, the Metarealm's interest lies in reducing the amount of further collateral damage and bloodshed that may occur if the war were to be restarted. And for this purpose, I reclaimed my position in the Skylord army in order to keep them from gaining the Key and to enlist your help for my cause."

"In what way?" I ask. What he's said so far intrigues me, but I keep my voice guarded.

"I would like you to use the Key to open Pandora's Pithos—"

"Um, what?" Daphne says, cutting him off. "That is exactly the thing we are trying to stop from happening."

"Please allow me to finish, Daphne," he says in that scolding teacher voice. "As I was saying, I would like you—with my help, of course—to journey into the Pithos, to use the Key to open the barrier between the Pits and the mortal realm . . ." He holds up his hand to stop Daphne's impeding protest until he finishes. ". . . where a band of like-minded Skylords will be waiting to help us kill the Keres, therefore neutralizing the threat of the Underlords' using them as weapons to win the war, and avoiding the full-scale destruction of this world."

I stand up straighter. His words surprise me, but not as much as they seem to surprise Garrick. He almost falls out of his beanbag chair.

"You know how to kill Keres?" he asks. "That's not possible."

"I don't know how to exactly, but I know that these two"—he points to me and Daphne—"have done it before."

"How do you know that?" Daphne asks.

"Do you want to tell her the rest, or shall I?" Ethan asks me.

"Did you tell him?" Daphne's question is directed at me this time. It's tinged with the suspicion that I have been sharing our secrets with the enemy. As if I've betrayed her trust.

"We both did," I say. "But not intentionally."

She glares at me.

"Remember when we stopped at that diner on our way to Vegas—the same diner we stopped at on our way back? That first stop, with just us and Garrick, and we told him about how we killed the Keres after the festival? How it was a combination of your voice and my lightning that did it? Well, if you'll recall, we weren't the only ones in the diner that day, and we weren't the only ones in the diner on the way back, either. There was a trucker at the bar. . . ."

Ethan waves his hand. "Howdy, folks," he says, dropping his scholarly voice for a down-home drawl. "Fancy seeing you again."

"You were following us?" Daphne asks. "You were just pretending to be a trucker so you could overhear our conversations? How long were you following us before that?"

"Now, that's a funny story." Ethan smiles. "I really was a trucker. You see, I've been on a bit of a sabbatical the last few years. Ever since my betrothed went missing." He sends a pointed glare at Dax. "I've been a bit conflicted about where my loyalties lie, so I thought I'd spend some time alone in the mortal world, sorting things out. And lo and behold, your little posse just happened to show up at my favorite milk shake joint on my route. Luckily for me, y'all talk real loud. Actually, I don't think luck had anything to do with it. That's what you call the will of the Fates. I saw it as the kick in the pants I needed to pick a side in this fight and do something."

Daphne shakes her head. I know she hates all this fate "mumbojumbo," but it's hard to call this situation a coincidence.

"I thought about following you, but then I noticed that you left your friend's car behind. I figured you'd be back for it at some point." He smirks. "Underlords are nothing if not predictable."

"So you gave up your glamorous life as a trucker and went back to being a Skylord Prince, only you're really working on behalf of the Metarealm?" Lexie asks. She's been strangely quiet—for Lexie—this whole meeting. Now she sounds mildly impressed.

Ethan nods. "And I would very much appreciate it if that bit of information doesn't leave this room." There's a growl to his voice, hinting at the danger that would befall anyone who shared his secret.

"And you knew all this when?" Daphne asks me, her arms crossed in front of her chest. It strikes me as a defensive pose—like she's walling herself off from me.

"Most of this is news to me," I say. "I had some suspicions when I saw him in the diner a second time, but I didn't *fully* put the trucker thing together until the day he showed up in our classroom."

"You mean you've known for almost a month and a half, and you didn't tell us?" Daphne asks.

"There were extenuating circumstances," I say.

She turns her angry glare on Ethan. "As in, you threatened Haden?" she asks him on the verge of a shout.

Ethan raises his hands. "We're getting off topic, and our time is growing short. I don't expect you to answer me now, but I ask you to spend some time considering my plan. I have seventeen loyal men waiting for my command. With Daphne's voice and our lightning, we could put an end to the Keres once and for all." He looks at his watch. "I believe your rehearsal time is about to start. I tried to deter them, but Terresa and Calix will be in the audience this afternoon, so really try to sell it. Terresa has made friends in the music department who have taken note of your clique's, as they put it, exclusive hangouts. She also suspects Daphne is of some importance to you, Haden, based on the way you reacted when you saw another young man dancing with her at the ball. Now, if you'll excuse me, I have to continue planning to avert an apocalypse."

chapter thirty-six

DAPHNE

"Well, that was an interesting turn of events," Dax says after Ethan leaves.

I can't exactly say that I share his nonchalance about it all. *Pissed* is more how I would describe my feelings. Haden knew a Skylord had found us before we even got back to Olympus Hills, *and* then he'd made some deal with him without telling us?

I know he'd been threatened by Ethan—who should bear the brunt of my anger—but at the same time, knowing that Haden had been keeping secrets from me again triggers just about every trust issue I've got.

"What do you make of his plan?" Dax asks Haden.

"I can't say it doesn't have its merits, but I don't like it. How can we know that any of Ethan's so-called loyal men, or even Ethan himself, can be trusted? They're still Skylords, after all. I don't fancy opening a door to the Underrealm for them, even if it is guarded by a couple of dozen Keres. And most importantly, I don't like the idea of letting Daphne go up against that many Keres, either."

"I'm not sure *let* is the word you're looking for," I snap.

As if he could *let* me do anything.

He looks at me. "Wrong choice of words, I'm sorry. But you can't deny that the last and only Keres we faced almost killed you. Your voice isn't powerful enough to take on a room full of them."

And that's when I feel like a hypocrite.

Because here I am fuming at Haden for keeping his arrangement with Ethan secret, but I still hadn't shared my burgeoning vocal powers with him. I told him and the others about my discovery of the scroll's song, but I haven't told them what happens when I sing it. They don't know that I can make raindrops dance in the air, let alone that I can command larger objects to move. By the end of the evening after the dance, I was rearranging all the wooden furniture in my room with only my voice. With my increased strength and some more practice, I probably could take on a few dozen Keres. I'm an asset in this fight, and Haden doesn't know it because I've been keeping my own secrets.

There's a rap on the door. "I need you all front and center," Mr. Morgan calls. Rehearsals are starting, so the rest of this conversation will have to wait for later.

The others get up and leave, but I stop Haden before he follows. "Will you wait for me after rehearsals? There's something we need to talk about."

"Fine," Haden says, his tone making it clear that he thinks the reason I want to talk is because I want to tell him off. "Though, for the record, it wasn't me whom Ethan was threatening to keep me quiet about our deal. It was you."

"I know," I say under my breath as he leaves.

And therein lies the problem.

Terresa and Calix are sitting in the back row of the auditorium, mixed in with some chorus members who are waiting to be called up by Mr. Morgan. Iris Thompkins, one of the scholarship students, sits next to Terresa, chatting happily at her like they're new BFFs—I guess we know who our unintentional mole is.

For the first half of the rehearsal, Calix and Terresa watch my every move, and I worry that they've finally gotten wise to who I *am* on their own—either that, or Ethan wasn't telling the truth about not sharing his intel with the other Skylords. Terresa's intense glare is so distracting that Mr. Morgan yells at me twice for tripping up my lines.

"Feeling up for having a diva moment?" I ask Joe as he walks over to show me his script. I nod ever so slightly toward our spectators.

"My pleasure," Joe says with a wink. Then he reels around, pointing his fingers toward the back of the auditorium. He squints like he can't see who's out there beyond the stage's light. "Someone out there keeps popping his jaw! I can hear it all the way up here. It's disgusting! How am I supposed to work like this?" He throws down his script. "That's it. Rehearsal is over!"

"Um, Joe," Mr. Morgan says. "Today is our first rehearsal with the full cast. You can't just call it off."

"Well, then, what am I supposed to do about the jaw popper over there? You either tell them to leave or I will."

"Those are the chorus members. . . ."

"Not those two," Joe says, while pointing out Terresa and Calix. "I don't remember casting those two. They could be pirates, for all I know. I don't need some kid recording my songs on a crappy phone and putting them up on YouTube before opening night. Either get them out of here or I'm leaving."

Mr. Morgan stands up and addresses the students in the back of the auditorium. "If you are not part of the cast, please leave.

Everyone else, there are no cell phones permitted, and you know it."

Calix and some random student with an iPhone in the back of the auditorium stand up to go, but Terresa approaches the stage instead. "Actually, my cousin and I were going to ask if we might join your tech crew. I guess you could say that lighting things up is one of my specialties."

Before Mr. Morgan can respond, Joe pretends to get hysterical. "No. No jaw poppers on my stage. All the crew positions are filled. Get out of my auditorium!" he yells, even though this auditorium is hardly his. Mr. Morgan looks flustered for a moment, like he's wondering what he's gotten himself into, working with a spoiled rock star, but then he tells Terresa and Calix that they need to leave.

Terresa goes, but she gives Joe a glare that makes me worry she might be able to "light things up" with her mind in addition to her hands. Still, I have to say I am happy to see her leave.

I relax into my role much more afterward. We are focused today on the second and third acts of the musical, which are both set in the underworld and outline the trials and travels of Orpheus and Eurydice as they search for each other and try to escape. Tobin and I both rehearse our solos, and then we have a duet toward the end, when my character is whisked off the stage (and across the lake once we move to rehearsing on the lakeside amphitheater as soon as it warms up a bit) and ripped back into the underworld. As we sing, I find myself connecting with the songs and the story more than I ever had during our previous read-throughs and rehearsals with the leads. I am so caught up in the emotion and the tragedy of it all that when Mr. Morgan calls it a day, I am surprised that three hours have already gone. I pass

Haden as we all pack up to leave, and looking over my shoulder, I whisper: "Meet me in the grove."

Haden is already on the defensive when he enters the grove. I can not only see it in his body language, but also in the tone he puts off—solid, rigid notes, forming a wall to fend off my attack.

"Relax," I say. "I didn't ask you here to yell at you."

"You didn't?" His inner tone softens ever so slightly.

"No, because I get it. You did what you had to do. But you're not the only one keeping secrets."

"I'm not?" He takes a step toward me, but his tone sounds hesitant and farther away.

"Stay right there," I say, holding out my hand. "Remember how I wanted to show you something before? That night I stayed at your house? Before all the craziness happened?"

He nods. His tone warbles as if the memory of that moment makes him anxious . . . or perhaps *nervous* is the better word.

"I want to try it again, only this time, it's going to be so much better."

Haden's tone suddenly spikes with a high note. I look at him, wondering what he was just thinking, but he glances away like he's embarrassed.

"Watch me," I say.

I open my outstretched hand. In it are a few green leaves, fresh buds from the early spring saplings that surround Orpheus's tree. I open my mouth and sing a series of notes like I'm doing a vocal exercise in Mr. Morgan's class, but it's the leaf buds that provide the key instead of a piano. I am singing their melody, and they respond by quivering in my hand almost instantly. When I had tried this with the raindrops and then in front of Haden, using a few wilted basil leaves, it had taken an extreme amount of concentration to get this far, but now this feels like nothing. I switch from the vocal exercises into singing the words from the scroll's song, keeping my voice in the same key as the buds. I toss them into the air and think, *Dance for me.* Instead of falling to the ground, the leaf buds float in front of me, twirling and spinning about each other, like partners in a dance.

"*Harpies,*" Haden whispers with awe, and steps forward. "Are you doing that?"

I smile as I sing. *He ain't seen nothing yet.* I'd chosen the grove for this demonstration not only for its seclusion, but also because I know extraordinary things will happen here when I sing—especially now that I know what I'm doing. I want Haden to see how powerful I am. I want him to know that I'm not just some lilting flower he needs to protect. That he doesn't have to succumb to threats on my behalf. I point to a pile of yellowed leaves that have been swept up against a large rock by the wind. I beckon them to join the dance, and they fly up from the ground, swirling and twisting into the air around Haden and me as if in a small whirlwind.

Next, I call the droplets of water that cling to the grass from the little rain shower earlier today. They bobble up into the air, floating around us as if it were raining in reverse. I can see the awe on Haden's face. I can hear his excited tone mingling with my song. But I don't stop until I've invited the trees to sway and the rocks to thump, adding a drum-line beat to the mix. Watching me, Haden smiles. He turns in a slow circle, seeming to try to take it all in at once.

As an extra touch, I command the dirt to move, filling in the holes that we dug in our search for the Key. Making the ground almost undisturbed.

I can feel my energy start to wane. The swirling dance starts to slow, so I end the song on a final note, letting it draw out until I have no more breath. When I stop, all the leaves and raindrops and the wind fall away. The trees go still and silent. I step back, gasping for breath, and then look at Haden.

"So . . . um . . . surprise?" I say.

He stares at me, completely dumbfounded. Or maybe a little afraid.

I quirk an uneasy smile. "So what do you think?"

"I love it." He takes two long strides until he's standing right in front of me. His hands reach for me, his fingers cupping my face, and he pulls me against him. "And I love you."

I gasp.

He leans in, pulling my face toward his.

He's going to kiss me.

I know he's going to kiss me.

And I am shocked by how much I want to let him.

I meet him halfway, stopping just a hairbreadth from his lips and let him finish. I expect his kiss to be hard and overwhelming, fraught with passion, but his lips come to me softly at first. Almost questioning. When my mouth parts in response, his kiss gains confidence and he grips me against him, one hand in my hair, the other pressing against the small of my back. My stomach feels hot as if it were melting against his abdomen, and I find myself wishing that our skin were touching there. Electricity pulses around us to the rhythm of a racing heart. I can feel every hair on my body standing on end, tingling in anticipation. With every movement of his lips, with every touch, he shows me what he has already said—that he *loves me.*

And that's when the heat in my stomach grows sharp.

Twisting. Almost like an ulcer. And what had felt so right only a moment before suddenly fills me with panic. Haden's lips implore for more, but I find myself unable to give. I push the heel of my hand against his chest, pushing him back. His grip on me loosens, and I start to pull away.

"What is it?" he asks, out of breath. "Did I shock you again?"

He looks at me with so much concern that tears prick at the corners of my eyes. I thought I had been out of breath finishing my song, but now I feel as though the wind has been knocked out of me. I can't speak. Can't think. Can't respond.

He lets me go.

"I'm sorry, Haden. I can't do this."

"What do you mean?" he asks, that look of concern growing even deeper.

"I just can't do *this*." I wave my hand between the two of us, because I don't even understand what I'm feeling enough to find the words to describe what I mean. "I can't say. . . ." My voice fails me.

"You don't have to say anything back," he says, like he's trying to reassure me. "It's all right—I just needed to say it. I needed to tell you. I've wanted to tell you for so long. It's why I refused my father's offer, why I wouldn't give you to him. I love you. I'm *in love* with you." Haden's words come tumbling out of him so fast, it's as if he's afraid he won't be able to say them if he hesitates for even a second. I know they're meant to comfort me, but they make me pull back even more. I'd suspected as much. Hell, deep down, I'd *known* it, but his admission only overwhelms me—a reminder that every threat we are under is because of me. Because he loves me, the world might very well end.

Suddenly that seems selfish on his part.

"You looked so happy," he says. "So strong. So powerful. I couldn't hold it in anymore." His tone is so earnest, it makes my heart ache, but it doesn't change the way I feel. "It is all right if you're not ready to say it back."

"It's not just that . . . I can't do any of this. I can't do *us*."

Both Haden's tone and face are stricken. "Do you not care for me, then?" he asks.

"That's not the reason." I can't lie. I know I have feelings for him.

"Then is it because you don't trust me?"

"Yes . . . no . . . I don't know." I shake my head, feeling like I can't say anything right. "That's not it, either. . . . "

"Is it because you can't see me as part of your future?"

That strikes a chord with me but not in the way that I expect. I'd worried that Haden and I could never work because we're from two different realms, but it's something more than that. . . . "I don't even know if I have a future anymore, let alone if you fit in it. What if the world doesn't exist in a few weeks?"

And it's all my fault.

How can he contemplate a relationship under these circumstances?

Haden makes a move toward me, his hand extended as if he wants to offer me comfort.

I wave to stop him. "I just can't do this. Not with everything that is going on. Not with the weight of the world on my shoulders. Not with not knowing if I even have a future past the next few weeks. I just can't."

He takes a step back. His inner tone has fallen completely silent. I can't read him at all. He searches my eyes, as if looking for a different answer.

"At least not right now," I whisper, and look away.

The cell phone that starts ringing in my jacket pocket might as well have been an explosion for how high I jump at the sound.

I turn away from Haden, fumbling to answer the call. Desperate not to have to look him in the eyes right now.

"Hello?" I say.

"What up, chica?" Lexie's voice fills my ear. "Guess who just got a booty call?"

"I'm pretty sure that falls in the TMI category of our budding friendship."

"Geez, not a literal booty call. Rowan called."

"He did?" I pull my phone from my ear and push the speaker button. I wave for Haden to listen but don't actually look at him. "She says Rowan called."

"Sure did," Lexie says. "He told me he wants to meet with Haden in the school parking lot tonight at midnight. Why do people always want to have secret rendezvous at midnight? Why not 11:27 or 4:30 in the afternoon?"

"Did he say anything else?"

"Yeah, he *claims* he'll bring the Compass, and then he said something about how Haden had better bring the money and the talisman, or he'll rip out Haden's spleen and feed it to him, or whatever. I stopped listening because the details were kind of graphic. . . . But the good news is that after he hung up, I got pinged on my Friends with Benefits app. Which means that I know where he was when he made the call. And the address is right smack-dab in the middle of a ritzy beach house community the next town over. What do you want to bet those are his new digs?"

"His new what?" Haden asks.

"His new house," I say.

213

"Oh. Right. Can you forward me the address?" he asks.

"Will do," she says.

I hang up the phone and tuck it into my pocket, but I can't bring myself to look up at Haden. We stand there awkwardly, neither one seeming to want to restart the conversation that had been interrupted by Lexie. I'd expected Haden to start arguing with me, to try to convince me to change my mind. But he doesn't.

Part of me is relieved that he respects my right to refuse him, but part of me is surprised he doesn't try to fight for me.

"I guess we'd better figure out how this exchange with Rowan is going to go down," I finally say.

He clears his throat. "Yes. I should do that. I'm going to go find Dax." His inner song is still silent, but it wouldn't take any supernatural abilities to hear the detached tone in his voice. I imagine if I were to look at him, I would see that impassive mask he wears when he pretends to be emotionless.

I wish I were capable of doing the same.

"Will you track down Tobin?" he asks. "I'm going to need him."

It isn't until Haden leaves that I realize he'd only used the word *I* in the last things he said to me. There was no *we*.

And that pains me more than I could have imagined, considering I was the one who had said there could be no *us*.

chapter thirty-seven

TOBIN

The walk home is always the worst part of my day. Between schoolwork, poring over Abbie's journal pages for some clue as to where she might be, plotting to get the Key out of the grove, and *actually* rehearsing for the school play, for most of the day, I don't have to think about having a conversation with *that woman* who calls herself my mother. But after all that is done, I have to walk home.

Because her latest form of punishment for my "uncharacteristic bad behavior" is taking away my car keys.

And when I'm walking home, all I can do is think about seeing her again.

The woman is a kidnapper, a liar, a thief, and a murderer . . . even if that last one is only by association. Every girl whom she's let be taken from this community has been given a death sentence. And then she does it to her own daughter? Every time I have to smile at her or pose for a picture or answer her questions as if nothing is wrong, it feels like I lose a small piece of myself.

I walk down the path leading to Olympus Row. I like to take the long way home. It takes an extra ten minutes if I pass through the shops. Longer if I stop in at Olympus Brew to ask the barista if Marta has shown up for her daily espresso—but the answer is always no. It's a little colder out tonight than it has been. Spring is unquestionably near, and winters are never really all that cold in Olympus Hills, but tonight there is a definite chill. I don't mind the cold, though. It helps me get in the right frame of mind for when I get home.

I pass the gelato shop and notice a dark-haired girl in a leather jacket sitting cross-legged on a bench out front and eating a scoop of bright orange sorbet. She smiles at me, and for a moment I think I'm having a vision of Abbie. But reality snaps back in as quickly as that thought crossed my mind. *Crap. It's Terresa.*

I hadn't seen the resemblance when Daphne had pointed it out to me—it had been six years since I'd seen Abbie, while only a few months for Daphne—but the way Terresa's nose crinkles with her smile sends a sudden memory of my sister through my mind. Even if Terresa's smile is obviously fake.

She stands up and waves to me like she's been waiting here for me.

"Hello, Tobin."

"Um, hi. It's Terresa, right?" I say, like I've barely noticed her in class.

"Look, can we just not pretend anymore?" she says, and takes a bite of her sorbet. "You know who I am; I know who you are. And we need to talk."

"What could we possibly need to talk about?"

"Well, let's see, there's the Key, for one. I know you all are close to finding it."

"I don't know what you mean," I say, and quicken my pace. My hope is that she won't follow, but of course that doesn't stop her.

She falls in stride next to me. "And then there's the matter of our sister."

I stop in my tracks. "I'm sorry, what?"

"You mean you don't see the resemblance? Ethan tells me Abbie and I look quite alike. Different hair and all, though."

"What the hell are you saying?" I ask, not wanting to believe her insinuation, even though the way she licks the sorbet from her spoon is so Abbie I want to scream.

"Abbie and I share the same father, obviously not the same mother. Frankly, I'm a little ashamed he would get involved with a *mortal*." She says the word like it's icky. I know she's talking about my mom, and I don't really disagree with the distaste in her voice on that account, but I don't miss the fact that I would fall under the class of "mortal," too.

"So what? Are you looking to set up a family reunion or something?" I say, coming to a dead stop. I don't want to believe that I share a sibling with her, let alone go for a leisurely stroll with her on the secluded lake paths. "What do you want from me, Terresa?"

"Well, I wasn't exactly looking for a gathering of relatives, but I was hoping for your help in getting Abbie back."

I spin around to face her. "You know where Abbie is?"

"No. But I know how to get her back."

"How?" I ask tentatively. I'd gotten my hopes up over so many leads in the last few weeks that have only led to one depressing dead end after another.

"You help me get the Key before your 'friends' turn it over to the Underrealm Court."

This insinuation implies that she doesn't know that Haden is a rogue Underlord. Which means Ethan really isn't working with her—or they're good at acting their parts.

"And how exactly does that get Abbie back?"

"Oh, don't be an idiot and just stop and think about it, Tobin. It is obvious that some lackey for the Underrealm has her hidden somewhere, just waiting for the gate to open again. Why do you think they want her as a Boon in the first place? They want to infuse Skylord DNA into their bloodlines. They are becoming more and more mortal with each passing generation of human Boons, and that scares them. She was meant to be breeding stock." The anger in her voice is hard to miss. It reminds me of how I felt when Dax first told me this.

How I still feel now.

"I know all that already," I say, matching her level of emotion. "But why do you care about Abbie's fate? You made it sound like you've never even met her."

"I haven't," Terresa says. "But the idea of someone I share blood with being bred with Underlords makes me sick. *They* make me sick."

"I know what you mean," I say about her last assertion.

"Then why in the names of Zeus and Hera would you want to help them? If we have the Key, we have access to the Underlords. They are trapped in the Underrealm with no way out. We could exterminate them once and for all and never have to deal with their lies or their manipulations or their murderous acts again!"

I take a step back. "That sounds like you're talking about genocide."

"Would that really be so bad? Don't forget what they've done to you. To your sister. To all those other girls they've taken for thousands of years. Do you call it genocide when you destroy a nest of poisonous spiders?" Her eyes have gone cold. She no longer seems overcome with anger, but is collected and confident in her statement. The resemblance to Abbie is gone. "That's what they are, Tobin. Every last one of them only cares about power and glory, about their own selfish desires. They are a race of murderers and rapists."

Her words have more of an effect on me than I expected. I realize now that a lot of the anger I was placing on my mother was meant for the Underlords, too. I just didn't think there was anything I could do about it. But now Teresa is telling me there is.

"I still don't see how this gets Abbie back," I say, thinking her offer sounds too good to be true.

"It's simple. With the Underlords gone, any lackey that has been gifted with a power granted by the Underrealm will have that power stripped. They will want to know why but will have lost communication with the Underrealm. Therefore, they'll all return here, seeking answers and direction. Humans are predictable that way. Whoever has Abbie will not want to leave her alone, and so they'll likely walk right into town with her under their guard. Even if they don't, it will be easy to pick them off one by one until we find someone who knows where she is. We kill all the Underlords, and Abbie is delivered like a packaged gift."

Her plan isn't exactly risk free, and I can see all kinds of ways it could go wrong, but it actually sounds like it might work. But there is still one big problem, as far as I am concerned. "Why should I believe you would hold up your end of the bargain?"

"My father wants Abbie out of the hands of the Underlords, and when my father is happy, I get what I want. Let's just say there's a big promotion in it for me."

I curl my fists at my sides. She's trying to exploit my affection for my sister for her own gain. "So your motives are purely selfish, as well. You sound just like an Underlord."

"Perhaps," she says. "But I'm not the one who stole your sister. They are. And they deserve to pay."

"Do I even get Abbie back, or are you just going to whisk her off to the Skyrealm to your father? Will he force her to marry Ethan? That doesn't sound much better than the people who stole her."

"Let's just say that once the Underlord threat is gone, I'm sure I can convince my father to let her go home. Ethan is a good catch. I'm sure he could scrounge up another fiancée in no time. With your help, Abbie could finally be free of both realms."

I stare at her, not knowing how I want to respond.

"Take some time to think about it. I'll contact you again soon." With that, she turns and walks back toward the gelato shop.

And I am left to go the other way, alone with my raging thoughts once more.

I'm on my front porch, digging in my backpack for my house keys, when my phone buzzes from my back pocket. My breath catches for a moment; I'm thinking it might be Terresa trying to contact me already for my answer (how she'd gotten my number, I don't know), but when I pull the phone out, I see it's Daphne. I don't feel like answering it, so I just stand there waiting for it to stop. When it does, I see that she had called me once before, right when I was talking to Terresa.

The phone buzzes with a voice mail that I also ignore.

I finally find my keys, and I'm unlocking the front door when a black Tesla pulls into the semicircle driveway behind me. Still not in the mood for talking, I wonder if I can get away with popping into the house, locking the door, and pretending I didn't see them.

"Hey, Tobin," Dax calls from the driver's-side window.

Too late.

"What?" I say, turning around. I don't make much effort to hide the irritation in my voice.

"Get in. We need your help."

No *please*. No asking if I *want* to help him.

"What for?"

"We're going to go steal us a Compass."

Stealing something has a strange appeal at the moment, so I comply. I get in the car and find Haden in the passenger seat. "Where's Daphne?"

"She's not a part of this," Haden says.

"Does she know that?" I ask. "That doesn't sound like Daphne at all."

Haden doesn't answer, and I wonder what's gotten him so cold at the moment.

"Haden and Garrick are going to meet Rowan for a supposed exchange," Dax says as he pulls out of my driveway. "We have our doubts Rowan even plans on bringing the Compass, so you and I are going to go stake out the address that Lexie got off her app. If it looks like the right place, we're going to break in and see what we can find."

"Sounds good to me," I say, surprised at how much more relaxing a little B & E sounds compared to eating dinner with my mother.

chapter thirty-eight

HADEN

It's twenty-five past midnight when Rowan finally pulls up on his motorcycle outside the school. I should have assumed he'd keep me waiting. I can only hope he didn't notice Dax and Tobin staking out his place, and isn't now showing up only to tell me where to find their bodies.

"Having trouble with the time?" I stand with my back leaned against my car, my arms folded casually in front of my chest, even though I feel anything but casual. "You see, the small hand points to the hour while the big hand points to the minutes."

"Funny." He smirks as he stands beside his motorcycle. "Since it was your lack of knowledge about time that sent you running back to the grove that first day."

"How do you know—"

"I know all about your various mistakes, Haden. Like how you tried to take Daphne through the gate the moment you met her. I give you points for gravitas, but your idiocy knows no bounds, does it?"

"Do you have the Compass or not?" I say, in no mood for Rowan's idea of small talk.

"You know that was the reason the Court insisted on sending

me, right? You almost destroyed yourself and the Cypher your first day here. You screwed up so royally, it didn't matter what the Oracle said. They shouldn't have sent a nursling without a nurse-maid."

"Does that mean you're waiting for me to suckle at your teat?"

Rowan's smirk falters, as he realizes his poor choice of words.

"Compass or no Compass?" I say. "I don't have all night. Unlike you, I have more important things to do than be someone else's glorified babysitter."

"Depends on whether you have my money and the talisman."

I pick up a black duffel bag next to my feet and toss it in front of him. He opens it and gives it a cursory inspection. There's only twenty thousand there—all we could get in cash advance before it raised a red flag on Simon's account—but I knew he wouldn't stop to count it.

He slings the bag over the back of his motorcycle. "And the talisman?"

I rap my knuckles against the hood of the car. One of the back doors opens, and Garrick steps out. He stands, hands shoved in his pockets, on the opposite side of the car. The Tesla acts as a barrier between him and Rowan.

"You brought the runt?" Rowan says. "How's he been working out for you?"

Garrick tries to hide his wince at being called a runt but fails.

"Just fine," I say, even though that's a lie. But I would still rather have Garrick in my entourage than my twin. "Talisman, Garrick?"

Garrick pulls a medallion on a long red leather cord out of his pocket. He holds it up, letting it dangle at his side.

Rowan starts to make a move toward him, but I step forward.

"Not until you show us the Compass."

Rowan eyes Garrick. "That doesn't look like my talisman."

"Simon's must have been the upgraded model. I found it in a turnip drawer in the refrigerator. Seems you were looking in the wrong place when you ransacked Simon's bedroom. Your talisman was destroyed. That's apparently what happens when you send a bolt of lightning through it when it's submerged in water." I hold up my hand to show him where the outline of the talisman is scarred into my palm.

"You destroyed my talisman?" There's a hint of panic behind his rage. "Do you have any idea what you've done?"

"What's the matter? You must be pretty desperate to reveal yourself to me after all this time. You can't handle a couple of months without constant direction from Father? I thought I was the nursling, not you."

"Not just direction, you idiot. I was supposed to report back to Ren that I'd secured the Compass. You might have gone off the rails, but they need to know that I'm taking care of everything else. Do you have any idea what's going on down there? Do you have any idea of the consequences if the Court isn't given assurances that everything is under control, that I can make you follow the plan—"

"You mean how the Court has designs on deposing Father? I'm afraid you're already too late for giving any assurances that you can make me follow Father's orders. That's as fried as your talisman."

"What did you do?" Rowan demands, his voice crackling with electric power.

"I paid Father a visit, using your talisman. He tried to convince me that he'd toss you aside as his favorite son and make me his heir in exchange for Daphne. And as tempting as it was to think of you being passed over for me, I made an unbreakable oath that I would never bring her to him."

"*Kopros*, Haden!" Rowan says, using my actual name for once. Which almost makes me take a step back. "Of all the addled things. Didn't he tell you what would happen if the Court gains control? Didn't he tell you about the Keres?"

I purse my lips, not wanting to show my concern. Part of me had wanted to believe that my father had made up the bit about the Court ripping through the Pits in order to get out of the Under-realm. That it was just a scare tactic—something he'd made up on the fly because it had been too terrible to believe that it might be real. But if Rowan is confirming it, it suddenly makes it feel all too real. And like Ethan's plan might not be so horrible, after all.

"The world is still standing. You don't see any Keres around here, do you?"

"For now," he says. "I can't promise the same for tomorrow. Or next week. Now give me the talisman. I need to make contact. I need to know what's happening down there." His voice is racked with desperation—a rare display of emotion on his part—and it almost makes me want to let him have the talisman.

When I don't respond, Rowan turns his attention on Garrick. "Give me the talisman, runt!"

"Compass first," Garrick says. His voice warbles, but I admire his resolve.

Rowan doesn't. Before I can react, he launches himself over the hood of the car. I fling a bolt of lightning at him but narrowly miss as he grabs Garrick by the shoulder. Another bolt ripples through me, but I don't dare throw it, for Garrick's sake. Rowan rips the talisman from Garrick's hand and then shoves him toward the ground. Garrick hits the pavement face-first, and Rowan slams his foot down on his back. I start to charge at Rowan as he holds the talisman aloft in one hand and a crackling sphere of lightning above Garrick's prostrate body.

"Move, and he fries," Rowan growls at me.

"What are you going to tell him?" I ask, referring to his realm-to-realm call with Ren.

"That I'll be the one bringing the Cypher back instead of you."

"You know that will never work. She will never pass through the gate willingly with you."

"Then I guess it's a good thing I still have the Compass," he says. "You know me, Haden. You know I can find a way to trick your girl into getting the Key for me. You didn't think I would actually bring the Compass tonight, did you?"

"No," I say. "In fact, I was counting on it."

"What?" he says.

"At 216 Sea Cliff Court," I say, reciting the address Lexie had texted me.

Rowan's usual smug look drops completely from his face. He shoves the talisman in his pocket and runs for his bike. I could try to stop him, but I don't. Dax and Tobin should have had plenty of time to get in and out of Rowan's place by now. Based on Rowan's reaction, I was sure they were going to find exactly what they were looking for.

As Rowan speeds away, I crouch down to help Garrick sit up. His lip is bloody, and bits of gravel from the pavement have been ground into his cheek. "I'm sorry," he says, rocking forward to hug his knees to his chest. "I let him get the talisman."

"Don't worry about it. In fact, I wish I could see his face when he tries to use it to place a call."

"What do you mean?"

"That wasn't Simon's talisman. I did find it in the fridge, but that thing Rowan took off with is something I dug out of the props Dax has been collecting for the play. Lexie's friend Bridgette brought it in. I guess it's a leftover keepsake from one of her mother's movies."

"A prop?" Garrick says. "You let me get my face split open over a prop?"

"I needed you to believe it was real so Rowan would buy it. You did great—"

"Stop it," he says, pushing himself up from the ground. "You should have told me."

"Garrick, I'm sorry, but I needed Rowan to believe it was real."

"And you didn't trust me to not give it away? Thanks a lot, *brother*. It's nice to know how you think of me. But I'm not your *Lesser* servant anymore. I'm not going to let you or Rowan or anyone else push me around. Not anymore."

Garrick walks away. My instinct is to order him to stop, but I know that would be the wrong move. He's right to leave. And I'm right to let him go.

I pull out my phone and send a text to Dax, warning him that Rowan is on his way home, and then sit alone on the curb, the silence of the night closing in on me. I haven't allowed myself to dwell on what happened with Daphne this afternoon because I needed to be ready for my meeting with my brother.

In the Underrealm, showing emotions turns you into prey to the likes of Rowan. Tonight, I'd needed to keep my feelings pushed down as far as possible so he couldn't exploit them, but now that he is gone, I can no longer hold them at bay.

Heartache rips through me like a storm breaking through a levy.

I am raw. I am drowning. I am gasping for air.

If I could turn off my emotions permanently to rid myself of this pain, I would do it.

I shake my head, rejecting that thought.

Don't despair, Dax had told me when I'd found him this afternoon. I've never been good at hiding things from him, and he'd known that something had happened by merely looking at me. I'd given him a cold, procedural retelling of the event, but he'd seen right through my mask. *She didn't rebuff you completely. She didn't say she doesn't care for you. I have a feeling she'll come around. Don't cut yourself off from her. Be open and patient, and she'll see you for who you really are. All is not lost.*

At the time, I had rejected his words for being meaningless platitudes. They'd bounced right off the shell that I had retreated into, but in the wake of my flooding emotions, I cling to them now like they're a life preserver.

I can't allow myself to be swept away in despair, and I can't allow myself to shut down. Not merely Daphne's future, not merely mine, or ours, but *everyone's* is depending on me. Once the Compass is in our possession, the real decisions—and the real danger—will begin, and a battered heart is not something I can allow to get in my way.

chapter thirty-nine

TOBIN

Dax and I sit in a car we've borrowed from Joe's collection two blocks away from Rowan's town house, waiting for his motorcycle to pass. He should have left almost fifteen minutes ago but we can still see the motorcycle in the driveway. A text pops up on Dax's phone asking if Rowan has left yet. It's from Haden. Dax takes another look at the house through his binoculars before replying.

I'm seeing some movement. He should be leaving soon, he messages. I can feel the anxiety starting to build as I try to psych myself up for another breaking-and-entering job. Seriously, when did my life become a James Bond movie?

Rowan finally comes out of the house, pulls out of the driveway on his motorcycle, and races off down the street, passing us without so much as a glance.

"Let's go," Dax says, hopping out of the driver's seat. We jog up to the door and, a moment later, Dax has it unlocked and we're inside.

"Where do we look first?" I ask.

"You start with the kitchen. I'll take the living room. Then we'll make our way upstairs. Make sure you check everywhere: behind boxes, air vents, the fridge. Everywhere."

Dax makes his way to the couch and starts pulling cushions off, so I head to the kitchen in the back. We work silently for about ten minutes before Dax announces that he's going to the dining room. I've almost completely destroyed the pantry and the cabinets under the sink when Dax comes back.

"Anything yet?" he asks.

"No, but I think I'm going much slower than you."

"Nothing wrong with being thorough. We just need to make sure we're out of here before he comes back. I'd say we maybe have another twenty minutes, tops."

I hesitate, not sure I know how to ask Dax the question that has been plaguing my mind since my encounter with Terresa.

"Dax . . . Do you really think this is the best way to get Abbie back?"

Dax stops pulling beer cans out of the fridge but doesn't look at me, as if he's contemplating my question. "What do you mean?"

"I mean, we've been so concentrated on helping the group find the Key, but they've hardly spent any time helping us figure out where Abbie is or if she is even safe. I feel like everyone seems to think that, if we find the Key, we'll miraculously find Abbie, too, or something. But maybe it's time I split off from the group and start concentrating all of my energy on Abbie. Maybe you should join me."

Dax doesn't answer immediately. "Haden needs me, Tobin. He needs your help, too. Maybe looking for the Key won't help us directly find Abbie, but who knows what leads might open up to us when we find it?"

"But are we doing enough *now*?" I ask.

"Believe me, Tobin, if I knew of a faster way to find Abbie, to make sure she's safe, to bring her home—I would move heaven and earth to do it." He finishes searching the fridge and moves on to the cabinets under the stove. "But I trust Sarah the Oracle. She said if I helped Haden find his true path, that I would be reunited with Abbie. So that's what I'm doing now."

"But why do you trust the Oracle?"

"She hasn't been wrong yet." Dax's phone buzzes with the arrival of a text. "*Kopros.* Rowan is on his way back. We've got maybe ten minutes with the way he drives. I'm going to head upstairs and check the bedrooms."

Dax's words about moving heaven and earth were meant to comfort me. To remind me that we are doing everything we can. To encourage me to be patient. Instead, they have me thinking about Terresa's proposition.

If I knew of another way, wouldn't I move heaven and earth, too? Wouldn't I do whatever it takes?

A sudden urge to break something comes over me. I move on to the living room and knock over the TV, just because I can. And, you know, in case the Compass is hiding inside of it. I go for a lamp next.

A few minutes later, Dax barrels down the stairs.

"Got it!"

"Where was it?"

"Can you believe that arrogant piece of *kopros* just left it on his bed? Now I'm kicking myself for not starting with the master bedroom," Dax says. "We'd better get going, though, before Rowan shows up." He eyes the damage I've caused in his absence. "I'd hate to be you when he sees this."

"Agreed."

We rush out the door and cross the street. I can hear the roar of a motorcycle not too far off. I pick up my pace to keep up with

Dax as we sprint for the car. We duck inside just before Rowan races by. He pulls into the driveway with screeching brakes, bounces off his bike, and throws his helmet at the garage door. He must have added a bit of lightning to his tantrum, because the helmet explodes with a loud flash and a crack. Lights from some of the neighbors turn on as he storms inside the house. Dax turns on the car and creeps away for another block, like we did when escaping from Ellis Fields, before he hits the headlights and accelerates onto the highway.

chapter forty

DAPHNE

I pace in front of my bedroom window, frustrated and annoyed that I'm being left out of the action. Dax had informed me via a phone call that Haden insisted that I stay far away from his meeting with Rowan, and from Dax and Tobin's search for the Compass. His logic made sense—I shouldn't be in the same place as the Compass with Rowan around—and I had consented to stay behind, but I couldn't help wondering if the real reason Haden had wanted me to keep my distance was because of what happened in the grove this afternoon.

My heart aches and my stomach throbs just from my thinking about it, and if I were in this pain, then how must my words have affected Haden? How would my refusal affect how he sees me? Would I only be the Cypher to him, and nothing more?

Kissing him had felt so right in the moment . . . until it didn't. And telling him I couldn't be with him had felt right, too. . . . So why does it hurt so much now?

Why do I feel like if there was one thing in this world I can't trust anymore, it's my own heart? Or maybe it's my head that's causing me so many problems?

I pace some more until my phone finally rings. "We've got it," Haden says.

Relief washes through me at the sound of his voice—it's measured and steady, and not cold like I had expected.

"Good. Do you want me to come meet you guys?" As painful as it would be for me to see Haden so soon, my hands are aching to wrap around the Compass again. I know it belongs to me the way I know that my right foot is my right foot, or my eyes are my eyes.

"No," Haden says. "We'll regroup tomorrow. In the meantime, you should stay away until the Compass is hidden in a new location. I've got Dax working on that now."

"Oh, okay." I'm quiet for a moment, not knowing what else to say.

"It's been a long day," Haden says. "I'm going to bed." I hear a dog bark both through my window and through my phone.

I walk out to my private family room and peek through the curtains. Haden's silent car is sitting outside the house. "Okay, good night," I say, and he hangs up. I wait for him to drive away, but he doesn't. I realize that, with a pissed-off, ripped-off Rowan in town, he's probably planning to stay out there all night.

My traitorous heart wants me to invite him to come inside, but my head tells me to stick to my words. I turn out the light and sit in the window seat, watching him watching out for me.

chapter forty-one

HADEN

On Monday, we reconvene for another war council—as I've come to think of it—but this time, we don't meet in the workshop behind the school's auditorium. Instead, we're in a cramped dressing room attached to the outdoor amphitheater on the north shore of the lake. Now that the weather is starting to turn warmer, Mr. Morgan has moved rehearsals here, where the final performance will be held. The outdoor setting is supposed to add to the drama and give the rock opera a more authentic feel—as most ancient Greek plays were performed in open-air theaters.

I respect the effect Mr. Morgan is going for, but I don't care for the change in locale as far as our group's secret meetings go. This dressing room is barely bigger than a closet, and with the lot of us—Daphne, Joe, Dax, Garrick, Tobin, Lexie, and even Brim, who's been sticking extra-close to me lately (as if she can sense my inner turmoil)—crammed in here, practically sitting on top of each other, tensions are running higher than usual.

What I had hoped would be a rational and calm strategy meeting to discuss our plan of action now that we have the Key is quickly devolving into an unhelpful debate.

"Have you guys considered just destroying the Compass and

leaving this 'Eternity Key,' or whatever we're calling it now, right where it is?" Lexie argues. "That way, *nobody* can get it."

"That isn't an option," I say. "Rowan confirmed my father's story about the Court planning on ripping through the Pits and releasing the Keres. Without using the Key to shore up the locks, both the Keres and the Underlords could tear through the barrier that separates this realm from Pandoras Pithos any day now."

"So then we team up with Ethan?" Daphne says, surprising me. For how angry she'd been about the deal I'd struck with him and how many trust issues she apparently has, she seems to have warmed up to the idea of working with him awfully quickly.

I take a deep breath, tempering myself before I say as much to her.

"I don't trust that guy. Yeah, he's hot—for a teacher—and all," Lexie says, like one's physical appearance would have bearing on their trustworthiness. "But how do we know he's not really just trying to play us? He could be pretending to hate Terresa and Calix just to throw us off."

"We could always give the Key to Terresa and Calix and let them solve our problem for us," Tobin grumbles. "Who'd mourn the deaths of a bunch of sociopathic underlords?"

I glare at him, not bothering to hide my irritation now. "You're talking about my home. And there aren't just people like my father and the Court down there—there are children and Boons and servants and other innocent souls. You think Terresa and the Skylords would discriminate in their killing?"

Tobin sinks back in his chair. "I was just kidding," he says, cowed.

"This isn't a joking matter."

"Back to Ethan," Daphne interjects. Brim is perched on her

knee, and Daphne strokes her furry back. "If he has the man power, why not help him open the Pits and let him help us take care of the Keres? And shouldn't we be trying to free the Boons, while we're at it? Other people's Abbies and Kaylas are trapped down there. We should be trying to save them."

The name Kayla pulls at my already-aching heart. My mother had died in the Underrealm just like all of the Boons eventually will, because humans can't survive in a realm without sun.

I shake my head. "I wish it were that simple. However, the Boons have all been through binding ceremonies. They've each eaten from a ceremonial pomegranate, binding them to the Champions who brought them there. We couldn't bring any of the Boons out of the Undderrealm, even if they wanted to leave."

Daphne hangs her head as if this idea pains her. I've always been impressed by her compassion. Brim pats her paw on Daphne's hand in a gesture I wish I could emulate.

"You mean, they couldn't leave unless the Underlords they were bound to were dead?" Tobin asks.

"That would be correct," I say, but don't want to dwell on the subject. What we're doing here is trying to prevent people from dying, not entertaining the possibility of letting my race be exterminated.

"But we can at least still use Ethan and his troops to help us go after the Keres," Daphne says. "They're our biggest threat, as far as I'm concerned."

"There are two problems with this idea," Dax says, leaning forward. "First of all, who's to say his Skylord posse will stop with merely the Keres when there's a door left wide open to them in the Underrealm? And, secondly, do you know where the barrier between this world and the Pits opens up to? It's in the middle of the mall in Washington, DC."

"Seriously?" Joe says. "The pit of hell opens up in the middle of DC? Why does that seem so fitting?"

"Yes, and imagine the damage if a couple of Keres slipped past us," Dax says.

"I've got half a mind to let 'em get free," Joe says. He starts to smile like he thinks he's so funny, but my glare shuts him down.

"Here's a wild idea," Garrick says. He tosses a green fuzzy ball up in the air and then catches it before it hits him in the face. "Why don't we just get the Key, give it to Rowan, and send him through the gate with it, and we all go see a movie?"

"And then have an *immortal* Ren and his *immortal* army come after us once they can open the main gates whenever they want?" I say. "And then restart the war with the Skylords, raining down death and destruction on all the realms? Yeah, good idea, Garrick." I throw my hands up, nearly smacking Joe in the face because of these tight quarters. "Will you all please take this seriously? This situation is as dire as it gets, and time is certainly not on our side. We're only a couple of weeks away from the equinox, which means the gate will open on its own, and I can bet Ren will have a crew of his finest Elites ready to come after us. That is, if he hasn't been deposed already. In that case, our time for planning could be up at any moment."

They all stare at me as if dumbfounded by my outburst. Brim hops from Daphne's knee to my leg, purring as if she thinks I need to be assuaged. Despite my efforts, I am still wearing my emotions too close to the surface. I take another deep breath to calm myself before explaining the plan I've been formulating while they've been bringing up useless arguments.

"One thing is for certain: we can't risk removing the Key from Orpheus's tree until the moment we're ready to use it," I say. "That way, it can't fall into anyone else's hands. However, that also means we need a window of time in which to get the Key and use it when no one else will be the wiser. Why not during the play?"

"During the play?" Daphne asks. Her eyes, meeting mine for the first time since we kissed in the grove, plainly show her doubts. "Like, in the middle of intermission?"

"No, I mean when most of us are on the stage, with Terresa, Calix, Ethan, and most likely Rowan staring right at us from the audience."

"How would that even work?" Lexie asks.

"There's a scene near the end of the play where Daphne's character, Eurydice, is dragged away back into the underworld and disappears. The way Mr. Morgan has it set up, Daphne will stand on a floating platform and be pulled across the water from the amphitheater to the grove island. The rest of us are onstage for the next fifteen minutes, during the resolution of the story, but Daphne isn't. What if she went for the Key right then? Dax could volunteer to be the stagehand who is supposed to wait for her on the other side, but really, he'll be waiting to help her get to the grove and provide her protection while she gets the Key—" I'm about to go on when I feel a sharp pain in my leg. Brim has sunk her tiny teeth into my thigh. "Apparently, Brimstone wants to go with you, Dax."

She releases my leg and meows in approval of my assessment.

"Sounds good to me," Dax says, reaching over to give Brim a good scratch. "I'm always happy for backup."

"The rest of us will join you three the moment the play ends," I say. "Before any of our adversaries suspect that we are up to anything."

"I could add a new song," Joe interjects, "to give her a few more minutes before the play is over."

"But what about curtain call?" Daphne asks. "That's why a stagehand is supposed to be waiting for me on the other side. They're supposed to help me get back to the stage as soon as the play is over to take my bows. If I'm not there, then someone might realize that something is up."

I stop for a moment. I hadn't realized that was part of the play process, but I should have. "Your character is veiled in the last scene, yes? Perhaps we send Garrick onstage pretending to be you. Dax, you could whip up a second version of Daphne's costume in the next couple of weeks."

"*Whip up* isn't how I would describe it, but, yes, I could do at least a makeshift version."

"He's too short," Daphne says. "I've got three inches on him."

Garrick scowls at her.

"He could wear heels!" Lexie says. "My mom has huge feet. I bet she has a pair that would fit him."

Garrick's scowl turns into a full-on glower. "First, you want to put me in a dress and now a pair of heels. What makes you guys even think I want to help you?"

Brim growls at him. I want to growl also, but I realize I shouldn't be surprised that he's being so difficult. Frankly, I'm surprised he even showed up today after what happened between us after the rendezvous with Rowan.

"Because the plan doesn't work without you, Garrick," Dax says.

"And then what are you even going to do with the Key?" Garrick asks. "Stick it up your a—"

"Garrick!" Dax snaps at him.

"*We'll* go through the gate without Ethan," I say. "And kill the Keres on our own."

"Say what?" Tobin asks.

"We don't need Ethan and his lackeys to do the job, and we certainly don't need to open the Pits to the outside world while they're still a threat. We can do it from the *inside*. Kill the Keres where they sleep, shore up the locks to the Pits so the Court can't bust through, and escape with the Key. That way, the Skylords can't get in and the Underlords can't get out; the war stays at a stalemate; and nobody else gets hurt."

"And then what do we do with the Key?" Daphne asks.

"We find a way to destroy it."

Daphne nods, the doubt in her eyes waning. "This all sounds completely insane but also kind of awesome," she says. "But do you think we can pull it off?"

"You've said that there are only a couple of dozen Keres in the Pits, right, Garrick?"

He shrugs. "Give or take a few."

"Are you sure?"

"I don't know; it's not like I went around giving the bloody soul suckers names or anything. No more than thirty, I would guess."

"We could do that," I say, nodding to Daphne.

She smiles at me as if she appreciates that I recognize how powerful she is. The sight of it soothes some of the aching in my heart. Like maybe there is still something between us . . .

"Whoa, whoa, whoa," says Joe. "Just a little while ago, you were claiming that would be too hard on Daphne. Why the rush to put her in harm's way now?"

I return Daphne's smile, though mine is small and tight. "Do you want to tell them, or shall I?"

"I will," she says, and then launches into an explanation of how she figured out how to manipulate objects with her voice and how the song from the scroll increases this newfound power tenfold. She even gives a small demonstration, channeling her voice to cause Joe's chair to lift several feet in the air with him still in it.

"This is brilliant," Joe says, beaming down at his daughter. "You're like a real Orpheus."

She lowers him back down, to the awe of the others. I love watching the happiness her power brings her.

"If I could solidify one Keres before," she says, "imagine how many I can help destroy now."

"It won't be easy," I say, "but I'm sure you could subdue several of the Keres at a time, while we three Underlords take them out."

Daphne nods to agree with me.

"So it's settled. The play is the day before the equinox, so no one will be expecting us to come through the gate. Tobin and Lexie can stay here, of course. Once Daphne, Dax, and Brim have gotten the Key, Garrick and I will meet them in the grove directly after curtain call, then the five of us will go through Persephone's Gate toge—" My voice catches like something is stuck in my throat. I try to clear it and go on. "We'll go through the gate with Da—" It happens again; this time, it feels like my throat is closing up when I try to say Daphne's name, and my thoughts muddle. I think for a second, backing up and trying again. "The plan is we'll use the Key to go through the gate, and then Da—"

I am stopped once again. I grasp at the thought that was in front of me—that we need Daphne to use her powers to help us kill the Keres, which mean she will have to come . . . that she will have to do . . . something. My thoughts go blank, and I stare at the others as they blink back at me. "I'm sorry. I have no idea what I was about to say. We need to . . ." But I can't remember what we need to do.

"Are you okay?" Daphne asks.

"Are you having a stroke?" Lexie says.

I shake my head. But maybe I am?

"*Kopros*," Dax says. "It's the oath. You made an unbreakable oath to never bring Daphne to the Underrealm. Which means you physically can't do it. You can't go together. It would be impossible."

"No. I made an oath never to bring her to my father. We're going to the Pits. That's different. Daphne and I will go toge—" *Together.* That's what I want to say, but the word slips away before I can wrap my mouth around it.

"You can't even say it," Dax says. "What makes you think you're going to be able to do it? The Underrealm is your father's kingdom, so whether you're taking Daphne directly to his throne room or to the Pits, the oath sees it as the same thing. It will be physically impossible for you and Daphne to go into the Underrealm together."

"But this doesn't work without her," I say, feeling my plan slip away from me. "She's the only one who can make the Keres corporeal. Without that, we can't kill them."

"Then we split up," Daphne says. "I'll go through first, and then you wait a few minutes and follow."

"I'm not sending you through the gate alone before me. We have no idea what might be waiting for us on the other side. And what if it doesn't work, and I'm not able to follow, after all?"

"I'll go with her," Dax says, stepping forward. "I'm going anyway. And, logically, Daphne should go through the gate first since we can't risk the gate's not letting her through if you go before she does. We'll wait ten minutes, maybe press forward, and then you and Garrick follow. If you can't go through the gate, then Daphne, Garrick, and I will go on to the Pits without you. We've both got lightning, and you know I've got better aim than you regardless, so face it, bro, you're the expendable one in this scenario."

"Thanks a lot," I say, folding my arms in front of my chest.

"The truth's the truth, my friend. But you have to admit, it's a good plan."

"It is a good plan, except you and Daphne will have to go through the gate as soon as you get the Key. Taking Brim with you, of course," I say, preventing the tiny cat from sinking her teeth into my leg once more. She's quite protective of Daphne. "She can help you subdue the gate guards who will be on duty on the other side. Once that's done, that should give you twenty minutes before I try to join you as soon as the play is over. I don't want you to move on unless you're sure I'm not coming through. Five of us against a couple of dozen Keres is far better odds than three." The fact that I am able to say these words out loud makes me hopeful that this version of the plan will work. "If Garrick comes through without me, then you can stop waiting."

"There's a problem with your plan," Garrick says, standing up from his beanbag. "I'm not going with you."

"Pardon?" I ask.

"I can't go back there. I can't go back to the Pits. That place . . . I just can't go back there again. . . ."

"We need you," I start to protest, but Garrick shakes his head.

He looks at me, his eyes rimmed with red. "I *won't* go."

Garrick ducks his head and runs from the room, with his arms wrapped around his chest. I think I hear a sob before the door slams shut behind him.

I sigh heavily, feeling like a *koprophage* for pressing him to return to the Pits—and try not to shudder at how nightmarish the place must be to cause that reaction from him.

"I'll go in his place," Joe says.

"You don't have any powers," Daphne says.

"A man doesn't need superpowers to try to protect his daughter." He stretches his hands out over his knees. "Use me as your messenger. If I come through the gate, then it means Haden isn't coming."

I nod, giving my consent to this plan. Daphne glares at me. Things may still be somewhat strained between them, but she cares about his safety.

"And how are you all planning on getting out?" Lexie says, with a shudder, as if she's happy to not be included in the plan. "Like my mom always says, never enter into any situation without an exit strategy. She means conversations at cocktail parties, but still."

"Once the Keres are dead," I say, "it will be safe to temporarily open the barrier between the Pits and the mortal realm. We just need to make sure we shore up the locks on our way out so no Underlords can follow us."

Joe nods. "I'll have my jet on standby in DC for you all."

"If we need more firepower," Daphne says, "maybe we *should* bring Ethan in on this. It's a modified version of his plan, after all."

"He's also a Skylord, which means he can't be trusted." I look around at each one of them. "In fact, the only ones we can trust are the people who are in this room right now."

chapter forty-two

TOBIN

Time seems to be stuck on warp speed, because the days between the big planning meeting and the upcoming play fly by at a breakneck speed. It's only three days before "Key Day" when I find myself sitting in the Olympus Brew again, nursing a coffee. I've been sitting here all evening after rehearsal, and I plan on staying until closing. My hope is that Marta—who doesn't seem to have set foot in Olympus Hills again since Joe fired her—will miraculously show up for a late-evening espresso. (The evil don't need sleep, right?)

This time, I wouldn't hold back. I'd confront her and not relent until she tells me everything she knows about Abbie. Who has her? Why? What do I need to do to get her back?

There has to be a better option than responding to Terresa, who's been sending me texts for the last week, asking to know if I've made up my mind about teaming up with her.

But it isn't Marta who is the last customer who comes in before closing. It's Lexie. She orders a frozen hot chocolate with extra whipped cream and a chocolate-chip muffin. It isn't like Lexie to ever eat carbs—at least not since eighth grade, when we'd celebrate Friday Pizza and Movie Night religiously—so I know she's upset before she even turns around with her order and notices me in the corner. Her face is splotched with red, like she's been crying.

At first, I expect her to leave, pretending she never saw me, but when I nod to her, she brings her food over to the table and sits across from me.

I watch her peck at the top of her muffin with her fingers and eat it a few crumbs at a time. I wonder if she's doing that for my sake, like she thinks I'll judge her if she bites right into it.

"Looks good," I say, because I'm not sure what else to do at the moment.

"You want it?"

I shake my head. "It's yours. Dig in."

She takes a sip of her cocoa and then breaks off a slightly bigger piece of her muffin. "Pear would have a fit if she knew I was eating this much sugar. We're supposed to be on the Paleo diet together ever since last summer. Then again, she's just barely graduated from getting her food through a tube to eating broth and Jell-O, so I'd say the diet pact is off." She sniffles and wipes at her nose with a napkin. I doubt it's the idea of Pear eating Jell-O for dinner that has her tearing up again.

"Pear's awake?" I ask. "I hadn't heard."

"Yeah," she says. "I got word a couple of weeks ago, but I hadn't gone yet. Not until today."

"Why did you wait?"

She wipes her nose again, and a stifled sob shudders through her. I realize that must have been the wrong question to ask.

"I guess I was afraid to see her. Or maybe it was guilt."

"Guilt?" I ask. "What happened to Pear wasn't—"

"My fault? I know . . . but, at the same time, I still felt guilty. Like survivor's guilt, you know. Because what happened to Pear had almost happened to me. I would have been the Keres's next victim if Daphne and Haden hadn't come along."

I nod.

"I don't remember much about what happened that night, but I do remember being terrified. I guess I was afraid to see Pear because I didn't want to see the results of what could have happened to me. I didn't want to hear her talk about being attacked, either, because it'd feel like reliving it. . . ." She takes another napkin and dabs it against her cheeks and eyes. "But then I realized that pretty much made me the worst friend in the world. So I sucked it up and went to see her today. . . ."

"How's she doing?"

"She looks terrible, and her mom says she's still not out of the woods yet."

"Did you get to talk to her? Does she remember much about the attack?"

Lexie nods and then shakes her head. For a second, she reminds me of a bobblehead—that is, until she bursts into tears. "It was even worse than I could have imagined. She said . . ."

"What?" I reach my hand across the table and place it over her fingers. "What did she say?"

Lexie shakes her head again. "She's still pretty out of it, and it's hard for her to talk because of the tubes they put down her throat while she was in a coma, but from what I could make out, it sounded like she'd not only been attacked by some sort of shadowy beast, as she called it, but also by a man."

"What?" A sick feeling pulls at my stomach. "What did she mean?"

"She said something like there was a guy in the grove, just standing there, watching while she was attacked. Like he was enjoying himself. Or like the beast had attacked her because he'd wanted it to. . . . She said she didn't remember anything else before she blacked out, except that it seemed like the guy had swirls of fire in his eyes."

"You mean an Underlord was there?" I ask, my anger surging.

She nods. "I didn't get much out of her before her mom came back from the cafeteria and shooed me out of the room. But do you think . . . do you think Haden was lying when he said he had nothing to do with Pear's attack?"

"No," I say, shaking my head. "My money would be on Rowan. He came through the gate after them."

Scum, I think, remembering what Terresa had called them. *Rowan was nothing but Underlord scum.* Haden and his two cousins may be different, but the rest of them make me sick.

"I wish there was a way to make him pay," Lexie says.

"Me, too." *I wish there was a way to make all of them pay.*

My phone in my pocket buzzes. I know it's another text from Terresa without looking at it. Lexie and I sit in silence until she's finished half her muffin. She pushes the rest aside, squeezes my hand, and then stands up.

I'm still seething when she says, "Thank you."

I look up at her, a little taken aback. "For what?"

"For being here. For letting me talk. I know we're not the best of friends anymore. . . ." She leans down and pecks my cheek with her lips. "Thanks for even wishing there were something you could do."

She picks up her purse and leaves before I can think of how to respond.

My phone buzzes once again. I pull it out and find three texts from Terresa, all saying the same thing.

Are you in?

I almost put it back in my pocket, but instead I answer back. I'll let you know my answer tomorrow.

I expect Terresa to be the one who is waiting for me on the front steps of the school in the morning, but instead it's Daphne.

She gives me this look like she can hear my inner tone from a mile away. At the moment, I curse her intuitive abilities, because I don't need her intruding on my feelings.

"Are you okay?" she asks, falling into step with me as we enter the building.

"Yeah," I lie.

She gives me a very pointed look. "I'm worried about you, Tobin."

"Don't be," I say.

Her look gets even more pointed.

"What I mean is that you shouldn't be worrying about me. I should be the one worrying about you. You're the one headed into the Underrealm in two days."

I am trying to distract her, but it doesn't seem to work. "I know you're not okay, Tobin. You sound like you're going to implode at any moment. You've just been so angry lately. . . ."

I shake my head. If she thinks the sound coming off me this morning is anger, then she's not as intuitive as she thinks she is. I'm not angry. Not anymore. I'm resigned.

I stop and put my hands on her shoulders. "I'm okay, Daphne, really. I'm just worried about you and how this quest of yours to the Underrealm is going to play out. That's all."

"Okay," she says, as if she hears the sincerity behind my words. She hugs me and I let her.

"Now, I gotta take care of something before music class," I say, when she finally lets me go. "See you in a few."

I know she's watching me go until I round the corner. I go down another hall until I see the person I'm looking for.

Terresa stands by her locker, chatting with Iris Thompkins, as if she were any other student. When she sees me coming, she excuses herself from the conversation and comes to meet me. I pull a folded-up piece of paper from my pocket and hand it to her.

"What's this?"

"A time and a location," I whisper. "Meet me after the play the evening after tomorrow, and I will take you to the Key."

She nods. I turn around and walk away briskly—only to almost run into Garrick at the end of the hall. "What?" I ask pointedly at his stare.

"Not a thing," he says, and lets me pass.

chapter forty-three

DAPHNE

Over the last two weeks, I've completely immersed myself in either rehearsals for the play or practicing honing my powers. I've even gotten in a couple of sessions with Haden, in which I use my power to send something flying in the air, and then he blasts it with a bolt. It's kind of like skeet shooting, but with lightning. He's polite to me—kind, even—but he doesn't ever try to touch me or press me more on our relationship status. Instead, he treats me like a comrade in arms.

I like the respect, but sometimes when I watch that concentrated look on his face when I'm teasing him by sending an object whirling in an erratic pattern before he can blast it, I find myself aching for more. A smile. A laugh. The touch of his hand on the small of my back. And then I curse my feelings for trying to betray my head.

The day of the play arrives too quickly. I wake early in the morning, worried that I'm not ready. But then I tell myself that there isn't more that I could possibly do to prepare. In the late afternoon, I get in one last vocal warm-up while using my voice to rearrange the clothes draped on wooden hangers in my closet, and then get set to leave.

I can't find Joe in the house, so I decide to head over to the amphitheater on my bike, but instead I discover Joe in the driveway. He's sitting on the teal green Vespa that he'd bought me for Christmas, and is wearing a leather jacket, a charcoal gray helmet, and aviator sunglasses.

"What are you doing?" I ask.

He smiles. "Your chariot awaits, mademoiselle," he says, and holds out another gray helmet for me.

"You're driving that to the play?"

"Bobby says he wants to buy it off me since you don't want it . . . but I thought it a shame to get rid of it without at least taking it for an inaugural ride. And, no, I'm not driving it; you're going to. What kind of rock star father would I be if I didn't teach my own daughter how to drive a motorcycle . . . or, er, motor scooter?"

"Right now?"

"No time like the present . . ." His voice trails off, and I gather his real meaning from the notes that swirl about him. He's trying to seize the opportunity for a daddy-daughter moment just in case. . . . Just in case he never gets the chance again . . .

"You seriously want me to drive this thing?" I ask, taking the helmet from him.

"It's easy," he says. "Just like riding your bicycle, but faster."

I strap on my helmet and climb onto the scooter seat in front of Joe.

Joe's assertion that it would be as easy as riding my bike doesn't exactly hold up, but I'm surprised by how fun it is to drive once I (sort of) start to get the hang of it. I even dare to speed up to a whole twenty miles an hour when I figure out that it's easier to balance, the faster I go. Joe laughs as my long hair in the wind whips him in the face.

I laugh, too, and I can't help thinking that this is exactly the kind of thing I have always wanted in a father: that person who teaches you how to drive, helps you with your schoolwork, and shows you how to be a better person. Joe may have his problems, but he is *trying*. He's been doing so much to help us and is doing everything possible to become a better man. I'd been carrying his sobriety coin in my pocket for the last few weeks as a reminder of the promises he'd made to me, but I had also still been carrying what remains of my anger toward him. And I'm tired of it. I'm tired of letting it weigh me down. So as we cruise along the lake-shore road, I decide to just let my anger go. To release it into the wind and let it fly away. And forgive Joe in my heart.

"Lean the scooter but not yourself," Joe says as we round the corner into the amphitheater parking lot. We pull to a stop—not too hard. Joe gets off first and then steadies the scooter as I swing off it.

"What do you think?" he asks.

"I love it," I say. "Do you think Bobby would mind if we decide to keep it? I think I'd like to do this some more *when* I get back."

"I was hoping you'd say that," Joe says, with a cheeky smile.

As I leave Joe to park the Vespa in the lot and I head toward the theater, I feel as though a change has come over me. I feel lighter and ever more confident about the tasks that lie ahead of me.

And like the wall around my heart is finally starting to come down again.

Haden is already backstage at the amphitheater when I come out of a dressing room with my hair and makeup done and my costume on. He's dressed in a rust red toga that shows off the finer parts of his body, while I wear a flowing white Grecian-style dress.

He doesn't smile when he sees me, but I can tell by his inner tone that he's relieved—and possibly happy—that I'm with him.

"I have something for you," he says. Other cast members are milling about, so he speaks softly as he slips something round and metal into my hand.

"The Compass," I whisper, wrapping my fingers around it. Warmth pulses through my hand, up my arm, and into my chest. It feels like what I imagine having one's sight restored after a month of blindness must be like.

"I can have Dax hang on to it and bring it to the grove so you don't have to worry about it while you're onstage."

"No, I'll keep it," I say, not wanting to let it out of my possession again, and tuck it into the secret pocket I asked Dax to sew into the side seam of my dress. It nestles next to Joe's sobriety coin, and knowing I have it on me gives me more strength.

Beyond the stage, I can hear the school band tuning their instruments, but I can still make out the shift in Haden's inner tone as it becomes softer and more fluid.

I look up to find him watching me. He starts to say something, hesitates, and then starts again. "I wanted to say something to you," he finally says.

I take a deep breath, part expecting, part dreading, and part hoping for another declaration.

"I want to apologize," he says.

"Apologize?" *Was he going to take back his words?* "For what?"

"For bringing you into all of this. I know none of what has happened to you is part of your big plan for your life, and I'm sorry that, because of me, your future is so uncertain. I also wanted to thank you for sticking with us. You didn't have to leave Ellis Fields and come back here with us; you didn't have to agree to go to the

Underrealm tonight. You could have stayed where it was safe and tried to forget about the rest of us, but the truth is we need you and you didn't run away from that." He brushes the backs of his fingers lightly against my shoulder, sending a tingling sensation down my arm. "I know this isn't what you envisioned for your life, but I'm glad we're doing this together."

I look down at my hands. *When did they start to tremble?* "You could have done differently, too," I say, realizing that now. He could have run away. Or stayed in Ellis. He could have said a big "screw you" to the mortal world and gone his merry way. No one had asked him to be a hero.

"I couldn't have done anything differently," he says.

"Why?"

"Because it wouldn't have been right."

My breath catches in my chest. I want to say something to him . . . tell him something . . . but I don't know the right words to express what I'm feeling.

"Yo, Daphne?" Tobin says, poking his head around the corner of the alcove where I've been standing with Haden. I am relieved to note that his inner tone sounds nervous but not angry like it had when I'd confronted him at school. "Joe's looking for you. He says you have a couple of surprise guests."

"I do?" I ask, completely confused.

I follow Tobin out of the alcove, with Haden trailing behind me. I can hear a string of tense notes accompanying him. Our plans for later tonight must have him paranoid, and I don't think he likes the sound of anything surprise-related.

"There you are, Daphne!" Joe says brightly as he comes through the curtains of the amphitheater, but his tone tells me something's got him worried. He pulls the curtain aside, and the two people I least expect to see follow him backstage.

"Mom? Jonathan?" I almost want to rub my eyes like a cartoon character to make sure I'm not seeing a mirage brought on by nerves.

"Hello, my little sprout!" Mom says as I throw myself at her. She hugs me tight, like she's tempted to never let me go. Or run off with me back to Ellis before I have a chance to escape.

"My turn!" Jonathan croons impatiently.

Mom releases me from her death-grip hug, only for Jonathan to scoop me up in his giant, bearlike embrace.

"What are you two doing here?" I ask, when he sets me back on my feet.

"Like we were going to miss your big debut!" Jonathan says.

Actually, that's exactly what I'd expected to happen. We hadn't really been speaking to each other since the Christmas debacle, and my mom doesn't travel—I knew crossing two state lines would be hard enough on her that I hadn't bothered to invite her to the play. I can tell from the uneasy tone that eeks off her that being here is no small sacrifice.

"Who are your friends?" Jonathan asks, indicating Tobin and Haden, who both stand protectively behind me. "I want to meet every one of your friends."

"Well, this is Tobin, my costar," I say as Tobin steps forward.

He shakes both my mom's and Jonathan's hands.

"The infamous Tobin Oshiro-Winters." Jonathan closes both of his huge hands around Tobin's. "We've heard a lot about you."

"And this is Haden Lord," I say, almost too reluctantly.

Haden follows Tobin's lead and shakes my mother's hand, then offers to do the same with Jonathan, but Jonathan doesn't return the gesture.

"Haden Lord? I haven't heard a *single thing* about you," Jonathan says, giving him a suspicious look. Like Haden's some secret boyfriend I've been keeping on the side. "Lord? I knew some Lords once. Where are you from?"

"Back east. New York."

"Oh really? I hail from Manhattan. What part of New York—"

"Jonathan, what do you think of the set?" I ask, trying to get his mind on design to deter him from giving Haden the third degree. "A lot swankier than that time you and I put on our version of Cinderella on the back patio, huh?"

"It's nice, yes. Where in New York?" he asks, undeterred.

"Upstate," Haden says, and I wonder how much more about New York geography he knows beyond that.

"No visitors backstage," I hear the stage manager call. "We're five minutes from curtain."

"Come on," Joe says. "I'll help you find your seats."

"We'll come find you right after," Mom says, giving me another squeeze. "You should see the bouquet Jonathan brought you all the way from Ellis for curtain call."

My heart sinks. I won't be here for curtain call. How will my mom react when she finds out I've gone missing? How will I explain to them where I've been when I get back?

If I get back?

"Yes. Bring all of your friends," Jonathan says, still eyeing Haden. "We'll go out for ice cream afterward."

"Break a leg," Joe says. I can tell by the look on his face that he's not only wishing me luck for the play but also for our journey to come. He moves like he wants to give me a hug but isn't sure I'll let him, so I wrap my arms around his shoulder and give him a tight squeeze. All while my mom gives Joe the side eye.

When I release Joe, he ushers Mom and Jonathan out, and I almost want to cry for the three of them not to leave. I'd known all along that what we are planning to do tonight is dangerous. Foolish, even. But I hadn't thought about how it will affect the people who love me if we don't succeed. Failure is not an option I've allowed myself to dwell on. Now, having seen Mom and Jonathan again, knowing what I'd be missing and who would be missing me, I can feel the *possibility* trying to close in on me.

"Hey," Haden says, giving me a little shake. "Are you okay?"

"Yeah," I say, but my voice sounds anything but sure.

"We'll make it back. I promise."

"You don't know that. . . ."

"I do. Because this right here," he says, indicating the stage, "this is your destiny. This is your plan. You're going to kill it out there, and everyone is going to love you, and it'll be the beginning of that big music-star dream you've always wanted. And I've made up my mind. There's no way I'm not getting you back here so you can go on to live it."

I look at him, warmth filling me because I know he means everything he says. My plans may have been derailed temporarily by all this Underrealm stuff, but it didn't mean that the future I'd planned couldn't be put back on track.

And the details might be hazy, but for the first time, I can start picturing Haden as part of it.

chapter forty-four

HADEN

"You ready for this?" Dax asks during intermission. He adjusts the golden trim on the shoulder of my red toga, which came loose during the last scene before the break.

"I just hope I don't forget the rest of my lines," I say, rocking back in my sandaled feet. I've gotten so used to wearing twenty-first-century teenager clothes that it feels strange to be back in garb similar to what I wore in my former life. Actually, it feels almost ominous, considering it is the Eve of the Return. The night before the equinox, when the gate will open on its own.

"I was talking about later," Dax says, pulling his hand away from my shoulder.

I take a deep breath. Through the curtains, I can see Daphne on the other side of backstage. She's dressed as Eurydice in a flowing white dress, having just acted out her death on her wedding night. "I know," I say to Dax. "Are you?"

He nods.

"Intermission is over in two minutes," the stage manager whispers loudly as he comes through the curtains.

A phone starts ringing on the table behind us.

"Whose phone is this?" the stage manager growls, picking it

up. "Mr. Morgan will flip if you don't turn it off. It interferes with the sound system!"

"Sorry, it's mine," Dax says, and grabs it out of his hand.

"I hit decline. You'll have to take the phone at least three hundred feet from the stage before you call them back. Unless you want Mr. Morgan to kill you."

"I hear you," Dax says, waving at the kid as he crosses to the other side of the stage to inform the rest of the cast that we are about to go back onstage for the second half of the play.

"Who was it?" I ask Dax.

"I don't recognize the number," he says. The phone beeps, indicating there's a message. Dax hits the play button and holds the phone to his ear.

"Aren't you afraid of Mr. Morgan's wrath—" I start to tease, but Dax holds up a hand to silence me. The look in his eyes tells me this is no joking matter. He clasps his hand over his mouth.

"It was Abbie," he says, through his fingers.

"What?"

He hits the speaker button and holds the phone up as he replays the message. A garbled, frantic voice speaks like a ghost: "Dax? Dax? It's me. I escaped. I've been running. I'm hiding at a place near my old town. Old Sutton Mill. Please, Dax, come. Before they find me again." The message cuts off, and Dax looks as pale as a harpy's underbelly. He hits the redial button, but the call doesn't go through.

"That's Abbie," Dax says. "I have to go to her. I have to go now."

"Dax, it could be a trap."

"It's not. I know Abbie. She wouldn't have left that message unless it was the real deal. No matter how much duress she was under."

"But how did she even get your number? It's a trick: the Sky-lords messing with us because they know we're up to something."

"I don't care. That was *her* voice. I have to go."

I grab his arm. "You can't go. What about . . ." *My plan. If Dax leaves, my plan is jeopardized. Who will protect Daphne as she gets the Key? Who will cross through the gate with her?* But I can't bring myself to say any of it. Because I know that if it had been Daphne who called, if that had been her voice ringing with fear through that phone, nothing anyone could say would stop me from going to her. Even if she doesn't feel the same way about me.

"I'll come with you," I say, pulling at the shoulder of my toga. "Give me a second to change."

"No," Dax says, clasping his hand over my shoulder. "If you leave, then the play can't go on, and if the play doesn't go on, then your plan is ruined. The mill is only about twenty minutes from here. I have to check this out even if it is a prank. I can get there and back before the play is even over. I *will* be back in time to meet Daphne in the grove; I swear it." He gives me a look that tells me that if he had water from the River Styx, he would make an oath on it right now.

"Take Brim, at least," I say, offering her up in my place. If I couldn't be there to protect Dax, then she would willingly do it for me. "She's in my duffel in the dressing room. Take her with you now so you don't have to return here before going to the grove."

"I will," he says. "I'll leave a message on your phone when we've made it back."

"Places, everyone, places," the stage manager calls. "One minute to curtain."

I place my hand on his shoulder, returning his gesture. Behind him, I can see Daphne and Tobin taking the stage. If something goes wrong, I will have to find a way to get the message to her that our plans have changed before she makes her grand exit and heads for the grove.

"Hades's speed," I say, and let Dax go.

chapter forty-five

DAPHNE

I stand on the stage of the amphitheater, clasping a goblet that supposedly holds water from the River Lethe, the river of forgetfulness in the underworld. My character has died on her wedding night and found herself in the underworld when she should have been celebrating with her new husband, Orpheus. She is overcome with grief.

Two handmaidens of Persephone have offered me the goblet, promising that if I drink from it, I will forget my pain, along with my former life, and find peace in my death.

I sing my response to them—Joe's words, written for me—in my most difficult solo of the night. The beauty of the song almost overcomes me as I channel Eurydice's emotions. The song ends as I dash the cup away, choosing to keep my pain in order to retain my memories of true love—a plot point that will come in handy when Orpheus comes to rescue his bride.

The handmaidens scurry away with the goblet, ducking their heads, as Haden, in the role of Hades, enters the stage. My character stands her ground as he sings to me about the folly of my choice to try to defy the order of his world.

I can tell by the notes that swirl around Haden that he is

nervous, but you wouldn't be able to tell by the way he carries himself. He is strong and proud and unbelievably attractive as he commands the stage. I would never guess that he had no idea what music was only six months ago—that he comes from a place where it is forbidden.

I watch him sing, letting his song wrap around me like a warm cocoon. I feel as though I could curl up inside of it and find refuge from the world.

That there is no other place I would rather be.

But it's not just the way he looks or the way he sings that has me so caught up in him. No, it's who he *is*. After our conversation before the play—his apology—I've realized something about him that I hadn't seen before. What he'd done by not giving me to his father hadn't happened just because he's in love with me. He didn't do it *just because* he wants me. He did it because it was the right thing to do.

And he'd done everything he's done since to see it through because it is what is right. Haden is good person . . . and I love him for that.

I love him.

The realization is so stark and plain; I don't know how I couldn't see it before. But at the same time, it's so overwhelming that I almost miss my cue as Haden's solo comes to an end.

He points at me and vows that if Orpheus tries to come for me, then he will throw every obstacle in his power in my husband's way.

I know I am supposed to look forlorn as I cast my eyes out over the audience, as if looking for Orpheus on the horizon, but my realization is so powerful that I am afraid everyone will be able to hear the swirling, tittering notes of happiness that radiate from my soul.

The lights go dark momentarily, indicating the end of the scene, and it's then that I see Rowan watching me intently from the third row in the audience. In front of him, I notice Terresa and Calix. They would be impossible not to pick out in the crowd, considering they are the only ones not applauding as the scene transitions into the next.

Lexie joins Haden from stage right while I take my exit to the left, where I continue to watch Haden from the shadows of the side curtains. I had been such an idiot for the last few weeks. I can't believe that I couldn't see how important we are together. Can't believe I'd thought clinging to my stress and anxiety was more important than letting myself be happy.

I love him.

And I promise myself I won't wait until we return from the Underrealm. I will tell him the words he's been longing to hear from me the very next chance I get.

chapter forty-six

HADEN

After my second duet with Lexie, she and I exit stage left, and I check my cell phone, which I've stashed on the props table. Either it isn't working because of the interference with the sound system, or Dax isn't back yet as he thought he would be. I know from watching the play over and over again that we are only minutes away from the moment when Daphne will be swept away to the island. Only minutes from her going for the Eternity Key.

Will Dax be there to meet her? Or will she find herself alone?

I need to find a way to get a message to her. I peer through the curtains. She's already taking her place on the platform. Too far for me to get her attention; besides, she's too focused as she sings to even notice me, short of my setting myself on fire and storming the stage.

For half a second, I contemplate it.

No. What I need is a messenger. A runner to meet her at the lake. To make sure Dax is there, or to tell her not to go through with getting the Key until I get there if he isn't.

My first thought goes to Joe. He had already volunteered to be our messenger if something went wrong. I'd seen him backstage during intermission; I could only hope he was still around. "Have you seen Joe?" I whisper to Lexie.

"Dressing room," she whispers back, and then sweeps onto the stage for her big solo, expounding on the woe of those who oppose the will of the gods. That means I have three minutes and thirty-four seconds before I'm needed onstage—and only ten seconds until Daphne is swept away.

I push my way through the chorus members who wait in the wings and make my way toward the dressing room behind the stage just as I hear the crescendo of music and the gasps from the audience as Daphne is drawn seemingly magically across the lake on a mechanical platform, indicating her being sucked back into the underworld because of Orpheus's folly.

"Where are you going?" I hear the stage manager whisper-shouting after me. "You're needed on deck."

I wave him off and throw open the dressing room door. I find Joe, but he's in no condition to run to Daphne. He's prostrate on the couch, seemingly asleep. My first instinct is to check his pulse, but as I lean over him, the smell of something acrid slaps me in the face. I pick up the opaque water bottle he'd been sipping nervously out of during intermission and sniff. It smells just as bad.

I shake my head in disgust. I'd actually believed Joe when he'd said he wanted to help protect Daphne. Maybe he'd believed it, too, when he said it.

I back out the door, searching for another option, while the stage manager whisper-yells at me again that I need to be out onstage. I want to tell him where he can shove his clipboard, and run for Daphne myself, but I also know that if I don't go out onstage, then every one of our enemies waiting in the audience will know that something is up. They'll descend on the place where they know Daphne last went—the island—and our chance to get the Key will be blown, or worse yet, one of them may find a way to force her to get it for them.

But I can't leave her there alone.

The stage manager grabs my arm. "Thirty seconds," he hisses at me. I am about to shove him away when I see Garrick skulking in the curtains. He's dressed in black like the other stagehands, holding a bag that contains the makeshift costume that is supposed to disguise him as Daphne. He was still dead set on not going with us, but had conceded to at least appear as Daphne onstage during curtain calls in exchange for the keys to Dax's Roadster.

"Garrick," I say, grabbing his attention. "Garrick, please, I need your help."

chapter forty-seven

TOBIN

When the play ends and the curtain pulls shut in front of me, I hear the audience burst into uproarious applause. I didn't expect any less. The play had been absolutely amazing.

The rest of the cast rushes the stage, ready to take their bows when the curtain opens again. Haden pushes through the incoming crowd, going the wrong way. He'd come stumbling onstage—the only hitch in the whole production—almost as if he'd been pushed by the stage manager a full ten seconds late for his last solo, and he looks even more flustered now.

"What's going on?" I ask him as he approaches. "Where's Garrick? He's supposed to be taking Daphne's place, isn't he?"

"He's not coming. I sent him to the grove to catch Daphne."

"Why?"

"Can't talk now. I have to get to her." He rushes off the stage. I try to follow him but slam into one of the girls from the chorus. We trip over each other, and by the time I've untangled myself, the curtain is rising again. In a choreographed move, the cast grabs hands and takes a bow. Then they raise their hands to applaud as Lexie moves to the front of the stage to take her bow with Haden as the king and queen of the underworld, only Haden isn't there. Lexie glances nervously at me but then sweeps down low in a bow and pops back up, blowing kisses to the audience, as if reveling in her solo time at the front of the stage.

The applause grows louder, and I know that I am supposed to take my bow with Daphne now. Or at least Garrick disguised in layers of veils, pretending to be Daphne. I follow Lexie's lead and take the front of the stage alone. It's hard to see past the stage's lights, but as I dip down for my bow, I see that the seats that Terresa and Calix had been occupying in the second row are empty. I have no idea how long they've been gone.

I step away to the side of the stage, clapping my hands with the other somewhat bewildered-looking actors. "Where are Daphne and Haden?" one of the chorus guys asks me. I shrug like I don't care and keep on clapping as Mr. Morgan takes the stage for his bows. He sweeps his arms out toward the front of stage left, where Joe Vince is supposed to rise out of the faux mist for his standing ovation. Only he doesn't appear.

Now everyone is confused, including the audience. As Mr. Morgan calls for an ovation of the band, I notice movement toward the edge of the audience and see Rowan making his way out of the crowd. Crap. He must know something's up.

The actor next to me grabs my hand and we all step forward for one final bow. As soon as he lets go, I bolt from the stage. I'm heading to a backstage exit when Joe comes stumbling from the dressing room. "Did I miss my cue?" he slurs. I don't bother to answer as he grabs on to the doorframe to steady himself.

I keep running, exit the school, and head for the jogging trails that will take me to the grove. I know I'm not supposed to go near the grove tonight, but Terresa's timing is off. She shouldn't have left already.

Something is going to go terribly wrong.

chapter forty-eight

DAPHNE

The mechanical pulley system that drags the floating platform to the island is faster than I remember its being in rehearsals. I brace myself, trying not to topple into the water, and in what feels like barely any time at all, I am almost to the island. The platform stops suddenly, a few feet short of the shore. I stomp on the platform a couple of times, thinking it's gotten caught on something, but it doesn't budge. "Dax?" I call out in a loud whisper, hoping he can pull me to shore.

When he doesn't answer, I call again.

I'd thought he was supposed to be waiting for me on the shore, but perhaps I am mistaken and he is waiting in the grove.

Hiking my white flowing dress up around my knees, I wade into the lake. The shock of the cold water on my legs makes my heart race. Or maybe that's just the anticipation of what is supposed to come next. The hem of my dress is soaked, and I'm shivering when I make it to shore.

My shoes, white ballet flats, squish into the sand. I look up at the steep, rocky, tree-lined hill I have to climb to get to the grove. Dax was also supposed to bring a change of shoes for me and I find myself wishing I'd been able to sneak a pair of hiking boots under my costume. Then again, the heavy Compass tucked into my secret pocket already creates enough bulk.

I look back at the amphitheater on the other side of the lake. I can hear the strains of music from the new song that Joe had added to give me the extra time I need to get to the Key, which means I'm already a few minutes behind schedule because of the platform malfunction. No use wasting more time shivering in the dark.

I can only hope Dax is waiting for me in the grove.

I climb the hill as quickly as possible, slipping just twice in my wet shoes. I make it to the grove, expecting to apologize to Dax for being late, only he isn't here. I cast about, calling his name softly— but urgently. No answer.

Crap. What am I supposed to do now?

Get the Key? Or wait longer?

Another couple of minutes pass by, and I am still alone. The Compass, in my wet dress, feels like it's weighing me down. I reach into my pocket, my fingers brushing over Joe's sobriety coin, and pull the Compass out.

I hear a rustle of bushes just beyond Orpheus's tree.

"Daphne?" Someone calls my name, but it isn't Dax who enters the grove. It's Garrick. He looks over his shoulder like he's worried he's being followed.

"What's going on? Where's Dax?"

"He isn't coming. Or he's going to be late. I don't really know," he says, looking a bit panicked.

"What do you mean, you don't know?"

"There wasn't really time for explanations," Garrick says. "Haden sent me to come find you. Dax disappeared or something?"

"Disappeared?"

"Or he's just late. I said, I don't know."

"Well, what are we supposed to do?"

"*I don't know.*"

Fine messenger he is. "Then why did Haden even send you?"

He glowers at me.

"I guess we stick with the plan," I say, yanking at my hair.
"Come on, we have to get the Key."

"Don't you think we should wait?" Garrick says, looking over
his shoulder again.

"Hear that?" I ask, indicating the cheers and applause in the
distance. "The play just ended. We've got to get the gate open so
we can pass through it before Haden gets here. We need to space
enough time between us so he can follow."

I wrap my fingers around the Compass and approach
Orpheus's tree.

"We?" Garrick asks, following me. "I'm just the messenger. I'm
not going through the gate. And I am not going back to the Pits.
Wait for Dax."

"Maybe he'll get here in time to help us, but we can't wait."

I try placing the Compass in the knot at the base of the
vibrating tree, and it sticks. "Stop being a pansy," I growl at
him—and then feel immediately guilty. I change tactics. "You
say you don't want to go into the Pits because you hate the Keres
so much. But instead of running away, why don't you help us get
rid of them? Stand up for yourself. Don't you think it would be
good to finally destroy the soul-sucking monsters that ruined
your life?"

Garrick ducks his head so I can't see his face. He has no inner
song at the moment—or pretty much ever—so I find it impossible

to read him. I don't know if it's a gesture of resignation to his fear or his acknowledging that I'm right.

I twist the Compass so the symbols on it line up with the symbols that are scratched into the tree's knot, and then give it a good whack with the heel of my hand. It slides into place with an odd-sounding click, and the symbols on the Compass light up with an ethereal glow. The vibration of the tree shifts into a steady, thrumming pulse, shaking the ground under my feet.

"Now what?" Garrick asks.

"Now I think I sing to it." I place my hands on the roots of the tree, soaking in the tone of its pulse. I start with a hum, finding the right pitch, and then begin to sing the words from the scroll. They're etched into my memory from how many times I've read it over. I just hope the tree will accept my English translation, since I am not sure I can sing the phonetically spelled-out Greek version that Haden made for me.

As I sing, the Compass begins to turn slowly back and forth inside the knot. It reminds me of a spinning combination lock. The symbols grow brighter. As I finish the song, the tree shudders, and a seam of light slits up its middle, lighting up the grove as if it were afternoon. So much for staying incognito. The crack of light grows wider and brighter as the tree peels itself open. The light is so bright now, I have to hold my hand in front of my eyes, and I step away from the tree.

The ground rumbles under my feet, almost knocking me over.

"Damn me to Tartarus," Garrick whispers, standing beside me. "It's really here."

I squint into the light and see the gleaming, golden, two-pronged staff floating where the tree once stood.

"The Eternity Key, Hades's Kronolithe," Garrick whispers,

affording the object a quiet reverence. He steps in front of me, bowing his head, and reaches for it.

"Not so fast," a voice rings through the grove.

A bolt of lightning explodes at Garrick's feet, sending him flying away into the thick trunk of a tree beside him. I hear his head smack, and then he slumps forward, lying face-first in the dirt. A crack of thunder rips the air, followed by the trill of amused laughter.

"Terresa," I say. "Fancy meeting you here."

She smiles, holding her hands out. White-hot lightning crackles up from her palms. "I've just come to collect what's been promised to me."

"Promised to you?"

"Let's just say that someone in your group wanted something more than he wanted you to have the Key. The desperate and angry always make the best deals."

chapter forty-nine

HADEN

"Tobin!" I say, when I reel around and see him behind me. I could tell I was being followed, but didn't expect my pursuer to be him. He was still dressed in his costume: a white toga and one of those stupid hats of his. "How did you catch up to me?"

"Shortcut," he pants. He clasps his hand to his side. He looks like he's been in a full sprint. "Nobody knows these trails like me."

"What are you doing? You should have stayed back!" I pick up my pace again, knowing I've wasted too much time already on this unexpected distraction.

"Terresa. She was gone," he says, jogging beside me.

"I know; that's why I left when I did."

"And Rowan," he says, and coughs. "If he took the same path as you did, he's only a minute or two behind us."

"*Kopros.* Not Rowan."

I fall into a flat-out run, not caring that Tobin can't keep up. In a firefight, he'd only be a liability. I'm on the part of the path that switches from asphalt to gravel, which means I'm still a half mile from the bridge that leads to the grove, when I see a beam of light shoot up from the island. I almost stop dead in my tracks but I force myself to run even faster.

"What . . . is . . . that?" Tobin pants from far behind me.

"The Key!" Frustration ripples through me, and I don't know if this meant Dax was where he was supposed to be, or if it meant Garrick hadn't even been listening when I told him to stop Daphne from getting the Key.

A roll of thunder comes from the island.

Or worse.

chapter fifty

DAPHNE

Terresa enters the grove with her fists full of lightning. A sinister snarl that I think is supposed to be a smile mars her face as she approaches the Key.

"A real Kronolithe," she says, eyeing the bident with gleeful malevolence. "Do you know the power this thing holds? It could grant an entire race immortality. Or wipe one completely out of existence." She extinguishes the bolt in one of her hands and wraps her fingers around the staff of the bident.

"What are you going to do? Open the gate and try to take on the entire population of the Underrealm on your own?"

"I've got a legion of Skylords waiting for my call. Calix is taking care of that for me right now." She hefts the bident in her hand, as if testing the weight. "But perhaps we should test this thing out first. See if it does what it's supposed to." She swings the bident toward me, and I jump away, scraping my arm against a tree.

She laughs. "Don't worry; you're not even worth killing. You're just the Cypher. You've already done your part. Now you're useless."

She holds the bident upright and marches toward the far end of the grove. "Now, where is that pesky gate?" She holds her hand out in front of her as if searching for some kind of energy signature.

"Terresa, stop!" I shout.

"Or you'll do what?"

I scramble after her, trying to grab her arm. She pushes me away. Hard. I fall back in a sitting position on the ground.

"You're nothing but a worthless human again." She takes another few steps. "Here we go," she says, standing in front of the archway created by two curved trees that cloak the gate. "Hmm, do you think I just jab it in?"

I rock forward on my knees. "I mean it, Terresa. Don't do this."

She thrusts the pitchforklike end of the bident into the archway and turns the handle as if twisting a key in a lock. A green light as brilliant as emeralds ripples out from the bident's prongs. Energy surges as the gate pulses to life. Terresa croons with arrogant joy, stomping her feet on the low, flat rock she's standing on.

"Terresa! Turn it off!" I demand, standing now.

She turns toward me. "Watcha going to do, sing at me?"

"Exactly." I let a low hum out of my lips and then direct all my attention to the rock she stands on. "Move," I command it, using that same low tone.

"Um, what?" Terresa starts to say, but then the rock flies out from under her feet. She falls sideways and hits one of the trees that forms the archway. The hand that holds the bident ricochets off the green light of the gate. She screams, snatching her hand away as if it were burned, and drops the bident in front of her.

I scramble for the bident. She makes a move toward me, but I command another rock to fly. This one hits her in the chest, knocking the wind out of her. I grab the bident, pulling it out of her reach, just as a motorcycle bursts into the grove.

chapter fifty-one

HADEN

A shrieking scream echoes from the grove. I pound across the bridge, knowing I'm only seconds away—and possibly seconds too late. My feet hit the gravel path again when an even more terrible noise fills my ears. The roar of a motorcycle. Coming from the other side of the island. Rowan must have ridden his bike around the lake and come over the footbridge on the other side. That way would have been too far on foot, but Rowan wouldn't even begin to care about the "no motorized vehicles on the footpaths" law.

He's going to beat me to Daphne.

I charge into the grove, just in time to see Rowan, dressed in motorcycle leathers and helmet, discard his motorcycle in the trees and charge at Daphne. She's holding a golden bident, the gate pulsing green behind her. Rocks fly through the air, seemingly flinging themselves at him. Then I realize that Daphne is using her voice to throw the rocks. A large one cracks against Rowan's helmet. It would have been a good blow if his head weren't protected. He keeps advancing on her.

"Stop!" I demand.

When he doesn't, I fling a lightning bolt at him. It narrowly misses and hits a tree branch above him. The branch explodes, sending shards of splintered wood raining down on both Rowan and Daphne. I shudder, realizing my mistake, but Daphne holds up her hand, and the shards stop midair right in front of her face, and then fall softly to the ground.

Rowan, probably shocked by what he's just witnessed, hesitates for a moment. That's when I make my move. Not wanting to risk possibly hurting Daphne with another stray bolt, I throw myself at Rowan, knocking him to the ground. I'm on top of him, pinning him to the ground with my knees.

I slam my fist against the face visor of his helmet. The plastic cracks. My knuckles scream with pain. I slam it again. Another crack. That's taking too long. I grab the bottom of his helmet and start wrenching it from his head. He screams in pain as I finally rip it loose. Blood oozes from one of his earlobes and from a cut just under his lip, where the cracked plastic must have caught his face. A surge of electricity shudders up my body, swirling in my chest and then exploding into my arm and hand. I'd had Rowan in this position once before. Only hours before leaving on my quest.

"Get back," I shout at Daphne.

She scrambles away, the Key in hand, to the other side of the grove. Well out of range of a blast.

"What are you going to do?" she asks.

"If he invokes *elios*—begs for mercy—I will only incapacitate him so he cannot follow us," I say. "If not . . . then I'll make sure he can't interfere in another way."

Rowan had called my bluff when I'd had him in this position before, but I hope to Hades he doesn't do it now. Maybe my emotions have softened me, but I don't like the idea of killing someone in front of Daphne. However, after witnessing him attack her and reflecting on his words about how he'd find a way to trick Daphne into giving him the Key, I fear I will have no other choice if he will not relent on his own mission.

"You don't have what it takes, little brother," Rowan snarls at me.

I raise my electrified fist, ready to show that I do, when a shout from somewhere else stops me.

"Help!" Tobin cries. I'd all but forgotten that he'd followed me into the grove. I search for the origin of his voice and find him lying on his side in the grass, only about twenty feet away. Terresa is crouched over him, her knee pinning down his shoulder, and an electrified knife held just in front of his throat. I had barely noticed her slumped against the archway when I tore into the grove. It is my failure not realizing she is still a threat.

"Give me the Key, Daphne, or your friend here loses his face," Terresa says.

Daphne takes a step toward them. "Leave him alone."

"Key first. Demands later."

Daphne moves closer. I can see her eyeing her surroundings, trying to find a way to attack Terresa without causing Tobin harm.

I want to tell her not to give the Key to Terresa, but there's no way I can ask that of her. Not when it's Tobin.

"Take it," Daphne says, holding the Key out in front of her.

chapter fifty-two

DAPHNE

I hold the Key out in front of me, offering it to Terresa. She will have to let go of Tobin if she wants it.

"Stop," I hear Garrick say. I'd almost forgotten he was here. "They're working together. Tobin and Terresa."

"What?" Tobin says, his eyes wide, looking up at me. "That's not true."

"She said she was working with someone," Garrick says, pushing himself up to standing. "She said someone in our group had told her in exchange for something he wanted. Tobin must've tipped her off about us coming for the Key tonight in exchange for information about Abbie."

"What? No," Tobin protests.

"How else did she get here so quickly?" Garrick says. "Unless she was tipped off?"

"No! I wouldn't betray you for her!"

"Oh, Toby," Terresa says in a saccharine voice. "Don't hurt my feelings. Didn't you enjoy our little date at the gelato shop? I thought you liked me, with all those notes you've been passing me at school. I especially liked the one where you wrote down the time and place I should be tonight if I wanted the Key. But maybe that's not the kind of affection we share. Maybe it's because I remind you too much of *our* sister?"

Our sister. I see it now. Terresa and Tobin have Abbie in common.

"I didn't tell her to be *here*!" Tobin cries.

"Oh, you know you left me a note. I could pull it out of my pocket right now, but you see, I've got this big old knife in one hand, and your life in the other."

"Let him go!" I shout at her.

"You going to throw another rock at me? I'm pretty sure I'm faster." She pulls the knife closer to Tobin's throat. He screams, and I can smell his burning flesh as her lightning sizzles against his neck.

At that moment, I don't care if Tobin is lying or not.

"Just take it, damn it!" I say, holding out the Key.

Terresa pulls the knife away from Tobin and reaches for the bident. Then she jerks suddenly, as if something hit her in the back. Her mouth forms the shape of pain, and then she topples forward over Tobin. What looks like a golden arrow protrudes from her back, just between her shoulder blades.

I look up to see where this arrow could have possibly come from, only to see the very last person in all of the world I expected to walk through the trees—a very large man with a very large bow, wearing a look that I can only describe as absolutely fierce, which contorts his normally jovial face.

I almost drop the Key in my utter shock.

"Jonathan?" I gasp.

"Actually, honey, I prefer the name Eros," he says.

Eros. *Cupid.*

Uncle Jonathan—who isn't really my uncle—is freaking Cupid?

This revelation should rock my world, but at the same time, it kind of actually makes a lot of sense.

Jonathan reaches over his shoulder and pulls another arrow from his quiver. This one is jet-black instead of gold like the one that juts out of Terresa's back.

"Holy crap, did you just kill Terresa?"

"Not with that arrow." He looks down at Tobin as he tries to push Terresa off him. "Be careful, son. She's going to fall madly in love with whomever she sees first when she wakes up."

Tobin stops shoving Terresa and raises his hands as if he's afraid to touch her again.

"Now tell me," Jonathan says, nocking the black arrow into his bow and then aiming it in the direction of Haden and Rowan. "Which one of these bastards is trying to steal my favorite niece into the Underrealm?"

"Whoa," I say, raising my hands. "This isn't what it looks like."

"I know this Lord family, Daphne. I know what they do to girls like you." Jonathan looks at me, that fierce expression still on his face. He catches sight of the bident in my raised hand. Recognition fills his eyes. "Where did you get *that*?"

"Like I said, what's happening here isn't what it looks like."

He lowers his bow slightly. "Then you'd better start explaining, Daph."

But before I get the chance, I catch a swift movement out of the corner of my eye. I turn just as Rowan smashes a tree branch against the side of Haden's head.

chapter fifty-three

HADEN

Terresa's threatening Tobin had pulled my attention away from blasting Rowan, although I'd managed to keep him pinned down. But Daphne's uncle's revealing himself as the god of love and pointing a black arrow in my direction is downright distracting.

When I get hit, I know it's my own damn fault for loosening my grip on Rowan just long enough for him to grab a fallen tree branch and swing it at my face.

I turn my head a split second before impact, so it's not a knock-out blow, but it's still enough to throw me off him, disoriented.

Rowan lunges at me as I try to shake off the blow, and before I can stop him, he clasps his hands against the sides of my face, pressing his fingers into my throat and my temples.

No, no, no, I think, but it's too late. I try to push him away, but I feel my body going limp. *No,* I think once more as darkness fills my brain. The last thing I see before my eyes slide shut is Daphne screaming my name.

chapter fifty-four

DAPHNE

I watch as Haden's body goes limp, and I know what Rowan has done. He's put him in a black sleep. A trick the Underlords use for rendering their opponents unconscious. I'd seen Haden do it once to Garrick. The boy had been unconscious for hours.

Rowan hauls Haden's body up with him as he stands in front of the pulsing green light of the open gate. He wraps his arm around Haden's throat in a stranglehold, even though I know Haden can't fight back at the moment.

"What do you want?" I ask him, using every ounce of my strength to stay calm instead of screaming.

Jonathan raises his bow, aiming the black arrow at Rowan's bloodied face. "Answer that question wisely, boy. I never miss my mark."

"Your love arrows don't scare me, you overgrown man baby," he sneers at Jonathan.

"Oh, this isn't a love arrow," Jonathan says, with a threatening yet cautionary tone. "This arrow will make you lose your capacity to love or feel love ever again. It will suck your happiness from your soul like a hydra would suck the marrow from your bones. You won't be able to experience pleasure to the point that you will seek out pain, just to be able to feel something. In a week, you'll go mad; in two, you'll be begging me to kill you; in a month, you'll do it yourself."

Rowan stammers. I blink at Jonathan. Ethan was right—Cupid isn't a baby.

He's a *badass*.

"Like I said, I *never* miss my mark, and since my niece seems to have some misguided affection for your captive, I suggest letting him go and running home, you—what is it they say in the Underrealm? Oh yes. I suggest you go running home—you overgrown nursling."

"I am a Champion of the Underrealm," Rowan says.

"And I'm a *god*," Jonathan says. "Your point being?"

"I was sent here with the sole purpose of making sure the Cypher returned to the Underrealm. My father wants the Key of Hades, but," Rowan says, turning his attention on me, "he also wants you delivered to him. Unlike my brother, I refuse to fail in my quest. However, I know you're not going to hand the Key over to me, and I know I can't physically force you through this gate without causing our own deaths. But that rule only applies to non-Underlords, which means I *can* drag Haden through. And you know how happy my father is going to be to see him. I'm sure he's got his execution party already planned."

"Don't you dare—" I start to say.

"Bring the Key to the Underrealm palace before the equinox is over, and you might be able to save him." Rowan hurls a bolt of lightning in our direction, almost as if having a tantrum, and takes a step backward, pulling Haden with him into the light. The archway pulses, sending a nearly blinding green flash.

I hear Jonathan's black arrow fly before I see it. It sails toward the green light just as Rowan twists and ducks, using Haden as his human shield. With another pulse of light, they vanish completely, arrow and all.

"No!" I scream, running toward the gate.

But someone stops me. Hands grab at me, pulling me back. It's not just Jonathan but Tobin, too. "You can't just run through the gate under duress, Daphne. It could kill you."

I'm so frantic that I'm not sure which one of them even said it. But I know he's right. I think of Terresa's burned hand from touching the gate when she wasn't ready. "Tell me you missed your mark," I beg Jonathan. "Tell me."

"I don't know, honey," he says, holding me to his chest. "They crossed through before it struck. It depends on if the arrow went with them."

Tobin releases me and searches the ground in front of the gate, but he confirms only what I already fear. "No arrow."

I breathe deep, trying to keep from losing it. Just because the arrow went through, it doesn't mean that it struck Haden. But deep down, I fear that isn't true. I feel something building inside of me, an emotion I can't quite explain, but I feel as though I am about to be torn in half. A sob escapes my lips.

Had I finally realized my love for Haden only to have his ripped away from me? If I found him and told him how I feel, would my words fall on deaf ears?

"Tell me there's an antidote," I beg Jonathan. "Please tell me."

"Not exactly . . . ," he starts to say, but a rolling clap of thunder cuts him off as swirling clouds blot out the stars above us. Another near-deafening clap follows.

"Skylords," I say. "Terresa said there was a whole legion of Skylords waiting for her call."

"I'm beginning to really hate Skylords," Tobin mutters. I glance at him, but there's no time to ask him the truth about him and Terresa.

A bolt of lightning streaks from above. It crashes in the middle of the grove. I close my eyes against the light, and when I open them, a man is standing in front of us. Jonathan lets go of me. He draws another black arrow in his bow and aims it at Ethan's heart.

Electricity pulses in the air as Ethan raises his hands. "I am friend, not foe."

"Do you know this man?" Jonathan asks, his bow pulled taut.

"He's one of my teachers, but I wouldn't call him a friend, necessarily. He's a Skylord Prince."

"Prince?" Jonathan asks.

"You don't want to shoot me with that," Ethan says, taking a step toward us.

Jonathan adjusts his aim to compensate for Ethan's movement. "And why is that?"

"Firstly, because there's an army of Skylords headed this way, and I am one of the few people in this world who might be able to get them to stand down. Secondly, because you're injured, and I can see your arm trembling."

I look at Jonathan and see for the first time that his shoulder looks as though it has been badly burned. His arm shakes, and I can tell now he's having a hard time keeping his bow aloft. That bolt of lightning Rowan had thrown just before he stepped into the gate—it must have hit Jonathan. Is that why he let the arrow fly?

"And, thirdly, Eros," Ethan says, stepping even closer, "because I am your son."

"Whoa, what?" I ask.

"I told you my father was from the Metarealm," Ethan says. "My mother, a Sky Princess, fell for Eros, the embodiment of love itself—only to be punished greatly for it—and her lover driven into hiding by the wrath of the Sky King. I've spent the last five years searching for him in the mortal world, because I knew he was living as a human after having his godhood stripped."

Jonathan's bow lowers, as if he can't hold it up much longer.

"Are you okay?" I ask him, but what I mean is *does Ethan speak the truth?*

He winces with pain. "I was bluffing earlier when I told Rowan that I'm a god. I may still have a few of my arrows, but my wings have been clipped, so to speak." He drops his bow and falls to his knees, gripping his shoulder just under the seared wound. He looks up at the Skylord. "You're Psyche's son? You're our child?"

"Yes, Father."

Ethan kneels beside him, inspecting his wound. I am kind of reeling at this information. It was hard enough processing the fact that Jonathan is Cupid, but Ethan is his son? And Psyche is a Sky Princess? The myth always said that she was a mortal who was granted immortality later in life—but I couldn't exactly claim that any of the myths in my textbook had gotten the facts just right.

"So you're really Cupid?" Tobin asks.

Jonathan nods.

"Did you know my sister, Abbie—I mean CeCe—was part Skylord?"

"Your sister?" Jonathan says. "I suspected she was at least part Skylord, but she seemed to want to keep it a secret so I never asked, and I wasn't too keen on revealing my own identity. Ellis is a safe haven. Many people there have secrets we don't talk about, but it

293

was the first place in the world I found where I could hide in plain sight, and I didn't want to do anything to jeopardize that." He clasps a hand over mine. "But believe me, Daph, if I had thought that the Underlords were using Olympus Hills as a staging ground for finding Boons again, I would've never let Joe bring you here. I thought it was a coincidence . . . until I saw your friend."

"I'm not a Boon," I say, almost indignantly. "I'm the Cypher."

"The Cypher? Well, that explains the Key." Jonathan looks at Ethan. "How is she? Your mother?"

"She will be better when she learns that I have found you."

Thunder claps in the distance, so loud, it makes me jump.

"I'm sorry. I know you must have questions, and I have many myself," Ethan says, "but we will have to save reunions for later. Skylords loyal to Terresa's cause are headed this way, which means, Daphne, if you're taking the Key through the gate, you need to ready yourself now."

I blink at him. I have to admit I'd expected Ethan to demand I give the Key to him, like Rowan and Terresa before him, insisting his plan for it was the only way to go. "You mean you're going to let me take it to the Underrealm palace? Just like that? Aren't you afraid of the consequences of the war that might follow?"

"I will let you go if you promise me one thing: that you will kill the Keres before you come home. I would go with you, but I am needed here to stop the Skylord army."

"I can't do that on my own. I need someone who can throw lightning. I need a guide." I look over at Garrick, who stands in the trees. "I need you to come with me, Garrick."

He bows his head.

"You know I'll get lost in five seconds flat without your help. I need you. Haden needs you. Heck, the world needs you."

Garrick steps out of the shadows of the trees. "Count me in, then," he says.

"Really?"

"Yes, I thought about what you said earlier. I want the chance to destroy the monsters who ruined my life." He gulps hard, looking at the gate. "But *you're* sure that's what you really want? To go with me? You can't be hesitant about it when we pass through the gate. You really want this?"

"Yes, I want to go with you."

"I'll come, too," Jonathan says, but I can hear the strains of pain radiating from him.

"No," I say. "You need medical attention." I turn to Ethan. "You'll make sure he's okay?"

Ethan nods.

"And someone needs to get my mother out of Olympus Hills. If Skylords are coming, I want her as far away from here as possible. And Joe, too. He was supposed to be here, but I don't know what happened to him."

"I'll make sure they're okay," Jonathan says.

I smile sadly, but gratefully, at him.

"Take this." Jonathan pulls a bright red arrow from his quiver. "You asked if there was an antidote to the black arrow. For most, there isn't, but considering you are willing to do all this to save Haden, then I am guessing this may work."

"What does this one do?"

"My golden arrows elicit passion—a mad type of love that will eventually wear off. But this," he says of the red arrow, "holds a true love spell. It will work only on someone who has found true love, solidifying it forever. I pricked myself by accident with one just before meeting Psyche—and once we kissed,

I knew there would be no other person I would love than her."

"And it can counteract the black arrow?" I ask, hope trying to mend the tear in my heart.

"If your love for him is true and his love for you is the same. You must pierce him with this arrow to activate the spell, but you must kiss him to seal it. Otherwise, after a fortnight, the spell will fail and the black arrow's poison will take hold of him forever."

"You mean I need to cure him with true love's kiss?" I ask. It sounds too surreal to be true. "Like stuff that fairy tales are made of?"

"I'm Cupid, honey," he says, brushing his hand through my hair. "Who do you think invented fairy tales?"

I smile, realizing that I shouldn't have questioned him.

"This arrow is one of my most precious, and the last red arrow that I possess. I do not part with it lightly. Since my golden bow—*my* Kronolithe was stripped from me—these arrows are the only remnants of my power." I look at the bow he'd dropped and realize it's one of the PE department's, which had been used as set dressing for the play. "When the last of the other arrows is gone, I will become fully mortal and die. So are you sure, Daphne, that this Underlord is worth it? I would hate to waste this arrow on him."

I nod. "Yes," I say. "He's most definitely worth it."

More thunder rumbles in the sky, growing closer still.

"You must hurry," Ethan says, clearly agitated over how much time we've spent.

Before he hands it to me, Jonathan whispers the word *mikro* to the arrow and it shrinks down so it fits in the palm of his hand. I gape, realizing that was why I'd never seen him carrying around a giant quiver of arrows before. "Now it's pocket-sized," he says, giving it to me.

I thank him for the precious gift and tuck it into the pocket of my dress for safekeeping. I stand and approach the gate as the smell of rain hangs in the air.

"Are you ready?" Ethan asks.

I steel myself. I am as ready as I'll ever be.

"Wait," Tobin says. "I know I don't have any powers or weapons or anything, but I want to come with you."

I start to shake my head. For all I know, he's the one who brought Terresa here.

"Please, Daph. I'm part of this team. I'm your friend. I said I'd help you and Haden back in Ellis Fields, when we all made our pact to follow him into the dark. Well, it's dark now, Daph. Real dark, and I'm not letting you go into it without me." The sound coming off him is so earnest, I can't help but believe him.

"Okay," I say as rain starts to fall.

I hold my hand out to Tobin, and he clings to it. Garrick follows at our heels. With the Key in hand and without a second's hesitation, I step into the green light of the gate with my two companions. With a pulse of light, the ground is ripped out from under my feet, and my whole entire world disappears.

chapter fifty-five

HADEN

I feel as though I am drowning in darkness, blackness pulling me under the surface of consciousness. I can't move. I have no control. A sharp pain radiates through my body, but I don't know from what or even where the pain is located. My arm? My chest? Is the pain even real? My mind kicks against the black, like it's trying to come up for air.

I think I hear a shout. Rowan? Or perhaps it was a cry. I am jostled. More pain shoots through me. I fight to open my eyes. More shouts.

I register a rocking sensation, as if I am on a boat.

The darkness pulls me under again.

chapter fifty-six

DAPHNE

When the pulling sensation stops, I almost lose my grip on the Key as I try to stop myself from toppling forward. Garrick, Tobin, and I have left the grove and are now standing in the middle of a stone archway pulsating with that same green light, at the end of a long ravine. Tobin stumbles next to me, clutching his stomach. A wave of nausea washes over me. Whatever form of transportation the gate uses, it causes motion sickness worse than any roller-coaster ride. I take a few lumbering steps away from the archway and wince at the sound of Tobin vomiting. I suck in a few deep breaths through my teeth, desperately trying to hold on to what lunch I was able to down before the play. Who knows when we will be eating again?

Eating. A thought hits me as I recall a part of Joe's play in which Orpheus is warned not to eat anything in the underworld or he will suffer the same fate as Persephone's—he'll be bound to the underworld for all eternity.

"Is it true that mortals can't eat here?" I ask Garrick. "Or does that only apply to Boons?"

He shrugs. "I don't know. I'm just a lowly servant, remember?"

"Just in case, don't eat anything while we're here," I warn

Tobin. "Not if you don't want to have to live down here for the rest of your life."

"Noted," he says. "But I don't want to even think about food right now."

He dry heaves beside the gate.

After I steady my stomach, my first act is to search for signs of Haden and Rowan. . . . The black arrow. The ground is stone, as if the ravine had been cut out of a mountain of rock, and there are no footprints. They were only a few minutes ahead of us, but as far as I can tell, there are no signs that they were even here.

I don't see any signs of the arrow at first, until I notice a small black, splintered fragment in the dust. I am careful not to touch it as I crouch down to inspect it. My heart throbs against my chest as I realize that it looks like the broken end of an obsidian arrowhead. And it appears as though it's smeared with blood.

A terrible image of Haden with a jet-black arrow protruding from his chest flashes through my mind. It wouldn't kill him, only make him dead inside.

That thought makes me sicker than the journey through the gate.

Garrick calls for my attention. He turns to the gate, the light casting a strange green pall on his face. "Give me the Key," he says, holding out his hand for the bident.

"Why?" I ask, feeling particularly possessive of it.

"We should lock the gate. If any Skylords get past Ethan, we need to make sure they can't get through the gate. It'll open up on its own when the equinox starts in a few hours, or at dawn actually, but in the meantime, we can slow them down."

"Good thinking," I say, but I don't hand over the Key to Garrick. I don't plan on handing it over to anyone until I see Haden's face again. Until I know he's been granted safety. I thrust the Key into the center of the pulsing green light, copying what I'd watched Terresa do, and twist the bident until the light starts to fade.

Stepping away from the gate, I look around, taking in the desolate ravine that is our surroundings. "Shouldn't there be guards?"

"Yes, there should be," Garrick says. "The gate only opens on its own twice a year, but there's usually a few guards stationed here just in case. And this close to the equinox, there should be more. Perhaps they're helping Rowan take Haden to the palace."

"I half expected Rowan to be waiting here for us," I admit. "Why wait for us to bring the Key to the throne room when he could attack us as soon as we were through the gate?"

"Maybe he was worried your god of an uncle was coming with you," Tobin says.

I look up at the sheer walls of rock that surround us on three sides. The only option for us is to move forward. "How far are we from the palace?"

"By foot," Garrick says, pressing forward, "an eternity."

"An eternity?" Tobin asks, attempting to follow. He stumbles again, and I steady him. The trip through the gate must have taken even more out of him than me. He leans his weight into my side, wrapping his arm around my back. I use the bident like a walking stick to help propel the both of us forward.

"As in, you'd never make it," Garrick calls back to us, his pace too quick for Tobin and me to keep up. "Between here and the palace are countless miles of the Wastelands. We venture through there, and we'll get torn to pieces by the shades—the souls of the dead—and eaten for breakfast."

"Then how do you propose we get there?" I ask.

Garrick stops at the end of the ravine. It takes Tobin and me a few seconds to catch up with him. The smooth-packed stone under our feet is now covered in sand. "We go by river," he says, pointing down the sandy bank in front of us to a snaking, turbulent river. "Acheron: the river of woe."

"I don't know how I feel about swimming in a river by that name," Tobin mumbles beside me.

"Beats being eaten alive by the dead," I say.

"We aren't swimming," Garrick says, continuing on toward what appears to be a boat dock on the riverbank. Tobin and I follow after him again. "We'll need to convince Charon, the river man, to take us by boat. Neither of you happen to have any money, do you? He has this thing about being paid."

I remember now that was another thing Dax was supposed to bring with him. Where he and Joe and even Brim have ended up instead of the grove fills me with worry.

"No room for a wallet in my toga," Tobin says, referring to the costume he's still wearing from the play. It strikes me as suddenly funny that Tobin and I are dressed in ancient Greek–style garb while Garrick is the one wearing black jeans and a black long-sleeved T-shirt during our venture through the underworld. At least Tobin is still wearing his fedora. That one little normalcy gives me comfort in this unfamiliar place.

My hand goes to the hidden pocket in my dress. The only two things I have in my possession, besides the Key, are Jonathan's arrow and Joe's sobriety coin. And there is no way that I am going to use Haden's antidote to barter for a boat ride. "I have Joe's sobriety coin," I say, taking it from my pocket. "It doesn't have any monetary value, but it resembles a bronze coin."

Garrick takes a look at it in my outstretched hand. "Charon is as blind as a bat; that'll probably do."

"Wait, a blind guy is going to steer our boat?" Tobin asks.

Garrick doesn't answer. He picks up his pace, practically running down the beach. He's too fast for me to keep up with while supporting Tobin. I look down at the coin. I don't want to part with it, knowing what it means to Joe—to me—but, at the same time, I know he would want me to use it if it would help. "I just wish I knew why Joe didn't make it to the grove," I say softly to Tobin. "I hope he's okay."

Tobin stops leaning on me and starts walking slowly on his own beside me. "About Joe . . . ," he says, a regretful tone coming off him. Like he doesn't *want* to say what's on his mind. "I saw him right after the play. . . ."

"Was he okay?" I ask.

"Yeah. I mean, no." Tobin takes a deep breath. "It's just that I think he was drunk. He could barely put one foot in front of the other. That's why he didn't come."

I squeeze the coin in my hand and shake my head. "That can't be. . . ."

But whatever else I am about to say gets drowned out by a shout from Garrick. The sound of it is so urgent that we respond by jogging down the beach. I pull ahead of Tobin and find Garrick huddled over what appears at first to be a pile of gray rags, but then I realize it's an old man dressed in tattered robes, curled in a fetal ball.

"You can keep your coin," Garrick says. "Charon's dead, and his boat is gone."

"You mean we're stranded?" Tobin asks as he appears behind us.

"As in, we're dead," Garrick says. "It's only a matter of minutes before the shades catch our scent."

chapter fifty-seven

TOBIN

As it turns out, the old boatman isn't dead but merely knocked out (unlike Garrick, Daphne bothered to check his pulse), but that still doesn't change the fact that we're stranded. The old guy isn't going to be waking anytime soon, based on how many times we jostle him, and there is no sign of his boat.

"Rowan must have commandeered it," Garrick says, pointing at several sets of erratic footprints in the wet sand on the river-bank. "It looks like there was some sort of altercation."

"That looks like too many footprints to be just Rowan," Daphne says.

"Perhaps the guards were with him."

"Then why would there have been a fight . . . ?" I start to ask, but then I picture Haden trying to escape. Maybe he wasn't as far under the black sleep as we had thought. "It doesn't make sense that Rowan would leave us stranded, either."

"Seriously," Daphne says. "Doesn't he *want* us to bring him the Key?"

"Maybe he's hoping the shades will kill us for him and then he can come back for the Key later—" Garrick swings around, look-ing in the direction of the horizon behind us. "*Kopros.* They're coming," he whispers, as if he hears something we don't.

I listen hard and catch a sound in the distance that reminds me of a moaning wind.

"Shades," Garrick says. "They've caught our scent faster than I thought. Do you have to smell so rank, Tobin?"

"I'm sorry; I sweat when I'm onstage . . . and, you know, about to be eaten by zombies."

A small, wispy bolt of lightning crackles up in Garrick's hand. It's not nearly as impressive as the lightning I've seen Haden throw. "Get behind me," he says, sounding braver than I have ever given him credit for.

"Wait," Daphne says. "Look, across the river. I think that's a boat!"

I follow her pointing gesture, straining my eyes to see what she's so excited about. At first, I don't see anything, but then I make out what appears to be the underside of a small, capsized boat. It looks like it'd been swept across the river from the dock and crashed into a small cove on the other side. It bobs in the water as the current pushes it against the rocks over and over again.

"We'll never make it!" Garrick says as the ethereal moaning grows closer. Between the sound of the encroaching shades and the rushing water, we have to shout everything we say just to be heard.

"Maybe we can bring it to us." Daphne runs out to the edge of the dock . . . and starts singing. For a moment, I think she may have lost her marbles, but then I watch as she raises her hands toward the capsized boat—and it bobs higher in the water than it had before. She increases her volume (really belting now), and the boat lifts up out of the water. Daphne twists her hands, and the boat responds by turning itself over so it's right side up. She beckons the boat to come to her. The vessel, slightly bigger than the two-man sailboats that many of the lakeside residents of Olympus Hills own, skids and skips across the water until it thumps into the front of the dock. Daphne flattens herself on the dock, grabbing the nose of the boat before it can be swept away again.

I stand, staring at Daphne in awe. She'd told us about this newfound power, but I hadn't seen more than her floating-chair demonstration of it until now. "That. Was. Awesome."

"The shades are getting closer," Garrick says. "And that boat has no sail." He points to where the mast of the small boat has been broken off. "And there are no oars. It's useless."

"Maybe we can just sit in it and float?" I yell.

"Rivers run backward in the Underrealm," Garrick says. "Look at the current: it runs in the opposite direction of where we need to go."

"I just lifted a boat across the water with my voice," Daphne calls. "I think I can sail this thing. Now hurry and get Charon into the boat before my arms fall off."

I grab the unconscious man, grateful that he's even smaller than I am, drag him to the end of the dock, and heft him into the boat. Then I grab the end of the dock and hold on while Daphne climbs in with the Key and settles herself against the broken stump of the mast.

The moaning sound turns to wails, and I see a line of shadowy figures coming over the ridge. I don't know if it's just my imagination, but it appears they have no faces save their gaping mouths.

"Come on!" I shout to Garrick.

He flings his bolt of lightning at one of the shades that advances ahead of the others with terrifying swiftness. The bolt misses, and Garrick stumbles backward, almost falling.

"Garrick!" Daphne shouts.

He rights himself and runs for the boat, the shade barreling after him. Garrick leaps from the dock, and as his feet touch down in the boat, I let go of the dock. The faceless shade shrieks and tries to take a swipe at me. The boat, caught in the current, carries us away from it just in time.

"I hope those things can't swim!" Daphne shouts.

I sigh with relief when it doesn't follow, only to have it drowned out by Garrick's shout: "We're headed for the rocks again!" Sure enough, the boat is careening toward the cove where Daphne had found it.

"I'm working on it!" Daphne shouts, before launching into song. Her voice warbles at first, but then gains strength as if she is fighting against the current. With the Key still clenched in one of her fists, she pushes her hands and arms out in front of her and then sweeps them back toward her chest in a fluid movement that almost reminds me of a mix between hula dancing and Tai Chi.

I want to ask what she's doing but realize that would break her concentration. Then I remember one of the lines from Joe's play about how Orpheus's voice was so powerful, he could even command rivers to change their courses. The boat lurches away from the incoming rocks, and I stare over the side of the boat, realizing that Daphne is pulling the water around the boat in a different direction from the rest. She's changing the current.

We've been sailing for what feels like an hour but could be longer, for all I can tell. There's no sun here, even though the sky (or whatever it is above us) is lit up by some sort of ghastly, dim light. It had been evening when we left Olympus Hills, but the time of day seems indeterminate here. I can tell Daphne's strength is waning. Her voice is beginning to sound hoarse, and the movement of her arms is much slower. The river is calmer here, wider, and without any rapids. I see what I assume is a tree branch drifting in the water and hope to hell—or, um, Hades—that it is as I reach for it over the side of the boat. I snatch it up and toss it to Garrick, and pick up another branch that I had collected earlier.

"Take a break," I call to Daphne. "Garrick and I can row for a while."

Garrick, who has been doing nothing while I manned the rudder through the rough patches, grumbles at this, so I throw him a cross look. Daphne drops her arms and sinks to the floorboards beside me, leaning her head against the mast, and sets the Key down beside her.

I let her rest while I dip my branch into the water like an oar. I hear a small sniffle, and I watch as she tries to blink away tears from her eyes before anyone sees. I may not share her ability to discern others' emotions through tones and all that, but it's obvious she's overwhelmed, exhausted, and worried about Haden. I kick myself for trying to tell her about Joe, but an even heavier weight pulls on me.

I need to confess.

"Daphne," I say softly. "I need to tell you something. . . ."

She opens her eyes, gives a small sigh, but doesn't look at me. Just watches the river straight ahead.

"Terresa did come to me. She wanted me to help her get the Key in exchange for help finding my sister. She wanted to use it to exterminate the Underlords. I'm not going to lie; I thought about helping her, briefly. I was tempted. . . . But I couldn't do it. Not when I thought about other people's sisters and daughters being down here. I couldn't let Terresa hurt them."

"What about the notes?" she asks, still not looking at me.

"There were no *notes*. Only one . . ."

She rocks her head so she's staring in the opposite direction from me now.

"I told Teresa that I was going to help her but then gave her a note with the wrong information. I told her the Key was hidden at Old Sutton Mill—the place where I used to play with Abbie. I said we were going to go for it after the play when we were supposed to be at a cast party. I swear, everything I told her was a lie. I was trying to draw her away from the grove, not lead her to it."

Daphne is quiet for a few moments.

"If that was really the case, then why didn't you just tell us beforehand?"

"Because you would have tried to stop me. . . . I was going to take her to the mill myself just to make sure she was as far away from the grove as possible."

"But, Tobin," she says. "Terresa might have killed you when she found out you were tricking her."

"I know," I say under my breath. In my head, I had convinced myself that I would be able to talk myself out of danger. That I could convince Teresa that we had merely been too late to steal the Key before the others went through the gate, or that I could run away while she was distracted by searching the mill, but I had also known that there was a possibility I would fail. It might seem crazy, but that possibility had seemed worth it to make sure all the other girls like Abbie in the Underrealm would be safe from Terresa's wrath.

Even if I didn't go to the mill with her, she still would have tried to hurt me. As evidenced by the throbbing burn from the electrified knife she'd held to my throat.

I paddle the boat, propelling us around a bend in the river. Daphne turns toward me now. "But how did Terresa know, then, before anyone else? It was like she was hiding in the grove, just waiting for me to unlock Orpheus's tree."

"Maybe someone else tipped her off as to our true plan. She was gone before things even went wrong with curtain call . . . like she already knew."

"Dax?" she asks. "He wasn't in the grove like he was supposed to be. Do you think he . . . ?" She lets the thought drop off as if it's too hard for her to contemplate.

"I don't know. . . ."

"*Kopros!*" Garrick shouts. He stands up so suddenly that it rocks the boat in his direction. He almost falls out, but Daphne grabs his ankle, pulling him back down. "Look!"

As we come fully around the bend, I see it in front of us: a whirlpool. The current grabs the boat, and we start to spin. Daphne tries to stand, in order to command the water, but we're turning too fast and she has to cling to the broken mast. I try rowing against the current with my branch, but it's swept right out of my hands. I can barely hear Daphne's singing over the raging water, but she's trying her best to propel us away from danger.

"Do something!" Garrick shouts as the boat goes careening toward an outcropping of rocks. He thrusts his branch against one of the rocks, but the push sends us back into the spin. The whirlpool has us now, water sloshing into the boat like a giant wet hand, trying to pull us under. I didn't even know rivers could have whirlpools (apparently they can in the underworld), but this one seems almost as if it were alive.

Just as the boat seems to be yanked out from under us, I hear Daphne's voice ring out with the force of a banshee's: "Let us go!"

The water pulling us under suddenly snaps down and then up, tossing the boat, and us, at the shore. I try to cling to the edge of the boat, but I topple out, hitting the water. I claw desperately around me, bobbing up and down, swallowing water, as I hear the boat crack against the shore. My hands find purchase on a plank of wood, and I cling to it as the current sweeps me away from the broken boat on the beach.

chapter fifty-eight

HADEN

I awaken on the deck of a large ship and know from the smell of the river that I am in the Underrealm. My head throbs, and the darkness still pulls at me, but I refuse to let it take me again. Every muscle in my body aches. A searing pain radiates down my arm from my tricep. I try to sit up but find that I have been bound. My legs are tied together, my costume toga has been stripped off my shoulders, and my arms are crossed over my chest like a corpse, with my hands bound flat against my bare skin—the standard procedure for keeping a captive Underlord subdued. I cannot use my lightning power without blasting myself in the chest.

I roll on my side toward the sound of footsteps. My vision is blurry, but I recognize the leather sandals that belong to the men who surround me—they are the garb of the Court's personal guard. There is some sort of ruckus, and another man is being pushed toward me. I had assumed Rowan was my captor and these guards his aides, until the guards thrust the man down at my feet. His legs are free, but his arms have been bound in a similar manner as mine. I cannot make out his face with my unfocused eyes, but I recognize his voice when he snarls at the guards: "This is treason!"

Rowan? Rowan is being treated as a captive?

"Rebind his legs," one of the men commands. "Lord Lex will not pay if either of them escapes."

A soldier stoops over Rowan with a leather cord, ready to follow the order.

"I am the son of the king," Rowan says. "Unhand me now, or my father will have your heads!"

"Whether your father is still the king is yet to be determined," the guard says, and he wraps the leather cord around Rowan's ankles while two other guards hold him.

"What do you mean? Where's my father? Where are you taking us?" he shouts as he thrashes against their hold.

"Don't worry, we're taking you to your father," the voice of their commander says. "Both you and your brother will stand in the judgment of the Court alongside him."

"Lex?" Rowan asks. "He's done it? He's staged his coup? And you treasonous harpies went along with it?"

"We serve at the pleasure of the Court," the commander says.

The man binding Rowan's legs laughs. "And the *payment.*"

Rowan spits in the man's face and receives a swift cuff to the cheek as retribution. Rowan's head snaps back, and he crumples to the boat deck next to me. My eyes gain some focus, and I see that his lip is cracked and he bears the marks of a beating. He must have tried to get away at some point.

"It's your failure that brought this upon your heads," says the commander. "Our orders were clear: if you returned through the gate *without* the Cypher or the Key, your father's claim to the throne no longer stands. The Court will dole out the proper punishment."

I start to gather what has happened now. Rowan must have

dragged me through the gate when I was unconscious, but without the aid of a communication talisman, he'd gone in blind to the coup. This troop of Lex's personal cronies must have been waiting to ambush him. I realize now the fallacy in my original plan, not accounting for the entire battalion of soldiers waiting on the other side, rather than only a handful of guards. We would have walked right into their hands.

"So you're taking us to trial?" Rowan asks the commander.

"We're taking you to your execution."

A guffaw of laughter ripples through the throng of soldiers as they turn away to their other duties. Rowan catches me staring at him. "This isn't over," he snarls at me. "Your failures will not be put on me."

I glare at him, rather than respond. I wish only that my hands were free so I could wrap them around his throat. Any restraint I'd felt in the grove is gone. I want to kill him. If I get my hands on him, I won't be doling out mercy.

I *will* kill him if it's the last thing I do.

My arm throbs with searing pain, and a thought engulfs me with rage: *everything has been taken from me . . . and I have nothing left to lose.*

"She's coming," Rowan whispers to me.

"What?" I ask, my voice sounding slurred.

"Daphne will bring the Key to the throne room before the equinox is over. I told her to do so in order to spare your life."

"You did what?"

"I told you I'd find a way to trick her into getting the Key for me. She'll bring it right to the throne room for me. Father and I will get out of this. We'll prove to the Court that his rule still stands." I have never loved my brother, but, in this moment, I have

314

never hated him more. Like it's the only emotion I'm capable of feeling anymore.

I won't just kill him; I will make him suffer first. He will not win.

Beyond the reedy scent of the river, I catch the floral aroma of pomegranate trees in bloom on the breeze. We are nearing the palace grounds. We will be face-to-face with our fates soon. I can feel the golden thread of my new destiny, the one I'd chosen for myself, slipping through my fingers.

"She'll come," Rowan says again, as if trying to reassure himself. This assertion seems completely irrational to me.

"How do you know that she will come for me?"

My arm throbs as if fire is ripping through it. Under the binding, I notice strange black markings radiating from a cut in my arm, as if black ink were spreading through my veins.

Rowan smirks like he knows something that I don't. "Because I saw the way she looked at you during the play. She loves you, Haden."

I have no reaction to his words. I feel as though I should, but I don't. I try to think back on the play, try to remember Daphne's face when we were onstage together. There had been one moment when I had been singing that she had seemed to look at me as if she was really seeing me for the first time.

Could that have been a look of love?

And if it was, why doesn't it seem to matter?

Why don't I care?

chapter fifty-nine

DAPHNE

"Happy birthday, Daphne!" My mother's voice rings out from behind me. The darkness blocking my sight disappears as she pulls her hands away from my eyes. "We love you, little sprout."

A cake, with teal green frosting, pink rosettes, and sixteen candles, sits in front of me at our kitchen table.

"I decorated it myself," Jonathan says, scooting next to me in his chair. "What do you think?"

"I love it," I say. "It's my favorite color."

"It's vanilla with buttercream frosting," Jonathan says. "I used that recipe from the Food Network I've been dying to try. It is completely *divine.*"

"Yes, it's delicious," Mom says, beaming at me. "You must try it."

She offers me a plate with a large slice of cake on it, even though I don't remember anyone cutting into it yet.

"But I didn't blow out the candles," I say, and when I look at the table, the rest of the cake isn't there. Just the slice that sits on my plate.

"Here, drink this with it," someone says, offering me a glass of milk.

"CeCe?" I say. I didn't know she was in the room until that moment.

"Uh, who else would I be?" she says, with a smile. Her hair springs out from her head like red coils, and she's wearing her favorite BREAKFAST AT TIFFANY'S shirt. "Try the milk."

I look at the glass she's set in front of me. The liquid in it resembles milky water more than it does actual milk. I don't want to drink it.

"Try the cake," Jonathan says.

Unlike the odd milk, the cake looks delicious. I pick up my fork, ready to dig in, but something stops me.

"Go ahead," the others urge. "Eat it."

Eat. Eating. Something about not eating. Something nags at the back of my mind, and the thought that I shouldn't eat the cake sticks with me.

I put down my fork. "Can I open my presents first?" I ask.

Mom and Jonathan exchange a look. Like something worries them. "Okay," Mom finally says. "You only turn sixteen once, and the birthday girl gets what she wants."

I remember the cake again—those sixteen candles.

"Strange, I could have sworn I was seventeen," I say out loud.

Another worried look passes between all three of them.

"Here, open mine first!" CeCe says, and I realize I am holding a small wrapped package. How did that get there?

"Open, open, open," the three of them chant when I hesitate.

"Isn't it beautiful?" CeCe says with her beaming smile.

I look down, and the box is already open. A delicate necklace bearing my name sits on the white fluff in the box.

"Isn't it beautiful?" she asks again. "I saw it and had to get it for you!"

"Yes," I say. "This is my favorite necklace."

Is my favorite? "Do I already own this . . . ?"

"Now eat your cake," my mother says, and the plate with the cake is in my hands again.

"Drink your milk," Jonathan says, holding the glass out to me.

There's a reason I'm not supposed to eat anything. . . .

I drop the plate on the table and stand up. "Something is wrong," I say, but I can't quite put my finger on it. Mom and Jonathan and CeCe crowd around me, smiling so brightly. I need air. "I need to go," I say, trying to find the door. It strikes me that there isn't one.

"Where would you go?" Mom asks. "Everyone you love is right here."

"Now eat your cake," Jonathan says, trying to make me take the plate again.

I thrust my hands into the pockets of my jeans. Something cold and metal touches my hand. I wrap my fingers around what feels like a coin. I pull it from my pocket. It's large and bronze with the number 1 engraved in the middle with a triangle around it. An inscription at the top says, TO THINE OWN SELF BE TRUE.

Be true. Truth.

"This isn't real," I say. "None of this is real."

Mom shakes her head. "What could be more real than being with the ones you love?"

But that's what's wrong with this situation. Not everyone I love *is* here.

"What about Joe?" I ask, holding out the coin. Something tells me this belongs to him. That he had given it to me. That it means something.

"Joe? We haven't seen him in years," Mom says.

But I know that isn't true. "I just saw him. . . ."

"Come sit, eat, drink your milk, be with your loved ones."

I shake my head. There's someone else missing. Someone else I *love* . . .

"Haden," I say, casting about the room. "Where's Haden?"

There is a reason he's missing. . . . There is something I need to do. I need to think. I need to remember. . . .

"Drink your milk, and it'll all be better," CeCe says, holding it out to me.

"I don't want the milk!" I swing my arm out, knocking the glass from her hands. It hits the ground and shatters, leaving a puddle that is nothing but water.

The others gape at me like I've lost my mind. Maybe I have.

"Where am I?" I whisper.

"You're in paradise, honey," Jonathan says. "Your own personal heaven."

I shake my head. That isn't true. Nothing here is right. This can't be my own personal heaven, because if it were, Haden would be here with me.

A door appears behind CeCe.

"Stay here," my mother says, a new glass of milky water in her hand. "If you drink the water of Lethe, then you will forget whatever pains you. You can stay here in this moment and be happy forever."

The water of Lethe—from the river of forgetfulness?

How do I know that?

"No," I say. "There's something I have to do."

The door in front of me opens, light flooding in from behind it.

Before they can stop me, I bolt through the opening.

I sit upright and realize that I have been lying on a slab of white stone—like an altar. I am cold and damp and shaking.

"Our patient is awake," someone says.

Three women in veils rush to my side.

"Where am I?" I ask.

"Elysium," one of the women answers, but I cannot tell which one, because their faces are covered. But by the sound of her voice and their hunched shoulders, I can tell that the women are very old.

"Elysium?" So that is what Jonathan had meant when he said I was in paradise. This is where the souls of the honored go when they die. The ancient Greek version of heaven . . .

The memory of the boat wreck comes back to me. I'd hit the rocks on the shore. "Am I dead?" I ask.

The three women shake their heads in unison. "Though you nearly were."

"What about my friends? Are they here, too?"

They shake their heads again.

And the Key? I nearly shriek, realizing it is gone.

"Did I have anything with me?" Or perhaps it is still with the boat? Or Garrick or Tobin has it?

"We found you washed up on our shore, alone. The Oracle bid us to bring you to her healing chamber. You were so far gone, we thought we would ease you into death with one of your fondest memories. Let you stay there if you so chose . . ."

"But you're a willful one," another of the women says. "It seems we will not be cutting your thread so soon."

My thread?

"It seems you had something more important to do than

dying," the second one says. "I guess we had better let you get to it."

"Yes," I say, pushing myself off the altar. My arm is bandaged and my muscles ache, but other than that, I feel fine. I don't know if the three have overstated my closeness to death or if they've worked some sort of magic on me. Whatever the case, I am grateful to them for pulling me from the river. "Thank you," I say.

I take a couple of steps and then realize that I have no idea where I am going. "Can any of you tell me the way to the Underrealm palace?"

"We like you," one of the old women says. "You have spirit. Because of this, we will send you with a guide. She will take you to the adamantine gate but can go no farther than that."

Another veiled woman, much younger, based on the way she moves, steps forward from a corridor, holding a lantern aloft. She doesn't say anything but bids me forward with her hand. She takes me through a series of winding hallways until we find a door. When we pass through it, I find myself standing on the bank of the river again. The wreckage of our boat lies in front of me.

"I sensed you would want to come here first," she says quietly.

I scramble to what is left of the boat, climbing over broken timbers and floorboards, searching for any sign of my companions or the Key. Neither Tobin nor Garrick are here, and even Charon's unconscious body is gone. For all I know, the Key has been washed away with them. The thought of losing my friends tries to pull me under, but I steel myself against a wave of grief. I can't let myself believe it's true.

"Do you still wish to move forward?" the veiled young woman asks.

I nod. Even if I don't have the Key anymore, even if our escape plan is all but ruined, even if we have little chance of surviving now—or maybe because of it—I need to bring the antidote arrow to Haden so he will know how much I love him before it's too late.

After we leave the shipwreck, I follow the woman along the shore. She moves quickly, as if floating, and at times all I can see is her lantern ahead of me. The ghostly sky has dimmed considerably, and I realize it is night here. My ears are pricked, listening for the moaning of the shades. They found us so quickly before, I don't know why they don't come for us now.

"We are on the shores of Elysium," the woman says as she stops to wait for me to catch up with her. "The shades cannot venture here. However"—she holds her lantern aloft, lighting up a great metal gate in the near distance. They remind me of what the "pearly gates" are supposed to look like, only totally obsidian black and topped with razor-sharp-looking spikes—"since you are not traveling by boat, you will have to go a less desirable route. It is faster, but beyond this gate are many dangers. Follow the path, and it will take you to a back-door entrance to the palace. But whatever happens, do not stray from the path or you may find yourself in the Pits, where the deadliest and most vile creatures of the Underrealm lie."

I take in a deep breath. "Got it. Don't get lost. . . . Are you sure you can't come with me?"

"I am a creature of light, and therefore can't cross the black gate," she says, stepping closer to me. She lifts her veil, and clasps her hand over my trembling one. "May the gods give you speed in your quest, whatever it be. I feel it is a righteous one."

I meet her eyes under the light of her lantern. They're jade green like Haden's, and I realize that I've seen her face before. In photo albums at home and in a picture that was on the wall in the Crossroads club back in Vegas.

"Kayla?" I ask. "Are you Kayla Reed?"

Haden's mother.

She blinks at me. "I may have been," she says. "But I do not recall anything of my former life. When I died, I was chosen to serve the Oracle. That is all I know."

I remember the glass of milky water that had been offered to me in my dream. I'd refused it, knowing it was from the river of forgetfulness. At the time, I couldn't place how I knew that, but now I remember that it was from a scene in Joe's play. Eurydice had refused the water even though it would make her forget her pain—make her forget her former life.

My heart swells with the thought of being able to tell Haden that his beloved mother isn't a shade. I can only hope he's still himself enough to care.

"Godspeed," Kayla whispers. She lets go of my hand and disappears, leaving me alone in front of the towering adamantine (aka impenetrable) gate. There are no handles or latches as far up as I can see.

Joe had once told me that he'd written the play for me. That he had intended it to be his covert way of teaching me about the perils of the underworld. So far, I'd used what I'd gleaned from the play to steer the boat, remember to refuse food, and to avoid having my memory wiped by the water of Lethe. I look up at the looming gate and remember in the story that Orpheus had played his lyre for the gate (or in the case of Joe's rock opera, it had been Tobin with his guitar), and the gate had been so moved by the beauty of his song that it had swung open on its own. I don't have a guitar, or a lyre for that matter, but I do have a song. I stand in front of the gate and direct my voice at it, imploring it to open.

I sing the words from the scroll's song, louder and louder, raising my volume until finally I hear the screech of metal against the stone path underneath, and the gate opens just wide enough for me to squeeze through.

I cross onto the path ahead of me in the darkness and find myself wishing that I'd thought to ask Kayla to leave me her light.

Sticking to the path, I stare at my feet as I go, with my arms stretched out in front of me in the darkness. Curtains of thick mist surround the path on both sides. I walk slowly for what feels like miles, wishing I could see more than a foot in front of my face. I have no idea if I am getting closer to the palace or possibly traveling in the completely wrong direction.

I am so startled when I hear voices up ahead of me, I practically jump. It sounds like a group of soldiers, from the accompanying sounds of marching feet. I am so panicked that my only thought is to hide—and take refuge in the mist. I step off the path, just one yard's length, and crouch in the mist until the voices pass.

Then a thought occurs to me—if I need to get to the palace, why not reveal myself to the soldiers and demand that they ... um ... take me to their leader?

I make a move to rejoin the path, and then suddenly realize that I don't know if the path is to my left or right. Is it in front of me or behind me? I try all directions, taking one large step like I'd had when I stepped off the path, but I don't find it.

Had I traveled much farther off it than I had thought?

I try shouting, calling out to the soldiers, but it is almost as if the mist drowns out my voice. I spin around, frantic, realizing that I have completely lost my way.

I stand still for a moment, breathing deep to stave off panic, and try to collect my bearings.

Convincing myself that I am certain I must have come from the right, I walk a good few paces in that direction. Only it isn't the path that I find but a door.

Was this the back door to the palace that Kayla had told me about? I can't make anything out in the mist, and without any other options, I do the only thing I can think of—I open it.

Through the doorway, the mist is gone, and in front of me is a long staircase that spirals downward. Oily torches line the walls, which remind me of a cavern. I follow their light down the stairs, descending for what feels like several minutes.

I am almost to the bottom, my legs aching, when I start to regret my decision, realizing that *down* is not the direction that I want to travel in the underworld. I start to turn, ready to run back up the stairs, but some sort of small creature skitters under my foot.

I trip, losing my balance completely, and tumble down the remainder of the stairs. I am too stunned to move for a moment. My arm aches under my bandage, and I wonder if I've broken something . . . possibly again. Cradling my arm against my chest, I manage to get to my knees. I am about to attempt to stand when I sense movement close by. Like a shadow shifting in the light of the torches.

Shadow? My heart slams against my rib cage as I look up and see a Keres looming only a few feet in front of me. I have lost my way, as Kayla warned, and found myself in the Pits.

The Keres sees me. I know it does. It stops midair, a floating shadow, and puffs itself out like a bird of prey, preparing for an attack. I stand and back away just as the Keres swoops forward—and then it stops dead only inches from my face. I am so shocked, I find myself paralyzed, breathing right into what I would consider the Keres's face, if it were corporeal. The shadow writhes, screeching and wailing, like a toddler having a tantrum, but it doesn't get any closer. Like some sort of invisible barrier is preventing it.

I take another step back, putting more distance between me and the Keres, which now appears to be trying to ram the barrier. Its fit must have caught the attention of a few of its fellow kind, because three more Keres approach the barrier. I am about to run for the stairs when the strangest noise catches my ear. It sounds like a voice calling out. It sounds like a person's voice, but it speaks some sort of screeching, sharp dialect that I don't understand. The four Keres facing the barrier turn away from me, and as if heeding the call, they float away, leaving me behind.

The voice goes on in that strange language, and I hear more sounds, as if one of the Keres is responding to it. More movement catches my eye as other Keres seem to drift in the direction of the voices. I may not be able to understand the language but I do understand tone, and I'm pretty sure the two are arguing. I climb a couple of the steps and grab one of the lit torches and hold it out in front of me. Black shadows swirl beyond the barrier, encircling the area where the voices are coming from. I start counting the shadow creatures until I can't keep track anymore. There aren't a couple dozen Keres down here as Garrick had claimed: there are hundreds of them. Maybe even thousands.

I drop the torch.

It thunks against the ground and rolls away beyond where the barrier seems to stand. The voices stop, and several Keres turn in my direction.

I run. Up the spiral staircase, my legs screaming with pain. But I don't stop. I make it out of the doorway, up back into the mist. Frantic thoughts fill my mind of me and Dax and Haden crossing that barrier to take on a handful of Keres, only to find ourselves overwhelmed by thousands.

How could Garrick have gotten their numbers so wrong? Or had the Keres gotten strong enough to exponentially multiply?

I think I hear someone following. Or at least there are footsteps that don't belong to me somewhere in the mist. At first, I think it is a Keres persuing me, but Keres don't have feet. Could it be the person who was conversing with them? Or perhaps another soldier?

I keep sprinting, realizing that I am turned around again, until I run right into what feels like a brick wall. I look up to find that I have collided into the chest of a very large man in armor. He grabs my arm before I can pull away. There are two more soldiers with him. "What are you doing here?" he growls. "Boons are not allowed—"

"You there!" one of the other soldiers shouts, and dives into the mist. He comes out a moment later, gripping a boy by the arm.

"Garrick!" I say, relieved to see a friendly face.

"Isn't this one of Ren's sons?" his captor asks the others.

"What are you doing with this Boon?" the man asks Garrick.

Garrick looks at me frantically. I wonder how long he'd been lost in the mist also.

"I am not a Boon," I say. "I am the Cypher. I am Garrick's . . . er . . . prisoner. Now take us to your king."

chapter sixty

HADEN

Rowan and I are allowed to walk on our own accord into the throne room, our hands still bound against our chests, and flanked by guards with electrified swords at our sides. The guard must have sent a runner ahead, because when we enter the room, the Court of Heirs looks as though they have been awaiting our arrival. Lex sits in my father's ebony throne, with the majority of the Court seated at his sides. I note that Lord Killian and Master Crue are not with him. Other Underlords crowd the room, as if spectators to a battle of gladiators.

My father sits, bound to a chair, in front of the Court. His crown, made of golden cypress leaves, has been laid out upon the altar, and his black robes and golden breastplate have been stripped away. He looks like nothing more than any other Underlord—except for the way he sits: his head held high, as if he were not a prisoner. As if he cannot be fazed.

But I know that he can. I'd seen his desperation when I refused to give Daphne to him. My throbbing arm is the only thing distracting me from screaming to the Court that he is merely acting.

Lex stands when we near the middle of the room. "The day of the equinox has arrived, Ren. Your sons have returned, as you predicted. However, I see they are empty-handed, as *we* predicted. Their failure is your failure."

One of our guards approaches Lex. "My lord, I have news," he says, giving him a slight bow. Lex nods for him to come forward. "Lord Rowan claims that the girl is coming. That she's on her way now."

"She's bringing the Key with her," Rowan says calmly but assertively. He'd spent the better part of our journey through the palace grounds making this same assertion to the guards, almost as if he were boasting.

A murmur ripples through the Court as the Heirs confer with each other. Lord Devlin leans forward and whispers something to Lex.

"The Court has grown tired of your family's false promises," Lex says, addressing us. The girl should have been ours seventeen years ago. I'm afraid we have grown tired of granting allowances—"

"She will be here before the equinox is over," Rowan says. "In fact, I don't think it will even take her that long. If these harpy-mouthed guards had merely waited at the gate as I instructed them, they could have intercepted her before now. So if it's anyone's failure that she isn't here yet, it's your own personal guards'."

"Lies," Lex says. "As if we are to believe that the girl could make it here on her own."

"She isn't just any girl," I say, my voice filled with so much anger that it doesn't sound like my own anymore. I realized too late that I have addressed him in English out of new-found habit instead of our archaic language, but I don't care enough to adjust that now. "She's more powerful than you could imagine—"

"Silence," Lex demands, switching to English as if I had issued him a challenge. He's doing his best impression of my father, but he shows his frustration too easily compared to Ren, who still sits regally in his captive chair, unmoving. "Your father has already been told his sentence for his ineptitude—banishment—but we've all had something extra-special in mind for you, Haden. *Death.*"

With that, I am seized by four of Lex's loyal guards and thrust down upon the altar. I almost laugh at finding myself in the same position I was in before I left the Underrealm, my head once again on the chopping block.

I should be afraid for my own life, but the agonizing pain in my blackening arm makes me think that death might be a welcome change.

Lex steps down from the throne. "I've been waiting for this moment for six months," he says, drawing his sword. "If your father were a true leader, he would have done this the first time: not made a mockery of our traditions by allowing you to continue on your so-called quest. As if *you* could have brought the Cypher to us."

Lex raises his sword. I glare up at him, daring him to do it. A loud shout sounding from somewhere in the antechamber beyond the throne room distracts him. It sounds like a quick skirmish. Lex lowers his sword slightly as the chamber doors burst open. I hear their footsteps before I see them, but then Garrick comes running into the throne room, holding Daphne by the hand.

"Haden!" she says when she sees me. "We're here."

"I can see that," I say. My head is still pressed against the altar.

A distant voice in my mind says with relief, *she came.* But I can't grasp on to it. The relief is replaced by anger that comes on so quick, I cannot think of why I would have been relieved to see her. I traded everything I ever wanted to keep her from this place, and now she comes waltzing in here of her own accord?

Why?

My furious thoughts are punctuated by the fiery pain that burns its way through my veins.

"What is the meaning of this?" Lex asks. "Who let this Boon in here?"

"I am the Cypher," Daphne says.

Another ripple of exclamations makes its way through the Court. Their excitement disgusts me almost as much as her ready admission. Daphne will have to fend for herself for her own stupidity.

"I've come because of Haden, which means he's fulfilled his quest. You have no grounds for punishment."

Two of the guards loosen their grip on me, and I am allowed to lift my head up from the altar, but I remain kneeling in front of it.

Ren stares at Lex, a satisfied smile sliding across his face. It is rare for my father to show such emotion. "Which means your grounds for this coup are unfounded. My bargain with the Court has been fulfilled," Ren says.

"You've already been deposed," Lex says. "The Court has given you a vote of no confidence, which means the title falls to me, as I am the next in line as Prime Heir. The crown is mine."

Lex reaches for the crown that sits on the altar in front of me, but then his hand stops. He strains, reaching for it, but he can't grasp it.

As if it were *impossible* for him to seize the crown.

Ren laughs. It's a horrible sound. "You forget about the oath I made," he says. "Before Haden left on his quest, I made an unbreakable oath that whoever brought the Cypher to me would become my Prime Heir."

I'd been too disoriented at the time to hear the oath that my father made when he dipped his dagger in the water from the River Styx at the Choosing Ceremony, but he'd told me about it later when he'd given me the chance to make my own oath to bring Daphne to him. He had said the word *whoever.*

I'd refused him then . . . for reasons I can't quite fathom at the moment. Had I fullfilled his oath without meaning to?

"You've lost your position, Lex," Ren says with a sneer.

"To whom? To Haden the nursling?" Lex rages. His sword is still drawn, and that distant voice inside my head tries to tell me that I should fear his wrath or that I should at least want to find a way to seize his weapon from him and run him through, but as pain pulses through my body, I find that I cannot even hold on to hate and anger at the moment. I simply do not care what he chooses to do with me. Only that he would make his decision faster.

"No," Rowan says. "I'm the one who got her to come. I should be the new Heir." The guards do not stop him as he walks toward the altar. Someone has loosed his bands, and he breaks them away, freeing his hands. "I am king now."

And I realize that is what he'd wanted all along. The reason he dragged me here and tricked Daphne into coming—he knew that he would become Prime Heir if he succeeded.

My apathy from only a second ago is replaced by burning hate once again at the idea that Rowan is going to win.

Daphne makes some sort of protest against Rowan's claim, but I don't care what she has to say. She let him trick her. This is all her fault.

That small, distant voice tries to whisper that I am wrong, that I *should* care. That Daphne's protection should still be my greatest desire, but she had already fulfilled her role in all of this, so what more use was she?

No, the voice whispers, but I don't know why I should care. The searing pain has spread to my chest now, with black, crawling tendrils spreading through my veins toward my heart. Perhaps it is some kind of poison. One that has left me with nothing but pain, anger, hate, and apathy to fill my cold shell.

The thought strikes me that when the black, inky poison spreads through all of my veins that there will be nothing left of me but the shell itself.

That nothingness feels as welcome as death.

Rowan smirks at me as he comes to stand by the altar. "I told you I would be the one who wins, *little brother.*" He stretches his hand toward the crown, but then snatches his hand back as if it's been burned. He tries to reach for it a second time but fails again.

"It seems it doesn't want to belong to you, either," I say.

"That's because it's mine," a voice says from the back of the chamber. Every head in the room snaps in the direction of the voice. Including mine.

Garrick steps from beside Daphne.

"What?" she asks, as confused as everyone else.

Apathy grips me once more, and I can't even muster the desire to be surprised.

Ren's eyes narrow into snakelike slits as he measures his Lesser son.

"What do you mean, runt?" Rowan barks at him.

"I'm the one who brought Daphne through the gate," Garrick says, walking toward the altar. "She said she wanted to go with me into the Underrealm of her own free will. I'm the one who delivered her here. Not Haden. Not Rowan. It was me." Garrick reaches for the crown. Nothing stops him, and he wraps his fingers around the wreath of golden cypress leaves and then lifts it from the altar. He holds it aloft for a moment, while everyone in the room watches him in awe.

"No!" Rowan shouts and tries to make a grab for the crown, but he's stopped as if by an invisible hand before he can touch it. One of the guards seizes his outstretched arm.

Garrick smiles at Rowan, his nostrils flared, and places the crown upon his own head.

The guards at my sides fall to one knee, and many in the Court do the same, acknowledging their new king.

chapter sixty-one

DAPHNE

When Garrick got the drop on one of the guards in the chamber outside the throne room and then freed me from my captor with a blast of lightning, I had expected him to try to make a run for it, but, instead, he'd grabbed me by the hand and burst through the throne room doors, in essence, delivering me to the Court.

I wonder now as he stands in front of the altar, the crowd bowing to him, if he knew that this is what would happen. Or if he'd only figured it out when Lex and Rowan were unable to claim the crown.

"This doesn't change anything," Lex says, addressing the Court. "Are you really going to claim this Lesser as your new king?"

Another regal-looking lord emerges from somewhere in the crowd of people—other Underlords, I presume—who fill the room. "The oath must be respected. It's been sealed and cannot be torn from the tapestry of the Fates. He is our king now, like it or not."

"Then kill the boy," Lex says.

"I'll do it for you, gladly," Rowan says. Two guards have him now but he speaks as if they'd happily give him a sword in order to kill Garrick.

"Do you not remember when that same suggestion against Haden at the Choosing Ceremony almost brought the wrath of the Oracle upon you?" the lord asks Lex. "Perhaps this is punishment for your insolence. I suggest others in the Court do not continue to press this matter, less they risk offending the Fates as well."

Another lord steps forward from the court of men who surround Lex behind the altar. "Ren's banishment still stands. We will accept the boy, but as far as Haden and Rowan are concerned, we were promised the Key. Where is it?"

All eyes from the Court fall on me, but I am empty-handed. "I don't have it."

Rowan points at me. "She was supposed to bring it here. That was the arrangement I made. I did my part. It should be here—"

"Banish Rowan with Ren," Lex says, like he can't stand listening to his excuses for another minute.

Rowan attempts to make a break for it but is soon subdued into a black sleep by one of the guards.

"And Haden?" the man from the Court asks once the hubbub is over.

"Haden's execution order still stands," Lex says, gesturing to the guards.

"What?" I shriek as the guards seize Haden once again. And he lets them. I expect him to struggle. I expect him to try to fight, but he just lets them place his head on the altar. *Like he doesn't care.* His face resembles that expressionless mask he used to employ so often when we first met. The one he used to pretend he was beyond feeling emotion. Only now I can't see the light behind his eyes. This time, he isn't *pretending*. . . .

What the hell is his problem? But then I see it. The thing I'd feared. His left arm under his bindings is streaked with black veins. They creep over his shoulder as if spreading toward his heart like spindly, poisonous vines.

He's been struck by the black arrow. And it's already affecting him.

Lex raises his electrified sword over Haden's neck, and a gleam of joy dances through his eyes. He revels in the moment. If he can't be king, he'll play executioner.

I need to do something.

I listen for the sound that Lex's sword makes, thinking I can cause it to leap from his hands, but the weapon is silent. That is when it strikes me—this room is void of ethereal sound. No notes. No melodies, no special tones coming from any person or object in this room. Come to think of it, I hadn't heard a single ethereal note since entering the palace.

I open my mouth with the idea to create my own music in hopes that it will be powerful enough to stop Lex's blade on its own, but when I try to sing, no sound comes out. I try humming, but the same thing happens. Silence.

I don't know why or how, but my music is gone. My power is *gone*. . . .

Lex raises his sword even higher.

"Wait!" I shout, almost expecting my voice not to work. Apparently, I can speak, but I cannot sing? "I don't have the Key *with* me, I mean. But I can get it. I hid it somewhere."

"More lies," Lex snarls.

"You'll never know if you kill Haden. I will never give it to you." I look at Garrick, imploring. "I hid it after the boat crashed. I can take you to it." I am lying, but I channel as much sincerity into my voice as possible as I approach the altar.

A couple of guards try to step in my way. "Stop," Garrick orders. "Let her come."

I'm standing only a foot from Haden now. "Do something, Garrick. You are king now, aren't you? Act like one."

The guards holding Haden look to Garrick for his answer, but before he responds, Lex swings his sword at Haden's neck.

"Stop!" I shout, feeling powerless.

A blast of lightning hits Lex's sword, and he drops it. He reels on the perpetrator: the lord who had stepped forward from the crowd to defend Garrick's place as king. The man stands his ground. "Let our new king decide Haden's punishment," he says.

While the Court is distracted, I make a run for Haden. I might not have my powers, but I still have my hands and feet. I try to grab him, but I am apprehended by two guards. They hold me up in the air by my arms. My muscles scream in response.

"What shall we do with her?" one guard asks, but his manner makes it unclear whom he is addressing—Lex or Garrick?

"Kill the lying witch," Lex says.

I look to Haden, and he doesn't even glance in my direction. One of the guards who holds me lifts his sword to my throat, while the other looks as though he wants to let me go.

"Halt!" Garrick commands, stepping in front of me. "Let her down."

The guards comply. Garrick steps even closer to me. "Promise your allegiance to me, Daphne, and I will lessen Haden's sentence. I will have him banished along with his father and brother."

"Why not just let him go?"

Garrick rocks forward and whispers so only I can hear. "I cannot do less than banishment. The Court wants him punished. If I let him just walk, I may lose what little hold I have on this crown." He turns away before I can argue and snatches a pomegranate from one of the fruit bowls that I imagine have been set out for the Court's refreshment, and carries it to the altar.

"What are you doing with that, Garrick?" Haden asks.

He's still kneeling, his hands bound, but the guards have let him raise his head once again.

"Saving your life," Garrick says.

"I don't need your help," Haden says, going from indifferent to angry. His emotions—all negative ones—are all over the place. I wonder how long until even those are gone permanently.

Garrick shakes his head as if he recognizes that Haden is no longer himself. He smacks the pomegranate against the altar. The fruit cracks open, dripping red juice on the white marble. "Come, Daphne," he says, sweeping his hand over the altar. "Bind yourself to me so you will be under my protection until you can bring me the Key, and I will let Haden live. He'll be banished to the mortal realm."

I kneel opposite Haden at the altar, and Garrick offers me the pomegranate. The juice running down his arm looks like blood. "Eat," he commands me.

"Don't do this," Haden says to me, but his voice gives away no emotion—only that he thinks I'm being illogical. "If you eat that, you'll be bound to this place."

"I know," I say.

"Let them kill me," Haden says to Garrick, anger seeping into his voice again. "Send her back to the mortal realm, where she can't cause any more problems." He sounds as though he is merely upset that I have delayed his execution, but I want to believe that there is at least an ounce of care driving his words.

Garrick shakes his head. "She's the only one who can take us to the Key."

Haden looks at me over the altar, his face only inches from mine. "Don't trade yourself on my account, Daphne. You have a future to go back to. I don't."

My heart aches as he says this, because I realize he is willing to die because he thinks he has nothing left to lose.

"Why would you do this?" he asks, like he thinks I'm being completely irrational.

I probably am. But I don't care.

I lean in closer to him over the altar and caress his cheek with my fingers. He does not react to my touch. I slip my other hand into my pocket and pull out the red arrow. I act before any of the guards have time to notice my weapon. "Because I love you," I say.

And stab him in the chest with the arrow.

G

chapter sixty-two

HADEN

She's stabbed me!

Has she tried to kill me herself?

I look at her, my apathy gone, and an emotion I can only call loathing pulses through my black veins for her betrayal.

Her eyes widen. "No, no, no," she says, and seems to lunge for me over the altar. Her hands go for my face, and I try to shake her off. She grabs me, both hands cupped under my chin, and she leans in as if she were about to kiss me. But just as her lips are about to touch mine, one of the guards pulls me away from her. Another takes her by the shoulders and holds her against the altar in front of Garrick.

A warm, pulsing sensation radiates from the arrow protruding from my chest. No blood spurts from the wound, but red, serpentine lines slither out from it under my skin, pushing back the black ink in my veins—as if sending it retreating toward the black cut in my arm.

The agonizing pain that has engulfed me since my arrival in the Underrealm lessens for the first time.

That small voice, the one that has been in my head, telling me that I am not acting like myself, grows louder.

"That's quite enough!" Garrick shouts. "Take him to the gate."

I hear Daphne protest. She's trying to tell Garrick that she needs to do something, but he doesn't listen. I am being dragged away from Daphne. Instead of feeling hate and betrayal, my instinct is to try to cling to her, but the fetters on my arms won't allow me to reach for her. My captors drag me toward the corridor that leads out of the throne room.

"Finish the binding ceremony!" I hear the Heirs demand. They tell her I will be killed unless she partakes of the fruit.

I twist in my captors' arms, just in time to watch Garrick offer the pomegranate to Daphne again. Before, I had seen her choice as illogical. A poor trade. But now I understand why she's doing it.

She loves me.

That thought melts through me as more warmth pulsates from the wound in my chest. Only moments before, I had felt incapable of caring, and now I care more than anything in the world about stopping her.

I thrash against my captors. Try to lift the leather straps that entrap my arms against the arrowhead protruding from my chest in an effort to cut them away. That effort fails.

I watch, horror-struck, as Daphne takes the pomegranate from Garrick and plucks one red seed from its flesh.

I have to stop her.

I channel the electric heat from my body into my arms. It pulses into my hands, and I send it crackling against my own chest. I electrocute myself in an effort to burn away the tethers on my arms. I writhe with pain as Daphne presses the red, gemlike seed to her lips, and I manage to rip one of my hands from the singed cords. I fling a bolt of lightning, blasting the pomegranate from her hands. She jumps back, and it falls to the ground as ash.

But I can tell from the look on her face that I hadn't stopped her altogether. She'd already swallowed the one seed.

"No!" I shout, but I am so weak from absorbing my own blast that I am unable to struggle anymore.

"Take Daphne to the chambers that are reserved for the queen," I hear Garrick say as I am dragged into the antechamber. I feel one of the guards' hands closing around my neck and forehead. I have become too much of a nuisance, and will be rendered incapacitated for our journey back to the gate. And there is nothing I can do to stop it.

When I open my eyes, I find myself back in the grove. For a fleeting moment, I think that I never left—that I had only suffered a terrible dream after being knocked unconscious by Rowan. But I take in my surroundings and realize that there has been a battle here. Burned trees, and blackened rocks that have been struck by bolts of lightning. I remember the throne room and Garrick ordering my banishment, and watching Daphne with the pomegranate as I was dragged away.

Daphne!

I scramble to the two arched trees that cloak the gate in the mortal world. The green glow is gone, but I still try to thrust my hand through the archway. Nothing.

I hear a faint groan that sounds distinctly female. It comes from somewhere in the grove. My heart pounds against my chest as I follow the sound. I let myself believe that it is Daphne, until I find Terresa lying near a copse of trees in the grove. She groans, cracking her eyes to look at me for a moment and then seems to fall asleep.

I search her pockets, looking for a phone. I need to know the date.

If I have been gone for more than thirty-two hours, that means the equinox has already passed. I find her phone and fumble it open. Then throw it against the ground and watch it break against a rock. It is too late. The equinox is over. Without the Key, Persephone's Gate won't open again on its own for another six months.

I am trapped in the mortal world, and Daphne is a captive in the Underrealm.

It is my hubris that brought this upon us. I'd thought I could choose my own path. Weave my own destiny. But the thread I'd been clinging to hasn't just slipped through my fingers, it has unraveled and snapped. Broken by my desperate attempts to keep hold of it.

In trying to keep Daphne out of the Court's hands, I caused her to give herself over to them.

I fall to my knees. I want to sob, but I can't seem to muster the strength for it. My arm throbs again, and I notice that the black inkiness in my veins has started to spread again, as if fighting back against the red. I don't understand the meaning of this, and the red arrow had disintegrated when I blasted my own chest.

Just as I feel utterly alone in my hopelessness, something small and furry brushes against my leg. "Brim?"

She yowls at me and jumps up on my knees. Her gray fur is matted with blood, as if she's been in a fight. "Where's Dax?" I ask.

She shakes her little head and then bristles, sniffing the air.

I cast about and find that we are not alone. Two others lie in the grove, not quite yet recovered from the black sleep. I have not only been trapped in a world that is not my own, but I have been left with Rowan and Ren as my companions in exile.

chapter sixty-three

DAPHNE

It was such a small thing—a pomegranate seed. It had sat like a plump red droplet of blood on the tip of my finger, like I'd pricked myself on a thorn. All I had to do was suck the sweet yet sour flesh from it. Let it dissolve on my tongue and allow the tartness to slip down my raw, parched throat. It had only taken me a moment to eat something so small. It had only taken a moment to change everything—to seal my fate to this dark place forever.

It didn't matter that Haden had blasted the rest of the pomegranate from my hand. It didn't matter that the rest of it had been destroyed. The one seed had been enough. I can feel a change starting to come over me. Starting to make me feel rooted here. The stronger the feeling grows, the more I know I need to escape.

Garrick had ordered Haden away before I'd had a chance to actually kiss him. There are less than two weeks left until the black arrow's curse will take him over completely. I'd already seen its effects in a mild form—once it was permanent, I could only imagine in terror what Haden might do to himself.

And unless I can find the missing Key, the gate won't open again until it's too late.

I pace the bedchamber where I have been sent to wait. The

bed, draped in filmy veils, calls to me. I am pretty sure it's been nearly two days since I slept. But I won't give in.

As I wait, I try testing my vocal powers again, but, once more, no sound comes out when I try to sing or hum. I remember Haden telling me once that music had been forbidden here ever since Orpheus used his powers to betray Hades. I had assumed it was just against the rules, but maybe it had been forbidden in a more literal sense. Like the palace itself had been warded against music?

Finally, there's a knock at my door. I check the little carved-out window and see Garrick standing outside. He still wears the golden-wreath crown. I pull the door open and beckon him inside. "What took you so long?" I ask as he enters. The longer I had been made to wait, the more I had started to feel like a prisoner.

"I wanted to find something for you," Garrick says. He holds out his hand, offering me a necklace. It's a pomegranate pendant, encrusted with rubies, dangling from a delicate gold chain. It looks positively ancient—like something you'd see encased in glass in a museum.

"I can't take that," I say. "It's too valuable."

"It is valuable. Many of the queens have worn it. The servants even whisper that it had once belonged to Persephone herself." He presses the necklace into my palm. "I want you to have it. My queen deserves the best."

"Your queen?" I ask. "I am not your queen."

"Yes, you are." There is something very wrong with the way Garrick looks at me. "You are bound to me. That makes you my queen."

"What?" I take a step back, realizing that Garrick's behavior in the throne room might not have just been a ruse for the Court's benefit. My head starts to spin as I realize that I have betrothed myself to *Garrick*.

"Are you okay?" he asks, stepping even closer.

"Yes, I'm just tired. I want to go to sleep." *And get him out of here as fast as I possibly can.* "Alone."

"Very well," he says. "You'll need your rest. We'll head out to get the Key first thing in the morning. My friends are very anxious to have it."

His friends?

I want to ask what he means, but I also don't want to give him any reason to stay longer. I need to get out of here.

"Good night," Garrick says as he takes his leave, shutting the door behind him.

Much to my horror, I hear him turn the lock.

So I am to be a prisoner here?

I run to the door and peer out the little window, wondering how I can unlock it without the use of my powers. As I watch Garrick walk away down the torch-lit corridor, I notice something that I didn't see before.

Garrick has two shadows.

chapter sixty-four

TOBIN

I stand in a cold, dank cell, shivering in my damp clothes. I was pulled from the river by a group of shades who would have devoured me if it had not been for the soldiers who arrived on horseback, scaring the faceless creatures away with electrified staffs. For a moment, I'd felt grateful to my rescuers. Until they informed me that I was being taken to the palace to be charged with trespassing.

The door swings open with a *thunk*. "The king will see you now."

I follow the guard down a long corridor lit with torches until we arrive at a room that resembles a private dining hall. My mouth waters from the smell of food that wafts through the doorway. I am ushered inside by the guard and told to sit in a high-backed, cushioned chair. I sink into it and drool at the spread in front of me (roasted meats and cheeses and bowls of fruit) that seems fit for a king.

"Help yourself," the guard says.

It has probably been more than a day since I have eaten, but I resist, thinking of what Daphne had said about not eating in the underworld. (I'm pretty sure this spread has been put here just to torture me.)

The door opens again and I hear someone enter. "This is the trespasser," I hear the guard say to the new person before he leaves.

"Hello, Tobin," says a familiar voice.

I pull my attention away from the smorgasbord in front of me to see Garrick take a seat in a wooden chair at the head of the table. He wears some sort of golden-wreath crown on his head. I laugh with relief at seeing him, and a plethora of questions come tripping out of me. "Are you a prisoner, too? Where's Daphne? Have you seen Haden? When do you think this king guy is coming? Do you think we can make a run for it before he does?"

Garrick laughs at my barrage of questions. He picks up a hunk of cheese from the buffet and bites into it like he has all the time in the world. "I am the king now," he says, pointing at the crown on top of his head.

I start to laugh again, but then I realize that he's being serious.

"How long was I in that river?" I ask. "Obviously a lot happened while I was gone."

"More than you'll ever know." He takes another bite of cheese and chews it as though he's thinking something over. "Actually, why not tell you everything? It's not like you'll ever get the chance to share it." There's a sinister edge to his voice that makes me question whether or not I want to hear what he has to say, but still, I sink deeper into my chair.

"You see," Garrick says, eating a hunk of meat with his fingers now. "I've been playing everyone since the day I arrived in Olympus Hills. Actually, much earlier than that, but let's stick to the topic at hand. Everyone looks at me like I'm some poor, pathetic Lesser boy, so I play that to my advantage. I had everyone fooled, including you." He takes another bite of meat, the grease dripping off his fingers. "Even Terresa. I'm the one who tipped her off, you know. I convinced her to pretend to be Abbie on the phone in order to lure Dax away into a trap at the mill. And then I drugged Joe so everyone would think he was drunk."

"Why?" I ask, still not sure if he's trying to pull some sort of prank on me.

"So Haden would have to turn to me to be the one to go after Daphne in the grove. Things almost went south when Terresa showed up a few minutes too early. Unbeknownst to her, she was just supposed to show up in order to scare Daphne into wanting to go through the gate with me to get away from her. I took a blast from her, and things almost fell apart, but luckily, Rowan was arrogant enough to get it back on track. Frankly, his dragging Haden through the gate was a far better motivator than our fleeing from a Skylord."

"But I thought you didn't want to go into the Underrealm," I say, remembering Garrick's protests—his tears over the idea of returning to the Pits. "What was the point?"

"Because I didn't just need Daphne to go through the gate with me; she needed to *want* to go through the gate with me. What better way to get someone to convince themselves that they want something than to make them try to make you want it? The more she thought I didn't want to go, the more she practically begged me to help her get there."

"Again, what was the point?" I ask, sinking even farther into the comfort of my chair. I feel like I should be getting angry, but my emotions remain even. Almost as if I can't muster the energy it would take to be mad.

"Because of this," Garrick says, pointing at his crown. "I knew that whoever took Daphne through the gate would become the next heir to the crown. We thought we were going to have to wait a while until we found the best way to get rid of Ren, but luckily, Lex had already taken care of that part. The Fates really seem to be smiling down on us lately."

We? Us? I think, noting that Garrick has switched from speaking in the singular to the plural, like Golem from Lord of the Rings. This strikes me as odd. . . . But then I can't remember why it should be strange.

"We did it so we would have the power to destroy the monsters who ruined my life."

"The Keres? But why deviate from Haden's plan? Why not just go along with his quest to kill the Keres in the first place?"

"I don't want to kill the Keres. The Keres are my friends. The monsters are the Underlords. My filthy brothers included."

I raise my eyebrows at him, the only incredulity that I can muster at the moment.

"The Keres practically raised me. I was only a small boy when I was banished to the Pits. I realized that they had a language of their own, and I learned to call them to me like Hades had once been able to. Everyone thinks they're mindless creatures, but I know they are cunning warriors who resent their imprisonment. As the first creations of Hades, they should be the true Heirs to the Underrealm. We want the Key for ourselves so we can destroy the Underlords, who have kept us imprisoned for centuries. And then from there," he says, smacking his greasy lips. "We'll take over the five realms."

"*We?* You keep saying *we* like you're one of them."

"I am one of them," Garrick says, rising from his chair in front of the fireplace. Two long shadows stretch out in front of him. "I am their emissary. Their ears and their eyes in the outside world. Their hands to get them the Key. Which I will have for them when Daphne takes me to the Key tomorrow." He straightens the crown on his head and smiles. "Maybe we didn't actually need the crown in order to get the Key, but it sure feels good to have everything Haden has ever wanted. Daphne included."

Daphne. A thought of concern for her flits through my head but is replaced by fatigue.

"Why are you telling me this?" I yawn. "Your villainous soliloquy is making me tired." I try to stretch as I yawn again, but my arms don't seem to want to move. I look down at them and see that the cushions on the armrests have snaked themselves around my arms. "What were we talking about?"

"I'm telling you all this because in a matter of minutes, you won't remember a thing I said, because you're sitting in the chair of forgetfulness. One of Hades's favorite punishments for those who didn't take him seriously. You'll sit in that chair, wasting away for all eternity, because you won't remember why you need to get up."

"Why not just kill me now?"

"Because this is more fun," he says, heading for the door. "And because we need collateral. If Daphne changes her mind about getting us the Key, we now have something to incentivize her with."

As Garrick leaves, I want to scream. I want to claw my way out of the chair.

But I can't remember why.

It's so comfortable here. I think I'll just sit a while longer. . . .

ACKNOWLEDGMENTS

I wouldn't be able to do what I do without the support and hard work of many amazing people. I guess you could say that it takes a village to raise a book. Much gratitude goes out to Ted Malawer and Michael Stearns of Upstart Crow Literary, along with the indelible crew at Egmont USA, namely: my new editor (who picked up the baton in the middle of this series and hasn't missed a step), Jordan Hamessley, and Andrea Cascardi, Georgia Morrissey, Margaret Coffee, Michelle Bayuk, Esther Lin, and Bonnie Cutler. (With a side-note shout-out to my old editor, Greg Ferguson, who helped me develop the first book in this series.)

Thank you to my many friends and family members who provide moral support and enthusiasm (and occasional great lunch companionship) with particular shout-outs to J.R. Johansson, Sara Raasch, Kim Webb Reid, Natalie Whipple, Sara B. Larson, Chersti Nieveen, Colleen Houck, Rachel Headrick, Angela Pederson, Michelle Sallay, Brooke Morris, Noreen Gibbons, and doubly to my parents, Nancy and Tai Biesinger.

Extra, extra special thanks go out to two great friends and beta readers, Sara Raasch and Jenilyn Collings. Your ideas and insights helped me take this story to a whole new level.

Squishy hugs go to my two amazing and (sometimes) patient boys. Between being an author and a mother, I have the two best jobs in the world.

Thank you to the many booksellers and librarians who help put books into the hands of readers—with special gratitude to the enthusiastic and supportive staff at my local indie, The King's English. And to you, dear reader, for picking up this book. I have always believed that a story doesn't live until it is read, so thank you for giving this one life.

Lastly, the most gratitude and appreciation goes out to my husband, Brick. You know I couldn't do this without your love, support, and talent. One of these days, I'm going to coerce you into sharing a byline with me. (Come on, you know it would be fun!) Thank you for always believing in me. I.L.Y.R.U.T.T.M.A.B.A.